LOST
EPISODE GUIDE FOR OTHERS

From one Lostie
to another
Robert Dougherty

LOST

EPISODE GUIDE FOR OTHERS

An Unofficial Anthology

by
Robert Dougherty

iUniverse, Inc.
New York Bloomington

Lost Episode Guide For Others
An Unofficial Anthology

iUniverse books may be ordered through booksellers or by contacting:

iUniverse
1663 Liberty Drive
Bloomington, IN 47403
www.iuniverse.com
1-800-Authors (1-800-288-4677)

ISBN: 978-1-4401-0288-2 (pbk)
ISBN: 978-1-4401-0289-9 (ebk)

Printed in the United States of America

CONTENTS

Season Two

Season Three

INTRODUCTION

Are you tired of people at work or in your own family raving about *Lost?* Do you hear people talk about smoke monsters and flash forwards and something called the DHARMA Initiative, while being completely unaware of what it all means? Do the words Jate, Skate and Darlton mean absolutely nothing to you? Or are you a "Lostie" who would like your friends and family to be as obsessed with *Lost* as you are?

There's still time to correct those grave mistakes. Maybe only two years left, but that's still something.

People say that it's almost impossible to get into *Lost* at this late stage. There's so many mysteries and weird, still unexplained things to explain, who could understand it at this point? It could take weeks to get it all. Maybe it'll still take weeks to read this book and catch up, but by reading about a few episodes each day, it might set a good pace.

Thanks to my episode summaries, flashback details, important details, talking points, and judgment if an episode is really worth watching, one can be caught up on *Lost* before Season 5 starts. Or they can be up to date quickly enough to catch up to Season 5 in progress. By the time the very final season begins in 2010, you'll be raving about the hatch blowing up and ranting about Nikki and Paulo like you were a fan from day one. At the least, you'll know exactly what episodes I just referenced to.

This is basically a guide for "The Others" who are outside the *Lost* fandom. If you purchased this, you would like to join us, or you are a Lostie who wants a friend or family to join. This book can get either process started.

By the time you finish, you won't be "One Of Them" but rather, "One Of Us."

GUIDE TO MY EPISODE GUIDE

Episode plot: A summary of the episode's main plot, which involves the episode's main character.

Other stuff: A summary of any subplots in the episodes. Often if the main plots and subplots are closely tied together, this section will not be needed.

Main character: Lists who is the focus of the episode.

Flashback details: A summary of the main character's flashback plot. If the flashbacks are crucial to understanding the main plot, they will be put first.

Important details in *Lost* lore: A list of all the important details in the episode which are crucial to the show's overall plot and history.

Amount of action: Ranges from little to fair to heavy.

New important characters: Lists any important characters that make their first appearance in a given episode.

Connections between characters: Lists the important relationships and conflicts in the episode, as well as any past connection that the survivors have.

***Lost* mysteries referenced:** Lists which specific mysteries are touched upon in the episode.

***Lost* mysteries introduced:** Lists which new mysteries are created from the episode.

Questions raised: List of the major questions and cliffhangers from the episode.

Talking point: A brief discussion of the various themes, as well as plot and character development, in an episode.

Other key issues: One or two supporting talking points.

Must see episode?: Lists whether the episode is worth seeing and is important to go over, or whether the viewer can skip it.

SEASON ONE

CHARACTERS YOU NEED TO KNOW FOR SEASON ONE

Jack Shephard-- played by Matthew Fox: Our brave doctor leader.

Kate Austin-- played by Evangeline Lilly: Our fearless fugitive female lead.

Sawyer-- played by Josh Holloway: Bad boy/anti hero/wise cracking con artist/Han Solo impersonator.

John Locke-- played by Terry O'Quinn: Formerly crippled man of destiny.

Hurley-- played by Jorge Garcia: The fat, funny comic relief on the island. But even comic relief fat guys have their curses.

Sayid Jarrah-- played by Naveen Andrews: Former Iraqi Republican Guard torturer.

Charlie Pace-- played by Dominic Monaghan: One of those one hit wonder rock star types.

Claire Littleton-- played by Emilie de Ravin: Pregnant Australian woman.

Sun Kwon-- played by Yunjin Kim: A married, seemingly passive Korean woman.

Jin Kwon-- played by Daniel dae Kim: Sun's seemingly controlling and domineering husband.

Michael Dawson-- played by Harold Perrineau: A man who has to learn to be a father to his son Walt.

Walt-- played by Malcolm David Kelly: A young boy with special and unknown powers.

Boone Carlyle-- played by Ian Somerhalder: Joined too much at the hip to his stepsister Shannon.

Shannon Rutherford-- played by Maggie Grace: Spoiled stepsister of Boone who's initially not much help to anyone else

Danielle Rousseau-- played by Mira Furlan: Seemingly crazy French woman who has been on the island for 16 years.

Aaron: The finally newborn baby of Claire.

Rose-- played by L. Scott Caudwell: Survivor who is convinced against all hope that her husband survived the crash as well.

Ethan Rom-- played by William Mapother: Kidnapper of Claire and the first of the mysterious "Others" to be seen up close.

Christian Shephard-- played by John Terry: Jack's cold father who is now dead, yet still walking around on the island. Also has several past connections to other survivors.

Vincent: Walt's dog and the island's resident animal mascot.

PILOT: PART 1

September 22, 2004 was an historic day. In our real world, it was the day *Lost* premiered, after heavy hype from ABC and from critics who had gotten a sneak peek. It was to be the first time the future Losties of the world would come together. It was the day shows like *The X-Files* and *Twin Peaks* got a new show that would be compared to them over and over. It was the day a massive cult of followers and a massive television phenomenon was born.

In the world of *Lost*, it was starting off as just another day. A group of strangers gathered together on Oceanic Flight 815, with various demons and challenges that we would come to know very well. One was out to bury his father once and for all, one was recovering from the loss of his dream trip, one was heading for prison, one was heading back home after killing the wrong man, one was being followed by a numerical curse, and so many others had past troubles they thought they would never recover from.

And on an island that nobody else could see or get to, a small but powerful community was going about their daily lives. Their leader, a man that had kept the threat of the outside world out for years, had received disastrous and impossible news about his spine. Meanwhile, their fertility doctor was distraught over not being allowed to return home.

Unknown to all of them, another man was living underground in a hatch built by their former enemies, keeping the world safe by pressing a button. However, he was late on this particular day. All the way back in London, a wealthy industrialist with mysterious ties to the island was waiting for the one opportunity and opening he needed to get back to it. But all these stories are for later seasons.

This is when everything changed for the passengers, the "other" people on the island, and for the world at large.

Episode Plot: After Oceanic 815 crashes, Jack Shephard saves as many people as he can from the wreckage, then meets Kate for the first time. After realizing the plane crashed far off course, the survivors hear the monstrous roars of something in the jungle.

The next day, Jack and Kate, with help from Charlie, go to find the wreckage of the cockpit in order to find the plane's transceiver. When they get there, they find the plane's pilot trapped inside. He confirms that they crashed 1000 miles off course and no one will be able to find them unless they make contact. But just before the survivors get the transceiver, the sounds of the monster are heard again.

Although Jack, Kate, and Charlie narrowly escape, the pilot's remains are later found on the top of a tree.

Other Stuff: The other survivors meet and try to stay calm. Jin orders Sun to stay close to him at all times, Locke sits in the rain with a smile during a storm, while Shannon remains confident that rescue will come soon.

Main character: Jack Shephard.

Flashback details: The initial turbulence of the plane crash is seen from Jack's point of view.

Important details in Lost lore: The island, the survivors, and the monster are all introduced.

Amount of action: Heavy during the opening sequence and the monster attacks.

New important characters: Everybody.

Connections between characters: Jack and Kate meet and bond for the first time.

Lost Mysteries Referenced/Introduced: The monster, the island in general.

Questions Raised: What is the monster? What, and where, is the island? Can the transceiver be used to send for rescue? How did the pilot's dead body get so high up? Why was Charlie behaving so strangely in the wreckage of the plane? Why was Locke smiling during the rainstorm?

Talking Points: Heroism is seen in the face of disaster, as Jack demonstrates in the very first moments. However, even heroes can be afraid, as Jack explains while telling Kate about his first solo surgery. But by only letting the fear in for a moment, Jack was able to overcome it, as Kate is later able to do during the monster's attack. Jack and Kate are also the first example of how a bond can form from the aftermath of a shared crisis.

It is also shown how various people can react from such a tragedy, and how pre-existing troubles can affect it. Jin uses his control over Sun to keep her from straying too far, Michael's inability to bond with his son Walt becomes more of a problem in this situation, and Shannon acts out in what will be typical behavior from her.

Other key issues: How the opening scene plays out more like a big screen action movie than what is usually seen on TV. After that opening hook, it is hard to turn away, even four years later.

Must see episode?: Yes. This is where it all began. Even though other episodes will introduce the show's biggest mysteries and characters, this is where it all came from. Every *Lost* newbie needs to see this episode first and foremost.

PILOT: PART 2

The first time we saw *Lost,* we were thrilled and excited and on our way to becoming Losties. However, the pilot wasn't over yet. Now that we had our first glance of the show, it needed to start building on that first strike. It needed to prove it could be a lasting success, and stretch out this premise that some were still skeptical about. So it was time to begin the *Lost* tradition of mystery, its characters secrets, and cliffhangers that would keep people watching to make them forget that there were no answers yet.

Therefore, certain characters that had barely been introduced in the first part stepped into the spotlight this time. Relationships and conflicts were beginning to form as the pursuit of rescue began. Mysteries were introduced about the island and its....unique residents, and about the survivors themselves. And right off the bat, someone who we had grown to trust turned out to be someone completely different. Even when a chance for rescue seemed to work, something would happen to dash it immediately and deepen the mystery about what this place really was.

Feel free to ask this question of Charlie's. "Guys.....where are we?"

Episode plot: After Jack, Kate, and Charlie return with the transceiver, Sayid attempts to fix it. He plans to go to higher ground to get a signal, with help from Kate, Charlie, Shannon, Boone and Sawyer. But the camp is already on edge, after seeing Sawyer attempt to fight Sayid and seeing evidence that there was a fugitive on board the plane. As Sayid and the others go up to get a signal, suspicions flare as to who that fugitive is, but they are interrupted when a polar bear runs through the jungle. Sawyer then shoots it dead just in time.

I did not write that sentence incorrectly. A polar bear was killed on a tropical island.

When the survivors get high up and can finally use the transceiver, instead of getting a signal, they get a message in French from a woman's voice. With translation from Shannon, they find out that the French woman is calling for help, saying "It killed them all." And that message has been playing on a loop for 16 years.

Other stuff: Michael and Walt continue to struggle to communicate, but that does not stop Walt from discovering the handcuffs of the fugitive. Walt then plays a game of backgammon with the mysterious, but happy, John Locke. After Locke teaches Walt the game, he asks "Do you want to know a secret?"

Michael also tries to talk to Sun, even though she cannot speak English. Jin then interrupts her when he notices that her blouse's top button is unbuttoned. Jin does try to give the survivors shellfish, but no one can understand him.

Jack stays behind to treat a man who has a piece of shrapnel in his stomach. After pulling it out, the man wakes up in a flash. He asks Jack, "Where is she?"

Main character: Another ensemble episode.

Flashback details: Charlie is seen in the bathroom before the plane crash, trying to flush his remaining stash of heroin. At the same time, the man with the shrapnel is revealed to be a U.S Marshal, escorting the fugitive on the plane....and that fugitive is Kate.

Important details in *Lost* lore: The island has polar bears. The French woman is heard for the first time. Kate is revealed to be a criminal. Communication with the outside world is impossible.

Amount of action: Fair. Sawyer and Sayid have a brief fight, with additional suspense and shock when the polar bear is shot. But there are no monster attacks, and the suspense is mainly from trying to contact the outside world, not with any chasing or fighting. Still, the action moves along fairly.

New important characters: Sawyer and Sayid receive a lot more focus and attention after their cameos in part 1. The U.S Marshal is also introduced.

Connections between characters: Sawyer and Sayid begin a rivalry, and Kate and Sawyer set off sparks for the first time. An obviously deep connection between Kate and the dying marshal is revealed. Boone and Shannon continue to squabble, as do Sun and Jin. Walt begins to form a friendship with Locke.

***Lost* mysteries referenced:** The mystery of the island, and what might be out there.

***Lost* mysteries introduced:** The mystery of the French woman, the polar bears, and Kate's criminal past. Also, there is a letter in Sawyer's pocket that he looks at before he goes off with Sayid's team. Locke is also a mystery onto himself.

Questions raised: What is the "it" that "killed them all" according to the French woman? Why has her transmission played on a loop for 16 years? Why is Kate a criminal? What is a polar bear doing here? What is Sawyer's letter? What is Locke's secret?

Talking points: There is conflict among the camp for the first time when Sawyer attacks Sayid, reflecting racist and xenophobic attitudes. Sayid was a member of Saddam's Republican Guard, which carries its own negative implications, although he has certainly been intelligent and helpful thus far. First impressions are obviously proven wrong throughout the episode, both with Sayid and with Kate as well. Even Sawyer, a very antagonistic character all through the episode, is briefly softened when he looks at his letter. Characters that started out appearing to be one thing may be something entirely different.

This also raises the issue of who you can trust. Kate is someone who Jack has trusted so much thus far, yet she may be more dangerous than he could have imagined.

Other key issues: Charlie's drug addiction, Boone and Shannon's bickering, and the revelation that Walt has only known his father for a few weeks.

Must see episode?: Yes. As the second part of *Lost's* introduction, it needs to be seen to compliment part 1 and fill in the remaining important parts of the series. It only confirms that this is no ordinary island, as these people may be there for some time to come.

TABULA RASA

Early critics of *Lost* could be forgiven if they thought the characters were archetypes to start off. There's clean cut hero Jack, attractive girl hero Kate, bad boy Sawyer, funny fat guy Hurley, mysterious but wise Locke, drug addicted rock star Charlie, etc. But *Lost* has made a habit of introducing typical, almost cliché like characters before shattering the stereotypes in the most surprising ways.

The first example of this trend is Kate, who had previously been shown as a supportive and strong heroine type. At least until we found out she was a fugitive being taken to jail by a U.S Marshal before the crash. Now the marshal is dying and trying to find her, while Jack, Kate's greatest ally thus far, is about to discover her secret.

"Tabula rasa" is a philosophical term for a clean slate where someone is blank and has no past or present. In this case, Kate and several other characters are a blank on this island, with their demons supposedly left behind in their past lives. But can someone really start over? Can a new future, and a new version of yourself, shine through in a whole new life? Kate is the first member of flight 815 to face that test, but she will not be the last.

Episode plot: In the jungle, Sayid decides not to tell the camp about the French woman's message, over Kate's objections. Back at the beach,

Jack discovers from the dying marshal that Kate's the fugitive. When Kate returns, she tells Jack about the message before asking him about the marshal. Jack says little about his condition, but the marshal is on the verge of death during the middle of the night.

When Kate goes to see the marshal, he grabs her before going into shock. Kate tells Jack that he should be allowed to die, but Jack then tells her that he knows she's a fugitive. So Kate goes to Sawyer and convinces him to shoot the marshal. Before he does, Kate has a final talk with the marshal in his tent. Afterwards, Sawyer goes in to shoot him…but he misses the marshal's heart, as he takes several more hours to finally die.

The next morning, Kate offers to tell Jack what she was arrested for, but Jack refuses. He says that "Three days ago, we all died. We should all be able to start over."

Other stuff: Sawyer starts to raid the dead bodies and the wreckage of flight 815, telling Jack that they're not in civilization anymore. Walt is looking for his dog Vincent, but Michael isn't providing much help. Walt's new friend Locke is able to find the dog, but lets Michael take the credit for it.

Main character: Kate.

Flashback details: Kate is sleeping in a barn at Australia, before being woken up by a farmer. She claims to be a visiting student, convincing the farmer to let her stay and do work for him. When she is caught with the money she had hidden in the farmhouse, she offers to leave, but the farmer offers to drive her to the train station.

When they get there, the farmer admits that he knew Kate was a wanted fugitive, as he turned her in to get the reward money. The marshal then appears, but Kate takes the farmer's truck and drives it until it is run off the road. After Kate escapes the crash and pulls the farmer out, the marshal is able to catch her and put Kate under arrest. They would get on flight 815 sometime later.

Important details in *Lost* lore: Jack refuses to ask about Kate's past, keeping the mystery of what she did alive.

Amount of action: Little. Suspense comes from the condition of the marshal and Kate's plight, but there are no action scenes on the island. There is a chase scene near the end of Kate's flashback.

New important characters: None.

Connections between characters: Kate gets closer to Sawyer to manipulate him, but finds a new reason to bond with Jack. Walt and Locke get closer, but Locke helps Michael try to bond with Walt at the end.

***Lost* mysteries referenced:** Kate's criminal past.

***Lost* mysteries introduced:** With the issue of what Kate did in the past unresolved, that becomes a full fledged mystery.

Questions raised: Does Jack continue to trust Kate, even after knowing the truth about her? What will Kate do now that her secret is safe again?

Talking points: The issue of euthanasia is briefly raised by Kate, but only as a ploy to kill the marshal before he reveals her secret. Sawyer's raiding of supplies, and his debate with Jack, highlights the conflict between trying to keep civilization alive in this new environment as Jack is, or living "in the wild" and embracing a lack of regular society as Sawyer has.

In an unfamiliar environment, not only is the question of society vs. anarchy raised, but the issue of whether someone can really start over and look past his- or her's- past mistakes. Jack believes that it is possible to start over, so perhaps Kate will embrace that as well and move beyond her criminal past.

Other key issues: Locke is revealed to have told Walt that "a miracle will happen", making it even more puzzling as to who Locke actually is.

Must see episode?: It is important in establishing Kate's past life, but we already had a glimpse of that in the pilot. Since there are no answers as to what made Kate a criminal, it isn't that important in the grand scheme of the *Lost* design.

WALKABOUT

By the time of *Lost's* fourth episode, the buzz was still going strong. But there were still skeptics who doubted the longevity of the show. And perhaps there were still those who watched the first three episodes, but were on the fence about whether to continue. Maybe you readers are on the fence right now. However, this is the episode that should turn that around.

Characters like Jack and Kate and Sawyer and Sayid had already gotten attention. One character that was largely in the background was John Locke, yet he was the most puzzling survivor even then. Whenever we did see him, he actually looked happy and was talking about secrets and miracles. Even among this group, it was odd behavior from someone who had just come out of a plane crash.

While everyone else was fighting, looking for answers or trying to cover up their pasts, Locke just sat there in his own little world that only Walt had gotten close to. Who was this Locke guy, and what was he so pleased about?

If you really haven't heard the secret from any other *Lost* fans, there's no way you're going to guess until I tell you.

Episode plot: Wild boars are going through the wreckage of the plane. Jack decides that they need to burn the fuselage down, even with dead bodies still inside. Worse yet, the food supply is running down in the camp. Just then, John Locke demonstrates his highly developed skill of throwing knives, and offers that they hunt down the boars for food. Kate goes along so she can work on the transceiver, with Michael going along so he can prove himself to Walt.

During the hunt, Michael is injured while Locke is knocked down. Locke then goes out by himself over Kate's objections. Before Kate and Michael can find him, they hear the roar of the monster. Locke is actually able to get a look at the monster, but instead of being scared, he is in awe. He later comes back with a dead boar.

That night, the fuselage is burned down while Claire reads the names of the dead bodies from the manifest. Locke claims to Michael that he never actually saw the monster. He then focuses his attention on something else in the burned wreckage....

Other stuff: In Jack's rush to burn the wreckage down, he insists that he's no good at this kind of thing. But Boone is able to convince Jack to talk to Rose, a woman who was sitting next to Jack at the time of the crash, and whose husband died in the tail section of the plane.

Jack strikes up a conversation with her and hints that his job as a doctor was "the family business." But Rose also insists that her husband and everyone in the tail section is alive, even though it's very unlikely that they could be. After all, the people in the outside world probably think everyone on flight 815 is dead too.

At that moment, Jack sees a man in a suit and tie in the jungle not once, but twice. Before he's able to get closer to this vision, Locke returns.

Meanwhile, Boone and Shannon argue over Shannon's inability to take care of herself. So she "proves it" by getting Charlie to catch a fish for her. Charlie successfully catches a fish, but he quickly realizes he's been used when Boone and Shannon start arguing again.

Main character: John Locke.

Flashback details: Locke is seen as an office drone in a box company, passing his time by playing an army board game. He is also planning to go to a "Walkabout" in Sydney, Australia. Although his boss says he can't do any of that stuff, Locke insists "Don't tell me what I can't do" and that this is his destiny. Locke calls a woman named Helen and asks her to come along, but she says "I'm not allowed to meet customers."

When Locke gets to Australia, the walkabout guide says that he can't go because he wasn't upfront about his "condition." He offers to send Locke back on flight 815, but Locke insists he can do it. When the guide says he can't, Locke explodes at him while chasing after him... in his wheelchair.

But when flight 815 crashes, he doesn't need the wheelchair anymore. The formerly paralyzed John Locke can walk again after the crash. The wheelchair is later seen in the burning wreckage on the island.

Important details in *Lost* lore: Locke was paralyzed before the crash, but the island has somehow given him the power to walk again. He's also the first person to ever see the monster, but does not tell anyone what it actually is.

Amount of action: Fair, thanks to the boars' raids and the monster's return.

New important characters: Rose, although she was already seen during Jack's flashback on the plane. But this is the first time she gets to fully introduce herself.

Connections between characters: Michael tries to outdo Locke during the hunt in order to impress Walt, but gets nowhere. Jack is able to bond with his former seat mate Rose, while Shannon tries to manipulate Charlie into catching fish for her.

***Lost* mysteries referenced:** The monster and its appearance, as well as the mystery surrounding John Locke, which is solved in a way.

***Lost* mysteries introduced:** With Locke revealed to be paralyzed for 4 years, it is not revealed how he got that way. It is not clear whether Rose is right about her husband being alive against all odds, or who the man is that Jack saw in the jungle.

Questions raised: What did Locke see when he saw the monster? Why did the monster spare his life? What does Jack mean when he says that medicine is the "family business"? How can the island make

Locke walk again? Why doesn't Jack participate in the episode ending ceremony? Who did he see?

Talking points: Kate's episode raised the theme of being able to overcome the past and start over, but Locke takes that to the extremes. Before, this island was just seen as creepy and something that had weird stuff walking around. But in Locke's case, it is a beautiful place where his destiny can be fulfilled, and he can become who he always imagined himself to be. That may also be why the horrifying monster isn't as terrifying to Locke as it is to everyone else.

There are some truly unique powers in this island, with Locke as the greatest example of it. But while the island is helping Locke, there are hints that it has more troubling effects on Jack as well, as his vision showed.

Other key issues: Shannon is not the nicest of people.

Must see episode?: Absolutely. The pilot ensured that people would start watching the show, but this episode ensures that people would keep watching the show for good.

WHITE RABBIT

Being a leader isn't for the faint of heart. But for the survivors, they have no reason to suspect that Jack Shephard is both a leader and someone faint at heart. Even though he has saved people and tried to keep the camp together in this growing crisis, he has concealed the part of him that has far less confidence. The nagging part of him that stresses that he doesn't have what it takes. The part that fears failure and tries to avoid it at all costs. The part that was given to him by his father.

In this episode, we first see the self doubt and demons that plague this previously confident and brave man. And it manifests itself in a way that would seem crazy on anywhere else but on this island. Jack is chasing something that is linked to *Alice in Wonderland's* White Rabbit, which leads him further down the rabbit hole of the island's wonderland. When he gets there, he doesn't find what he's looking for, per se. But he does find something much more valuable to himself and the camp as a whole.

Even with all his weaknesses, the part of Jack that is a leader, a healer, and a protector manages to take over at the right time. With that, the perception of who Jack is, and the reality of who he is, are finally one and the same.

Episode plot: Charlie alerts Jack to a woman drowning in the ocean. Jack does everything possible to save her, but fails. Afterwards, he sees the same man in the jungle that he saw at the end of "Walkabout." Meanwhile, the camp is running out of water, and turn to a tired and worn out Jack for help, but he is distracted. He goes off into the jungle to find the man, discovering that it is his father…which is impossible, because he's dead. But Jack goes in search of him anyway, nearly falling off a cliff in doing so. Locke is able to save him at the last minute.

Jack shares his concerns with Locke, who tries to reassure him that this might all be happening for a reason, due to his obvious conviction about the beauty of the island. Locke then goes off to let Jack continue on his search. That night, after seeing his father again, Jack follows the vision and finds his father's coffin, as well as a cave with a fresh spring of water. However, the coffin is empty, and Jack tears it apart having failed to find his father's body.

When he returns, the camp is in turmoil about the water, but Jack, now finally at ease with being the camp's leader, breaks it up. He tells them about the cave and stresses that they all need to band together. He says "If we can't live together....we're gonna die alone."

Other stuff: While the water crisis goes on, Boone blames Jack for not being able to save the woman. After Jack leaves, Claire collapses due to a lack of water. When Kate goes to get the camp's remaining water bottles, she discovers that they are gone. An investigation turns up Jin and Sawyer as suspects, but they are cleared. Finally, Boone is found as the culprit, as he tried to take over rationing of the water from Jack. A fight ensues until Jack returns and breaks it up.

Main character: Jack Shephard.

Flashback details: Jack is first seen as a boy, having been beaten up for trying to stop a fight and save a classmate. His father, a successful spinal surgeon, tells Jack in response that he shouldn't try to be a hero, because he doesn't have what it takes and he can't live with failure.

Days before flight 815 crashes, a grown up Jack is told by his mother that his father is in Sydney, Australia. Jack's mother says it's because of what Jack did to his father, and Jack goes to Australia to find him. He finds out that his father was heavily drunk and missing, and he is later found dead of a heart attack and high alcohol levels.

Jack then makes the arrangements for his father's coffin to go on flight 815. Although the Oceanic ticket agent doesn't let him take the coffin at first, Jack tearfully convinces her to do it, needing to bury his father for good.

Important details in *Lost* lore: The introduction of Jack's long standing daddy issues.

Amount of action: Fair. Jack swims in the ocean to save someone, then runs all around the jungle and almost gets himself killed as a result.

New important characters: Dr. Christian Shephard, Jack's father.

Connections between characters: Boone gets into a mini-rivalry with Jack. Jack's feelings about leading the entire group are in question until he finally makes the choice to be their leader. Locke also helps Jack along in his quest for self-discovery. This turns out to be the only time in the history of *Lost* that these two characters get along.

***Lost* mysteries referenced:** The mystery from the last episode about who Jack sees in the jungle. The sounds of the monster are also briefly heard during Jack's trek.

***Lost* mysteries introduced:** The ultimate fate of Christian Shephard's body.

Questions raised: Is Jack really seeing his father, or is it all in his head? If it's all in his head, then where is his father's body? Is Locke right in stating that all of this could be happening for a higher purpose? What conflict happened between Jack and his father that made him go to Australia? What will happen when Jack takes everyone to the caves?

Talking points: Leadership is brought into question, and whether Jack has what it takes to be one, or whether he believes he has what it takes to be one. Once again, it becomes clear that the events of the past heavily influence the decisions of characters in the present.

The island's supernatural powers continue to grow, this time working an influence on Jack. If it really wasn't Christian Shephard that Jack was following around, and it wasn't in his head, then the island itself was up to something. It did ultimately lead Jack to a place with fresh water and shelter that calms the anxieties of the camp, letting Jack become a leader after all. And the reference to *Alice in Wonderland* is one of *Lost's* first notable references to literature.

Other key issues: Locke's continued belief that the island is beautiful, and how Boone's attempt to question Jack's leadership results in theft.

Must see episode?: Yes. It is our first in depth glimpse at Jack's character, and introduces themes that are recurring throughout the character's struggles to be a leader. However, future Jack flashbacks tend to repeat those themes more often than they should.

HOUSE OF THE RISING SUN

For the most part, *Lost* is a diverse show filled with people from all walks of life, and from all corners of the world. As such, it may be easy to think that *Lost* is almost like *Survivor,* where people from many different backgrounds have to fight the elements and learn to get along at the same time. But *Survivor* is just a game show, as their different "castaways" will get to go home by the end. *Lost's* survivors have conflicts and secrets that often have life threatening or life changing consequences.

One example of diversity is the Korean couple, Sun and Jin. They had largely stayed in the background so far, with their premises already established. Jin was a controlling husband while Sun was his wallflower of a wife. Unable to speak English, they couldn't really communicate with the other survivors, nor did Jin particularly want to. A simple enough pairing, with simple enough stereotypes.

But as Sun gets the flashback treatment for the first time, the *Lost* model stays the same. Everybody, no matter how different and no matter how simple they seem at first, has shocking secrets.

Episode plot: As the survivors prepare to go to the caves that Jack discovered, Michael is caught off guard when Jin attacks him from out of nowhere. He thoroughly beats Michael up before he is finally pulled away and handcuffed to a piece of plane wreckage. Since Jin cannot explain himself in English, no one knows why he attacked Michael, but Michael attributes the attack to racism. Until it is settled, Jin will remain handcuffed.

Later on, when Michael is chopping bamboo, Sun approaches him. She says she needs to talk to him...and she says it in perfect English. Stunned that Sun can speak English, Michael finds out that Sun was keeping it a secret from Jin. Sun also explains that Michael had found a watch several days ago that belonged to Jin. Or rather, it belonged to Sun's father, who Jin was going to deliver the watch for in Los Angeles. Sun asks for Michael's help to resolve the matter.

Later, Michael approaches Jin with an ax and cuts him loose, throwing the watch back to him. He demands that Jin stay away from him and Walt, leaving without having to give away Sun's secret.

Other stuff: The other survivors are impressed by the caves, their supply of water and the shelter they provide. Since it would take too much time to carry water back to the beach, Jack suggests they all move to the caves. Sayid objects, stating that they have a worse chance of getting rescued if they are not on the beach. To him, moving to the caves is a sign of giving up.

Soon, the survivors split apart, with Hurley, Jin and Sun going to the caves with Jack, while Sawyer, Shannon, Boone and even Kate stay on the beach with Sayid.

Meanwhile, Charlie tries to sneak away with his last amounts of heroin, but winds up standing on a beehive. After escaping with more than a few stings, Charlie is confronted by Locke. Charlie mentions that his guitar is still missing, but Locke insists he will find it soon.

Later on, Locke confronts Charlie again and says he knows about his drug addiction. Locke asks Charlie if he wants his guitar more than his drugs. Charlie answers yes, eventually handing over the heroin to Locke. He then points up to show that Charlie's guitar is up above on some tree roots.

Main character: Sun.

Flashback details: Sun is seen at a dinner party in Korea, while Jin is a waiter. The two are deeply in love, but they cannot yet get married due to Sun's father, a powerful business man. Days later, Jin tells Sun that her father has agreed for them to get married, provided that he works for him. As time goes on, the newlyweds are able to spend less time together due to Jin's commitment and his work.

One night, Sun is shocked to see Jin come home with blood all over his hands. In a panic, Sun asks him what happened and what exactly he does for her father. Jin slaps her, saying he does whatever her father tells him.

Later on, Sun is seen taking English lessons, as she is planning to leave Jin and the country. They are going on flight 815 so Jin can deliver a watch for Sun's father in Los Angeles. Sun makes plans to leave Jin before they board, then head to America on her own to start her life over.

However, when Sun is about to do it, she sees Jin with a white flower, which was one of the gifts he gave her while they were still in love. Sun cannot bring herself to leave, so she goes back to Jin's side... sealing her fate as a survivor of flight 815.

Important details in *Lost* lore: Sun can speak English, while Jin was some kind of enforcer for her father in the past. The caves are introduced, resulting in the survivors splitting up into different camps. Charlie also attempts to give up his drug addiction.

Amount of action: Fair. Jin delivers a thorough beating to Michael, who in turn threatens him with an ax. Charlie has to fight off bees, though that's more comedic than thrilling.

New important characters: Sun's father, who is mentioned a lot but is never seen.

Connections between characters: Jin and Michael's conflict reaches a boiling point, while Sun and Michael get a little closer. Jack has a split up with Sayid and Kate over where to stay on the island. Locke bonds with Charlie in an attempt to cure him of his drug addiction.

***Lost* mysteries referenced:** None

***Lost* mysteries introduced:** Two skeletons that appear to be hundreds of years old are found in the caves. Jin is introduced as an enforcer in his past life.

Questions raised: What exactly did Jin do for Sun's father? Has he killed someone before? What are the skeletons in the caves? What is truly the best strategy for the survivors: stay on the beach, or go to the caves? Has Charlie really renounced his addiction? Is there any hope left for Sun and Jin's marriage?

Talking points: The racial conflict between black people and Koreans is mentioned by Michael as a theory for the attack, but is incorrect. The skeletons in the cave suggest that this island is a lot older, and has a lot more history, than we know of.

We also see the slow dissolution of a marriage through Sun's point of view, yet it is that past love which keeps Sun from leaving and escaping the crash of flight 815. Even in a bad marriage, she holds on because of the good they had before, as many other couples in real life may have.

Other key issues: Locke is becoming quite a busy body, having stepped in during another character's crisis two weeks in a row.

Must see episode?: Yes. It is a smaller, character driven episode that provides the first showcase for Yunjin Kim, and adds important new layers to the Sun/Jin dynamic. They are still minor characters thus far, so this may be uninteresting to some viewers as things begin to slow down.

THE MOTH

Countless movies about singers have taken all the suspense out of a singing star's life story. They rise from humble beginnings, become gigantic stars, succumb to drugs and other temptations, and inevitably decline because of them. The story is as old as time with little circumstances that make it different. Charlie Pace isn't that much of an exception, except that his third act comeback will have to be on an island.

In effect, this episode has the classic three act *Behind the Music* structure, only spread out differently. The flashbacks show the first two acts of a traditional rock story: the rise and drug fueled fall. The third act of redemption takes place on the island, along with withdrawals and a cave in. And since this is in the early days of *Lost,* Charlie's eventual redemption is not the end of the story. Technically, this is the first act of his third act.

Episode plot: Charlie is going through withdrawals after giving Locke his drugs, so now he wants them back. But Locke tells him that he will only give back the drugs after he asks for them three times. In the process, Charlie becomes more unstable, which Jack takes notice of as he organizes the move to the cave. When Charlie snaps at Jack, it causes a cave in. Charlie is able to get out in time, but Jack is left trapped.

Michael takes charge and organizes an effort to remove the rocks, while Charlie goes and asks Locke for the drugs again. Locke tells Charlie a story about a nearby moth, and how it would be weaker if he let it out of its cocoon too soon. Charlie then returns and finds a way into the caves himself, but gets trapped in a smaller cave in. However, after he gets Jack free of the rocks, he finds another way out and leads Jack to safety.

That night, Charlie asks Locke for the drugs one last time, then throws them into a fire.

Other stuff: Meanwhile in the jungle, Sayid wants to find the source of the 16-year-old recording by the French woman. Enlisting Kate and Boone's help, Sayid has them activate three separate antennas at different parts of the island. With that, Sayid can triangulate the recording's signal. But Kate and Boone have to leave after they find out about Jack, so Sawyer and Shannon fill in for them.

After the two actually do what they're told for once, Sayid turns on the transceiver to get a signal…and is then knocked out cold by an unseen figure.

Main character: Charlie Pace.

Flashback details: Charlie is the lead singer of the band "Drive Shaft" with his brother Liam. But Charlie is thinking of leaving the band, due to the various temptations of the rock lifestyle. After Charlie leaves a confessional, Liam shows him that they have gotten a record contract and are about to make it big. Charlie agrees to sign, on the condition that they walk away if he feels uncomfortable.

Drive Shaft becomes huge, with the hit song "You All Everybody." But Liam succumbs to a heroin addiction, which disrupts the band and his relationship with Charlie. Finally, the toll becomes so big on Charlie that he starts to take heroin himself.

Years later, the band is broken up and Charlie is a full blown addict. By then, Liam has gotten clean and has started a family in Australia. Charlie goes there to talk Liam into reuniting the band, but he refuses. Charlie angrily leaves him and heads off to board Flight 815.

Important details in *Lost* lore: The story of Charlie's one-hit-wonder success. Although he would be tempted by drugs later in the series, this is when Charlie kicks the heroin habit for the first time. The attack on Sayid reveals that someone doesn't want him to find rescue. Michael also reveals his profession as an architect, which comes into play later.

Amount of action: Little, save for Jack and Charlie's painful ordeal in the caves and the attack on Sayid.

New important characters: Charlie's brother Liam.

Connections between characters: Locke is able to help Charlie kick his drug addiction, albeit in weird ways. Jack and Charlie also manage to bond during their ordeal. Kate and Sawyer have another round of arguing/flirting.

***Lost* mysteries referenced:** The French woman's message.

***Lost* mysteries introduced:** Sayid getting attacked.

Questions raised: Who attacked Sayid? Is Charlie off drugs for good? Are the caves really safer than the beach?

Talking points: The costs of the rock star lifestyle are shown, as well as the balance between rock star Charlie and devoted Catholic Charlie, which was severed due to the rock star side of him.

The episode has heavy dramatic irony, as Charlie goes from innocent to drug addict while his brother Liam goes from drug addict to family man. This also reinforces the theme that the characters past have an impact on their actions on the island.

Other key issues: More Jack/Kate hints, as well as Kate/Sawyer moments.

Must see episode?: So-so. This is important for followers of Charlie, but doesn't have a huge impact in the grander *Lost* story.

CONFIDENCE MAN

Every show has a bad boy and anti-hero. Someone who's not a downright villain, but isn't really a welcome presence among the heroes. Someone who is always out for number one and who will usually cause great trouble to get ahead. Sawyer has clearly been that figure so far.

Aside from Hurley, Sawyer has been *Lost's* comic relief, only his zingers are mean spirited and filled with insulting nicknames. But his photogenic looks and his flirting with Kate are enough for *Lost* fans, especially the ladies, to ignore his vast flaws. In this episode, Sawyer's hoarding and selfishness leads to a near fatal result for one character, added sexual tension with another, and a painful confrontation with two others. In between, we find out a barely surprising detail about Sawyer being a con man.

However, even this flashback is a bit of misdirection, leading to a plot twist that puts Sawyer in a whole new light. But it is not one bright enough that he would want sympathy for it.

Episode plot: Boone rummages through Sawyer's stash of stolen supplies, getting beat up in the process. Jack finds out that Boone did it to find an inhaler for Shannon, who suffers from asthma. Kate goes to Sawyer and asks for the inhaler, but Sawyer will only give it up for a kiss. But Kate then brings up the letter that Sawyer keeps carrying around, figuring that it makes Sawyer a human after all. In response, Sawyer makes Kate read it. The letter is from a young boy, who says that "Mr. Sawyer" conned the boy's mother, leading to his father killing her and himself.

Shannon suffers an asthma attack, leaving Jack desperate to get the inhaler. Sayid, who already suspects that Sawyer knocked him out in the jungle, offers to get the information out of him. After Jack and Sayid capture him, Sayid begins to torture him. Finally, Sawyer agrees, but he will only give the inhaler to Kate.

When Kate appears, Sawyer reiterates that he will give her the inhaler for a kiss. But after the two finally kiss....for some time....Sawyer says he never had it. Sayid then returns and attacks Sawyer, but winds up stabbing him in the arm.

After Jack treats him, Kate comes by with Sawyer's letter. She has re-read it and figured out the truth about it. It was written by Sawyer as a young boy. It turns out that when Sawyer was a child, a con man conned his mother, which led to his father killing her and himself. In addition, Sawyer isn't even his real name, as it was the name of the con man. In trying to find the man, he changed his name to Sawyer and became a con man himself, becoming the very man he was hunting. Sawyer refuses Kate's sympathy and sends her away.

Other stuff: Although Sawyer never had the inhaler, Sun is able to help Shannon out. Since Michael is the only one who knows that she speaks English, she enlists his help in making a plant that improves her breathing.

Charlie begins to bond with Claire as he tries to get her to move to the caves. Using pretend peanut butter, he charms her into agreeing.

After Sayid's torture and near killing of Sawyer, he resolves to leave the camp. Having sworn never to torture anyone again before today, Sayid plans to go into exile after breaking his vow. But he also plans to spend his time exploring the jungle and their location.

Main character: Sawyer.

Flashback details: Sawyer is working one of his cons on a woman named Jessica. He proposes that she invest her money in an oil deal, and she gets her husband to agree. At this point, we believe that Sawyer's con will lead to the husband killing his wife, and their son later writing the letter to Sawyer. However, when Sawyer sees their son, he calls off the deal, as he perhaps realized that he couldn't do the same thing that the man who ruined his family did.

Important details in *Lost* lore: Sawyer's past as a con man, as well as his tragic past involving the deaths of his parents. This episode also features Kate and Sawyer's first kiss, and the beginning of the bond between Charlie and Claire. Sayid and Sawyer's rivalry also comes to a head. It is revealed that Sayid was a torturer in a past life, but had vowed to quit until now.

Amount of action: Substantial, both in the torture scenes and the sexual tension moments.

New important characters: None.

Connections between characters: Jack and Kate get into conflict over Sawyer, while Kate and Sawyer's connection heats up. Charlie and Claire begin to bond, while Sun and Michael work together to help Shannon.

***Lost* mysteries referenced:** Sawyer's letter, the issue of who attacked Sayid in the jungle.

***Lost* mysteries introduced:** Sayid's history as a torturer, Sawyer's revelation that a con man destroyed his family.

Questions raised: Who is the con man that ruined Sawyer's life as a boy? What will happen to Sayid now that he is leaving the beach? What is the state of Kate's relationships with Jack and Sawyer? Why did Sayid vow to stop torturing until now?

Talking points: Sayid's rush to judgment about Sawyer leads to violence, just as Sawyer's earlier rushes to judgment about Sayid were incorrect. However, Sawyer did little to convince him that he was innocent. In fact, Kate pointed out that Sawyer is going out of his way to be hated.

It is clear that the tragedy he witnessed as a child really messed Sawyer up, as he actively seeks to be just like the con man he has been hunting. Sawyer's self loathing clearly fuels his trouble making on the island, but it is not something he wants to be pitied for.

Other key issues: Charlie seems to be well on the mend from his drug addiction, having moved on to attach himself to Claire.

Must see episode?: Yes. This is where the Kate/Sawyer "Skate" pairing really got started, plus some of the characters really dark sides are explored as well.

SOLITARY

Lost prides itself on the diversity of its cast. One prime example is Sayid, a character who doesn't fit the traditional profile of a lead character, especially in today's climate. A former soldier in Saddam's Republican Guard, Sayid has shown and stated that he was a torturer in his past life. But no one would suspect Sayid had such a dark history after talking with him for a while, unless he told you himself. Still, Sayid has clearly been making strides to leave behind his old life and start anew. But those efforts clearly hit a big snag in the last episode.

The results of that incident lead Sayid to explore on his own, where he gets closer to solving a big mystery. A mystery involving someone who has also led a solitary life filled with regret and violence. Someone who has also been stranded on the island for some time and who has some experience in torture and death herself. And even though this person is quite insane, she has quite a few interesting tidbits to tell while she puts Sayid through his ordeal.

Episode plot: Sayid goes far along the island coastline, where he discovers a cable leading into the ocean. Going into the jungle to find the other end of that cable, he gets himself caught into a trap.

Sayid is taken to some kind of hut, where he is tortured with an electrical current while a female voice asks "Where is Alex?" Sayid explains that he has crashed onto the island, and talks about the distress signal he heard that has been playing on a loop for 16 years.

At that point, the woman reveals herself. It is the very same French woman who sent out that distress call 16 years ago.

The woman's name is Danielle Rousseau, a member of a scientific team that crashed onto the island many years ago. She claims that something happened to her team, which is why she stated in her message that "It killed them all." She also claims that the carriers of this "sickness" were "The Others." Half crazed, Rousseau states that she hears these "Others" whisper in the jungle, which makes Sayid disbelieve her story.

After Sayid fixes a music box for Rousseau, he tries to escape. They then hear the roaring sound of the Monster, which makes Rousseau take off. Sayid then tries to escape and finds Rousseau in the jungle a moment later. Sayid tells her that he knows she really killed her entire team, but Rousseau claims she did it because they were "sick."

She pleads for Sayid to stay with her, but he cannot, as he now wants to return to the camp and help the survivors get off the island. Rousseau warns Sayid to watch his friends closely. Before he leaves, Sayid gets Rousseau to tell him that Alex was her child.

That night, when Sayid treks through the jungle, he begins to hear the exact same whispers that Rousseau was talking about.

Other stuff: Hurley is worried that everyone is becoming too tense, and seeks to lighten things up somehow. He does so by finding golf clubs and creating a golf course. Eventually, Jack and some other survivors take his advice and enjoy a relaxing round of golf. Even Sawyer joins in by making bets, reliving the tension he caused in the last episode.

In the meantime, Walt continues to bond with Locke, much to Michael's dismay. While Michael is out playing golf, Locke begins to teach Walt how to throw knifes.

Main character: Sayid Jarrah.

Flashback details: Sayid's past as a torturer in the Republican Guard is explored. One day, he is called upon to interrogate a woman involved in a bombing plot. The woman happens to be an old friend from Sayid's childhood named Nadia. Despite their connection, Sayid goes through with his "interrogations" although Nadia is not worried.

As time goes by, Nadia refuses to talk and the toll of torturing her takes a lot out of Sayid. Finally, Sayid's superiors order that Nadia be executed. But Sayid instead tries to help her escape, as he has planned out an escape route. However, Sayid himself cannot escape with her.

Nadia writes a message on the back of a photo of herself, which we later find out reads "You will find me in the next life, if not in this one." It is the same photo that Sayid carries with him on the island.

Important details in *Lost* lore: We find out why Sayid renounced his duties as a torturer. But more importantly, we discover the identity of the French woman, who she is, and how she went crazy. Even more important in the long run, there is the first mention of a group called "The Others."

Amount of action: Fair, due to the suspense in Sayid and Rousseau's encounters.

New important characters: Danielle Rousseau, a new survivor named Ethan, and Sayid's former love Nadia.

Connections between characters: Sayid and Rousseau meet for the first time. Walt grows closer to Locke. Hurley allows everyone else to finally relax, and Sawyer begins to thaw the chilly relationship between him and the other survivors.

***Lost* mysteries referenced:** The French woman and her distress call, Sayid's past as a torturer, and the Monster.

***Lost* mysteries introduced:** The story of how Rousseau crash landed and survived on the island, whispers on the island, mentions of a "sickness" and of people called "The Others."

Questions raised: Is Rousseau's story accurate? Is she crazy, or is she telling the truth about her past, or both? Is there a sickness? Who or what are The Others? Why are they whispering in the jungle? Did Sayid ever try to find Nadia again?

Talking points: Sayid comes face to face with his existence as a torturer in the past, as love makes him leave behind the lifestyle. In the present, he is on the other side of the fence as the one being tortured. Rousseau and Sayid share certain similarities, although she has lost her mind while Sayid has managed to remain sane and go on with his life.

This could be a cautionary tale for Sayid, or it could be that although she is crazy, she might be right about some things. After all, we now know that the survivors are not alone on this island.

Other key issues: Hurley comes through as the lighter, happier element of the show, and of this camp in general.

Must see episode?: Somewhat. We get some key answers about Rousseau, but they raise even more questions in the process. This is a tactic that will become very common in *Lost.*

RAISED BY ANOTHER

In the midst of all the worrying and fears for their lives, the survivors also face the prospect of new life being born. Claire, the very pregnant Australian woman on the plane, has somehow maintained her pregnancy even after this terrible crash. Eventually she's going to have to give birth, but how can she do that under these circumstances? As it turns out, this was a responsibility she was hoping to avoid.

As Claire suffers physical or perhaps just mental danger, she is revealed as a prospective mother who never wanted to keep her baby after giving birth. However, this plot line manages to introduce aspects of fate and destiny into the equation....while ending things with a substantial new threat on the horizon.

Episode plot: Claire has a nightmare where Locke says "He is your responsibility, but you gave him away, Claire. Everyone pays the price now...." She wakes up to find blood on her hands. Jack believes that she dug her nails into her hands, but Claire isn't so sure. Charlie tries to comfort her, however.

The next night, Claire has a hand cover her mouth while another hand puts a needle into her stomach. As a result of this incident, Hurley decides to take a census to find out who everyone is, in order to get a better idea of who is dangerous. Meanwhile, Jack comes to believe that

Claire imagined the attack due to stress. When he tells this to Claire, she leaves the caves.

Charlie runs after her, but soon Claire starts to feel contractions. Charlie finds Ethan and asks him to find Jack. But Claire is not having the baby now. Still, Charlie manages to calm her down and make her feel better.

Back at the caves, Hurley returns with the results of his census. He reveals that when he compared the census to the flight manifest, he found something shocking. One of the names on the census was not on the manifest. One of them was not on the plane.

When Charlie and Claire start walking back to the caves, they suddenly find Ethan there, staring intently at Claire.

Other stuff: Jack and Kate go back to their now traditional flirting pattern, while Kate is concerned that Sayid hasn't been back for a week. But Sayid returns near the end, looking delirious from his encounter with Rousseau and his trek back to the caves. He states breathlessly that they are not alone.

Main character: Claire Littleton.

Flashback details: When Claire got pregnant, she was taken aback, but her boyfriend Thomas reassured her. Claire then went to see a psychic named Richard Malkin, on the advice of a friend. But when Malkin reads her, he immediately sends her away in a frightened manner.

Not long afterwards, Thomas gets cold feet and leaves Claire. Later, she returns to get another reading from Malkin. He says that it is important that Claire keep the baby and not give it up for adoption, as she had begun to plan. Absolutely no one else other than Claire must raise this child, or else it appears something terrible will happen. Claire leaves and then has to endure months of phone calls from Malkin, urging her to change her mind. But by then, she has made arrangements to give the baby away to an adoptive couple.

At the meeting to finalize the deal, Claire tries to sign the agreement, but her pen runs out of ink. Finally she gets second thoughts and leaves. Claire rushes to Malkin and demands to hear his plan. He tells her that there is a couple in Los Angeles that will adopt the baby, and she needs to get on Flight 815 to meet them. He insists that it cannot be any other flight on any other day.

Later on the island, a talk with Charlie leads Claire to realize that Malkin put her on 815 on purpose, knowing that the plane would crash. This would leave her to raise the baby herself after all.

Important details in *Lost* lore: The importance of Claire's baby and the possibility that the plane crashed for a larger purpose. In the end, we also meet a native of the island for the first time, as he is perhaps one of the "Others" that Rousseau talked about.

Amount of action: Little, save for Claire's attacks.

New important characters: Psychic Richard Malkin, who may have foreseen the crash of 815.

Connections between characters: Charlie and Claire continue to get closer, and even have their first fight due to the question of whether Claire imagined her attacks.

***Lost* mysteries referenced:** The Others, whose existence seems to have been confirmed by Ethan.

***Lost* mysteries introduced:** Claire's baby and how valuable it may be.

Questions raised: Did the psychic really know that the plane would crash? What is the significance of Claire's baby? What happened to Sayid on his way back from Rousseau's? Who is Ethan? What does he want with Claire?

Talking points: For the first time from someone other than Locke, we get a sense that all of this might be happening for a reason. Maybe it is fate that caused the plane to crash, for a larger purpose than the survivors might know. Once again, there is a sense that this island causes people to confront their biggest fears and challenges from their pasts. In this case, it causes Claire to confront her fear about being a mom.

In addition, the show's first human antagonist is introduced in island native Ethan, but he is certainly not the last.

Other key issues: Hurley proves to be quite useful for the second straight episode.

Must see episode?: Yes, if only for the big reveals and the setup for the bigger stuff to come in the next few episodes.

ALL THE BEST COWBOYS HAVE DADDY ISSUES

By now, nearly every main character on *Lost* has had a flashback episode to set up their pasts. As the designated hero of the show, it is fitting that Jack becomes the first character to get a second flashback. And it serves to pretty much repeat the same recurring element of the first one, regarding his troubled relationship with his late father. But it fills in a few gaps and sheds some light on Jack's current actions on the island, as per usual for *Lost* flashbacks.

Jack is someone who never gives up in trying to fix something or save someone. In the past, that part of him came into a direct confrontation with his father, which was the last conflict they ever had. In the present, Jack's determination comes into conflict with an even more sinister and unknown enemy. However, the biggest discovery of all is made far away from him.

Episode plot: After Jack finds out that Ethan's name wasn't on the manifest, he rushes out with Locke to find Charlie and Claire. By then, they have already been taken. Jack starts chasing after the trail while Locke goes back to form a search team. Kate and Boone come along and catch up to Jack, who has been going in circles. Locke finds the right trail, and they soon discover that Charlie has left behind his finger bands as a trail to follow. However, there are two trails being left, so Jack and Kate go to follow one while Locke and Boone follow another.

Fueled by guilt over not believing Claire's claim that she was attacked, Jack presses on. He finally hears a scream and runs, but slips on the ground. When he looks up, he finds Ethan standing over him. They fight and Ethan manages to defeat him quickly. He warns Jack that he will kill one of them if Jack does not stop tracking him.

When Jack regains consciousness, he vows to keep going. He soon finds Charlie's last finger band, then looks up to see Charlie hanging from a tree. Jack brings him down and tries to revive him, but it appears that he is dead. Still not giving up, Jack relentlessly pounds on Charlie's chest and keeps giving him CPR until he finally starts breathing again.

That night, Jack asks Charlie what happened, but he can't remember much. All he does know is that the only thing "they" wanted was the still missing Claire.

Other stuff: When Locke goes to form a search team, Michael volunteers to come along, but he is turned down. Walt again takes Locke's side over Michael's in the matter. Later, he thoroughly beats Hurley in Locke's favorite game of backgammon, then tells Sawyer that Sayid is back.

Looking for revenge over his torture, Sawyer goes over to Sayid's resting place. Sayid tells him that he met Rousseau and heard whispers in the jungle, proving that there may be others on the island. A stunned Sawyer then leaves without taking any revenge.

As for Locke and Boone, the two talk about their respective past lives while on one of the trails. Though they are actually on the wrong trail, the two continue their trek through the night and through a rain storm. Once Boone figures out they are lost, he wants to go back. Locke tosses him a flashlight to help him on his way, but it falls on the ground, making a metallic clanking sound. The two start to dig in order to unearth this metal buried under the ground.

Main character: Jack Shephard.

Flashback details: Jack is in the middle of a surgery, trying to save a woman who is near death. Despite all his efforts to revive the patient, she dies. Another doctor tells him to call the time of the death. That doctor is Christian Shephard. As it turns out, this was his surgery, and Jack was called in to take over in the middle of it. Jack concludes that his father made a mistake during the surgery, accusing him of being drunk.

The next day, Christian is ready to file the report on the patient's death, but plans to leave out how he was impaired. He tries to convince Jack to help him cover it up, fearing that the truth will end his career. But Jack doesn't want to help him until Christian actually apologizes for his harsh treatment of him while he was growing up. He further butters Jack up by talking about his "extraordinary skills", and insists that Jack would be destroying Christian's life if he told the truth. Finally, Jack agrees to sign the false report.

The patient's husband sues the hospital and a hearing is called regarding the surgery. Jack backs up his father's story, which should ensure that Christian will avoid any trouble. As they conclude the hearing, it slips out that the patient was pregnant and Christian knew about it. Outraged at his father's deceit, Jack finally tells the whole truth.

This was to be the last time Jack and his father spoke before Christian went to Australia and drank himself to death.

Important details in *Lost* lore: The incident that ended the relationship between Jack and his father, the kidnapping of Claire, and the discovery of something metal on the ground.

Amount of action: Substantial, with Jack and Ethan's one sided fight and Jack's intense revival of Charlie.

New important characters: None.

Connections between characters: Jack and Locke have a bit of a spat in regards on how to track Charlie and Claire. Walt again takes Locke's side over Michael. Locke and Boone connect over tracking Charlie and Claire, before making their big discovery. Sawyer actually turns down getting revenge on Sayid, while Jack and Kate work closely together again.

***Lost* mysteries referenced:** Ethan and his mysterious work. Also, we find out what Jack's mother meant in "White Rabbit" when she said Jack needed to find his father "after what you did."

***Lost* mysteries introduced:** The metallic surface found in the jungle.

Questions raised: Why did Ethan only want Claire? Where are they now? What did Locke and Boone find? Why didn't Sawyer strike at Sayid? Was it plausible that Jack miraculously saved Charlie after he was unconscious for so long?

Talking points: Once again, the island gives a character a second chance to redeem a past mistake. Jack once again tries to save a dying person against all odds, after he failed to save his father's patient in the past. Jack himself says that he won't get away with this "again", equating Ethan to his father. Whereas his father screwed up enough so that Jack couldn't save his patient, this time Jack was able to save Charlie when it looked utterly impossible. In this case, Jack's obsession with going above and beyond for someone paid off.

Meanwhile, the mysteries of the island itself are beginning to show themselves, with the confirmation that "Others" are around, and that the island itself may be hiding something underground.

Other key issues: This is more confirmation that Jack's "daddy issues" cut him incredibly deep. Even heroes have their weak spots, as Jack was willing to cover up for his father's actions until the very end. The flashbacks of both this episode and "White Rabbit" tell quite a story when compared side by side.

Must see episode?: Yes. Jack goes through the emotional ringer again, Ethan's plot gets murkier, and things are set up for the season's most important plot line.

WHATEVER THE CASE MAY BE

Lost was packed with action and further mysteries about the island in the last few episodes. For this show, *Lost* stepped back and went back to a character driven story. Putting Claire's kidnapping aside as a mere subplot, it was Kate who took center stage this time with her second flashback.

Kate has already been revealed as a fugitive and a criminal, as well as the object of two vastly different men's desires. Both of those recurring elements come into play, with a bit more light shed into Kate's criminal past while Jack and Sawyer get caught in the middle. Kate's mysteries are not as closely related to the island and important plot lines as the other characters are, but once in a while the show needs some breathing room. And in true *Lost* fashion, we are both closer and farther away to figuring out Kate by the end of things.

Episode plot: Kate and Sawyer discover a waterfall and start to take a swim. Underwater, Kate discovers some plane wreckage, as well as a Halliburton case which is of some interest to her. She gets Sawyer to help her recover it, but does not tell her why it is important. Sawyer takes it back as a result, and is able to keep Kate from taking the case back that night.

Sawyer tries to open the case himself the next day, but nothing works. Kate manages to take the case while he's distracted. Sawyer tracks her down, and offers to let her have it if she tells him why she wants it so much. Again, Kate will not answer.

Finally she goes to Jack and tells him that the case belonged to the US Marshal who arrested her. In addition, it contains four guns inside. The key to opening it is on the dead body of the marshal, and Jack reluctantly agrees to dig it up.

After they do, Jack stops Kate from taking the key for herself. He then goes to Sawyer and threatens to cut off his medication if he doesn't give him the case. Sawyer agrees, but not before warning her about Kate. Jack and Kate meet in the cave to open the case, which indeed has four guns inside.

But the object that Kate is looking for is in a small envelope. It turns out to contain a small toy model of an Oceanic airplane. Jack asks Kate what it is and starts yelling when she doesn't give a straight answer. Finally, she yells out that it belonged to the man she loved... and to the man she killed.

Other stuff: Sayid now no longer believes that he heard any whispers in the jungle, now doubting Rousseau's stories. But he has maps from Rousseau's hut, although the notes and directions are in French. Since Shannon was able to translate Rousseau's recording, Sayid asks for her help. However, they don't get anywhere and the little bits that Shannon can translate are ramblings. But by the end, the two are able to bond.

Charlie is still in a traumatized state after Claire's abduction. Rose tries to help him out by sharing her continued belief that her husband is alive. Finally, Charlie breaks down in tears as Rose makes a prayer for him.

Locke and Boone are going out in the jungle more and more, claiming to be looking for Claire. However, their true goal involves the metallic surface they discovered, which turns out to be the door of a hatch. Locke is determined to get it open.

Main character: Kate Austin.

Flashback details: Kate is applying for a loan at a bank under the alias "Mrs. Ryan." At that point, a team of bank robbers charge in and take over, demanding access to the bank vault. It is later revealed that Kate is working undercover as part of the robbery.

The team leader pretends to threaten Kate's life if they are not taken to the money, which eventually works. When they get to the safety deposit boxes, Kate shoots the team leader before he kills the employee. Turning on all the robbers, she only wants access to safety deposit box #815. Once she gets it, she takes out the only contents inside, a small envelope which is later found to have the Oceanic toy airplane inside.

Important details in *Lost* lore: A further look into Kate's criminal past, as well as the revelation that there was a man she loved before Jack and Sawyer, who apparently died as a result. There is also official conformation that there is a hatch underneath the island.

Amount of action: Fair in the flashback scenes, but the island scenes have action that is mainly centered on opening the case, and on the usual Jack/Kate/Sawyer tension.

New important characters: None.

Connections between characters: Locke and Boone are now joined at the hip to open the hatch. But while Boone isn't looking, Shannon may have found something with Sayid. Rose and Charlie bond over their grief and faith. On the Jack/Kate/Sawyer front, Kate and Sawyer again have the closest sexual tension while Jack and Kate square off in a more emotional way.

***Lost* mysteries referenced:** Kate's criminal past, Rousseau's maps, the fate of the tail section of the plane.

***Lost* mysteries introduced:** The hatch, Kate's dead love.

Questions raised: What is the hatch? Who was the man Kate loved and killed, and what does the toy airplane have to do with him? Why is Sayid bonding with Shannon despite his situation with Nadia? Where is Claire? How will the newly discovered guns come into play?

Talking points: Charlie and Rose explore the different ways to deal with grief and the lost of a loved one. In both cases, they were struck by initial trauma, but turned to faith in hopes that they would see their lost loves again. Will that be rewarded?

Kate's past, both with love and with her fugitive past, keeps getting murkier. Considering how she used the robbers to get the toy airplane, it is no wonder how she is able to use and fool men like Jack and Sawyer so often.

And in the usual *Lost* pattern, instead of answering more questions about the recent abduction of Claire and the existence of the Others, there is a new mystery tacked on regarding the hatch.

Other key issues: Fans of the Pixar film *Finding Nemo* will recognize that Shannon's song in French was "Beyond the Sea" as heard in the movie's end credits.

Must see episode?: Somewhat. The hatch and the Sayid/Shannon bond is further set up, but the rest is mainly for the "shippers" of the main *Lost* couples. If you aren't a fan of those by now, this will be a filler episode.

HEARTS AND MINDS

Some *Lost* characters have an easy time getting huge fan support. Locke, Sawyer, and Hurley were instant fan favorites, while Jack, Charlie, and Sayid also have fair sized fan bases. But despite the popularity of some *Lost* survivors, there are always at least one or two characters that aren't so lucky. Boone and Shannon filled that bill in the first season. Actually, Boone was regarded as okay, while Shannon got the brunt of *Lost* fans hatred. But since Boone was so attached to Shannon, it didn't help his cause.

In this episode, we find out just how attached Boone was to Shannon, and still is. But Locke has a little something to say about that as the hatch mystery takes up even more focus. We know that *Lost* fans would easily choose Locke over Shannon if they were Boone, but Boone needs a bit more convincing.

Episode plot: Boone notices that Shannon is getting closer to Sayid, but Locke wants Boone focused on opening the hatch. However, Boone tells him that they should start sharing their discovery with the others, or at least with Shannon. When Boone goes off to see her, Locke knocks him out with his knife.

Boone wakes up to discover that Locke has tied him to a tree. Locke is making some kind of substance in a coconut bowl, putting it on Boone's face while explaining that he is doing this for his own good. Locke leaves his knife just out of Boone's reach before he goes.

Soon, Boone hears Shannon screaming, since it appears Locke has tied her up too. Now armed with the proper motivation, he reaches far enough to get the knife and cut himself free. Unfortunately, the sounds of the monster are heard not far away. Boone runs to Shannon and cuts her loose before the monster comes.

On the way back, Boone finally tells her about Locke and the hatch, but then the monster comes again. This time, the two are separated. Boone rushes to find Shannon, but finds her lying by the stream, clearly dead.

That night, Boone attacks Locke and tells him that Shannon died. Locke merely asks why there's none of Shannon's blood on him. Indeed, the blood is gone. Locke then shows Boone that Shannon is nearby, talking with Sayid.

The material that Locke put on Boone's head only made him hallucinate that Shannon had died. As it turns out, Boone reveals that he felt relieved when he thought Shannon was dead. Locke tells him that it's time to let go, and Boone, now a full disciple of Locke's, follows.

Other stuff: The camp's boar supply is running low, due to Locke failing to catch them because of his work on the hatch. Desperate for some food, Hurley turns to Jin and tries to ask for help in catching fish. Since they can't understand each other, it's not an easy task.

Sun on the other hand, has done well for herself by making a garden, which Kate helps her with. But Kate soon realizes that Sun can understand her, and can speak English as well. Sun eventually gets her not to tell anyone, especially Jin.

Jack's suspicion of Locke starts to grow, although Charlie insists that Locke is the best person to save them all.

Main character: Boone.

Flashback details: Boone is working at a tennis club when he gets a call from Shannon, who yells for her to come and get her in Sydney. When he gets there, he finds Shannon with her boyfriend Bryan, as she has a bruise on her face. Boone then goes to file a complaint with a detective. In the process, it is revealed that Boone and Shannon are only step-siblings, as Boone's mother married Shannon's father when they were kids. When the police can't help Boone, he goes to bribe Bryan with $50,000 dollars in return for him leaving Shannon.

Boone then goes to bring Shannon home, but soon discovers the truth. Shannon and Bryan made up the entire domestic abuse story in order to scam the money from Boone. Boone responds by getting into a fight with Bryan, which he loses. That night, Shannon visits him in his hotel after Bryan took off with the money. She insists that Boone fell for the scam because he loves her.

And as step-siblings, it's a tiny bit less disturbing to see that they had sex afterwards. But Shannon dismisses the whole thing the next morning before they leave to go on flight 815 together.

Important details in *Lost* lore: Locke fully turns Boone over to his side with the hallucination ordeal. Boone and Shannon's....relationship is discovered, and Jack starts to have suspicions about Locke for the first time.

Amount of action: Fair, although most of the action sequences were in Boone's fevered imagination.

New important characters: None.

Connections between characters: Locke gives Boone a major test, which he winds up passing. It winds up resolving Boone's feelings, family wise and other wise, towards Shannon, causing him to give his full loyalty to Locke. Meanwhile, Shannon is evidently closer with Sayid now.

Kate discovers Sun's secret, as Sun finally has someone other than Michael to really talk to. Hurley and Jin have comical experiences together as Hurley tries to catch fish with him. Jack starts to suspect Locke is lying to the camp. In the past, Sawyer is seen being dragged through the police station Boone is visiting.

***Lost* mysteries referenced:** The hatch, the monster.

***Lost* mysteries introduced:** None.

Questions raised: Has Boone really learned to let go of Shannon? Was Locke right or wrong to do what he did to Boone? Did he do it to help him, or just to keep the hatch a secret? Can Sun's secret of speaking English stay a secret much longer?

Talking points: Leaving aside the issues raised by the sex scene, Boone and Shannon appear to have a relationship straight out of a soap opera. And like he did with Charlie and Jack, Locke uses his unique perspective, or a dangerous extension of his island faith, to solve Boone's internal crisis.

But if Locke went this far to do it, it proves how his determination to open the hatch is becoming something else entirely. He is outright lying to the camp and manipulating Boone to keep things under wraps. How much farther will he go later?

Other key issues: We get back to the issues of actually surviving and getting food on the island, as Jin and Sun seem to be doing well for themselves, albeit separately.

Must see episode?: Perhaps for the soap opera like sex scene between step-sibs and for Locke's weird little plan. Otherwise, there isn't much impact on the larger *Lost* story in this episode.

SPECIAL

While other survivors are dealing with leadership, hatches, lies and secrets of their own, Michael's problems are perhaps even more difficult. Ever since the crash, things with his estranged son Walt haven't improved a bit, and Walt's bonding with Locke hasn't helped. When he's not dealing with that, he's usually in the middle of Sun and Jin's conflict. Michael certainly envisioned problems when he was first called upon to take care of Walt, but these situations go beyond that. So it's no wonder that he suggests building a raft to get out of here, in the middle of his latest showdowns with Walt and Locke.

But once again, the way a character acts on the island is quite different from what we see of them in their flashbacks. Once more, the most startling and surprising details come out of another character's past, which opens the door to the supernatural. And even when some hope arrives, another conflict and mystery reappears once more.

Episode plot: Michael's latest Locke-related conflict with Walt is about Walt learning to throw knives. Locke insists that Walt should realize his potential, stating that he is "special." This throws Michael for a loop as he drags Walt away.

That night, Michael confesses to Sun that even though he doesn't know how to communicate with Walt, he can't let him grow up on this island. The next morning, Michael takes action and tells the other survivors that he wants to build a raft. However, they are too busy analyzing Rousseau's maps to give him much support. So Michael gets Walt to help him get started, although he is busy reading his comic books.

Walt eventually sneaks away to see Locke, although this time Locke tells him that he should be with his father. But Michael doesn't see this part and immediately starts to yell at Locke when he finds him. Walt defends him by yelling about Michael being absent all his life. In response, Michael throws his comics into the fire.

Later, Walt is gone again, but this time he's not with Locke. Michael and Locke join forces to find him. Walt is walking Vincent in the jungle, until Vincent suddenly runs away. When Walt chases him, he instead finds one of the island's polar bears. By the time Michael and Locke find him, he is trapped between some tree stumps while the polar bear tries to bring him down. Working together, Michael and Locke climb above Walt, as Locke grabs him while Michael distracts the bear.

Other stuff: Charlie is out looking for Claire's diary. He immediately suspects Sawyer and turns out to be right. With Kate's help, Sawyer hands it over. Afterwards, Charlie struggles to resist reading it, but finally gives in. He brings the diary to Jack's attention, specifically a part about a dream regarding a black rock. Sayid realizes that it could be the "Black Rock" Rousseau wrote about in her maps.

Meanwhile, Locke and Boone go out to find Vincent, but soon see another figure.....the long lost Claire.

Main character: Michael Dawson.

Flashback details: Unlike the Michael on the island, Michael was happy with being a dad in the past. Walt's mother was Michael's girlfriend Susan, and Michael couldn't stop doting on Walt when he was very young. However, Michael's relationship with Susan soured when she took a job in Amsterdam, taking Walt with him.

Michael could barely live with not seeing Walt, especially after hearing that Susan is seeing her boss, Brian Porter. Michael vows on the phone to go to Amsterdam and get Walt back. He is then hit by a car five seconds later for his trouble.

As Michael recovers, Susan visits and tells him that she is marrying Brian and wants full custody of Walt. Afterwards, there is a flashback of Walt, as he is reading a book about birds while Susan and Brian talk. He tells them to look at the book, but they pay no attention, until a bird just like the one in Walt's book crashes into the window.

Michael gets the next flashback, as Brian visits him to tell him that Susan has died. Brian wants Michael to take custody of Walt, even though Michael has completely forgotten about him by then and has lost his desire to get him back. Brian is abandoning Walt because he is "special" noting that "things happen when he's around." With no choice, Michael heads to Sydney to meet older Walt for the first time.

Important details in *Lost* lore: Walt is revealed to have "special" abilities. Another island polar bear is discovered. Michael begins his quest to leave the island on a raft. Rousseau's maps reveal a location called "The Black Rock." Claire finally returns.

Amount of action: Fair, due to the polar bear attacks.

New important characters: Walt's mother Susan.

Connections between characters: The triangle between Michael, Walt and Locke comes to a climax, as Michael finally begins to fix things with Walt and stops seeing Locke as a threat. We also see the very big difference between how Michael regarded Walt in the past compared to their relationship on the island. Michael also manages to open up to Sun about his worries.

***Lost* mysteries referenced:** The polar bears, Claire's disappearance, and Rousseau's maps.

***Lost* mysteries introduced:** Walt's powers, the Black Rock.

Questions raised: How did Michael finally stop trying to get Walt back in the past? What are Walt's powers? Is there any connection between Claire's dream and Rousseau's map? Where has Claire been? How did she get back, and where is Ethan? Is Michael going to succeed in building his raft?

Talking points: In the flashbacks and the present, fatherhood drives Michael in vastly different ways. The juxtaposition between his feelings back then and his feelings now are quite different, which again proves that things aren't always what they seem with these characters. But for the first time, progress has been made for Michael and Walt, and that may be what fuels his efforts to finally leave the island. Yet it appears that with Claire finally back, it will have to wait.

An entirely different dimension is raised regarding Walt. Now we know that he indeed has some kind of power, but it is unclear whether he really knows it. If anyone knows, it's Locke, and perhaps that's why he's taken such an interest in him. The island has already worked in great ways for Locke, so perhaps it has expanded Walt's powers as well. But how do Walt's abilities fit into the larger story?

Other key issues: It is interesting that Jack and Sayid were more interested in going over Rousseau's maps than in taking up Michael's offer to build the raft. Perhaps they have already settled into the island too much.

Must see episode?: Yes. Michael and Walt's relationship is seen in a different light, new mysteries are introduced, and there's even a cliffhanger for good measure.

HOMECOMING

After weeks of being absent, Claire finally comes home. But for those expecting answers as to what happened to her, why she was taken, and who Ethan is…don't bother. Since Claire lost her memory, even she doesn't know. So we're stuck with focusing on Charlie as he takes measures to protect Claire, even though she has no idea who he is anymore. Unfortunately for both of them, Ethan didn't have a similar memory loss.

If there are a whole group of "Others" on this island, Ethan shows that they are not playing around. With the threat of real war on the horizon, the camp must take measures to defend themselves. But is Charlie ready for that responsibility? Can he take care of someone despite his past? In a way, he does prove himself. But in another way, he probably does it too well.

Episode plot: Locke and Boone bring Claire back to the caves, but Claire is not happy to see them. In fact, she has no idea who they are. After a month away, Claire has lost her memory. Charlie tries to fill her in by giving her the diary, reminding her that Ethan is the bad guy.

The next day, Charlie and Jin's walk through the jungle is interrupted by Ethan. He knocks Jin out and grabs Charlie by the throat, demanding that Claire be brought back to him. If she isn't, he will kill one survivor each day, saving Charlie for last. Afterwards, Jack and Locke form a lookout team to stand guard during the night. But it is not enough as Ethan indeed kills a survivor named Scott.

Claire is uneasy about everyone avoiding her and not letting her in on what's going on. After she finds out from Charlie, she insists that she can take care of herself and volunteers to be part of the retaliation against Ethan. Locke warns Jack that this is Ethan's territory, so Jack reveals the existence of the marshal's guns, which gives the survivors the advantage back.

With Claire as bait, Jack, Locke, Sayid, and Sawyer plan to ambush Ethan after he comes to get her. Charlie comes along as well, using the gun that the marshal was carrying. The trap is set, and Ethan takes the bait. Jack catches him before he gets away with Claire. This time, Jack gets even by defeating Ethan in a fight.

With the others surrounding him, they prepare to take Ethan back to question him about who he is and who he works for. But that plan is shattered when Charlie shoots and kills Ethan instantly.

That night, Claire tells him that she remembers their imaginary peanut butter conversation weeks ago, and that she does want to trust him.

Other stuff: Little goes on that is unrelated to the main plot this time.

Main character: Charlie Pace.

Flashback details: After Drive Shaft broke up, Charlie is in the throes of drug addiction. He still manages to get together with a girl named Lucy, who gets him a job working for her father. But eventually, Charlie goes through withdrawal and tries to steal a valuable cigarette case for drug money. His symptoms also ruin his job, where he passes out and the other employees find the case in his jacket.

Later, he tries to explain himself to Lucy, who shuts the door on him and says that he will never be able to take care of anyone.

Important details in *Lost* lore: Claire has amnesia after her ordeal with Ethan. For the first time, someone in the camp is murdered. Ethan too is killed before he can give out any answers.

Amount of action: Heavy.

New important characters: None.

Connections between characters: Charlie and Claire have to start all over again due to Claire's memory loss, but they make a little progress by the end.

***Lost* mysteries referenced:** Ethan and the Others, Claire's kidnapping.

***Lost* mysteries introduced:** Claire's amnesia, the issue of what happened to her during her time with Ethan,

Questions raised: How did Claire lose her memory? Did Ethan do anything to her or the baby? Was Charlie right to kill Ethan before he could have answered any questions? With Ethan dead, is the threat to the camp over?

Talking points: Charlie tries to prove that he can take care of someone in both the past and present. He fails in the past, and perhaps went too far in trying to succeed in the present. His execution of Ethan also leaves a lot of questions unanswered. Now the best hope in getting answers will be to repair Claire's memory, which could take some time. By now, it has become a full fledged *Lost* tradition to stop just short of getting some questions answered.

Other key issues: After near misses with Charlie and Shannon, someone in the camp finally is killed. But thus far, *Lost* has still never actually killed off a full fledged major character.

Must see episode?: Yes, if only to bring half-closure to the Ethan storyline. But the rest of the episode, including a Charlie flashback that is all but useless, is a letdown. Once again we are left with more questions than answers.

OUTLAWS

The *Lost* survivors have already dealt with various ordeals since surviving the crash. But despite attacks from mysterious Others and a monster, the biggest weapon to use against them has been the past. They can survive plane crashes and actually start to adapt to a desert island, but compared to their pasts on the mainland, this is a piece of cake. We've seen Jack's conflict with his father, Kate's lifetime of running away, Locke's paralysis, Sayid's history of torture, Charlie's drug fueled rise and fall from the top, and Sun's broken marriage. But no one's past has shaped who they are and why they do what they do on the island more than Sawyer's.

The deaths of his parents through the actions of a con man literally transformed Sawyer into the hardened, sarcastic, cynical man that the survivors have to tolerate. The search for this man has made Sawyer do some pretty underhanded things. In this episode, we see how it made him cross the biggest line of all. But before he did that, he had time to talk with a very unlikely kindred spirit.

Episode plot: A boar is going through Sawyer's tent late at night. When he goes after it, he hears some strange whispers saying "It'll come back around." The next day, Sawyer goes after the boar again and hears the same whisper before the boar charges past him.

Sawyer goes on a full blown hunt to kill the boar, taking the only gun from the marshal's suitcase that Jack hasn't put back. Kate eventually tags along, asking in return that he gives her whatever she wants from his stash in the future, with no questions asked. That night, the two make camp and play a round of the popular college game "I Never." Through this game, it is shown that Kate was once married and that both Kate and Sawyer have killed a man in their pasts.

The next morning, Sawyer wakes up to find that the boar has attacked his campsite, but left Kate's alone. Locke then comes around to their camp. He and Sawyer talk about the boar and how Sawyer thinks it has a personal vendetta against him. Locke senses that Sawyer is projecting the boar as something else from his past.

Kate and Sawyer are soon able to track down the boar's baby. Sawyer grabs it in order to lure the boar out, which makes Kate leave out of disgust. When he goes after her, he finally finds the boar. Sawyer stares the boar down for a long moment, with his gun pointed at it, but he cannot shoot it. Shrugging off the whole thing, he and Kate go back to camp.

Sawyer then finds Jack and gives him back the gun. A comment that Jack makes afterwards brings to mind an important part of Sawyer's flashback....

Other stuff: Claire is starting to remember more things about Charlie, who is still living with killing Ethan. Hurley notices this and brings it to Sayid's attention. When Sayid confronts him, Charlie denies feeling any guilt over having killed Ethan. Sayid shares that he had his own troubles after he killed his first man, and reassures Charlie that he is not alone. Afterwards, Charlie is able to clear his mind enough to take a walk with Claire.

Main character: Sawyer

Flashback details: The episode starts by showing Sawyer as a young boy. He was under his bed when his father killed his mother and then himself, due to their altercation with a con man named Sawyer.

Later, a grown up Sawyer is encountered by a former partner named Hibbs. He tells him that he found "the real Sawyer." His real name is Frank Duckett, and he runs a shrimp station in Sydney. Sawyer flies over to Sydney and purchases a gun to kill him. But when he goes there to do it, he cannot pull the trigger.

Sawyer drinks his troubles away at a bar, where another American is sitting nearby and getting drunk. The two men strike up a conversation. The man shares that some men are meant to suffer. After all, "That's why the Red Sox will never win the Series." In his case, he was a chief of surgery who lost his job due to his son ratting him out. Although his son thinks he hates him, it is not true. In fact, the man is proud of his son for being a better doctor and man than he is. If he wanted to, he could call him right now, tell him he loves him and fix everything between them. But he won't because he's too weak. He then advises Sawyer that if his business in Sydney will ease his suffering, then he needs to go do it.

The man's name? Dr. Christian Shephard.

That night, Sawyer is back at the station and finds Duckett taking out the trash. He walks up to him and shoots him in the chest. As Duckett lies dying, Sawyer pulls out the letter he wrote "Sawyer" when he was a boy and starts reading. But Duckett interrupts, telling Sawyer that he has Hibbs's money. Sawyer realizes that Hibbs tricked him into killing a man who owed him money. Duckett says "It'll come back around" before he dies in front of the stunned and heartbroken Sawyer.

Sometime later on the island, Jack repeats his father's line about the Red Sox never winning the series. Sawyer now realizes that he was talking to Jack's father at the bar, as he finds out that he died. Jack asks him why Sawyer asked about his father. With the chance to now tell Jack that Christian loved him all along, he merely says "No reason...."

Important details in *Lost* lore: Sawyer killed a man who he thought was the con artist that destroyed his family. Kate has been married before. Sawyer had a conversation with Jack's father before he died, where he revealed that he really didn't hate Jack for what he did to him. Sawyer now knows that, even though Jack doesn't.

Amount of action: Fair.

New important characters: None

Connections between characters: Kate and Sawyer get the majority of time together this time. Sawyer's past connection to

Christian Shephard is also revealed. Sayid and Charlie relate to their respective violent acts, which paves the way for Charlie to begin getting close to Claire again.

***Lost* mysteries referenced:** The mystery of who destroyed Sawyer's family. The jungle whispers also return. Claire's amnesia begins to clear up.

***Lost* mysteries introduced:** None.

Questions raised: Did the boar really represent the man Sawyer had killed? Why did he hear the whispers? Why did he ultimately spare the boar? Why didn't Sawyer tell Jack that he met his father? Will he ever? When did Kate get married?

Talking points: The tragedy of Sawyer's past only increases. The man who conned his parents never actually killed them himself, but now Sawyer has killed the wrong man in cold blood. Sawyer truly did go above and beyond making himself over to become this man. Yet by sparing the boar, he might have taken a small but key step towards his recovery.

We are beginning to get a larger picture about how these survivors are connected to each other. Call it a "Six Degrees of *Lost*" phenomenon. Although these people don't appear to have met each other directly before the crash, they are showing some indirect connections that indicate the hand of destiny in all this. Perhaps they are all together now for a reason.

Other key issues: In the main love triangle, Sawyer appears to have the lead now, at least in this episode.

Must see episode?: Yes. Unlike recent episodes with Kate and Charlie, Sawyer's second flashback really sheds some new light on the character in very surprising ways. The Sawyer/Christian scene alone is one of the season's high points.

...IN TRANSLATION

First impressions have been shattered time and time again on *Lost.* No one is ever who they appear to be, even con men and struggling fathers. But an exception could have still been made for Jin. All we have seen of Jin so far is that he's a controlling, antagonistic husband. His wife Sun learned English behind his back and almost left him before flight 815 boarded. Through Sun's first flashback, she got the impression that he might have been a killer for her wealthy father. Combined with his altercations with Michael, Jin has proven to be a pretty hard person to be around. Surely an exception could be made to judging this book by its cover.

However, that is not how *Lost* rolls. We got Sun's point of view about how their marriage fell apart, but we did not get Jin's. When we do, events on the island and events from the past are seen in a whole new light yet again.

Episode plot: Jin and Sun's latest argument consists of Jin trying to cover Sun up when she goes out in a bikini. Michael tries to break them up, but Sun slaps him. Later, she explains that he tried to get Michael away before Jin attacked him, but Michael is done trying to get involved in their business. He is focused on building his raft, which is coming along very nicely with the help of Walt and Sawyer, who has bought himself a trip onboard.

That night, the raft is set on fire and destroyed. Immediately, Michael believes it was Jin who did it. Sun then sees Jin going through the cave's medical supplies, with his hands burned.

That morning, Jin is by himself in the jungle before Sawyer attacks him. He drags Jin to the beach, where Michael accuses him of destroying the raft. Jin cannot respond in English and can barely understand the accusations, so he is unable to defend himself. Michael punches him over and over until Sun finally calls for him to stop in English.

With her secret out, Sun tells them that Jin didn't burn the raft, knowing that he tried to put the fire out instead. Locke then steps in and states that the problem is the people that have attacked them and killed them before. He yells "We're not the only people on this island, and we all know it!!" The survivors stop suspecting Jin, who is still shocked that Sun can speak English.

Later, Jin packs up and starts to leave the caves. Sun pleads for them to start over, but he doesn't listen. She then tells him in English that she was going to leave him. When she asks once again for them to "go back to the beginning" Jin replies in Korean that "It's too late" and leaves.

Surprisingly, Jin then goes over to Michael and starts to help him rebuild the raft. As for Sun, she walks on the beach in her bikini without any worry.

Other stuff: Sayid tells Boone about how he and Shannon have gotten closer. Boone warns him that Shannon often uses people that can "take care of her." This gives Sayid some pause and he begins to draw away from her. Once Shannon realizes that Boone got to him, she prepares to confront him. Locke talks her out of it, advising her not to worry about what Boone said, saying that "Everyone gets a new life on this island."

The night after the raft burns, Locke and Walt are playing backgammon again. Locke then asks Walt why he burned the raft. After Locke promises not to tell anyone, Walt confesses that he's tired of moving around all the time, and he likes it on the island. Naturally, Locke understands this very well.

Main character: Jin.

Flashback details: The time line of Sun's first flashback is now seen from Jin's point of view. Jin asks her father, Mr. Paik, for permission to marry Sun. He gets it, but only after promising to work as a personal "assistant" for Mr. Paik. Jin has to undergo "management training" right after the wedding, which delays their honeymoon.

Sometime later, Mr. Paik asks Jin to "communicate his displeasure" to the head of the Korean Secretary for Environmental Safety, who has closed down a Paik owned factory. When he does so, Jin merely tells the man about it, which makes him relieved for reasons that Jin isn't too clear about.

The next day, Paik calls Jin and voices his displeasure, sending him back to the house with an associate who will deliver the real message. After realizing that this man plans to kill the secretary, Jin rushes in and merely beats him up before he can be shot. He tells him to open the factory, adding that "I just saved your life."

This is the reason why Jin came into his house with blood on his hands in "House of the Rising Sun." After Jin slaps Sun and says he does whatever her father tells him, he is then seen scrubbing the blood off his hands and breaking down in tears.

Sometime later, Jin visits his father, even though he told Mr. Paik that his father was dead. He was ashamed of his dad for being a fisherman, but now he comes over to ask for forgiveness. Afterwards, he tells his father about Sun and their material troubles. Jin is advised to make his final delivery for Mr. Paik, which is to go on flight 815 and deliver a watch to Los Angeles, and then never come back.

As it turns out, at the same time that Sun was about to leave Jin before flight 815 boarded, Jin was about to quit his job and stay in America to repair their marriage. But it may be too late now.

Important details in *Lost* lore: The work that Jin did for Sun's father is revealed, as well as his overwhelming guilt and shame over it. The raft burns down because of Walt, but it is now in the process of being rebuilt. Jin and everyone else discover that Sun can speak English. Locke briefly hints to Walt that his father was "not cool."

Amount of action: Fair.

New important characters: Sun's father is seen in person for the first time.

Connections between characters: Sun and Jin's marital difficulties reach the boiling point, as does the conflict between Michael and Jin. Shannon learns to put Boone aside and focus on her relationship with Sayid. Walt confides to Locke that he burned down the raft because he likes being on the island.

***Lost* mysteries referenced:** Jin's violent work for Sun's father is revealed. Locke brings up the Others as culprits for the raft attack, although it was only to cover up for Walt.

***Lost* mysteries introduced:** None.

Questions raised: Is this it for Sun and Jin's marriage? Why is Jin now helping Michael rebuild the raft after what happened? Will Walt try anything else to avoid leaving the island? Can the raft be rebuilt?

Talking points: After 16 episodes of Jin being a cold and unloving person, he shows just how conflicted and heartbroken he really was. It turns out that both Jin and Sun had secret plans and frustrations that they could not communicate to each other. Yet now that everything is out in the open, they seem farther apart than ever.

We also see that Locke isn't the only person who prefers life on the island. Still, it looks like Walt's efforts were for naught as construction resumes on the raft. With Michael having made plans to include Walt and Sawyer on this trip, it appears that the prospect of leaving the island is more of a reality.

Other key issues: Locke again tries to solve other character's problems, this time with Shannon. But he most likely advised Shannon to disregard Boone's complaints so that Boone could stay focused on the hatch again. Still, even after Boone learned to "let go" of Shannon, he meddled with her and Sayid anyway. Perhaps he hasn't let go as much as Locke would want.

Some more perceptive fans noticed that when Jin visited the secretary's house, Hurley was seen on a TV for some reason.

Must see episode?: Yes. It provides a much needed new perspective on Jin while advancing some first and second tier stories on the island.

NUMBERS

4, 8, 15, 16, 23, 42. Thanks to *Lost,* these numbers will live on in pop culture for all time. None of these numbers had a huge significance beyond math and sports stats beforehand. The number 23 is a fairly infamous number on its own, as Jim Carrey would go on to prove. But aside from that, these numbers together were nothing special. The numbers 8 and 15 combined to make Oceanic Flight 815, but beyond that...

Yet with this episode, *Lost* fans would become numerologists, if only to find anything else that related to these numbers. Out of all the *Lost* obsessions, this is undoubtedly among the top five. They speak to the very heart of this story and all its mysteries, as well as the power of the island itself. And who would have expected that it would be Hurley, the fat comic relief of the show, to expose this massive power?

4, 8, 15, 16, 23, 42....

For this episode, we need to explore the flashback details first.

Main character: Hurley.

Flashback details: Hurley is wearing the uniform of a fast food worker at his house. He watches the local lottery, where the winning numbers are 4, 8, 15, 16, 23, and 42. These are the exact numbers on

Hurley's lottery ticket. He faints after realizing he has won over 100 million dollars.

At a press conference for Hurley, his grandfather suffers a fatal heart attack. Later, more tragic events happen to people around Hurley. On top of that, the new house he bought for his mother burns down, she suffers a broken ankle at the same time, and Hurley is arrested on suspicion of owning drugs. Hurley is convinced that he's become cursed after winning the lottery. Soon, he suspects the numbers themselves caused the curse.

Hurley travels to a mental institution that he was once a resident of. He finds a patient named Leonard, who keeps repeating the six numbers. Since this is where Hurley got the inspiration to use the numbers in the lottery, he asks Leonard where he got the numbers from. When Hurley tells Leonard what he did with the numbers, he becomes hysterical and yells "You've opened the box!!" But Hurley does find out that he got the numbers from a friend who heard the numbers in Australia.

Hurley travels to Australia to find the friend, and instead finds his wife. He discovers that Leonard and his friend heard the numbers from listening to a looping radio broadcast that came from the Pacific Ocean. Afterwards, they both suffered from terrible luck. Although the wife believes that the numbers are not cursed, Hurley leaves to go on flight 815 no less reassured.

Episode plot: Michael needs a new battery to charge the distress beacon on his raft. Sayid dismisses the idea of getting one from Rousseau, however. Hurley believes otherwise after seeing the numbers 4, 8, 15, 16, 23, and 42 all over Rousseau's maps. Hurley then goes out to the jungle to find her.

Jack, Sayid, and Charlie track him down and stop him from falling into one of Rousseau's traps. Hurley claims he's going to get a battery from her, and the three come along. They reach a bridge, which Hurley is able to cross without much trouble. Charlie crosses it too, but the bridge then falls apart.

Although Jack and Sayid are far away, Hurley wants to go on anyway. Charlie starts to accuse Hurley of acting crazy, which makes Hurley very upset. As he starts to tell him why he's on this trip, gunshots are heard. Hurley runs away but then runs into the source of the shots, which is Rousseau.

Hurley tells her that he was on flight 815 with Sayid, then shows her the maps. He wants to know why she drew the numbers. When she says she doesn't know, Hurley explodes at last and demands some answers.

Rousseau then confesses that when her scientific expedition crashed onto the island, they were following a radio transmission where a voice repeated the numbers over and over. After they crashed, the rest of her team became sick before they could figure out what the numbers meant. It was the numbers that brought Rousseau to the island, which led to the misery and losses she suffered over the last 16 years. As such, she agrees with Hurley that they are cursed.

Relieved that someone finally agrees with him, and finally convinced that he's not crazy, Hurley hugs her. He then returns to Jack, Sayid and Charlie with the battery.

That night, Hurley shares with Charlie that he thinks he's cursed. When Charlie disagrees, Hurley shares his biggest secret. Back home, he's worth 156 million dollars. But Charlie believes he is just joking and leaves in frustration.

The final image is of the hatch door. Upon a close up, something is shown imprinted on it.

It is 4, 8, 15, 16, 23, and 42.....

Other stuff: Locke asks for Claire's help on a "project." She helps him build something, although she has no idea what it is. Later at night, she tells Locke that it's her birthday and shares that she wanted to give her baby up before the crash. When they are done, it is shown that Locke didn't build something related to the hatch, but instead built a crib for Claire. Locke wishes Claire a happy birthday.

Important details in *Lost* lore: 4, 8, 15, 16, 23, and 42. The numbers are also tied to Rousseau crashing on the island, as well as the hatch. Also, Hurley is a millionaire and perhaps a former mental patient. Hurley's real name is Hugo Reyes.

Amount of action: Fair.

New important characters: Hurley's family, as well as mental patient Leonard.

Connections between characters: Hurley and Charlie square off over Hurley's obsession. However, Hurley finds answers from Rousseau after all. Claire is able to confide in Locke, who takes time away from the hatch to build her a present. In the past, Hurley owns a box company in Tustin, which is likely the box company Locke worked at.

***Lost* mysteries referenced:** Rousseau's past, the hatch.

***Lost* mysteries introduced:** The numbers, Hurley's past at a mental institution.

Questions raised: What in Heaven's name are the numbers? Are they truly cursed? What are they doing on the hatch? What role did they have in causing Rousseau to crash on the island? How deeply are the numbers connected to the island itself? Was Hurley really a mental patient?

Talking points: The island's history and mysteries are now deeply connected to these numbers, for one thing.

It is always the person you least suspect who might be crazy and/or cursed, which is Hurley in this case. But there are just too many incidents involving these numbers to believe Hurley is crazy, although he could be both crazy and right. His fear and determination to prove he's not crazy have certainly made him weary. Even if he could tell someone about this, they would dismiss him just like Charlie did at the end.

Although we found out a lot of secrets, they don't help out anyone except Hurley. But it could be bad news for Locke and Boone if the hatch is infected with the numbers.

Other key issues: Rousseau is also made into a more tragic and less crazed figure due to her own affliction with the numbers.

Must see episode?: Perhaps one of the most important episodes in *Lost* history, so yes.

DEUS EX MACHINA

The incredible story of John Locke is one of *Lost's* most famous tales. Paralyzed for four years until the island healed him, Locke has risen further than any other character on the show. He has overcome a great deal and become the man he always thought he was meant to be. Until now, Locke's greatest test seemed to be his paralysis. But we are about to see that he didn't have it easy even before he went into the wheelchair.

On the island, Locke faces the greatest threat to his new faith, in this case the hatch. But he presses through, hoping that the island will give him what he needs just like it did before. However, Locke is a man who dealt with a lot of tragedy and sorrow in his life. Even on the island, and even for someone as favored as John Locke, that kind of pattern cannot be changed so easily.

Episode plot: The efforts to open the hatch are going nowhere. None of Locke's plans work and Boone is starting to question his judgment. Locke is now waiting for the island to send him a sign. It finally does when Locke sees a vision of another plane crashing into the island. He also sees a vision of Boone covered in blood.

Locke comes to believe that finding this plane will give him what he needs to open the hatch. However, his legs begin to become useless again, leaving Locke once again unable to walk. With that, it is up to Boone to lead the way.

When they get to the spot where Locke saw the plane crash, there is indeed a plane hanging in the trees. Since Locke can no longer walk, Boone has to go up himself. He explores the plane and discovers that it is full of statues of the Virgin Mary, which contain large quantities of heroin inside. The bodies of people dressed as Nigerian missionaries are also found, but there is nothing inside that can help them. There is a radio, however.

Boone tries to use it to make contact and actually gets in touch with a voice. After he says he was a survivor of 815, a voice seems to say "We're the survivors of flight 815!" Just then, the plane starts to give way. Miraculously, Locke is then able to walk again, but by then the plane crashes to the ground.

Locke carries a badly injured Boone back to the caves, where Jack begins to treat him. Locke claims he fell off a cliff, but then takes off before Jack can ask him any more questions.

That night, Locke cries over the door of the hatch, asking the island why it did this. Almost as a response, a light shines through the window of the hatch door....

Other stuff: Sawyer is coming down with headaches. Kate is able to get Jack to look at him. Jack asks him a series of questions about his sexual history as part of the treatment, but he knows that has nothing to do with this. The headaches are due to farsightedness, which start to go away when Jack and Sayid are able to give him glasses.

Meanwhile, raft reconstruction is underway, with Jin helping out Michael although communication between them is still unsuccessful.

Main character: John Locke.

Flashback details: 10 years ago, Locke had more hair and he was working at a superstore. He is stunned when the birth mother who gave him away turns up. Locke asks her about his father, but she says he was immaculately conceived. He debunks this when he hires a private investigator and discovers the identity of his real father, Anthony Cooper.

Locke tracks Cooper down, finding that he is a pretty well off man. The two begin to bond, as Locke learns how to hunt from him.

But Cooper is on dialysis, needing a kidney transplant. Locke comes through for him, offering his kidney to him. He goes under the knife, happy to do this for his father.

When Locke wakes up after the surgery, Cooper is gone. His mother then shows up and delivers the devastating news. She was paid by Cooper to make up the immaculate conception claim so that Locke would track him down. The only reason Cooper even wanted to see him was to get his kidney, as bonding with him was all part of a con.

Locke leaves the hospital and tries to see Cooper, but his guard will no longer let him in. He drives away and then breaks down in tears.

Important details in *Lost* lore: Locke finds his father in the past, who turns out to be a con man. The Nigerian plane is also discovered, along with the possible existence of other survivors. Boone is left gravely injured. The light from the hatch indicates that something is indeed down there.

Amount of action: Minimal, save for Locke's insane vision and the plane crash.

New important characters: Locke's father, Anthony Cooper.

Connections between characters: Locke and Boone are at odds until Locke has his vision. However, this attachment leads to disaster for Boone. Jack, Kate and Sawyer are put together again, but their interactions are more playful this time around.

***Lost* mysteries referenced:** Locke's paralysis, the hatch.

***Lost* mysteries introduced:** The Nigerian plane and a possible survivor of 815 on the other end of its radio.

Questions raised: Why did Locke lose the ability to walk again? Why did he receive the vision? Was he meant to stay on the ground while Boone went up and got himself injured? Will Boone live? Why did a light shine from the hatch? Was it a sign from the island, or something else altogether?

Talking points: The power of the island to heal Locke has always been thought of as a positive thing, by Locke and by the audience. However, now there may be a darker side to that power. If the island gave him his legs for a reason, it took them away again for another reason, leaving Boone to pay the price. Locke may indeed have a grand destiny ahead of him, so perhaps that's why he was spared from going up to the plane, with Boone as the sacrificial lamb in his place. Even the grandest miracles seem to come at a cost on this island.

We are no closer to discovering why Locke was paralyzed in the first place, but we got a sense of another great tragedy in his life. Locke said that "it was meant to be" before he found out he was conned by his father. His faith blinded him to the truth, just as it blinded him on the island and left Boone to suffer for it. Locke's standing as an all knowing and wise figure certainly went down a few pegs this time around.

Other key issues: Even at Boone's life threatening crisis, Locke still feels the need to cover up the hatch. With this incident, it may not stay secret for long.

Must see episode?: Yes. Disappointing when compared to "Walkabout", but it serves as a setup for big things to come.

DO NO HARM

Since the crash of Oceanic 815, it has been Jack Shephard's job to keep the survivors safe. As a doctor, it was also his job to keep his patients and those he cared for safe. His determination to save people has been well established in both the present and the past. But now for the first time, we see Jack faced with a task that even he may not succeed in. As a result, he goes above and beyond in ways that are more disturbing than heroic. Even heroes fail, although Jack refuses to see that at all costs.

As a tragic milestone of *Lost* is reached, naturally a more positive milestone is reached not too far away. But even as tragedy and hope are balanced out, for Jack the tragedy is foremost on his mind. This in turn causes a divide between him and another survivor that will forever alter the course of life on the island.

Episode plot: With help from Sun and Kate, Jack works on treating Boone's deep injuries. Despite the long odds, Jack promises Boone that he will save him. But the heavy loss of blood and a nasty leg wound make this a difficult promise to keep.

It becomes clear that Boone needs a blood transfusion. After Jack sets his leg straight, Boone says that he is A-negative before slipping into unconsciousness. However, no one really knows their blood type, and those who do don't have A-negative blood. So Jack gives him some of his O-negative blood to buy some time.

During this procedure, Boone briefly wakes up and starts to tell Jack the truth about how he got injured. He also mentions the hatch and how Locke told him not to tell. Before he goes further into it, he becomes unconscious again.

The transfusion doesn't work, and Jack now focuses on the leg. Since it is now filled with blood, Jack wants to cut it off. With Michael's reluctant help, Jack makes a guillotine that will cut the leg. Sun protests that Jack can't do this, but in the full throes of his obsession, Jack screams out "Don't tell me what I can't do!"

Before Jack can do this, Boone wakes up one more time. Knowing that he will die, Boone tells Jack to "let him go" relieving him of his promise. Jack can now only watch Boone slip away into death. Boone starts to ask Jack to tell Shannon something, but he dies before he can complete his last request.

The next morning, Jack tells Kate that he believes Boone was murdered. He walks off determined to find John Locke.

Other stuff: During the treatment of Boone, Kate runs off to get alcohol bottles from Sawyer. On the way back, she hears moaning from Claire. At long last, she is about to deliver the baby. Jin stumbles onto the scene, leaving Kate to tell him to get Jack. When he gets there, Sun is able to translate his message for him. But by then, there's no way for Jack to go there himself, so he instructs that Kate will have to deliver the baby.

Meanwhile, Shannon has not been informed of her brother's condition because she is off with Sayid. He has taken her on a picnic at a secluded spot on the island.

Back in the jungle, Jin and Charlie are helping Kate take care of Claire. Kate is the only one among them who can deliver the baby, despite her worries. Claire is worried too, fearing that the baby will know that she wanted to give it away. Kate finally gets her to calm down and start to push the baby out. She talks her through the labor, and finally the baby comes out almost at the same time of Boone's death. It is a boy.

The next morning, Claire returns to camp and the survivors all surround her to greet the new baby. Shannon and Sayid then return from their night out, leaving Jack to finally tell them what happened. Shannon is then seen sobbing over Boone's body as Sayid silently watches.

Main character: Jack Shephard.

Flashback details: Jack is seen helping a friend with a bowtie, just before a wedding rehearsal. As it turns out, the groom is none other than Jack. He is getting married to Sarah, a woman who suffered a devastating spinal injury that Jack was miraculously able to fix. Afterwards, the two fell in love and got engaged. As the wedding draws closer, Jack is uneasy that he has not been able to write his vows.

The night before the wedding, Jack is able to confide his fears and concerns to his father. He worried that he only proposed to Sarah out of obligation after he saved her life. Christian reminds Jack that he's good at commitment, but not at letting go.

On the wedding day, Jack still has not written any vows. However, he goes through with it by speaking vows directly from the heart. He says that she fixed him instead of the other way around. With that, the wedding goes through perfectly.

Important details in *Lost* lore: For the first time, a major character of *Lost* dies, after a few near misses. At the same time, Claire's baby is finally born. Jack's hatred of Locke is also established, as well as the fact that he was once married.

Amount of action: Heavy, though it's the medical treatments that serve to deliver the action.

New important characters: Claire's baby, Jack's former wife Sarah.

Connections between characters: Jack nearly loses it trying to save Boone, although Boone absolves him right before he dies. Kate takes care of Claire and helps her finally give birth. Jin and Sun are briefly on speaking terms again when she translates Jin's message from Kate. Shannon and Sayid have their most romantic outing, though it prevents her from saying goodbye to Boone. Jack is left convinced that Locke murdered Boone and is determined to track him down.

***Lost* mysteries referenced:** The hatch, Claire's baby.

***Lost* mysteries introduced:** Jack's marriage, which most likely fell apart somehow despite the happy wedding day.

Questions raised: What was the history of Jack's marriage? What will happen when Locke finally returns after Boone's death? What has he been up to? What will Jack and Shannon do now? Now that the baby is finally here, what will happen to it?

Talking points: Letting things go continues to be a common problem for Jack. In the past, he had doubts about whether he was really ready to get married, but he put those worries aside to fulfill his commitment. Since Jack is likely not married now, it may have been the wrong decision.

In the present, his commitment to saving Boone takes him to the very edge of reason. He is only brought back by the very person he went besides himself to save. Even after Boone's death, it appears Jack has not fully learned his lesson, as he turns his commitment and obsession towards getting revenge on Locke.

Christian Shephard once told young Jack that he shouldn't try to be a hero, because when he fails, he won't have what it takes to move on and let go. For all of Christian's faults and sins, this may be the one thing that he was right about. Now Locke may be the next one to pay for it as a result.

Other key issues: The link between death and life comes to mind many.....many times.

Must see episode?: Yes. A milestone episode in both happy and tragic ways.

THE GREATER GOOD

In the aftermath of tragedy, emotions usually take hold over logic and reason. In some ways, this is a good thing as people can come together for healing. In other ways, the emotions of anger and revenge come to the center. For the first major death in *Lost* history, it is these negative emotions that are driving both Jack and Shannon against Locke, while Sayid is caught in the middle.

Love has made Sayid do some life changing things. It made him leave behind his life in Iraq and has fueled him to find his former love ever since. Now, his newest love puts him in a position to take action for her brother's death. But "there is always a choice" to make. Which one will Sayid make this time?

Episode plot: Shannon's grief over Boone and Jack's determination to blame Locke for it have only increased. At the funeral for Boone, Sayid delivers a brief eulogy. Just then, Locke finally returns.

He admits that the death was his fault and tells them about the plane they found, and how it fell. Locke says nothing about the hatch, though. Jack explodes and demands to know where he was as he attacks him. Although Jack is suffering from fatigue, he does remember that Boone said something about a hatch. Sayid manages to overhear this as well.

Later, Locke brings Boone's belongings back to Shannon and can only offer his condolences to her. Shannon has no words for him, but she has words for Sayid. She wants his help for revenge against Locke.

Sayid asks Locke to take him to the plane. As they walk, he asks Locke questions about his story, which he is able to answer. The two arrive at the plane, which backs up Locke's story. But Sayid still doesn't believe Locke is telling the whole truth.

So as a sign of trust, Locke shares a secret with him. When Sayid was knocked out in the jungle while trying to get Rousseau's signal, it was Locke who knocked him out.

Locke argues that it was for the camp's own good, since Rousseau's message did say "It killed them all." Still, even when Sayid asks about the hatch, Locke does not tell the truth. However, Sayid is left convinced that Locke did not have Boone killed. But Shannon is still far from satisfied.

While all this is happening, Jack has finally gone to sleep due to Kate grounding up pills in his juice. Although Jack is rested again, someone has stolen the key to the suitcase with the guns. He assumes it was Locke, but Sayid soon realizes that it was Shannon.

When Sayid, Jack and Kate find Shannon, she has a gun pointed at Locke. She demands that Locke confess to killing Boone, commenting that even Jack believed it. Sayid cannot talk her down and has to tackle her just as she gets a shot off, which only grazes Locke.

That night Shannon sits alone, with Sayid not daring to try and talk to her. He goes to Locke instead, saying that he believes Locke is their best hope for survival, but that he does not trust him. Sayid then demands "no more lies" from Locke and insists to be taken to the hatch.

Other stuff: Claire and her baby are trying to settle down in the camp, as Claire is still worried for his safety. Charlie swears to look after the baby while Claire gets an overdue nap. But the baby will not stop crying, as nothing Charlie or Hurley do can keep him quiet. However, there is one thing that soothes him…the sound of Sawyer's voice. Claire wakes up to see Sawyer reading an automotive magazine, which stops the baby's crying.

Meanwhile, work on the raft progresses even further, as Walt expresses concerns about how safe it will be.

Main character: Sayid Jarrah.

Flashback details: CIA agents have Sayid arrested in an airport, in order to secure his help. Essam, an old university friend of Sayid's, is a member of a terrorist cell that's planning an attack in Melbourne. The CIA offers to give Sayid the location of his lost love Nadia if he infiltrates the cell. So he heads to Australia to make contact with Essam.

Sayid soon integrates himself with the other members of the cell. Essam is to be a suicide bomber in the attack, but he is not yet fully committed. As a result, Sayid wants to get him out before the attack, but the CIA agents insist that he needs to go through with it so they can take the cell down. They remind Sayid about Nadia, suggesting that they can arrest her if anything goes wrong. So Sayid returns to Essam and convinces him to go through with the attack, saying it will be for the greater good.

On the day of the attack, Sayid and Essam are instructed to drive a truck full of explosives into their target. But Sayid again has second thoughts. He confesses that he is working for the CIA and advises Essam to leave quickly. Furious, Essam points his gun at Sayid, but turns it on himself before the CIA arrives.

Afterwards, the CIA tells Sayid that Nadia is in California. A flight to her location leaves in two hours. But Sayid wants to bury Essam per Muslim custom. As such, he asks to be put on a flight for the next day, which is on Oceanic Flight 815.

Important details in *Lost* lore: Jack and Locke's rivalry begins in full force. Shannon tries and fails to kill Locke. It is revealed that Locke stopped Sayid from finding Rousseau's signal in "The Moth." The hatch is no longer a secret.

Amount of action: Substantial.

New important characters: None.

Connections between characters: Three characters are in conflict with Locke. Jack turns on him for believing that he killed Boone, while Shannon actually tries to kill him, but Sayid comes to believe he is innocent. Sayid and Shannon's relationship hits a brick wall as a result.

***Lost* mysteries referenced:** The hatch, the plane, Sayid's attacker in the jungle, Nadia.

***Lost* mysteries introduced:** None.

Questions raised: Was Locke telling the truth when he explained why he attacked Sayid? Will Sayid and Shannon's relationship ever be the same? What will happen now that Sayid knows about the hatch? Is the raft ready to sail soon? Will Jack continue to blame Locke for Boone's death?

Talking points: Sayid wrestles with the greater good in both the past and present. He convinces Essam that his attack is for the greater good, just as he convinces himself that using him to see Nadia again justifies his lie. But he stops believing that at the end, although it still costs Essam his life.

In the present, he tries to help Shannon strike back at Locke, but realizes he is not to blame for what happened to Boone. Still, he seems to regret having to stop Shannon, since "there's always a choice." But in the end, he chooses to save Locke for the greater good of trying to get off the island and discover more about the hatch.

Will that ultimately serve the greater good? Now, as then, the question doesn't seem to have an easy answer.

Other key issues: Who knew that Sawyer's voice was a sure fire cure for baby crying? It's a wonder Josh Holloway couldn't retire from acting to get into that business.

Must see episode?: Yes. We have a tiny bit of closure for the Boone storyline and a clear setup for the final few episodes of the season. The end is coming closer.

BORN TO RUN

In the early days of *Lost,* the survivors started to realize that no one was coming for them. Over time, they started to adapt to surviving on the island. But now, with Michael taking rescue into his own hands, the castaways can dare to dream again. As the chance for finding rescue comes closer to reality, they feel that their time on the island is almost over. But what would they go back to if it was?

For Kate, the answer is not very promising. As a fugitive from the law, the very discovery of her would put her back into custody. However, she is determined to get a spot on Michael's raft anyway. She obviously has a plan to avoid being caught again, just as she has plans for getting on that raft. Once again, Kate is ready to run away just like she always does.

But running away has cost Kate too much already in the past. And on this island, there are still some prices to pay for repeating one's mistakes as well.

Episode plot: Michael's raft is almost finished, but according to another survivor, science teacher Dr. Arzt, it must sail immediately to avoid monsoon season. Kate rushes to Michael and asks for a spot on the raft, but his passengers are already set. Walt, Jin, and Sawyer are going with him. However, Michael starts to have second thoughts about how useful Sawyer will be at sea.

Sawyer finds Kate trying to alter the passport of Joanna, the survivor who drowned in the beginning of "White Rabbit." Knowing that she is a fugitive, Sawyer figures out Kate wants to pose as Joanna when they get rescued, then go back on the run. Although Sawyer won't tell anyone, he refuses to give up his seat on the raft for her.

Sometime later, Michael takes a drink of water and falls down to the ground. When Jack examines him, he concludes that the water was tainted. Once Michael wakes up and finds out, he accuses Sawyer of trying to poison him. Jack then becomes suspicious of Kate when she asks if Sawyer will be taken off the raft.

Soon after, Michael announces that Kate is going on the raft now. Outraged at the accusation that he poisoned Michael, Sawyer spills the truth about Kate. He downright accuses her of poisoning Michael, since she will do anything to survive and escape. Kate admits she was a fugitive, but maintains she did not poison Michael. Yet Michael doesn't believe her, as he puts Sawyer back on the raft again.

That night, Sawyer tells Kate that the raft will sail tomorrow. He revealed her secret to get back on the raft since, to him, there's nothing left on the island worth staying for. Meanwhile, Jack figures out the culprit behind Michael's poisoning was Sun. Once he tells her this, she confesses that she was trying to poison Jin so that he would not leave the island and possibly die at sea. Jack promises not to tell, but warns her that she needs to say goodbye soon.

But afterwards, Sun is shown talking about the plan with Kate. Sun may have done it, but it was Kate's plan all along.

Other stuff: With Sayid now fully aware of the hatch, he and Locke bring Jack into the loop. Naturally, the three disagree about what should be done about it. Jack is uncertain, while Sayid believes that it is dangerous. Jack is also upset at Locke for keeping this secret from him.

Later on, Walt comes up to Locke and tells him that he didn't poison Michael, fearing that Locke would believe he did since he burned the raft down. Locke believes him as he prepares to say goodbye to him. But when he touches Walt's arm, Walt goes into a kind of trance, telling Locke "don't open that thing."

That night, Walt confesses to Michael that he burned the first raft. Michael takes it well, suggesting that they don't have to leave after all. But Walt is now convinced that they need to go immediately.

Main character: Kate Austin.

Flashback details: While at her latest hideout in a motel, Kate gets a note that makes her break down into tears. Later, she goes to a hospital where a woman named Diane Janssen is being treated. There, she finds a man named Tom, who was Kate's old sweetheart and is a doctor at the hospital. Kate needs his help to get close to Diane, so he arranges an MRI scan for her.

As they wait for morning, the two reflect on their past, even though Tom is married now. They go out to a field and dig up a time capsule they made in the late 80's. Inside it is childhood toys and a tape recording of their younger selves. There is also an Oceanic toy airplane.

The next day, Tom is able to get Kate into the hospital so she can see Diane before her surgery. As it turns out, Diane is Kate's mother. As she sleeps, Kate starts to apologize for everything she has done. But when Diane wakes up, she screams at seeing Kate and yells for help.

With the meeting ruined, Kate has to run away again. Tom stays with her and refuses to go. She gets into her car and drives through a barricade of police fire, escaping capture. However, one of the bullets hits Tom and kills him. A distraught Kate has to run away and leave behind the body, as well as Tom's toy airplane.

Important details in *Lost* lore: The raft is almost ready to leave, while the hatch's existence is revealed to Jack. We find out who the man Kate loved and "killed" was, and where the toy airplane came from.

Amount of action: Little.

New important characters: New survivor Dr. Arzt. In the past, we meet Kate's former love Tom and her mother Diane.

Connections between characters: Kate and Sawyer are more at odds than ever as they may have ended up saying goodbye to each other. Jack and Locke continue to square off, while Walt makes amends to Michael for burning the raft. Sun has clearly not moved on from Jin, a fact which Kate is able to exploit.

***Lost* mysteries referenced:** The hatch, Kate's fugitive past, Walt's powers.

***Lost* mysteries introduced:** Walt's strange warning for Locke not to open the hatch.

Questions raised: What will Kate's standing in the camp be now that everyone knows who she was? What is her standing with Sawyer? What will happen regarding the hatch, now that Jack knows about it? How did Walt know, or sense, that opening the hatch was dangerous? How will the raft's launch go tomorrow? Will Sun be able to say goodbye to Jin? Where did this Arzt guy come from all of a sudden?

Talking points: Once again, the more we find out about Kate's past, the less we really know. Though we know who owned the toy airplane and who Kate indirectly killed, there's still no clue as to how her criminal past began and why her mother was so afraid of her.

With rescue close at hand, Kate's desire to avoid getting caught makes her go farther than she's ever gone on the island to get ahead. But instead of success, this scheme may have cost her a place on the raft, a place with Sawyer, and her standing with the camp. This time, she may be in a corner that is too big for her to get out of.

The mystery of the hatch only deepens thanks to yet another weird ability from Walt. It's already been revealed that the cursed numbers are on the door, so maybe Walt's on to something. Now the raft mission becomes more important than ever before.

Other key issues: Jack and Locke's new conflict has gone beyond Boone's death and turned into a full blown leadership battle. Probably not the best time to start that sort of thing.

Must see episode?: Somewhat. The raft is finally set up to go and the hatch gets closer to blowing open, but the rest is just for Kate fans and Kate/Sawyer people.

EXODUS- PART 1

At long last the end is about to come, at least for this first chapter of the *Lost* story. By this point, *Lost* was a full blown hit with the most obsessive fans on TV. After almost a full year of teasing and puzzling fans, the stage was set for a kind of climax. A show that began with a plane crash was now ending an unlikely wave of success towards a possible rescue, as well as the discovery of the island's biggest secret. The two biggest questions on everyone's minds were if rescue would be possible, and what was in that hatch.

But in one fell swoop, a new question would be raised. A third threat which had been forgotten about for a while came back with a vengeance. We knew this wasn't a deserted island, thanks to Danielle Rousseau and Ethan. But once Ethan was shot, the prospect of having evil people on the island that were hunting the survivors down was forgotten. At least until that crazy French woman returned to remind us.

It's not enough that suspense has to be drawn from a raft launch and opening a mysterious hatch. We have to have Others ready to attack as well. That's a season finale for you, or at least the first hour of it.

Episode plot: Danielle Rousseau comes to the beach camp for the first time with the warning "The Others are coming." 16 years ago, when Rousseau first came to the island, a large pillar of black smoke was detected. A week later, her daughter was taken from her. Now Rousseau believes the Others are coming again, this time for the survivors. Their only options are to run, hide, or die.

Due to her mental state, Jack does not believe her. In any case, the survivors are focused on launching Michael's raft. However, the test run damages the raft. The arguing over it is interrupted when they find a cloud of black smoke on the horizon, just as Rousseau warned. The Others are coming indeed.

Jack figures out that the best way to hide everyone is to finally open the hatch. Rousseau still has a large quantity of dynamite that they can use. However, it is located at the infamous and unknown Black Rock. Jack, Locke, Kate, Hurley, and Dr. Arzt plan to go to the Black Rock with Rousseau to get the dynamite.

Before Jack leaves, he finds Sawyer and gives him a gun, just in case something goes wrong on the raft. With their goodbye imminent, Sawyer finally tells Jack about the time he met his father in Sydney before the crash. He tells Jack about how Christian said he loved his son and was proud of him, which makes Jack nearly break down in front of Sawyer.

Later, the journey to the Black Rock begins. It is briefly interrupted when the sounds of the monster are heard, as well as Dr. Arzt's panicked screams. However, it does not get them. Rousseau claims that it is "a security system" for the island. Afterwards, the group finally arrives at the Black Rock.

And of all things, the Black Rock is a large sailing ship right in the middle of the jungle.

Other stuff: Once the raft is repaired, it is soon time to say goodbye. Walt finds Shannon, offering to give Vincent to her while he's gone. Since Vincent was good company for Walt after his mother died, he figures that Walt can help Shannon cope with Boone's death. For once, Shannon looks moved.

Later, Sun finally gets to say goodbye to Jin. She leaves him with a notebook of English nautical words written in Korean, believing it will help him make contact if rescue is found. With that, Jin starts to cry. He apologizes to Sun for everything that has happened, believing that he has been punished for his past actions by being stuck on the island.

But now he has to go on the raft because he's going to save Sun. The two finally reconcile and declare their love.

In a near silent montage, the raft is dragged onto the beach and the survivors say their goodbyes to the departing crew. A bottle filled with written messages from those left behind goes on the raft as well. Finally, the crew pushes the raft to sea and goes onboard. Vincent chases after it, but a teary eyed Walt has him go back. The raft sails out to sea perfectly as Michael, Walt, and Sawyer celebrate. Those left on the island cheer and wave them goodbye, as Sun and Jin stare longingly at each other while the raft leaves.

But in the distance behind this happy celebration, the pillar of black smoke is still rising.

Main character: None. This episode has multiple flashbacks of several characters on the day flight 815 took off.

Flashback details: Walt and Michael stayed in a hotel room the night before they boarded flight 815. The two get into an argument, where Walt says that Michael is not his real father.

For Jack, he had a drink at an airport bar, where he struck up a conversation with a woman named Ana-Lucia, who sat at the tail section of the plane. He offered to see her again during the flight.

For Sawyer, he was in an Australian police station the day before the flight, as we briefly saw in Boone's flashback. Sawyer head butted the Minister of Agriculture while drunk, presumably after he killed Frank Duckett. He was put on flight 815 to be deported out of Australia. Sawyer's real name is revealed to be James Ford.

For Kate, US Marshal Edward Mars is introducing her to a security officer. He explains that he needs to bring five guns onboard in the Halliburton case because of how dangerous Kate is. Mars explains her history and how her actions got her childhood love killed. When he taunts her by asking his name, Kate jumps on him. With that, the marshal is able to get the five guns he needs.

For Shannon, she is bored waiting for a first class seat, with the still alive Boone failing to get one. She also tells a security guard that Sayid, a.k.a. "some Arab guy" left a bag unchecked nearby.

For Sun, she brings Jin coffee while listening to a couple gossip as they watch them. Since she does know English, she understands everything. This distracts her enough to spill the coffee on Jin's lap.

Important details in *Lost* lore: The possibility of an attack by the Others is raised. The hatch is now closer to being opened. The raft finally sails off. Sun and Jin finally patch things up. Vincent is left in Shannon's care. Jack finally learns that Sawyer and his father met in Australia. The Black Rock is revealed to be a ship in the middle of the jungle. Dr. Arzt's first name is Leslie.

Amount of action: Fair.

New important characters: Ana Lucia, who Jack met before the plane crash. This is explained further in Season Two.

Connections between characters: Rousseau appears to the camp and is met with skepticism before her warnings are proven right. Jack and Sawyer have somewhat of a bonding moment. Walt helps Shannon by giving her Vincent, while Sun and Jin come together again. The survivors on the beach and on the raft share a sad but hopeful farewell.

***Lost* mysteries referenced:** The Others, the hatch, the monster, the Black Rock, the kidnapping of Rousseau's daughter.

***Lost* mysteries introduced:** The black smoke, the fact that there's a ship in the middle of the jungle.

Questions raised: Will the raft find rescue? Will the dynamite from the Black Rock finally open the hatch? Will it make a difference before the Others attack? Will the Others attack? Is Rousseau telling the truth? Is the monster really just a security system?

Talking points: As the first season finally comes to a climax, we are reminded of just how far the survivors have come. Many of them are seen at the low points they were in before the crash, in contrast with what they have become now.

Whereas Walt and Michael didn't know each other or even like each other before, they are fully united now. Whereas Sun and Jin were on the brink of marital collapse before, they have rediscovered their love for each other, just before it was too late. Even rivalries like the one between Jack and Sawyer have thawed, if only for a moment, in the face of a possible goodbye. Even Shannon's spoiled and grief stricken heart is touched for a while. For once, the survivors can say that they have triumphed, both in getting the raft out to sea and in overcoming so many personal demons. In this instance, we catch them at their lowest points, and at their highest.

But *Lost* would not exist without some danger, as the possible attack by the Others signifies. Is this triumph to be short lived?

Other key issues: *Lost* composer Michael Giacchino is such a huge behind-the-scenes part of the show's success. No scene proves this better than in the final five minutes of this episode.

Must see episode?: One of the best in *Lost* history.

EXODUS- PART 2

So here we are. Only two hours now remain in one of the most acclaimed seasons in recent TV history. The expectations for *Lost* fans were high, as they must be high for those of you who really don't know what happened next. This is where we would finally get some answers. This is where we would find out what the hatch is all about. This is where we would discover if the raft mission was successful. This is where The Others other than Ethan would finally make their appearance. This is where all the waiting for answers and payoffs would finally be rewarded.

Or would it?

Episode plot: After discovering the Black Rock, Jack, Kate, and Locke go searching for the dynamite. Leslie Arzt tries to instruct them how to hold the dynamite so that it doesn't go off. Moments later, he is blown to bits when the dynamite goes off in his hands. But the other survivors are able to handle the dynamite as Rousseau takes her leave.

On the beach, Sayid is leading all of the remaining survivors to the caves before the Others attack. Charlie insists on a gun, but Sayid advises him to focus on taking care of Claire. Rousseau then returns and asks for Sayid, so Charlie goes to get him. She then focuses on Claire and the baby, asking to hold him. Suddenly, Claire gets a flash of her memory back, as she remembers that she scratched Rousseau the night before Ethan kidnapped her.

When Charlie returns with Sayid, the baby is gone. Claire screams that Rousseau took him away. Charlie blames Sayid for letting Rousseau near her, but Sayid shuts him up by grabbing his throat. Sayid realizes that Rousseau is going to the black smoke with the baby, concluding that she wants to give him to the Others in exchange for her daughter. Before he and Charlie head into the jungle, Claire pleads to Charlie to get "Aaron" back.

Jack and Locke have another dispute, this time over who gets to carry the dynamite. After drawing straws, Jack and Kate win the right to take the sticks.

On the raft, Michael, Walt, Sawyer and Jin keep sailing away, but have not found anyone yet. They hit some trouble when the rudder breaks off, with Sawyer diving into the ocean to save it. Michael is relieved until he discovers that Sawyer brought a gun.

Sayid and Charlie rush through the jungle to find Rousseau. Along the way, they find the Nigerian plane again. This time, Charlie finds out that his drug of choice, heroin, is inside.

Meanwhile, Jack and his team head back for the hatch. But they are interrupted when the sounds of the monster are heard again. For the first time since "Walkabout" Locke sees the monster. But in this case, it does not spare him. Instead, it drags him off with a tentacle of what looks to be black smoke. Jack and Kate chase after him as he is about to be dragged down a hole. Locke insists that he'll be all right, but Jack has Kate throw dynamite down the hole, which releases the monster's grasp.

Sayid and Charlie are delayed again when Charlie runs into one of Rousseau's traps. Charlie insists on staying put, even though he is bleeding badly in the head. Sayid stops it by putting gunpowder on the wound and lighting a match.

It is now night, as Jack and company are close to the hatch. Jack questions Locke over why he wanted to be dragged down with the monster. Locke explains that he was being tested as a man of faith, while Jack is a man of science. With that, he explains his belief that all this has happened for a reason and that the island has brought the survivors here. It is their destiny to be here because they have all been chosen, and their path will end at the hatch. Jack insists that he doesn't believe in destiny. Locke replies that he does, but he doesn't know it yet.

On the raft, Sawyer is using their radar to search for any oncoming ships. Michael confronts him about why he is on the raft, figuring that he either wants to be a hero, or he wants to die. But they are interrupted when the radar picks up a signal.

Sayid and Charlie finally reach the black smoke, but no one is there except for Rousseau. She is saddened because no one has come, confessing that she thought she could get her daughter back. Sayid gently gets her to give the baby back to him, while Charlie accuses her of making the whole thing up. She insists that she heard whispers, but Charlie is convinced the Others never existed. Rousseau still swears that "The Others said they were coming for the boy..."

Jack's team is finally at the hatch, preparing to light the dynamite. Jack confides to Kate that they're going to have "A Locke problem" if they survive this night. As Hurley helps Locke, he drops his flashlight. He then sees the numbers 4, 8, 15, 16, 23 and 42 on the door. Hurley panics and yells that they can't open the hatch because "The numbers are bad!" Locke ignores him and lights the fuse. Jack dives to get Hurley out of the way before the door finally explodes open.

On the raft, Michael is reluctant to use their only flare to signal whatever's out there. But as the radar signal starts to disappear, Michael gives in. The flare works, as a boat comes out to meet them. The survivors cheer as Michael explains everything to the boat's captain. But the captain says, "Only the thing is....we're gonna have to take the boy."

Danielle Rousseau's whispers were true. They were just about the wrong boy.

The captain turns off his light as Sawyer draws his gun. But Sawyer is shot first and falls into the water, with Jin diving after him. The ship's crew raids the raft and grabs Walt, throwing Michael overboard. A woman throws an explosive onto the raft. It explodes just as the boat leaves with a screaming Walt pleading for help from Michael. Michael yells out Walt's name in tears as he fades away from view. The raft burns in the sea with it's two other occupants nowhere to be found.

Sayid and Charlie return to the caves, with Aaron in tow. The survivors rejoice as Claire hugs Charlie, who now has a hidden Virgin Mary statue filled with heroin in his backpack.

Finally, there is a montage of everyone getting on flight 815 just before takeoff. To contrast it, the scene cuts back to Jack and Locke running over to the hatch's now open door. They look down the deep exposed tunnel, and what they see is.....

We will not know until Season 2.

Main character: None. Again, the flashback format shows what the characters did before flight 815 took off.

Flashback details: After Sun spills coffee on Jin, he goes to the bathroom to clean it off. There, he is met by a representative of Mr. Paik, who reminds him to deliver his watch to Los Angeles and not run away. He tells Jin that he will never be free.

Charlie wakes up that morning in a hotel room with a girl, looking for his stash of drugs. The girl attacks him for the drugs before he's able to escape.

Sayid leaves a holding room after Shannon told airport officials about his bag. Meanwhile, Michael and Walt are waiting around and are still not talking. Michael calls his mother and starts to ask her if she can take care of Walt, before he notices Walt nearby.

Hurley wakes up late for his flight, due to another string of bad luck. He comically rushes to the airport, while seeing his numbers at various places. At the last minute, he is able to get on the plane.

Locke is waiting in the airport, clearly still upset over not being allowed to go on the Walkabout. Due to his condition, Locke has to be carried on the plane. He can't even reach an airport pamphlet after he drops it.

Important details in *Lost* lore: Rousseau tried to attack Claire during her ordeal. The Others do in fact exist, and they were coming for Walt. Walt is now gone, with the fate of the other raft dwellers in the air. Claire's baby is now called Aaron. Locke has another encounter with the monster, which is far less friendly than before. The monster appears to contain black smoke. Charlie is tempted by heroin again. Hurley discovers his numbers on the hatch. At long last, the hatch is opened and we still don't know what's in it.

Amount of action: Substantial.

New important characters: The Others and their ship captain, who was labeled in the credits as "Mr. Friendly"

Connections between characters: The rivalry between Jack and Locke deepens further. Many of the survivors stayed in the same hotel before going on flight 815. Sayid and Charlie team up and squabble over the search for Aaron and Rousseau. Walt is revealed as someone important to the Others.

***Lost* mysteries referenced:** The Black Rock, the Others, the hatch, Rousseau's daughter, the attacks on Claire, the numbers and their place on the hatch door.

***Lost* mysteries introduced:** Walt's kidnapping.

Questions raised: What's in the hatch? Why was Walt kidnapped? What will happen to Michael, Sawyer, and Jin? What's in the hatch? Will Charlie go back to his heroin addiction? Why did the monster attack Locke this time? Is Rousseau really not so crazy after all? How will Hurley deal with facing the numbers again? What's in the hatch? Will there be "A Locke problem" in Season 2? Why didn't we find out what's in that hatch?

Talking points: Once more, the episode shows the low points of the survivors before the crash. But this time, their exploits on the island do not turn out any better.

After merely hinting at the true divide between Jack and Locke, the *Lost* powers are no longer being subtle about it. Science and faith are having still yet another showdown, this time on a mystery island. On the under card is fate vs. coincidence, a debate which Sun and Claire briefly have in the caves.

Perhaps the Others taking Walt isn't surprising, since they previously took Rousseau's baby daughter and a pregnant Claire. Whatever they are, they like taking kids. What significance do children have to the island?

It seems "The Moth" wasn't enough to keep Charlie away from drugs, as it looks like the sequel to that battle is coming soon.

Other key issues: It is unclear why the *Lost* people needed two hours to do part 2, since most of the major events could probably be compressed down to an hour. Especially since little is actually answered.

Must see episode?: Season finales are always must see, although compared to how good part 1 was, this is pretty disappointing. Aside from Walt's shocking fate, absolutely nothing is explained. *Lost* has always teased fans, but this was their biggest stall for time yet. On to Season 2.

SEASON TWO

CHARACTERS YOU NEED TO KNOW FOR SEASON TWO

Desmond Hume-- played by Henry Ian Cusick: A Scottish man separated from his lost love and stranded inside the hatch.

Ana Lucia Cortez-- played by Michelle Rodriguez: A former Los Angeles cop who leads flight 815's tail section survivors.

Libby-- played by Cynthia Watros: A former psychologist who forms a bond with Hurley.

Mr. Eko-- played by Adewale Akinnuoye-Agbaje: A brutal Nigerian drug lord who reformed and turned to the priesthood after his brother suffered for his crimes.

Bernard-- played by Sam Anderson: Rose's husband, who has indeed been alive all along with the tail section survivors.

Henry Gale-- played by Michael Emerson: A man literally caught in a net who is suspected to be one of "The Others."

Penelope Widmore-- played by Sonya Walger: Desmond's lost love that has been separated from him for three years.

MAN OF SCIENCE, MAN OF FAITH

At this time in the previous year, *Lost* was an unknown show working with an unlikely premise. No one believed a show on an island could be stretched out for a long period of time. One year, millions of crazed fans, and a Best Drama Emmy Award later, *Lost* returned with high expectations and impatient followers.

The season finale opened the hatch, but teased us out for three hours by not showing what was in it. But heading into Season Two, *Lost* had no choice but to finally start explaining it. Everyone's imagination ran wild in predicting what would be down there. With little spoilers leaking out as to what the real answer was, it could have been anything.

But give this to the *Lost* powers. No one could have guessed what it ultimately was, or how we first saw it.

Season Two begins now.

Episode plot: A man is seen waking up to the sound of a beeping noise. He gets up and starts typing on a computer. With that, he turns on the Mama Cass song "Make Your Own Kind Of Music" and goes about a daily routine. He appears to be in some kind of home from the past, so this might be a flashback.

But just then, an explosion is heard from outside.

The still unseen and unrecognizable man runs over to a series of mirrors, which he uses to look down the hall. We follow it until we go up.....to see Jack and Locke staring down the hatch.

Without knowing it until now, we have just seen inside the hatch for the first time.

Back on the ground, Hurley is repeating his numbers and is convinced that they're dead. Jack is convinced that they cannot hide everyone in the hatch from the Others, especially with a broken ladder inside. He prefers to explore it tomorrow, but Locke is impatient. Kate then notices that the hatch door has the words "QUARANTINE" written on the back. Locke eventually agrees to head back with the others. On the way, Hurley tells Jack about the numbers and his curse, but Jack isn't too helpful.

When they return to the caves, Jack explains about the hatch and how they can't use it. He promises to watch over them until the sun rises, then they'll plan their next move. Locke however, is heading for the hatch right now, tired of waiting. Soon after, Kate decides to go with him.

Kate proves to be useful as Locke has her tied to a cable and lowers her down inside the tunnel. She goes down slowly, but she then yells that something is down there. Suddenly a huge bright light shines through the tunnel. When it fades away, Kate is gone.

Jack soon becomes worried and goes down to the hatch himself. After seeing that both Kate and Locke are gone, he climbs down. Once he's on the ground, he goes through a series of passageways. He passes by a mural with the numbers on then, as well as a spot that seems to have a strong magnetic force. At that moment, "Make Your Own Kind Of Music" blares in the background again.

Jack then finds himself in a kind of underground dome, containing computer equipment over a few decades old. At the center is the old computer that the man inside used at the beginning of the show.

Before Jack can examine it further, Locke appears. The man inside the hatch has a gun pointed at his head. Jack barely cares, demanding to know where Kate is and taunting Locke about his destiny. The man demands that Jack lower his gun, or he'll blow Locke's head off, "brother." This word triggers a memory in Jack....

Other stuff: Back in the caves, Shannon has already lost sight of Walt's dog Vincent. Sayid helps her, but the two get separated. She then hears the jungle whispers and then sees a very unlikely sight. Walt is standing in the jungle and speaking backwards. But when Sayid finds Shannon, Walt is gone. She asks about the Others when Jack's team returns, but Charlie still insists that Rousseau made the Others up.

Main character: Jack Shephard.

Flashback details: Years ago, two victims of a car wreck came to Jack's hospital. Jack had to choose between performing surgery on the man or woman. The man's name is Adam Rutherford, who has the same last name as Shannon and is probably her father. Jack focuses on the woman, who turns out to be Sarah, his future wife.

Due to the severe damage to Sarah's spine, Jack tells her she is unlikely to walk again. For that, he gets a lecture from Christian Shephard about his cold bedside manner, explaining that patients like to hear that they have a chance. Jack prefers to tell the truth rather than give false hope, however. Later, Jack explains things to Sarah's current fiancée, who doesn't seem happy with her condition.

Once Sarah goes into spinal surgery, Jack ignores his own philosophy and assures her that she is going to walk again. But he is convinced that he was unable to keep his promise. He even tells her the next day that he was unable to fix her. But Sarah doesn't believe him because she can move her toes. Jack confirms it by feeling her legs, breaking down in shock and happiness.

Yet the key part of this flashback came the night earlier. Jack was jogging around in the L.A Coliseum, lost in his own regret. Someone else was there with him, as the two began to talk after they stopped running. The Scottish accented man explains that he's training for a race around the world. Jack tells him about his problem and that he knows he failed to fix Sarah, but the man asks "What if you did fix her?" Jack believes that would be a miracle. Before the man leaves, he says his name is Desmond, telling Jack "See you in another life."

One life later, Desmond is revealed as the man inside the hatch.

Important details in *Lost* lore: The contents of the hatch are finally revealed, which include a man who Jack has met before. Walt mysteriously appears to Shannon. Jack is seen fixing his future wife in the past, despite his belief that it could not be done.

Amount of action: Little.

New important characters: Desmond.

Connections between characters: Jack and Kate's dancing around, as well as Jack and Locke's clash, only continue. Shannon, who was previously connected to Walt through Vincent, sees him again even after he was kidnapped. Jack and Desmond meet in the LA Coliseum years ago, and then meet again in the hatch.

***Lost* mysteries referenced:** The hatch, the numbers, Walt's kidnapping.

***Lost* mysteries introduced:** Desmond, the actual contents of the hatch, the Quarantine warning on the hatch door, Shannon seeing Walt.

Questions raised: Now that we know what's in the hatch, what is it all for? Who is Desmond? What is the significance of Desmond and Jack meeting years earlier? How could Walt possibly be in the jungle? Where did Kate go? Where are the others from the raft? Was it a miracle that Jack could fix Sarah? Why is the word Quarantine on the hatch?

Talking points: Jack's clear belief in science and rationality didn't start on the island. His lack of reassurance and helpful beside manner is clear both on the mainland and on the island, as Hurley points out. Even his father was someone who tried to soften the blows, albeit with false hopes.

But it appears that for one brief moment, Jack was proven wrong about not having faith. As such, it led to him getting married. Yet since we know this marriage couldn't have lasted, Jack may not have believed that this was a miracle for long.

The survivors have tended to have had unknown and unlikely connections with each other in the past. However, Jack and Desmond's encounter takes the cake.

Walt's powers have been established to the point that it may explain why the Others wanted him so badly. But if those powers could get him seen by Shannon, even after last season's finale, that says something.

Other key issues: The numbers are not only on the hatch door, they were found inside the hatch as well. Where else are they?

In addition, when Walt's backward message is translated, it says "Don't push the button."

Must see episode?: Obviously, since it's the season premiere. The opening scene alone is one of the best moments in *Lost* history. Except for the other looks in the hatch and the introduction of Desmond, not much else matches that opening, however.

ADRIFT

The season premiere reunited us with most of the *Lost* survivors, but not all of them. Michael, Sawyer and Jin were still stranded in the middle of the ocean, with Walt taken away by the Others. If viewers were waiting for any answers about what would happen to Walt..... well, it's still been a long wait. But Michael, Sawyer and Jin's fates were discovered here. In the meantime, we would find out more examples of how Michael fought to be a father years ago, as his damaging road to get him back in the present was about to begin.

However, Jack and Locke's group wasn't forgotten about either, as we got a few more clues about the hatch and about newcomer Desmond. The next episode would blow things wide upon on those fronts, but they helped pass the time in this episode first.

Episode plot: Moments after the Others blow up the raft, Sawyer emerges from the ocean, shot but still alive. He finds Michael, who was drowning, and brings him back onto what's left of the raft. Jin is nowhere to be found, however.

Through much of the night, Michael and Sawyer bicker over using the flare gun and Walt's kidnapping. In the meantime, Sawyer's wound has attracted a nearby shark. The raft soon breaks apart, with Michael on one part and Sawyer on another. Finally they find a pontoon from the raft, and Michael shoots the shark with Sawyer's gun while they swim to get it.

As daybreak occurs, Michael vows that he will get Walt back, while the current washes them back to the island and back "home" as Sawyer points out. When they get to land, they find Jin rushing towards them, with his hands tied up. The one English word he yells is "Others!" as Michael and Sawyer find a gang of people on the beach heading towards them.

Other stuff: We return to the hatch, but not where we left off. Instead, we flashback to when Kate was taken hostage and Locke goes down to the hatch to find her. When he gets inside, Kate is on the floor out cold. Desmond then appears with his gun, asking "Are you him?" Not knowing what he means, Locke says he is "him" anyway to see what's going on. But when Desmond asks the cryptic question "What did one snowman say to the other?" Locke is caught in the lie.

Locke is questioned by Desmond as Kate wakes up and starts moving around, as she discovers a huge room of food in the process. Locke tells Desmond about the plane crash, but then an alarm goes off. Desmond rushes to a computer and orders Locke to type in the number sequence of 4, 8, 15, 16, 23, 42. This silences the alarm and sets a timer on the wall back to the number 108. Before Locke can inquire any further, Jack is heard coming down.

Main character: Michael Dawson.

Flashback details: Many years ago, Michael fought his girlfriend Susan for custody of baby Walt, wanting to go to trial despite his lack of money. But at the hearings, Susan's lawyer gets Michael to admit he doesn't know much about Walt at all. However, Michael refuses to give up until Susan convinces him that he couldn't provide for Walt like Susan and her fiancée Brian could. Finally, Michael gives up and says goodbye to young Walt at the park. They would not meet again for many more years.

Important details in *Lost* lore: The first appearances of the hatch computer and timer, and the reintroduction of the numbers.

Amount of action: Little.

New important characters: The unknown group of people at the end who may or may not be the Others.

Connections between characters: Michael and Sawyer both bicker and work together to save themselves. Meanwhile, Locke and Desmond have their first meeting in the hatch.

***Lost* mysteries referenced:** The numbers, the hatch, the Others.

***Lost* mysteries introduced:** The hatch computer and how the numbers relate to it.

Questions raised: Have Michael, Sawyer and Jin found the Others? What happened to Jin during Michael and Sawyer's ordeal? What did pushing the numbers on the computer do? Are we going to move forward in the hatch showdown any time soon?

Talking points: We revisit how Michael, who was reluctant to be a father at the beginning of the series, was obsessed with being one at the early stages of Walt's life. But we see how he finally gave him up and how he won't make that same mistake again.

Other key issues: Viewers used their TiVo's to find out that the shark in the ocean had a logo on its fin. That logo would be cleared up soon enough.

Must see episode?: If only to get more info on the hatch and to see some of Michael and Sawyer's bickering. But this is mostly filler to hold us over until the next episode.

ORIENTATION

There are some *Lost* episodes in which nothing is the same on the show again after watching them. We've recapped some of them and there are still more than a few left to come. One of those is certainly this episode, due to the introduction of some very key details.

From this point on, *Lost* fans would have to add "The button" and "The DHARMA Initiative" into their vocabulary for all time. After this episode, the series spent an entire year figuring out the mystery of the button, while only making slight progress on the DHARMA Initiative. But be warned that once this episode introduced the purpose of the hatch, many fans jumped ship when it became clear the whole season would revolve around it. This is where the first bump in *Lost's* ride to the top began to show for several viewers.

For the rest of us? We're gonna have to watch it again.

Episode plot: Once again, Jack and Desmond are seen holding each other at gunpoint in the hatch. As for Kate, she's gotten into the vents and jumps down to tackle Desmond. But this makes Desmond accidentally fire his gun at the computer where Locke typed in the numbers moments before. With the computer damaged, Desmond fearfully remarks "We're all gonna die...."

An impatient Jack demands that Desmond explain himself. Desmond finally tells him that three years ago, he entered a sailing race around the world and crash landed onto the island. A man named Kelvin took him into the hatch and taught him how to press the numbers into the computer, saying that it would "save the world." Kate goes off to get Sayid's help in fixing the computer. As Desmond frantically tries to repair it, he gets Jack and Locke to watch a video that will explain things further.

The video is an orientation film from 1980, hosted by a man named Dr. Marvin Candle. He works for an organization called the DHARMA Initiative, which lived and worked on the island many years ago. Funded by a corporation called the Hanso Foundation and created by scientists Karen and Gerald DeGroot, the DHARMA Initiative performed unique experiments on the island, harnessing it's very unique properties.

The hatch is called "The Swan" and is one of six DHARMA stations on the island. Due to an "Incident" those who live in the Swan must enter the numbers into the computer every 108 minutes to prevent an unspecified disaster. This is why Desmond is so worried about repairing the computer before the timer hits zero.

The ever skeptical Jack pretty much mocks Desmond, pointing out that pushing the button could just be another experiment. Locke takes the opposite view, of course. In any case, Desmond's efforts to fix the computer short it out, causing him to leave before the timer hits zero. Jack leaves as well, saying that Locke is on his own.

Kate returns with Sayid and they work with Locke to fix the computer, while Jack tracks Desmond down in the jungle. There, Jack continues to yell that nothing will happen. Finally, Desmond remembers seeing Jack and running with him three years ago, remembering that Jack was running after his surgery on Sarah. After Jack tearfully admits that he married her and that they aren't married anymore, Desmond once again tells Jack "See you in another life" and goes away.

Back at the hatch, the computer is fixed and now Hurley is with Kate, Sayid and Locke. Once Locke starts typing the numbers, Hurley begins to panic. Jack returns and tells Locke the final number, since Desmond had told him the sequence minutes earlier.

But instead of pressing the button, Locke wants Jack to do it, saying that manning the button is a two man job. After still another debate over their respective beliefs, Locke finally gets Jack to take a "leap of faith" and he presses the button. Locke then begins to take his shift as Jack leaves.

Other stuff: Michael, Sawyer and Jin are taken by the people on the beach and put into a pit. Michael demands to know where Walt is, but no one answers him.

Sometime later, a woman is placed into the pit with them. After Michael introduces himself, the woman realizes they are passengers on Oceanic 815, just like her. This is Ana Lucia, the woman who talked to Jack before they boarded the plane. She is a survivor from the tail section of the plane that broke apart before the crash.

Sawyer makes an escape plan, still carrying his gun. But while he works it out, Ana Lucia takes the gun. She is then lifted out of the pit by a guard, who asks her what information she got out of them.

Main character: John Locke.

Flashback details: Locke is in group therapy after his father conned him out of his kidney. There, he finds a fellow patient named Helen and the two begin to bond. But Locke is still obsessed with his father, parking outside his home every night. Anthony Cooper actually comes out to him one day, coldly telling him to get over it and to stop stalking him.

Locke is still undeterred, even after he and Helen have been dating for six months. Helen knows this and confronts him outside Cooper's gates one night. She pleads with him to move on, asking for a "leap of faith." Finally, Locke agrees and leaves with Helen.

Important details in *Lost* lore: The introduction of the DHARMA Initiative and of the button that may or may not be saving the world. From this point on, the *Lost* characters will be working at the hatch to press the button for the rest of the season. Also, Locke had a girlfriend named Helen, though it is not the Helen he called on a phone sex line before his walkabout journey. We are also reintroduced to Ana Lucia, whose appearance is a clue that the new people on the beach are not the Others.

Amount of action: Most of the action is from the overload of new information.

New important characters: Locke's girlfriend Helen, Dr. Marvin Candle, and Ana Lucia. She was seen before, but she is now introduced as a regular character.

Connections between characters: The debate and feud between Jack and Locke reaches yet another climax. Jack and Desmond's past encounter is referenced again. Michael, Sawyer and Jin meet Ana Lucia for the first time.

***Lost* mysteries referenced:** The purpose of the hatch and button, and the numbers connection to both, is revealed.

***Lost* mysteries introduced:** The DHARMA Initiative, the truth about the button, and Ana Lucia.

Questions raised: What is the DHARMA Initiative? Does the button really save the world? Where has Desmond gone to? What will happen now that Hurley has found the numbers yet again? What role will the hatch play for the future of Locke and the survivors? How many more battles are Jack and Locke still yet to have? Who is Ana Lucia? Who are the people she is with, if they are not the Others?

Talking points: The faith vs. science debate continues to go on and on and on, with Locke coming out on top for now. In contrast, we go back to Locke's far darker and uncertain past, when he first learned to take a leap of faith from Helen. Doing so resulted in some long overdue happiness for Locke.

But since we know he and Helen aren't together now and we still haven't seen how Locke got crippled, this probably did not last. So it's not quite an origin story as to how Locke became the man of faith.

We also have another key clue as to the island's past. The Others reside on it now, but now there is an entirely new group in the DHARMA Initiative, which doesn't seem to be around anymore. What is the connection between them, if any?

Other key issues: Sayid, perhaps speaking for *Lost* fans who were getting tired of the Jack vs. Locke wars, brushes aside their argument as irrelevant to the key issue of fixing the computer, just like a good soldier.

Must see episode?: Yes, as one of the key parts of *Lost's* entire mythology. The consequences of discovering the button and the existence of the DHARMA Initiative still reverberate to this very day.

EVERYBODY HATES HUGO

This episode title seems like a bit of a misprint. Hugo of course, is the real first name of Hurley, one of *Lost's* most beloved characters by fans and by the survivors. Why would anyone, much less everyone, hate him? Some may remember that Hurley was in a mental institution and is cursed. In his paranoid mind, this title would be cause for worry. When it's put together with the hatch, the numbers and a large room of food, it becomes the basis for even more dangerous, and downright weird, paranoia.

Episode plot: Hurley has a strange dream where Jin is appearing in the hatch, speaking English next to a costume of a giant chicken. Jin says "Everything is going to change" as well as "Have a cluckity cluck cluck day, Hurley" before Hurley wakes up. Kate reminds him to type those infamous numbers into the computer, before taking her shift to press the button. Hurley is less than thrilled over his new job at the hatch as "head of food rationing."

Charlie later finds Hurley and wants to know about the hatch, but Hurley has no answers for him. Hurley later finds a confident in Rose, however. Jack warns them that soon everyone else will have to be told about the hatch, as well as the giant room of food inside. First they have to make an inventory of the food, which is Hurley and

Rose's job. Hurley soon becomes convinced that this job will make him unpopular.

Meanwhile, Charlie finally gets answers about the hatch from Locke, who also tells him about the room of food. Charlie then finds Hurley and asks for some peanut butter for Claire, but Hurley can't do this until his task is done. Charlie gets mad at him and goes off, confirming Hurley's worst fears. Hurley then goes to Locke and complains about how things are changing, which is a good thing to Locke. But it is certainly not good to Hurley.

Desperate, Hurley finds some spare sticks of dynamite and plans to destroy the food. Rose finds him in time and tries to talk him out of it. Hurley breaks down with his worry and fear that things will start to fall apart because of him, much like they did after his lottery win. He then calms down, not knowing what he should do.

That night, Hurley comes to a decision about how to ration the food, spreading it around to everyone on the beach. For once, everyone is smiling and getting along with no worries as they share their food, all thanks to Hurley.

Other stuff: Sayid and Jack begin to explore the rest of the hatch, finding some blocked doorways and an unseen power source covered by concrete. To Sayid, this power is comparable to Chernobyl. Before they go any further, Jack hears a noise...which is actually Kate coming out of the hatch shower.

Meanwhile, Claire spots the message bottle from the raft, which has washed up from the beach. She and Shannon go to tell Sun about it first, leaving it up to her about what to do. Sun then buries the bottle from sight in her garden, not wanting anyone else to know but clearly fearing the worst about Jin.

Jin, Michael and Sawyer are still alive, but are still the prisoners of Ana Lucia and her group of survivors from the tail section. After some time, they are let go from their pit, since now everyone believes they are from 815 and are not from the Others. They lead the three away into the jungle.

One of the new survivors introduces herself as Libby, while the large man who stood as guard in the pit apologizes to Sawyer for the initial misunderstanding. The group arrives at another DHARMA Initiative hatch called the Arrow, a storage room where they stay for the night.

At the end, one of the tail section survivors comes to Michael, Jin and Sawyer. He asks them if a woman named Rose survived the crash with them…and introduces himself as Bernard. Rose's long held, almost impossible belief that her husband survived the crash is indeed true. Bernard has tears of joy when Michael says Rose is alive and well.

Main character: Hurley.

Flashback details: In the aftermath of Hurley's lottery victory, Hurley doesn't come forward to claim his money, not wanting things in his life to change. He remains working at Mr. Cluck's Chicken Shack, whose mascot is the chicken from Hurley's dream. Hurley winds up quitting anyway when his boss reprimands him for eating the shack's drumsticks. His best friend Johnny quits in solidarity and the two go out on the town.

After taking some gnomes and using them to make the message "Cluck You" on their ex-boss's lawn, Hurley and Johnny promise to remain friends no matter what changes. But when they get to a convenience store, the press is interviewing the man who sold Hurley the winning lottery ticket. He then points Hurley out to the crowd and they rush to him, now knowing he won the lottery. Johnny is upset that Hurley didn't tell him, as their friendship is the first of many things that is about to change for Hurley.

Important details in *Lost* lore: The rest of the survivors discover the hatch. The people holding Michael, Sawyer and Jin hostage are all fellow 815 survivors. Rose's husband really is alive.

Amount of action: Little.

New important characters: More new characters from the tail section survivors, like Libby and Bernard.

Connections between characters: Charlie and Hurley's friendship is strained for a time, while Hurley finds some help from Rose. We also see how Hurley's past friendship with fellow chicken employee Johnny was ruined.

***Lost* mysteries referenced:** The hatch, the button, the numbers, the new group of survivors, and the fate of Rose's husband.

***Lost* mysteries introduced:** Another new DHARMA hatch.

Questions raised: Now that we know the new group of characters are fellow 815 survivors, what is their story? When will Rose and Bernard be reunited? What is this new group going to do with Michael, Jin and Sawyer? What will Sun do now that she knows something happened to the raft?

Talking points: Hurley's fear of change becomes a big part of his actions in this episode. Plus his solution to blow up the food raises his mental state back into question. Only a crazy person would believe he could prevent being unpopular by blowing up massive amounts of food that the survivors need, after all. But with his unpleasant experiences and past, maybe it's excusable. He is probably right about the numbers being cursed, after all.

Other key issues: Battles over faith have been a huge part of the season thus far. Since Rose's faith that her husband is alive is actually correct, that gives another point to faith.

Must see episode?: Not an especially essential episode. Yet after the drama and endless arguing thus far this season, the happy, sentimental ending is a good and overdue relief.

...AND FOUND

So far this season, the discovery of the hatch and the button has dominated talk on the beach. As such, worry and concern over the raft has faded back a bit. But for Sun, the new knowledge that something happened to the raft has brought that back into focus all too well. For all the new information and new characters introduced so far, the fact still is that the camp is not fully united yet. Now, the separation and fear over that fact is starting to take its toll for both Sun and Jin. Yet even that pales in comparison to Michael's ever growing hysteria about Walt, which begins to bring about its own consequences as well.

Episode plot: Ana Lucia orders her group out of the DHARMA hatch, planning to find the other survivors on the beach. First, they stop in the jungle to gather food. Michael goes off with Libby, while Jin helps Ana Lucia and Bernard get fish and Sawyer rests from his increasingly infectious gun wound. However, Michael runs away to find Walt on his own.

Jin goes to find him, accompanied by the larger guard from the pit, who is named Mr. Eko. The other survivors continue on their way to the beach. Jin and Mr. Eko go on their own, as Jin soon finds a dead body through a stake. Mr. Eko calls him Goodwin, who was one of the Others.

Jin soon finds footprints, but they are not Michael's. Mr. Eko gets Jin to hide in the bushes, where they see the Others themselves walking by, only from the knees down. One of them is a child carrying a teddy bear.

Michael is finally found at a waterfall, yelling for the Others to come get him. Jin finally reassures him by saying "You find Walt, Michael" which convinces Michael that he won't be able to do this by himself. With no real chance of finding Walt now, Michael comes back with Jin and Eko.

Other stuff: Sun and Claire discuss what might have happened to the raft, with Claire more confident that Jin will be fine with Michael and Sawyer. Sun then panics over something else entirely, as she has lost her wedding ring.

Jack helps Sun go through her things to find the ring, but they have no luck. Jack's own story about how he lost his own wedding ring and found a replacement doesn't help much, either. Hurley's own suggestion that Vincent the dog ate the ring is even less helpful.

Sun finally tears apart her garden just as Locke comes by. Sun is amazed by Locke's calm, as he explains that it's because he isn't lost anymore. He only found himself when he stopped looking.

When Kate tries to help, Sun finally lets out her real fear by telling her she found the message bottle. Kate, now fearing for Sawyer's safety, looks inside to try and find a message from him, but Sun stops her. In the process, she finally finds her ring in the sand, smiling in relief and with a new hope that Jin may be okay as well.

Main characters: Sun and Jin.

Flashback details: Sun and Jin's actions in the days before they met are examined. Sun's parents are trying to set her up for marriage, as she does strike up a bond with a man named Jae Lee. But he wants to marry a girl in America instead, and saw Sun just to reassure his own parents.

Jin is busy trying to get a job at a hotel, while his friend suggests from an astrology book that he will find love soon. Jin is focused on his work, where he is hired as a doorman at the hotel, though his boss looks down on his poor background. Finally Jin quits when his boss insults him for letting a poor boy inside to go to the bathroom.

Afterwards, Jin walks down a bridge, where a woman in an orange dress catches his eye. Then he bumps right into Sun, in their very first accidental meeting.

Important details in *Lost* lore: Sun and Jin's first meeting is revealed, and the Others are briefly seen again.

Amount of action: Little.

New important characters: Mr. Eko is introduced by name for the first time, while we get our first glimpse of the late Goodwin. Jae Lee is also introduced in flashbacks.

Connections between characters: Sun and Jin are brought together in the past, as Sun gravely worries for him in the present. She and Kate have a bonding moment at the end, while she also gets respective help from Jack, Hurley and Locke. Ana Lucia and Sawyer also start bickering and trading barbs as they trek through the jungle.

***Lost* mysteries referenced:** The Others.

***Lost* mysteries introduced:** A dead Other named Goodwin.

Questions raised: Who is Mr. Eko? Is Sawyer in serious trouble from his wound? What will Michael do to find Walt now? How long will it be until Sun and Jin are reunited?

Talking points: Loss is taking an ever increasing toll on Sun and Michael, in different ways. But Locke, as usual, has the answer by suggesting that things are only found after you stop looking. It worked for Sun in regards to her ring, while it also worked to bring Sun and Jin together when they weren't expecting it. Perhaps that will work for Michael as well now that he's stopped searching for Walt alone. Such a tactic may soon pay off for Sun and Jin's reunion as well.

Other key issues: The Others are starting to show up ever so slowly, as their knees are shown and one of their dead bodies is also seen.

Must see episode?: No. With the plot concerning the search for a wedding ring, Sun's worry that Jin is dead when we know he isn't, plus the foregone conclusion of finding a desperate Michael, there's not much to advance the big picture.

ABANDONED

Lost may be a unique, one of a kind show, but it can also be one big popularity contest. On the upper end of that contest are characters like Locke, Sawyer, Hurley, Charlie and Jack, while others like Kate, Walt and Michael are in the middle tier. To many *Lost* fans, the character at the bottom of the popularity totem pole is Shannon, who was pegged as a spoiled, whining character almost from day 1. With her brother Boone shot dead in Season One, Shannon's luck just kept getting worse, with only Sayid there for her.

As time goes on, it's become clear that the *Lost* creators are quick to eventually respond when characters become unpopular. Since Shannon was the least popular back then, this episode was least likely to break people's hearts. However, some were indeed touched and a bit shocked when *Lost* killed off a main character for the second time ever.

But *Lost* is a survival of the fittest show where the most beloved characters are least likely to die. So the last minute sympathy for Shannon came too little, too late.

Episode plot: Sayid and Shannon share a romantic night together. But it is interrupted when Shannon sees Walt for the second time. She screams to get everyone's attention, but no one believes she saw Walt, not even Sayid.

Shannon uses Vincent to try and find Walt, but he only leads her to Boone's grave. Sayid sees her and believes she is mourning. She then takes off and Sayid tells her that she couldn't have seen Walt, knowing that Sun and Claire found the message bottle. Shannon remains upset that Sayid doesn't believe her and goes deeper into the jungle.

Meanwhile, the tail section survivors are getting closer to the beach. However, Sawyer is becoming gravely ill from his wound. The survivors have to make a stretcher to carry him, over Ana Lucia's objections. They have to carry the stretcher over a hill, but as they do so, one of the tail section survivors named Cindy literally disappears. Just then, low whispers are heard, which signal that the Others are nearby. The group starts to run, fearing they will be attacked.

Sayid catches up to Shannon, who expresses her fear that he doesn't believe in her and will abandon her as soon as they're rescued. But Sayid reassures her that he does love her and believe her. As they hug, Shannon sees Walt yet again, who makes a "Sssh" sound. This time Sayid sees him as well. Shannon then runs towards Walt and Sayid chases her.

As Sayid runs, a gunshot is heard and Shannon stumbles back into view, having been shot in the stomach. The source of the gunshot is then seen. The shooter is Ana Lucia, having fired her gun out of fear that Shannon was an Other. Shannon falls into Sayid's arms and dies on the spot.

The remaining tail section survivors, along with Michael and Jin, are stunned to see what has happened. Sayid cries over Shannon's body, then he stares menacingly at Ana Lucia.

Other stuff: During Shannon's screaming fit at night, Charlie gets upset that she woke Aaron, which catches Claire a bit off guard. Later that day, Locke helps her with the baby, as Claire expresses concern that Charlie is acting like Aaron's father. She says that he could be a religious zealot for all she knows, due to the Virgin Mary statue he has around him. Locke, knowing what that statue really is, looks concerned.

Main character: Shannon Rutherford.

Flashback details: Shannon is working as a ballet instructor when she hears that her father has died in a car accident, which was hinted at in the season premiere. At the funeral, she is reunited with Boone.

There, she tells him she is working to get an internship at a dance company in New York.

Shannon does get the internship, but her rent has bounced. Her stepmother, who has hated Shannon since she married into the family, is no help either. She tells her that her father left no will, but instead a living trust that passed to her. She refuses to give Shannon any money for her trip to New York, kicking her out of her house.

Boone tries to ask the stepmother for money, but gets nowhere as well. Shannon asks to move in with him in New York, but he's moving out after getting a job from his mother. Shannon soon becomes offended that Boone doesn't think she can make it on her own, rejecting his offer to lend her money.

Important details in *Lost* lore: The show has its first on island sex scene between Sayid and Shannon. This may help explain Shannon's prompt death the next day. The murder is also the first meeting between the tail section survivors and someone from the beach.

Amount of action: Fair.

New important characters: Another tail section survivor named Cindy, who is promptly taken away by the Others. Shannon's evil stepmother also appears.

Connections between characters: Sayid and Shannon's relationship is consummated and just as quickly brought to an end. Locke and Claire also pair up to take care of the baby, with the subsequent information about the Virgin Mary statue foreshadowing a rift between Locke and Charlie. Ana Lucia also makes it on Sayid's revenge list by killing Shannon.

***Lost* mysteries referenced:** The fate of Walt, the Others, the Virgin Mary heroin statues.

***Lost* mysteries introduced:** The fate of Cindy.

Questions raised: What will happen now that Shannon is dead? Will Sayid be able to kill Ana Lucia? Why does Walt keep showing up in the jungle? Can Sawyer hold on a bit longer? What will Locke do now that he suspects Charlie of using heroin again?

Talking points: In killing off Shannon, the *Lost* masterminds almost seem to be breaking the fourth wall. Shannon repeatedly comments about how no one believes she can do anything and is useless. This sounded familiar to fans who had said the exact same thing for over a season. This wouldn't be the first time *Lost* would use this technique in killing off unpopular characters.

By this time in the season, Ana Lucia was well on her way to becoming an unpopular, heavily criticized character herself as well. So killing Shannon was basically the passing of the torch of *Lost* unpopularity.

Other key issues: With the out of nowhere abduction and whispers, the Others are entering the realm of the supernatural. But as we will learn in a year or two, that really isn't the case with them.

Must see episode?: Yes. Those who hated Shannon or thought she got a bad break will each get something out of this episode, as it gets us out of the rut of the last two episodes.

THE OTHER 48 DAYS

The formula for a *Lost* episode had become well established by now, mixing present action with flashbacks from the mainland. But at this point in the season, with the main survivors and the tail section ones on the verge of meeting, they stepped back to break the formula. For the first time, a flashback would not only be on the island, it would take up the entire episode. While our main cast struggled during their first 48 days on the island, the adventures of the tail section band raged on behind their backs, as well as ours.

The tail section people were having a hard time integrating into the show as it was, so this technique came just in time for them. Many of their ordeals were the same as the original cast, dealing with Others and moles and characters who mirrored the likes of Jack and Locke. But each separate ordeal has led each group to the same place, over Shannon's dead body with the prospect of more blood on the way. Before that can be resolved, it's time to take a step back and relieve each day all over again.

Episode plot: On the day of flight 815's crash, the tail section landed on the other side of the island. Ana Lucia, like Jack, immediately took charge by saving the children onboard. She also saved Bernard, who was stuck in a tree in his airplane seat. A man named Goodwin builds a signal fire for the rescue that isn't coming. But that night, while the regular survivors heard the monster for the first time, the Others came to the tail section side and kidnapped three adults. Mr. Eko is able to kill two of them, but takes a vow of silence from then on in.

The survivors stay on the beach, but then face another attack from the Others on day 12. Seven adults and two children are taken, but this time Ana kills one of them in response. From the Other's dead body, Ana finds a list of names of all the people they have kidnapped. No longer safe on the beach, the survivors trek into the jungle.

After making camp, Ana creates the pit/prison cell, putting a man named Nathan inside. Suspecting Nathan to be an Other, she starves him and questions him about where the children are. Goodwin finds out that Ana will move on to torture, then frees Nathan from the pit. Goodwin then promptly snaps Nathan's neck.

The tail section survivors soon find the DHARMA Arrow hatch, as well as a radio inside. Ana and Goodwin go up to higher ground to get a signal. While they wait, Ana reveals that she's figured out Goodwin is an Other, realizing that his clothes were actually dry right after the tail crashed into the water.

Goodwin doesn't deny it, saying that the children the Others took are better off. Nathan was killed because he wasn't a good person, which is why he wasn't on their list. A subsequent brawl results in Goodwin being impaled with a big stick, exactly where he was found two episodes ago. With the camp safe from Other attacks now, the survivors rest up.

On Day 41, Bernard actually gets a signal from the radio. This is the day when Boone made his radio call on the downed plane. As it turns out, the person Boone was talking to who said "they" were the survivors of 815 was Bernard. But Ana is convinced that Boone is an Other trying to trap them, not pursuing it any further. She storms out and is met by Eko, who has gone 40 days without speaking. At last he tells her everything will be okay, and Ana finally breaks down and cries.

Days later, Jin washes up on shore from the raft and is taken by Cindy and Libby. While Ana and Eko debate whether he is an Other, Jin escapes. From then on in, the events of the last several episodes are replayed, ending once again with Ana Lucia shooting Shannon and Sayid kneeling over her body.

Main characters: The tail section survivors.

Important details in *Lost* lore: The ordeals of the tail section survivors during the first 48 days on the island are revealed. We also learn that the Others had a spy in their camp just like Ethan in the original survivors' camp. According to Goodwin, the Others have only taken children and "good people" thus far on their list.

Amount of action: Heavy.

New important character: Fellow Other spy Goodwin.

Connections between characters: The episode shows how the tail section survivors came together, despite some friction over Ana's leadership. Ana and Goodwin also connect before they fight to the death. Bernard is also revealed to have talked to Boone right before his fatal accident.

***Lost* mysteries referenced:** The Others, Goodwin, the source of Boone's radio call.

***Lost* mysteries introduced:** The existence of lists to determine who the Others will abduct.

Questions raised: Why and how have the Others decided to abduct "good people" and children? How do they make their lists? Why have they taken more people from the tail section group? Is the parallel between Ana Lucia and Jack's respective leadership a fair one?

Talking points: The adventures of the "tailies" draws obvious parallels to our regular survivors. Ana Lucia took charge like Jack did, as her group battled the Others more fiercely than the regulars did. While Ana Lucia is supposed to be like Jack, her temporary companion before 815 took off, Eko's vow of silence evokes faith not unlike Locke's. Only Eko's is based more on religion.

But unlike the regular survivors, the tailies were less organized and had to move around more, plus they lost many more people to the Others. By the Others new found moral standard, does that mean there are more good people on the tail section side? Many fans would doubt that claim.

Other key issue: As if the abduction of Walt and Claire weren't enough proof of this, the Others have a really big fetish for taking children and the unborn. That's because they weren't creepy enough.

Must see episode?: Yes, as it provides a unique one shot experiment and brings the parallel experiences of these two bands of survivors full circle. What's more, for those who are fed up with the survivors being split up so far this season, this episode signals that this trend is almost over.

COLLISION

After one thirds of this season, the union of two bands of *Lost* survivors is finally at hand. Of course, it comes through the circumstances of one band's leader killing an original character, but nothing's perfect, especially on this island. This is also a chance for *Lost's* newest least favorite character, Ana Lucia, to explain herself and try to get some sympathy back. Like Jack, she also has a history of trying to save lives and be a hero. Unlike Jack, she has less control over her emotions and triggers even more tragic consequences as a result.

But while this union is forged by death, there are also reunions that flourish. Kate and Sawyer are finally brought together again just in time for Jack to save his life, while two *Lost* couples finally come back together. And the foreshadowing of a new connection between two men of respective but powerful faiths is upon us as well, which figures strongly into the rest of Season Two.

Episode plot: Moments after Shannon's death, Sayid leaps into action to kill Ana Lucia, but Eko is able to knock him out. Ana Lucia, fearing what will happen when Sayid wakes up, orders Eko to tie him up with vines from Sawyer's stretcher. When Libby objects, Ana shuts her up at gunpoint. Eko then picks up Sawyer's body and goes to find other original survivors.

When Sayid awakens, Michael gives him water and tells him what happened. Sayid reacts especially strongly to the news about Walt's abduction. The other survivors demand to know what Ana is up to and what she will do to Sayid. Finally she asks Michael to get her supplies from the hatch, so that she can survive away from those that would take revenge on her. Michael then goes off to arrange this and runs into Sun in the process.

Jack and Kate are in a middle of a golf game, which is interrupted when Eko comes out of jungle with Sawyer's body, asking for the doctor. They take Sawyer into the hatch and Jack begins to treat him. Eko also meets Locke for the first time, explaining to him what has happened.

Once Jack has finished treating Sawyer, he learns of the situation outside and demands that Eko bring him to Sayid. Eko, seeing the nearby gun rack, refuses to help. Michael then returns with Sun, filling in the rest of the details for Jack, who then grabs a gun. Eko stops him, stating that "Ana Lucia made a mistake." This stops Jack, as he clearly remembers his meeting with her before 815 took off. Eko agrees to take Jack with him alone, but without any guns.

Back in the jungle, Ana Lucia starts to question Sayid. He asks if she is going to kill him. In talking about his own experiences of torturing and killing men, Sayid seems ready to accept his death now. In response, Ana shares her own experience being shot as a cop in Los Angeles, saying that she still feels dead. She then unties Sayid and is prepared to let him take Eko's blade and kill her. But Sayid responds that it would be useless since "we're both already dead" and leaves to take Shannon's body away.

Finally, the remaining tail section survivors arrive on the beach. As a result, the two overdue reunions of Sun and Jin, plus Rose and Bernard, come to pass. In the jungle, Sayid carries Shannon's body past Jack, who is brought back together with Ana Lucia.

Main character: Ana Lucia Cortez.

Flashback details: Ana Lucia is seen returning to work at the LAPD after having survived a shooting. She insists on being put back on patrol despite the reluctance of her mother, who is also her police captain. Ana gets her wish, but is clearly still troubled after drawing her gun to settle a mere domestic disturbance call.

Later on, Ana's mother tells her they've found the man who shot her, who has already confessed. But when Ana is called upon to identify him, she says it isn't him. As a result, he is released. She was lying on purpose, as she follows him late at night and waits to trap him alone.

Once he is in a parking lot, Ana comes up to him with her gun. He asks if he knows her, and Ana responds by saying "I was pregnant" before shooting him repeatedly until he is dead.

Important details in *Lost* lore: The original survivors and the tail section ones are brought fully together, with the respective reunions of Sun and Jin, Kate and Sawyer, Rose and Bernard, and Jack and Ana Lucia to a lesser extent. Locke and Eko also have their first meeting.

Amount of action: Fair.

New important characters: Ana Lucia's boss/mother and the man who shot Ana while she was pregnant.

Connections between characters: Aside from all the reunions and new meetings, Ana Lucia and Sayid have their obvious tensions in the aftermath of Shannon's shooting. But despite their obvious quarrels, they share their respective history of death and violence before they came to the island.

***Lost* mysteries referenced:** None

***Lost* mysteries introduced:** None

Questions raised: Now that the two groups are finally together, what will happen now? What will happen to Ana Lucia once everyone else finds out what she did? How will Sayid recover from Shannon's death? Will Sawyer be able to get better that he's back with Jack and Kate?

Talking points: Ana Lucia's major back story tragedy is perhaps one of *Lost's* more cruel fates. But it does explain her protectiveness towards the children during the previous episode's flashback. Though fans still had a hard time with her, her past certainly fits right in with the other depressing ones on the show.

Eko's role as the conscience of the tail section becomes clearer in his first confrontation with the regulars, and in his success in keeping Jack from coming out shooting. As the show already works towards drawing comparisons between Eko and Locke, it would appear that Eko is a more peaceful and less obsessive version of Locke. At least for now.

Other key issues: Once more, *Lost* scores major points with another silent emotional montage set to Michael Giacchino's soaring music at the very end.

Must see episode?: Yes, as it finally brings a close to the separate plot lines this season and brings everyone back together. But it was still a little too late for some impatient fans, nonetheless.

WHAT KATE DID

By this point, *Lost* fans were just about ready to accept that the answers to some really big mysteries would take a while. The larger questions about the island, the Others, the monster and such would probably not be answered for several seasons. But until then, the show passed it's time solving some of the smaller, character based mysteries to make it seem like things are moving along. One such mystery they solved right before going on holiday break in Season Two was about Kate.

In Kate's first three flashback episodes, we came close to finding out why Kate had been on the run for so many years, but never got the answer. But this time, the answer came right away and with a bang or two. All it took was Sawyer finally coming back, a few hallucinations/ visions, and even a kiss or two to finally get it out of her.

As such, this time we're going to start off by going over the flashback details first.

Main character: Kate Austin.

Flashback details: A younger Kate is outside her home when her stepfather Wayne shows up drunk. Kate has to put her to bed while fending off some rather inappropriate advances. But Kate is able to get him into bed, and then leaves the area on her motorcycle. A second later, the house blows up into a million pieces with Wayne in it.

Kate stops at a diner where her mother is working. She points out an injury her mother suffered on account of Wayne, but she brushes it off. Kate then shows her a homeowner's policy and explains that she will be taken care of now. Her mother starts to realize what that means after Kate takes off.

Sometime later, Kate has her first meeting with U.S Marshal Edward Mars, after he arrests her before she gets away to Tallahassee. Kate was turned in by her own mother and is driven off by Mars to be arraigned. But while they are on the road, a black horse runs into view and Mars winds up crashing into a telephone pole. Kate subdues him and kicks him out of the car, seeing the black horse staring at her before she drives off.

Kate finally heads to a U.S Army recruitment station, where her real father, Sergeant Major Sam Austin works. During their talk, Kate reveals she found out that Sam was actually her step father and Wayne was her real father. Sam kept this from her fearing that she would kill Wayne as a result, which she has. Sam also cannot help Kate hide out, but gives her a head start before he calls the police.

Episode plot: Sawyer is still sick inside the hatch, but is able to ask Jack "Where is she?" and says "I love her" to Jack's obvious uneasiness. Kate is outside and is shocked to see a black horse standing nearby. She then returns to the hatch to care for Sawyer, where she is shocked again when she envisions Sawyer grabbing her neck and hissing "Why did you kill me?"

Jack later returns to see Sawyer lying on the floor and Kate nowhere to be found. He goes outside and finds her, wanting to know what happened. Still very much distraught, Kate lashes out and apologizes for not being as perfect and good as Jack. Softened, Jack pulls her close, then Kate kisses him deeply and without warning. She just as quickly takes off again.

Kate finds Sayid at Shannon's new grave, confessing that she might be going crazy and seeing things. Since Sayid also saw Walt before Shannon's death, he's in no position to judge about going crazy himself. Kate then returns to the hatch and takes Sun's place in caring for Sawyer.

Thinking that Wayne has possessed Sawyer, Kate confesses to having blown him up, not being able to live with herself after finding out he was his biological father. But even after this, Kate couldn't help being reminded of Wayne whenever she and Sawyer had gotten close. This finally wakes Sawyer up and back to his old self.

Kate later takes Sawyer back outside, then sees the black horse once again. After confirming that Sawyer can see it as well, Kate goes up to it and pets it, relieved that she's not seeing things after all.

Other stuff: The two camps of survivors are now fully together. Hurley catches Jin and Sun coming out of their tent together, giving a knowing thumbs up. Later, the camps hold a funeral for Shannon as Sayid tearfully gives the eulogy. Ana Lucia stays away, despite Eko's reassurance that people understand what happened. Jack soon comes up to her afterwards and the two resume their connection from before the plane crash.

Inside the hatch, Locke explains to Michael about the hatch and how people are taking six hour shifts in pressing the button. As Michael inspects the area, Eko goes to get Locke's attention.

The two sit down as Eko begins telling the Bible story of Josiah. As it turns out, it is a lead in for Eko to show Locke a Bible he found in the DHARMA Arrow station, which contains the missing parts of the Swan Orientation video inside. They work to splice the missing reel back into the original film, as Locke marvels at how this must have been fate. But Eko responds "Do not mistake coincidence for fate."

Locke and Eko watch the restored orientation film. The missing piece has Dr. Marvin Candle explaining that the computer must not be used for anything other than entering the numbers and pressing the button. If the computer is used for anything else, it may trigger another "incident."

However, at this same moment Michael hears a beeping noise on the computer even though the timer is not close to hitting zero. The screen shows the word "Hello?" Michael enters some text in response, typing his name and asking who this is.

The response then typed on the screen is "Dad?" as Michael looks on in shock.

Important details in *Lost* lore: Kate's original crime and father issues are finally revealed. The island once again shows ghosts and strange animal life. The missing pieces of the Swan orientation video are discovered, as Michael seems to have finally connected with Walt again.

Amount of action: Fair, due to all the information.

New important characters: Kate's late abusive father, and her much better Army stepfather.

Connections between characters: The Jack/Kate/Sawyer love triangle is back in the spotlight. Locke and Eko have another big meeting while Jack and Ana Lucia reconnect.

***Lost* mysteries referenced:** Kate's past, the hatch orientation video, the fate of Walt

***Lost* mysteries introduced:** Kate's horse reappearing on the island, whether Walt is really able to talk to Michael on the computer.

Questions raised: Now that Kate has erased memories of her father from her relationship with Sawyer, what is next for them? What will happen now between Jack and Kate? How does Ana Lucia fit into this triangle? Is Michael really talking to Walt now? Will using the computer for communication really trigger disaster, as the video now says?

Talking points: Add Kate to the list of *Lost* characters with father issues, only these ones aren't as creepy or violent. And this one also brings Oedipal themes into the Kate and Sawyer connection, so that makes things a bit more uneasy.

The nature of Kate's visions also raises more questions about the island. Did it bring about these visions to help Kate, or was it just in her mind? The island has played its part before in bringing back old conflicts and wounds for the survivors. In this case, it seems Kate has benefited from the experience, at least when she's not further complicating the triangle.

Other key issues: Locke and Eko continue to come together, but Eko's warning about fate suggests that although these two may have faith, their interpretation of it is quite different.

Must see episode?: Yes to a point, as it solves a mystery for once, gives out a few new hatch tidbits, brings back some weird island visions and ends on a cliffhanger for the holiday. The rest is mainly for the shippers.

THE 23'RD PSALM

As you may have picked up already, the new cast of *Lost* characters had a hard time fitting in. Ana Lucia was already a scapegoat for a season that many thought was dragging on, while Libby was barely doing anything thus far. The one new character that people were getting fond of was Mr. Eko, the mysterious and imposing new man of faith. He often didn't say much, but what he did say added to his intrigue. New regular actor Adewale Akinnuoye-Agbaje also had the fortune of being able to say more with a stare than many could with their words, much like Terry O'Quinn and Naveen Andrews.

So when *Lost* came back from holiday and word was that Mr. Eko would finally get a flashback, hopes were high that the season could be uplifted. This time, their patience was rewarded.

Episode plot: Claire finds Eko carving Bible scripture into his club. Offhand, she remarks that Eko would probably have a lot in common with Charlie, due to Charlie's Virgin Mary statue. However, this sets Eko off in fear and he rushes to find the statue.

There, Claire finally finds out that it is full of heroin and Eko rushes to find Charlie. He grabs him and demands to know where he got the statue, then orders that he take him to "the plane." Eko is actually referring to the downed plane filled with heroin. But how he knows about it isn't revealed until the flashback.

Charlie and Eko trek towards the tree that the plane crashed into, though Charlie is still upset that Eko's discovery ruined things with Claire. They find the corpse of the Nigerian man from the plane, as Eko realizes that it is not "his brother." But before they go any further, the sounds of the monster are heard.

Charlie climbs up a tree, but Eko stays behind. The monster is then finally seen in full for the first time as a giant cloud of black smoke. Eko stares the monster down as it surrounds him, displaying images from his past and seeming to read his mind. Finally, it goes back and disappears without attacking him.

Once things die down, Eko and Charlie finally find the plane. Eko goes inside and finds what he was looking for, the dead body of his brother. He hugs the body and sobs, silently asking for forgiveness and taking the crucifix around his brother's neck.

When he comes out, Eko gives Charlie another Virgin Mary statue to compensate for the one he broke. They then burn the plane as Charlie asks if Eko is really a priest. In response, Eko puts on the crucifix and says he is. The two recite the 23'rd Psalm together as the plane burns down.

Charlie returns at night to see Claire still upset with him. Believing him to be an addict again, she tells Charlie not to come near her or Aaron. Charlie then goes off and places his new Virgin Mary statue next to the five he already has in a hiding place. Obviously he's more tempted than ever to actually use the drugs again.

Other stuff: In the aftermath of Michael contacting Walt on the hatch computer, he keeps it a secret, but gets Locke to teach him how to use one of the hatch rifles. When it's his shift on the computer, he contacts Walt again. Walt types that "they are coming back" and asks Michael to come for him. At that point, Jack returns and Michael has to delete the text. Though Jack reassures Michael that they will go find Walt soon, Michael is already set on his path.

In an ending montage, Kate is giving Sawyer a haircut while Jin is helping Ana Lucia integrate into the camp and Hurley and Libby meet for the first time.

Main character: Mr. Eko.

Flashback details: As a young boy in Nigeria, Mr. Eko lived peacefully with his brother Yemi. But one day, guerilla warriors stormed their village. They take Yemi and demand he shoot an old man. But before they can kill him for not doing so, young Eko takes the gun and shoots the man himself. It spares Yemi, but it results in Eko being taken away and being labeled a "born killer."

When he's all grown up, Eko is now a powerful drug dealer and warlord. Another dealer meets with Eko, wanting to get his supply of heroin out of the country. Eko agrees and buys them at a low price, then slits his throat.

Later, Eko finds his brother Yemi all grown up and now a local priest. Eko wants a plane from his church so he can fly the drugs out of the country, offering him enough money to fund polio vaccines for his village. But Yemi refuses, not wanting anything to do with Eko's business. The next time Eko comes by, he asks Yemi to sign papers that would make him and his associates' priests, so they can charter a plane themselves. This time, he threatens to burn the church to the ground if Yemi refuses, so he reluctantly takes the deal.

Now passing as a priest, Eko and his crew put the heroin inside the Virgin Mary statues and prepare to take off. But Yemi rushes into the scene, begging him not to do this. Just then the military arrives and opens fire, with one of the bullets hitting Yemi. Eko quickly gets him on the plane, but Eko himself is kicked out by his associates before the plane takes off...with the island its unintentional destination.

When the carnage is over, the military men mistake Eko for a real priest as he is overcome with guilt.

Important details in *Lost* lore: Mr. Eko's back story is revealed, and with it comes the answers about the Nigerian plane on the island. The monster is at last seen in full, along with its mind reading powers. Charlie's potential relapse is also discovered by Claire. Hurley and Libby also begin their future relationship.

Amount of action: Heavy.

New important characters: Eko's brother Yemi.

Connections between characters: Eko is paired up with Charlie, another character with ties to religion in his past. Eko's connection to the dead men inside the plane is also revealed. Charlie and Claire's relationship seems to be severed at this point, however.

***Lost* mysteries referenced:** The monster, the downed plane full of drugs, Walt's connection to Michael on the computer, Charlie's potential drug relapse.

***Lost* mysteries introduced:** The fact that the monster is really a cloud of black smoke.

Questions raised: Now that we know what the monster looks like and some of what it can do, what do we make of it? What do we make of Eko's brutal past compared to what he is now? Is Charlie and Claire's relationship finished? Will Charlie relapse for good? What does Michael plan to do now?

Talking points: The lines between good and evil, faith and sinning, light and dark have been blurred on *Lost* ever since the early days. But in Mr. Eko, those lines are more of a criss cross than ever before on this show. Even his origin calls this into question, as his first murder made him a monster, but it saved his brother's life and allowed him to do good.

Now that we know how Eko became a priest, albeit a fake one at first, it calls into question whether this really is enough to redeem his brutal past and whether one like his can be wiped clean. His 40 day vow of silence after killing two Others certainly shows he's committed to it.

That is the emotional center of the episode, but the biggest single scene is the long awaited full screen view of the monster. Of course, knowing what it looks like doesn't take away its mystery. Just like with Locke, when Eko stared it down for the first time it didn't do anything to him. Why have they been so lucky while others haven't?

Other key issues: Charlie's past as a devout Catholic is brought back into focus during his trials with Eko, right as he may have hit the breaking point in his war against returning to drugs.

Must see episode?: Yes. It is mostly a one off episode, with the biggest overall contribution to *Lost* being the appearance of the monster. But it solves a few minor mysteries and offers one of the season's best character based episodes.

THE HUNTING PARTY

Since the discovery of the button, Jack has largely been sidelined as a leader. He's managed to steer clear of any science vs. faith debates with Locke for once, while dealing with his latest Kate problems and reconnecting with Ana Lucia. But although it's been a down period for Jack, the arrival of the tail section and the abduction of Walt makes it clear that further conflict with the Others is inevitable.

Michael, a ticking time bomb since Walt's kidnapping, finally goes off just in time for Jack to get one step closer to that war. And despite being paired with his two least favorite people, Locke and Sawyer, Jack is on his way to find Michael before the worst happens. But leaders aren't always in control, even of their own feelings.

Episode plot: Jack's day begins by waking up to see Locke unconscious and Michael gathering guns from the hatch. He's going after Walt himself and Jack cannot come with him. Michael locks Jack and Locke in the armory and takes off. They are locked in until Kate and Sawyer come in and get them out.

Jack, Locke and Sawyer head to find Michael, but Jack orders Kate to stay behind and take care of the button. Clearly, that's not why Jack really doesn't want to be around her. They head into the jungle to try and track Michael, though Locke questions whether they can really tell him not to go off and find his son. Soon they hear some gun shots and rush forward, where they discover three shell casings from Michael's gun.

At night, the party has lost the trail and Locke argues that they wouldn't be able to get Michael back if they did find him. But Jack and Locke's argument is interrupted by the bearded Other Mr. Friendly, who kidnapped Walt. Knowing who all of them are, Friendly suggests they start a fire and have a chat.

Friendly tells them that Michael won't find the Others, also reassuring them that Walt is fine. He chastises the survivors for intruding on the island, telling them that they're only alive because the Others let them live. Jack disagrees with his assessment of how strong the Others are, then Friendly yells out "Light em up!!!" and a whole group of torches are lit by the Others in the shadows.

Friendly suggests that Jack leave before their "misunderstanding" turns into something else, but he refuses. With that, Friendly calls out his trump card. Kate, who tried to follow Jack, Locke and Sawyer, is dragged into view by the Others. With Kate at gun point, Jack and his team have no choice but to surrender their guns. Kate is then let go as Friendly and the Others leave, with Jack not too happy about it.

The next morning, Jack finds Ana Lucia and talks to her about what happened. He then asks how long it might take to form an army against the Others.

Other stuff: At the camp, Hurley tells Sun and Jin about Michael's mission. Jin wants to go off and join Jack's team, but Sun refuses to let him, worried for his safety.

Inside the hatch, Charlie and Hurley look over an old record collection. Charlie wonders if Claire misses him, while Hurley wonders if he has a shot with Libby. Sayid, still grieving Shannon, walks in awkwardly at that moment.

The next morning, Jin tells Sun that he didn't like being told what to do, but Sun reminds him that she had to be told what to do for years. Jin immediately gets the point. Locke returns to the camp and helps Claire take care of Aaron in Charlie's place.

Main character: Jack Shephard.

Flashback details: In the aftermath of Jack's miracle surgery on his wife Sarah, Jack has become more sought out. An elderly man with a spinal tumor asks Jack to perform surgery on him, hoping for a miracle. Although Christian Shephard warns against it, Jack agrees. While he prepares for the surgery, he forms a connection with the man's daughter, Gabriella. Christian cautions Jack not to get too close, knowing he couldn't live with himself if things got too far.

Meanwhile, Jack's marriage with Sarah is hitting a rough patch, as Jack is throwing himself into work more than usual. But the work doesn't pay off, as the old man dies in surgery. Jack blames himself and goes to apologize to Gabriella, leading to the two sharing an emotionally distraught kiss. A guilt ridden Jack leaves quickly and goes back home, where he confesses to Sarah and vows to fix their marriage.

But it's too late, as Sarah also has something to confess. She's been having an affair for some time. Sarah comments that Jack will always need "something to fix" and leaves.

Important details in *Lost* lore: Michael goes off on his own rescue mission and doesn't return. Jack, Locke and Sawyer have their first extended confrontation and conversation with one of the Others. We find out how Jack's past marriage crumbled.

Amount of action: Fair.

New important characters: Gabriella.

Connections between characters: Jack and Kate have a rift between them, with Jack going to Ana Lucia right afterwards. Jack and Locke find something different to argue about this time, while Jin and Sun have a brief fight but are able to make up. Sawyer also gets another confrontation with Mr. Friendly, the man who shot him on the raft. Locke also questions Sawyer about his nickname and where he got it from.

***Lost* mysteries referenced:** The Others, Walt's kidnapping, bearded Other Mr. Friendly, how Jack's marriage ended.

***Lost* mysteries introduced:** What happened to Michael after he left.

Questions raised: Where is Michael? Is Jack really going to form an army with Ana Lucia? Will Jack and Kate be okay after this latest ordeal? How powerful are the Others?

Talking points: Once again, Jack's obsessive drive to fix something and someone costs him in the past and present. It ended his marriage, it stopped his own rescue mission and now may lead him into crossing the line with the Others. Also once again, Christian is a surprise voice of reason for Jack in the past, knowing him and his emotions all too well.

Now not only is Walt gone, Michael has disappeared as well. In both cases, they won't be heard from again for some time.

Other key issues: After seeing the rifts and breakdowns of many key relationships lately, Jin and Sun's make up and new found understanding after their brief fight is a nice change of pace.

Must see episode?: The showdown with Friendly is a definite highlight, but otherwise it just repeats the same themes from Jack's other flashback episodes.

FIRE + WATER

Lost has done some very weird things in the past, stretching the limits of believability and science fiction. But few episodes have as many weird and unusual sights as this episode has, which in this case actually isn't a good thing. After regaining some forward momentum in recent weeks, things are brought to a halt. This is thanks to Charlie indulging in weird fantasies and a downright creepy obsession to help Aaron, continuing his recent downward spiral.

Episode plot: Charlie has a bad dream where he is playing his piano on the beach, then hears Aaron crying from inside. It carries Aaron out to sea before Charlie wakes up. He rushes to see him, but Claire tells him that she needs some space after their recent troubles.

Charlie then hears Aaron crying again and sees the baby being carried out to sea again in his cradle. He then sees more visions where Claire tells him to "save him" and Hurley is wearing robes like in a Bible painting. Charlie wakes from his dream, as this time he is standing in the ocean with Aaron in his arms. Claire gets even angrier and slaps him.

Charlie then tries to convince Locke he's not crazy, but Locke already suspects Charlie is using heroin again, knowing about the Virgin Mary statues. He advises him to give Claire time to trust Charlie again. Charlie instead goes to Eko, who suggests that Charlie's visions could be a sign. He interprets them to mean that Aaron should be baptized. Charlie goes to tell Claire about it, but gets nowhere as Kate watches over her.

Locke watches Charlie head to his hiding place, finding that the Virgin Mary statues are gone. Locke took them away, convinced that Charlie is using, but Charlie says he was planning to destroy them all. No longer trusting Charlie, Locke goes off to help Claire get away from him.

That night, Charlie starts a fire near the camp as a distraction to take Aaron again. Trying to baptize him, Charlie doesn't get far before Locke and Claire find him. Locke asks Charlie to give him the baby, but Charlie goes off into a rant about how Locke isn't Aaron's father or family. Locke points out that Charlie isn't either. Finally Charlie gives Aaron up, then is knocked out with three punches to the face by Locke.

The next day, Claire finally agrees to have Aaron baptized, but by Eko. As this goes on, Locke finally locks up the Virgin Mary statues inside the hatch.

Other stuff: Hurley starts to ask around about the tail section survivors and Libby in particular. Sawyer needles him about his potential new "love connection." But soon afterwards, Sawyer also points out to Kate that Jack and Ana Lucia are spending more time together.

Hurley gets his chance with Libby when they do laundry together inside the hatch. Hurley suspects that he has seen Libby somewhere before, even before the plane crash. Libby says that he stepped on his toe before he boarded, as the two are on the road to bonding.

Main character: Charlie Pace.

Flashback details: Charlie is seen as a boy receiving a new piano on Christmas, as his mother tells him he has to use it to "save" the family.

Years later as Charlie and his brother Liam are in Driveshaft, Liam's girlfriend has given birth to a baby daughter. But Liam is still a drug addict, as Charlie covers for him.

Driveshaft is in its final days of stardom, as the band films a reworked version of "You All Everybody" for a diaper commercial. Liam is still addicted on the shoot, as Charlie tries desperately to get him back on track. He tries to put together a new song for the band, but Liam can only ask if they have any more heroin.

Finally, Liam is able to get off his feet and try to repair his family, starting by selling Charlie's piano. He breaks up the band to repair himself, leaving Charlie all alone.

Important details in *Lost* lore: Aaron is baptized and Driveshaft is seen breaking up in the past. We also see Hurley and Libby begin to bond.

Amount of action: Little.

New important characters: Charlie's parents.

Connections between characters: Charlie and Claire's relationship continues to suffer, while Charlie's relationship with Locke, the man who helped him get off drugs, completely falls apart.

***Lost* mysteries referenced:** None.

***Lost* mysteries introduced:** Libby's past.

Questions raised: Are Charlie and Claire finished? How close will Claire and Locke get now that Locke has made himself Aaron's new protector? What are Jack and Ana Lucia up to? Does Hurley really have a shot with Libby?

Talking points: After being stuck in the hatch all year, Locke seems to have finally found something else to do by looking after Claire. But his wrong assumptions that Charlie was on heroin again suggests he went about it the wrong way. Though with Charlie's behavior, it's a little hard to blame him.

And it goes without saying that this is one of the odder, weird and off the rails episodes in the show's history.

Other key issues: Seeing Driveshaft sing an awful parody of their hit song brings to mind all those lame song parodies seen in so many commercials over the years.

Must see episode?: One of the least must see episodes in *Lost* history.

THE LONG CON

As much as we may bond and feel for the *Lost* characters, it is hard to remember that these are people we may not like so much if they were real. In real life, it may be harder to handle Jack's hero complex, Locke's often damaging faith and Sayid's brutal skills. In the case of Sawyer, he may be a hot guy that the lady fans can fawn over, and he may provide the show's best lines, but he is a con man.

Sawyer may be a bad boy type and anti hero, but the man still always looks out for himself and doesn't often care who he steps on to get ahead. For some fans of his, that may be hard to remember and to care about. But episodes like this make it clear that Sawyer is to be dealt with at one's own peril.

Episode plot: Jack locks up the guns from the hatch inside the gun vault, with Locke warning Jack that Sawyer is ransacking and selling items again. So Jack goes into Sawyer's tent and takes some meds that Sawyer stole from the hatch. Since Sawyer's tent was ransacked while he was gone on the raft, he's not too happy about starting from scratch again. Kate tries to help him out, but is taken aback when Locke tells her about Ana Lucia helping Jack put together an army. However, Ana is concerned that people feel too safe to want to go out and fight.

Later that day, Sun is tending to her garden and is suddenly attacked by an unseen assailant. She is dragged off and knocked unconscious, though Kate and Sawyer hear her screaming. They don't find her in time to get her attacker, however. In the aftermath, Ana Lucia is ready to attack the Others, but Locke and Jack are more skeptical.

Kate and Sawyer do their own investigating, with Sawyer noting how the attack is different from the other Other attacks. He believes that the attack was staged by Ana Lucia to con everyone else into joining the army.

As Jack tends to Sun, Kate hints about Sawyer's theory with him, but Jack doesn't take it well. Yet as Ana Lucia talks to him about how people are more eager to fight now, Jack begins to suspect her. Just then, Sun wakes up and is ready to talk. Although she doesn't remember anything and can't say who was responsible, Jin is convinced it was the Others and demands a gun. Kate and Sawyer come to believe that Ana's objective was to get the guns from the vault. She gets Sawyer to go to the hatch and try to warn Locke.

When Sawyer gets there, he tells Locke that Jack's team will be coming for the guns, which will be easy since Jack knows the combination. He convinces Locke to change the combination and volunteers to push the button for Locke while he hides the guns.

Later, Jack goes down to the hatch and opens the vault, finding it empty. Sawyer is no help, so Jack goes to confront Locke on the beach. As they argue, Sawyer then appears firing three shots into the air with one of the hatch guns. During the entire ordeal, Sawyer was able to get all the guns himself, having conned Jack, Locke and Kate the entire way through in a "long con."

Now Sawyer is back in a position of power and is once again the man people need to trade with to get something. Only this time, Sawyer's big supply is guns. He isn't telling anyone where he hid them, saying "There's a new sheriff in town."

Kate confronts him afterwards about how he pulled this off, accusing him of being part of Sun's attack. She then says he did all this just so everyone would start to hate him again. Sawyer responds that he cons and she runs, as nothing can change their stripes.

When it's over, Sawyer goes to the jungle and talks to the person who really did attack Sun...Charlie. He joined in just to help Sawyer humiliate and con Locke for revenge, though he doesn't want any of the locked up Virgin Mary statues. Charlie says that Sun can never know he attacked her, but asks Sawyer why he put all this together. Sawyer merely states that he's not a good person, and never did one good thing in his life.

Other stuff: Hurley comes over to a still depressed Sayid, telling him about Bernard's radio and suggesting they could use it to contact the outside world. Sayid isn't interested, but Hurley says he suggested it to help cheer him up.

That night, Sayid is able to help Hurley work on the radio, playing around with the signal. Suddenly they do start to hear a radio broadcast playing Glenn Miller's "Moonlight Serenade." The music could be coming from anywhere, so it is of little help. But Sayid and Hurley still listen to it, now a bit more relaxed.

Main character: Sawyer.

Flashback details: Sawyer is performing another one of his cons. But this time his mark, a young woman named Cassidy, is on to him. She also wants to learn about his cons. So Sawyer takes her under his wing and performs a series of cons with her. However, Cassidy wants to perform a bigger con.

Sawyer explains that this sort of thing is a "Long Con" where the con artist makes the mark ask for a favor as if it was their idea. It would take a lot of money, but Cassidy explains that she is actually worth around $600,000 dollars. So she volunteers to perform the favor of getting this money for a con, as if it were her idea.

Sawyer is performing this Long Con on Cassidy, but his partner Gordy suspects he is getting cold feet. He tells him to finish the deal or he'll kill them both. When Cassidy comes to Sawyer with the money, he confesses that she was the long con. He takes Cassidy's money and puts it in a duffel bag, telling her to get to a motel while he takes care of Gordy. She agrees and they part ways.

Once she leaves, Sawyer starts counting Mississippi's before pulling out another duffel bag from under a table. He had given Cassidy an empty bag and left the bag with the money inside. Having finished his long con successfully, Sawyer heads off.

Important details in *Lost* lore: Sawyer takes control of the survivors gun supply.

Amount of action: Fair, due to all the con action.

New important characters: Sawyer's mark/old partner/girlfriend Cassidy.

Connections between characters: Sawyer manages to get the best of and further alienate Jack, Locke and Kate in one fell swoop. Charlie's new hatred of Locke also leads him to attack Sun. Hurley manages to get Sayid's mind off Shannon for a precious few moments. In the flashback, Sawyer orders food in a diner from a woman who turns out to be Kate's mother.

***Lost* mysteries referenced:** The Others, though they are used as scapegoats this time.

***Lost* mysteries introduced:** Sawyer's theft of the guns.

Questions raised: Has the balance of power on the island shifted with Sawyer's power play? Did Sawyer do all this just because he wants to be the bad guy in everyone's eyes? Will Charlie's role in Sawyer's plan be discovered? What becomes of the plan to form the army now?

Talking points: This season has become more and more dark and dreary for many characters. In Season One, these people were making progress towards overcoming their dark pasts and moving forward towards redemption. Now they seem to be taking giant steps backward.

Jack's leadership is struggling, Locke is losing his touch, Sayid has lost another loved one, Charlie has slipped to the brink of downright evil and Sawyer purposefully undid all the progress he had made. The only bit of uplifting character progress seems to be made by Mr. Eko, a newcomer and a former drug lord.

Other key issues: The *Lost* writers are getting more and more self conscious as Hurley remarks that the radio signal could have come from "any time," taking a jab at their own penance for weird plot twists.

Must see episode?: For Sawyer fans and for fans of lots of cons, it is. But it doesn't really move anything that forward in the grand scheme. Neither has the last few episodes, for that matter. However, that is shortly about to change.

ONE OF THEM

There are two ways to look at this episode. One is how *Lost* fans viewed it when it first came on. When it premiered, it seemed like just another episode where a brand new plot element was introduced, rather than answer any of the old plots. In this case, the discovery of a captured man who might be one of the Others. Since the Others were ever so slowly starting to reveal themselves, this wasn't all that mind blowing. Even though Sayid got to command this episode, it didn't seem gigantic at first.

The other way to view it is within the context of time. Once you get done looking over every single *Lost* episode, you'll understand what this means. It is only after seeing every episode that you can go back and see that this may be one of the most important episodes in *Lost* history. It may even be the most important, period. Not for what happened in this episode itself, but for who we met for the very first time.

From the very first shot of Michael Emerson as Henry Gale, *Lost* would never be the same show ever again. Even if we didn't know it yet.

Episode plot: Sayid is met by, of all people, Ana Lucia. She tells him she saw an Other, but when Sayid investigates, he finds it is Danielle Rousseau. Sayid tells Ana to go back and tell no one about what happened. He then goes forward to reunite with Rousseau, who tells Sayid she was looking for him.

She leads him to a tree where she shows that she has caught a man in a net. The man, distraught with fear, says that his name is Henry Gale, but Rousseau is convinced he is an Other. Sayid lowers the net anyway and cuts it open, but as Henry runs away, Rousseau shoots a bow into his back. She tells Sayid to take him to Jack, and warns that "for a long time, he will lie."

Sayid brings Henry Gale into the hatch, where Locke is the first to see them. A panicked Henry starts to explain that he crashed on the island on a hot air balloon, having buried his wife three weeks ago. Jack then comes in and starts treating him. As he does so, Sayid convinces Locke to put Henry in the armory and change the combination so Jack can't come in. Sayid wants to interrogate Henry alone.

Once Locke changes the combination, Sayid brings Henry into the armory and closes the door before Jack can get in. Locke keeps Jack subdued, explaining that what Sayid is doing is part of the war that Jack was ready to declare on the Others.

Inside the armory, Sayid begins asking Henry questions about his life and what he is doing on the island. Henry explains about his hot air balloon trip and his wife's sickness, and then asks who Sayid is. Sayid talks about his career and how he discovered his capacity for violence, then says "My name is Sayid Jarrah, and I am a torturer."

Sayid goes on to ask Henry more detailed questions about his life and his story. The more he goes on, the more angry and closer to violence he gets. He finally breaks down when he demands Henry answer him about his wife's death and how he buried her.

Overcome with grief over Shannon, Sayid yells that Henry would remember every detail about burying someone he loved…if his story was true, that is. Henry asks if Sayid lost someone, to which Sayid answers that it was an accident. He says that the woman who killed Shannon was afraid someone was coming to hurt her.....someone like Henry.

With that, Sayid's beating of Henry begins. Jack overhears it and is determined to get inside the armory. But as Locke tries to stop him, the timer begins to sound as the button needs to be pushed. Jack will only let Locke go push it if he gives him the combination, daring Locke to let the countdown go to zero. Finally Locke opens the door for Jack. While Jack tries to get Sayid off of Henry, Locke rushes to the computer.

But the countdown has hit zero, and hieroglyphics begin to appear where the timer's numbers are. Before anything else happens, Locke successfully enters the numbers and presses the button. At last Jack gets Sayid out of the armory, leaving Henry inside to recover from his wounds. Yet Sayid catches a meaningful glare from Henry before the door closes.

Sayid returns to the beach, where he tells Charlie about Henry. He says he feels no guilt for his torture, because it seems people have forgotten what the Others are capable of and what they have done. He asks Charlie if he's forgotten as well.

Other stuff: Sawyer's victory in the past episode is tempered by the annoying sounds of a tree frog outside his tent. When Jin won't help him out, he goes to Hurley after discovering Hurley's hidden stash of food. During their search for the frog, Hurley becomes fed up with Sawyer's fat nicknames, reminding him that everyone still likes him, unlike Sawyer. In response, when they find the frog and Hurley wants to keep it, Sawyer crushes it in his fist.

Main character: Sayid Jarrah.

Flashback details: In the middle of the Gulf War, American soldiers capture Sayid and demand to know where his commanding officer is. When Sayid says he doesn't know, the soldiers show that they already have the officer, Tariq, captured. They want Sayid to translate the interrogation of Tariq, as they want him to give up the location of a missing American pilot.

When the interrogation goes nowhere, an American commander named Inman talks to Sayid. He tells him that since Tariq won't talk to the Americans, he wants Sayid to get the information out of him. To get him riled up, Inman shows him a video of a village being gassed under Tariq's orders. It is also a village where Sayid had family members. Inman then hands Sayid a box of tools for torture. Sayid uses these tools to torture Tariq into admitting that the American pilot died two days ago.

Sometime later, Sayid is driven to the desert as the Americans are leaving Iraq. Although Sayid vows never to torture anyone again, Inman tells him in Arabic that Sayid will need to know something one day, as now he has the tools to get it. The Americans leave as Sayid starts walking back to Baghdad.

Important details in *Lost* lore: The survivors capture suspected Other Henry Gale, as the beginning of Sayid's life of torture is revealed. The hatch countdown goes down to zero for the first time.

Amount of action: Heavy.

New important characters: Henry Gale and the American soldier Inman.

Connections between characters: Jack, Locke and Sayid all meet Henry Gale for the first time, as Sayid tortures him, Jack tries to stop it and Locke approves of it. Hurley and Sawyer also have an odd little mission in the jungle. In the flashback, one of the soldiers who takes Sayid is Kate's Army stepfather.

***Lost* mysteries referenced:** The Others, the button.

***Lost* mysteries introduced:** Henry Gale.

Questions raised: Who is Henry Gale? Is he an Other? Even if he is, was Sayid right to torture him over Shannon's death? How will he treated in the wake of Sayid's torture? Does the appearance of symbols on the timer suggest the button really does do something if the countdown reaches zero? What more will Sayid do to prove Henry is one of them? Was there any point to Hurley and Sawyer's tree frog search?

Talking points: In continuing with the trend noticed in the last episode, Sayid has also returned to his old dark self with the capture of Henry Gale. Whether that is entirely good or bad depends if Henry is an Other, of course. The whole term "Other" is also debated at the end when Jack points out Rousseau first thought Sayid was an Other too, so Locke says that to her, everyone is an Other. Now the lines between "one of them" and everyone else are blurring even deeper.

Other key issues: Henry gives a rather shifty look to Sayid right before he is taken away, even after he has taken a massive beating. Do not think this is the last time that will happen.

Must see episode?: Hurt by a useless subplot, but otherwise yes. Maybe it isn't as good individually as other landmark *Lost* episodes, but time will prove it to be quite the turning point in the show's history indeed.

MATERNITY LEAVE

In the course of having so much action on *Lost,* some plots and entire characters can be left in the wayside. Claire is one of those examples. Aside from yelling at Charlie and looking worried about Charlie, Claire has had very little to do since giving birth to Aaron. What's more, it's even easier to forget she was kidnapped last season, plus she still has amnesia about what happened. But with *Lost,* one remembers these little forgotten plots just in time to devote a whole episode to them.

For only the second time, flashbacks take place on the island, so the flashback details will be incorporated into the episode plot section. We also get a blast from the past via a return visit from an old dead Other, while a new potential Other begins to settle into the hatch.

Main character: Claire Littleton.

Episode plot: Claire becomes worried when Aaron develops a fever late at night. As she waits for Jack, she finds Rousseau instead and is not too happy, since Rousseau kidnapped Aaron the last time they met. But Rousseau knows Aaron is sick and says Claire "doesn't remember." This triggers Claire to see a series of images from her still foggy memory.

The next day, Claire goes to see Libby in hopes that she can help her recover her memory. Libby starts to meditate with her, trying to get past her memory regression. This helps Claire flashback to when she was inside a medical hatch, discussing the baby with a doctor. Soon enough, as the doctor injects her, he is revealed to be Ethan Rom. This jumps Claire back into the present, now remembering Ethan fully. Convinced that Ethan drugged her and that those drugs are now affecting Aaron, she is determined to find the medical hatch where Ethan kept her.

Kate volunteers to help her and gets Sawyer to give her a gun. They plan to find Rousseau so that she can find the medical hatch for them. Claire leaves Aaron in the care of Sun, who asks her "Are you sure you want to do this?" This triggers another flashback where Ethan drugs Claire again, then takes her into a nursery room with baby toys and pictures.

She lies down peacefully, while Ethan goes to speak with Mr. Friendly, who is actually without his beard. He scolds Ethan for capturing Claire before he finished his list of survivors to take. Friendly also worries about what will happen when "he" finds out about this.

Claire then returns back to the present and brings herself to head off with Kate. In the jungle, the two track down Rousseau, where Claire asks her to bring her to where she scratched Rousseau's arm during her attack. Rousseau brings them further into the jungle, but does not know where she's supposed to go next. Claire yells that Rousseau scratched her here when she tried to bring her back to the Others, but Rousseau calls her a liar. Kate holds Rousseau back by pointing her gun, though Rousseau actually wants her to shoot.

As this goes on, Claire runs away to a tree stump, then has another flashback to when she and Ethan talked on that stump. Ethan reveals that the Others will be taking her baby away after Claire gives birth. But Ethan reassures her that the Others are "good people" and will take care of the baby.

Claire then recovers and runs some more until she finds a set of leaves. As Kate and Rousseau return, Claire pulls the leaves back to reveal a door with the DHARMA logo on it. The door leads to the inside of a stairwell leading to the medical station.

The three women explore the station, as Kate discovers a locker filled with fake beards and fake rags, much like the clothes the Others have worn. Claire's search triggers another flashback, where she is awakened by a young girl. She tells Claire to be quiet, saying that the

Others are going to take the baby. In her drugged state, Claire panics and calls for Ethan, but the girl knocks her out with chloroform and takes her out of the medical station. She mutters that Claire will thank her for this one day and leaves her in the jungle.

When Claire snaps out of it, she, Kate and Rousseau find the examination room where Ethan drugged her. Claire searches for a vaccine that will cure Aaron, but finds nothing. She yells that Rousseau should know where it is, then has her final flashback.

In it, Rousseau finds Claire in the jungle while Ethan and the Others are looking for her. Claire wakes up and tries to get Ethan's attention, but Rousseau tries to stop her. The ensuing fight is how Claire scratched Rousseau's arm, resulting in Rousseau knocking Claire out with her gun. This gave her the amnesia, but also gave Rousseau time to drag her closer to her camp, where she eventually woke up and came back to her friends.

Kate, Claire and Rousseau leave the hatch, with Rousseau stating that she also didn't find what she was looking for, just like Claire. But Claire tells her about the girl who saved her in the hatch, figuring that it could very well have been Rousseau's daughter Alex. She tears up in relief and hope.

Claire returns to the camp and is told by Jack that Aaron's fever is gone. Relieved, Claire gives Aaron a sock she knitted for him in the hatch. She shares that she wanted to give him up before he was born, but now vows that they will never be separated again.

Other stuff: The captured suspected Other Henry Gale is still locked up in the armory, as Jack and Locke debate on what to do with him. Locke wants a long term plan, but Jack ridicules that by comparing it to Locke's lack of a long term plan for the button. Henry overhears this and suggests they let him go.

Eko later comes into the hatch and oversees Jack hiding Henry. He confronts Jack about it and asks to see Henry himself, or else he will tell everyone else about him. When Eko gets the chance to see Henry, he confesses how he killed two of the Others over 40 days ago. He asks for forgiveness, then pulls out his blade and cuts off two bundles of hair on his chin.

Afterwards, Locke comes into Henry's cell and the two begin to talk, with Henry commenting on how Jack seems to be "calling the shots." Locke claims that he and Jack make decisions together, but Henry clearly doesn't believe it. Neither does Locke, as he leaves the armory and smashes a dish on the sink in anger. Henry listens to this intently, almost suspiciously so.

Important details in *Lost* lore: Claire's memory fully returns as she remembers everything about her time in Ethan's custody. We also get our first suspected glimpse of what may be Rousseau's lost daughter Alex, as she saves Claire's life. It is also revealed that Rousseau also saved Claire from the Others and did not attack her. There are also hints that the ragged and native look of the Others may be fake.

Amount of action: Fair.

New important characters: Alex, if indeed the girl is Rousseau's Alex.

Connections between characters: Claire, Kate and Rousseau have their own little hunting party as the truth of Claire's past experiences with Rousseau and Ethan are discovered. Henry Gale is introduced to Eko, while putting his two cents in about Jack and Locke's leadership feud.

***Lost* mysteries referenced:** Claire's abduction by Ethan and her forgotten time in captivity, Rousseau's lost daughter, and Henry Gale.

***Lost* mysteries introduced:** The existence of a "him" that outranks Ethan and Mr. Friendly in the Others power structure.

Questions raised: Is Rousseau's daughter with the Others? If so, why did she go against them and save Claire and the baby's life? Will Aaron continue to get sick? Was Henry Gale trying to make Locke upset on purpose by bringing up his feud with Jack? Why would he do this if he isn't an Other, as he says?

Talking points: This is a rare moment when *Lost* actually brings a character arc and mystery to a definitive close. It tied up pretty much all the loose ends about Claire's time with the Others, except for why they took her and what they wanted with Aaron. But let's be lucky for one miracle at a time. Now that this arc is closed, Claire will probably have to go back to pining over and being mad at Charlie, however.

Back in the hatch, Jack and Locke are right back to their usual, endless arguments. Only this time, someone is there to exploit it. For the second straight episode, Henry Gale mostly acted confused and frightened about everything around him, then gave some mysterious hint that there is something suspicious about him.

Other key issues: After all those times where Jack and company went trudging around the jungle, it is nice to see three of the female characters go on their own little adventure by themselves.

Must see episode?: Yes, as it brings closure to an almost forgotten Season One mystery. Albeit one that has slid down the list of important mysteries by now.

THE WHOLE TRUTH

Pregnancy is often a dangerous thing to introduce on a TV show. The arrival of a new baby often signals that writers have run out of ideas and introduced a new kid to hide it. It is credited for making plenty of 80's sitcoms "jump the shark" as it were. But those were on shows where there are only a few main characters, whereas *Lost* has about 15 of them. As such, having a character get pregnant shouldn't produce much backlash for a show like this. Especially for a show that was facing enough backlash by this point.

So on *Lost,* introducing the possibility of Sun being pregnant isn't a show killer. In fact, it introduces a whole new plot for Sun to get mixed up in. In the meantime, some more immediate forward action takes place in the hatch, as the mystery of Henry Gale sucks up more characters and gets a tiny bit creepier by the end.

Episode plot: Concerned that Sun will be attacked again, Jin overcompensates by wrecking Sun's garden so she can stay close to the camp. Once Sun does return, she begins to look sick. She then goes to Sawyer and asks for a pregnancy test.

After Sun gets a pregnancy kit, Kate sits with her as she waits for the results. The result is positive, with Jack later confirming that Sun is indeed pregnant, which makes Sun a bit nervous.

Jin is fishing at the beach as Sawyer tells Bernard that Sun is pregnant. They both congratulate Jin, but he cannot understand what they are saying. This starts to distress Jin, as he later goes back to fix Sun's garden. When Sun finds him, he confesses that he wants to stop fighting with her. He needs her since she is the only one that can understand him. With that, Sun finally tells him that she is pregnant.

Other stuff: Locke has become impatient with having Henry in the hatch, seeking Ana Lucia's help in finding out the truth about him. He doesn't bother to tell Jack about this plan, however.

Ana goes inside the hatch and has a talk with Henry, as he retells his back story about crashing in a balloon and his dead wife. This time around, Ana volunteers to let Henry draw a map to where the balloon crashed, as she plans to look for it and see if it matches the story. Henry is still afraid that they will "crucify him" to make him a scapegoat for their war with the Others, but he draws a map anyway.

Ana takes Sayid and Charlie with her to find the balloon. Once they rest in the jungle, Ana shares with Sayid that she knows no one likes her. also knowing that Sayid has an especially good reason not to. But Sayid says that she was just trying to protect her people and that the Others are really to blame for Shannon's death. He anticipates that once they find out Henry is indeed one of them, something will have to be done.

Henry is still in the hatch as Jack takes him out of the armory to give him breakfast. He eats with Jack and Locke, then brings up Ana Lucia and how he drew a map for her to find the balloon. Locke didn't even know about this, which gives Henry another chance to point out Jack and Locke's lack of trust.

Henry then theorizes that if he really was "one of them" he would have sent Ana Lucia and her party into a trap, where his people would go get them and use them to trade for Henry. But he quips that it's a good thing he really isn't one of them, then asks if there's any milk.

Main character: Sun.

Flashback details: Sun and Jin hit another snag in their marriage when they cannot conceive a baby. In the meantime, Sun is already planning to leave Jin and go to America, as her former love interest Jae Lee is teaching her how to speak English.

Sun and Jin go to a fertility specialist, who tells them that Sun cannot have children. Jin explodes in rage and storms out of the room. However, Sun later tells Jae Lee that she is relieved she can't have a baby. Jae Lee then confesses that he would like her to stay with him, as things are left up in the air between them.

The fertility specialist later finds Sun and tells her he lied about Sun not being able to have babies. As it turns out, Jin is the one who is infertile, having a low sperm count. The doctor was afraid to tell the truth due to Jin's connections to Sun's father.

In the present day, Sun tells Jin that he is the infertile one, but reassures him that the baby is indeed his. Convinced, Jin declares that the baby is a miracle, but Sun isn't too sure.

Important details in *Lost* lore: Sun is discovered to be pregnant, but how she got pregnant remains a mystery. Ana Lucia's mission also brings us a step closer to finding out the truth about Henry Gale.

Amount of action: Little.

New important characters: None.

Connections between characters: More stormy details about Sun and Jin's past are discovered, as they take another step forward to a new beginning in the present. Ana Lucia and Sayid have a bit of reconciliation as they search for Henry Gale's balloon, while Henry puts more doubt into both Jack and Locke.

***Lost* mysteries referenced:** Henry Gale.

***Lost* mysteries introduced:** Sun's pregnancy and whether she got pregnant via another man.

Questions raised: Who is Sun's baby's father? If Jin really is the father, how was he able to get her pregnant after all? Will Sun's pregnancy make her a target of the Others like Claire was? Will Ana Lucia, Sayid and Charlie find Henry's supposed balloon? Was Henry teasing Jack and Locke with his story about setting a trap, or was he telling the truth?

Talking points: In the beginning, Jin appeared to fall right into the second season trend of characters returning to their old, rotten selves. But in contrast to the likes of Sayid, Sawyer and Charlie, Jin is able to resist old temptations and maintain his new found goodness. Having no one else to speak your language certainly helps.

For all the debates and battles for leadership between Jack and Locke, they are both proving to be quite inadequate lately. Jack keeps getting blind sided by Locke, while Locke was kept in the dark by Ana Lucia, and they both continue to get played by Henry Gale. Maybe it's time for some new blood on the top of the food chain.

Other key issues: The episode took time to remind us that Rose and Bernard are still around on the island.

Must see episode?: To a point, as it introduces an important new plot in Sun's pregnancy. But other than that, not much is of interest except for the latest confrontations with Henry, especially at the end.

LOCKDOWN

As *Lost* continued to face charges of a slump in its second season, one of those most vulnerable to the charges was John Locke himself. In Season One, Locke was the mysterious man of the jungle who searched high and long for his destiny. But in Season Two, Locke was just stuck pushing a button and having countless arguments with Jack. The man of action and of faith was not being rewarded too much for his beliefs, which made fans that loved him in Season One a bit frustrated.

Locke was getting in a rut that needed to be fixed fast. So what better way to do so than to give him a race against time, discover a new mystery, and have his first, but not last, extended face off with the man still calling himself Henry Gale?

Episode plot: Henry's "hypothetical" speech about sending Ana Lucia, Sayid and Charlie into a trap makes Jack order him back into the armory. This makes Henry question Locke again about why he lets Jack order him around. This time, Locke just locks him up again, in no mood to be needled by Henry now.

In the jungle, Ana's team is making no progress in finding Henry's balloon. As it rains, Sayid argues that they've given Henry more time to think of an escape. But just then, Charlie finds the grave where Henry said his wife was buried. Once they realize it has stopped raining, the survivors look up to see the balloon hanging in the trees.

Later, as Locke does some exercises in the hatch, a mysterious voice is heard through the speakers. It is a garbled voice, but by the end it is heard performing a countdown. When it gets to zero, blast doors inside the hatch come down. They lock Locke inside the hatch living area and away from the computer. Locke manages to put a claw under the final blast door, while Henry keeps asking what's going on from his cell.

Once Locke gets himself situated, he explains to Henry what has happened. He needs help to get out and press the button in time, but there's no one around except Henry. With no choice, Locke has to enlist Henry's help, as Henry makes him promise that he won't let his people hurt him anymore. Locke lets Henry out and they start trying to lift the blast door up. They use a toolbox to prop the door up and Locke tries to slide under it, but the box gives way. The door crushes Locke's legs, making him immobile once again.

Now it is up to Henry to find a way out and get to the computer. He tries to get into the vents but trips and falls, then finally wakes and heads up just as the timer alarm starts to sound. With only seconds left, Locke yells for Henry to press the button, but the clock then hits zero.

Suddenly the lights go completely out, replaced by hidden blue lights that highlight the door Locke is trapped under. Now a huge map is visible on the door, seeming to document all the locations on the island. At the center of the map is a gigantic question mark. Locke tries to memorize each detail, but then the regular lights go back on and the timer is heard reverting back to zero. The lockdown also ends as the blast doors are lifted back up.

Locke crawls back towards the computer, calling out for Henry. But Henry comes up right behind him and helps him up. Relieved, Locke thanks him for staying. Henry treats his wounds and explains that he did press the button.

They are interrupted by the search party returning to the hatch, along with Jack and Kate. Jack grabs Henry and Sayid points his gun at him, as Locke demands to know what's going on. Sayid tells Henry that they found the grave and his balloon just as he told them. But Sayid still did not believe him and dug up the grave for himself. What he found was not the body of a woman, but of a man. He then searched the man and found a wallet, which he shows to Henry.

Inside the wallet is a driver's license with a picture of a black man, identified as Henry Gale.

Henry just stares at Sayid as Locke is left silent at this latest betrayal.

Other stuff: After Jack leaves the hatch at the beginning of the episode, he stumbles onto Sawyer, Hurley and Kate playing poker. Jack claims to know a lot about the game, so Sawyer invites him to play. The two have their usual banter and ego boosting as Jack cleans Sawyer's clock in the game. So Jack suggests they play for all the meds Sawyer took from the hatch.

As it turns out, Jack easily wins that match as well. Sawyer is surprised Jack didn't ask to play for the guns, but Jack responds that he'll get them when he needs them, leaving Sawyer a bit taken aback.

At night, Jack and Kate discuss the game as they head for the hatch, then they see a light coming down towards the jungle. They run to the source of it and see some large packages of food with the DHARMA logo on it. Before they can investigate further, Ana Lucia's search team shows up and meets with them.

Main character: John Locke.

Flashback details: Locke is living together with Helen and making plans to propose to her at a picnic. But instead he is stunned when Helen reads an obituary for his father, Anthony Cooper.

The two go to the funeral as Locke finally gets some closure with his father, saying that he forgives him. But he is suspicious of a white car nearby that leaves right after the proceedings. That car later shows up again to him. Locke is stunned to see Anthony Cooper, alive and well, inside.

Cooper explains that he faked his death to avoid two men he betrayed in one of his cons. There is $700,000 in a safety deposit box, which Cooper wants Locke's help to retrieve. Despite Locke's initial refusal, he still finds himself helping his father anyway.

After he withdraws the money, Locke returns home to see the two men who are pursuing Cooper. Locke lies and says he hasn't seen Cooper since his death. The men leave, but Helen is now suspicious herself.

Later, Locke goes to his father's motel and hands him the money. Just as Locke refuses a cut of the money, a knock is heard.

Cooper answers it and sees Helen, who asks "Are you him?" and then slaps him in the face. Once Locke sees her, he desperately follows her and tries to apologize for lying. She doesn't want to hear it, leaving Locke to pull out his engagement ring and propose to her in desperation. She refuses and drives off, leaving Locke alone as Cooper departs as well.

Important details in *Lost* lore: Henry is finally revealed to be an Other. Locke discovers a mysterious invisible map of the island. The flashback shows how Locke's former relationship ended.

Amount of action: Heavy.

New important characters: None.

Connections between characters: Locke and Henry have to work together and actually seem to bond before the truth about Henry finally comes out. Jack and Sawyer face off in poker, with Jack's victory putting him back in good graces with Kate. In the flashback, Locke is seen inspecting the house of Sayid's lost love Nadia before he encounters Cooper again. Helen also uses the same line "Are you him?" that Desmond asked Locke in the hatch.

***Lost* mysteries referenced:** The button, Henry Gale.

***Lost* mysteries introduced:** The hidden map with the question mark on it, who Henry Gale is now that we know he's lying, the drops of DHARMA food.

Questions raised: What was that map, and will Locke be able to figure out what it means? Now that Henry is an Other, who is he really? Why did Henry come back for Locke and press the button if he is an Other? Where did the DHARMA food come from? How is Jack really going to get the guns?

Talking points: In the past and present, Locke suffers for trusting in the wrong men. He helped Cooper despite knowing better and losing Helen in the process, then he went on to trust Henry in the hatch. Granted, he really had less of a choice in the hatch with time running out there, but Henry still got him on his side before being exposed.

Despite seeing how Locke was so easily taken advantage of in his past, it's clear he still hasn't learned his lesson about that sort of thing. Does that put in some new doubt about whether he's right to trust the island and the button? Or will Henry's lies finally be a wake up call for him?

Other key issues: At least *Lost* outwardly admitted that Jack and Sawyer's poker showdown was pretty much the equivalent of getting out a ruler and measuring, as Kate quips.

Must see episode?: Yes, as it finally puts some of the bigger new and old mysteries this season front and center, instead of burying them in subplots. With Henry exposed and a new mystery around that might get us closer to solving the hatch, some forward momentum is at last regained.

DAVE

When we first got Hurley's back story in Season One, it revealed him to be much more important and complex than just being the funny fat guy. For one, it introduced the all important numbers and Hurley's curse. But while everyone was obsessing over the numbers, there was also the hint that Hurley may have been in a mental institution, well before he even discovered the numbers. How crazy could Hurley have been, given his usually jolly attitude? In this episode, it's pretty crazy as it turns out, in both Hurley's past and present. As such, the flashback materials need to be recapped first.

Main character: Hurley.

Flashback details: Hurley resides in the Santa Rosa Mental Health Institute, which he has been in for two months at this point. His doctor, Dr. Brooks, is monitoring Hurley's diet, but they wind up arguing about the influence of another patient named Dave.

Though Hurley says Dave is the most normal person there, he is also encouraging Hurley not to take tests and to cheat on his diet. He also tells Hurley not to take his pills, as Hurley keeps them in his mouth even as Dr. Brooks takes a picture of him and Dave.

Later, Dr. Brooks finally brings up the accident that made Hurley have to be committed. His weight apparently caused a deck to collapse and killed two people, though Dr. Brooks tries to convince him it wasn't his fault. He brings up that the accident made Hurley almost catatonic and made him punish himself by overeating. Hurley yells that Dave was right to call Dr. Brooks a quack, which makes the doctor take out the picture he took of Hurley and Dave that day.

The picture only shows Hurley, with Dave nowhere to be found. This is due to Hurley having made Dave completely up in his imagination.

That night, Hurley sees Dave again as he encourages him to escape from the institution and go find more food. Hurley realizes that Dave is just the part of him that doesn't want to get better and wants to keep punishing himself with food. So Hurley goes back inside the institution and locks Dave outside, now on the road to recovery.

Episode plot: Hurley is trying and failing to get into shape with Libby, confessing that he is "sick" and showing her his hidden stash of food. So Libby gets him to throw it all away, which he finally does with a smile. But before they get closer, they are told about the new supply of DHARMA food that dropped out of the sky last night. Hurley is taken aback, then gets upset when the hoarding survivors suggest he should be in charge of food rations again. As he does so, he gets a glimpse of Dave and finds his slipper.

At the beach, Hurley winds up eating some DHARMA crackers, which triggers Dave's reappearance. Hurley then goes to ask Sawyer for some meds, which causes Sawyer to start making fun of him for being nuts. This is the breaking point for Hurley in regards to Sawyer's insults, as he attacks him and repeats Sawyer's various insulting nicknames. Enraged over being called crazy, Hurley goes to stay in the deserted caves.

Later, as Hurley eats from a jar of peanut butter, Dave returns again. This time they have a long talk in which Dave says that Hurley isn't even on the island and that the island isn't real. Hurley is still in the mental institution, having dreamed the entire series. He imagined winning the lottery and discovering the cursed numbers and having Libby like him, since all of that could have never happened in reality, according to Dave.

Hurley actually becomes convinced as Dave takes him to a cliff. He tells him that once Hurley jumps off, he will be back in the institute and this long hallucination will have ended, returning him to his old life. Dave says "See you in another life" and then jumps off himself.

Hurley seriously considers jumping just as Libby finds him. He repeats Dave's claim that none of this is real, especially Libby liking him. Libby counters by saying she is real, recounting her terrible experiences with the tail section survivors, which Hurley couldn't have made up. But Hurley is still barely convinced, until Libby finally proves she does like him by kissing him. At last, Hurley is convinced and is able to return to normal, heading off with Libby.

But in one final flashback, the scene returns to Hurley getting his picture taken with Dave. This time, the scene goes back to show that Libby, medicated and alone, was a patient in the institution as well.

Other stuff: In the aftermath of Henry being exposed, he is tied and bound in the armory as Ana Lucia and Sayid interrogate him again. Locke, with his legs still injured, is unable to walk without crutches and is now out of the loop.

Henry says that the real Henry Gale died four months ago, after crashing and suffering a broken neck. But Sayid found a note that the real Henry wrote to his wife after he crashed, which pokes a hole in the story. The fake Henry pleads that he didn't kill him as Sayid starts to ask about the Others.

Henry says that the Others leader, who isn't Mr. Friendly, will kill him if he talks. Sayid pulls out a gun and is ready to pull the trigger as Henry begs for his life. Ana Lucia pushes Sayid back just as he fires the gun and misses. Locke hears the shot from his bunk, getting more and more upset that he doesn't know what's happening.

Finally Locke gets himself up to talk to Henry. He asks why he let himself be captured, thinking it was to find out about the hatch. Henry instead calls it a joke and also comments that God can't see the island better than anyone else can. He then explains that when he crawled through the vents and went to press the button, he let the countdown go to zero and the timer reset itself. Now he claims he never entered the numbers and nothing happened when he didn't. Locke says he's lying, but Henry replies that he's done lying.

Meanwhile, Eko is gathering wood to begin building a church for the island, with Charlie volunteering to help.

Important details in *Lost* lore: Hurley is confirmed to be a former mental patient who suffers from hallucinations and seeing imaginary friends. Libby is also discovered to be an ex-mental patient as well. Henry finally admits out loud he is an Other and that they have a leader who would kill him for answering Sayid's questions.

Amount of action: Fair.

New important characters: Hurley's imaginary friend Dave.

Connections between characters: Hurley and Libby get closer and have their first kiss in time to stop him from killing himself. Eko and Charlie come together again to build a church. Sayid once again interrogates Henry and almost kills him this time, but Henry lives to plant some real doubt in Locke's mind about the button. For the second straight episode, a character repeats one of Desmond's old sayings, in this case Dave.

***Lost* mysteries referenced:** Hurley's past in a mental institution, Henry Gale, the button, the DHARMA food drop.

***Lost* mysteries introduced:** Libby's past in a mental institution, who the Others leader is, whether Henry really pressed the button.

Questions raised: Is Hurley cured of his hallucinations? What is Libby's past? Was Henry telling the truth about the button and the Others leader? Is Locke about to stop believing in the button? What does Henry mean when he says God can't see the island better than anyone else can?

Talking points: *Lost* fans tend to come up with many wild solutions to the whole great mystery. Some keep saying it's all purgatory, even after the creators deny it many, many times.

One of the wildest theories was that the whole series was all in Hurley's mind, a la the *St. Elsewhere* finale. It would seem that the writers pretty much made this whole episode just to discount that theory and make fun of it. But having that kind of jokey/semi serious self parody has its good and bad qualities. At this stage, fans would rather see real answers than spend a whole episode discounting a wild fan theory.

Other key issues: The Others weird sense of morality is brought into question again as Henry screams "I am not a bad person!!" before Sayid almost kills him.

Must see episode?: Perhaps for Hurley fans, though it may discourage them to see Hurley taken to the brink of insanity this thoroughly. But yet again, the main plot in an episode really isn't that important, while Henry Gale's subplot in the hatch is.

S.O.S

By this point in the story of *Lost,* the flashback structure has been used for just about everyone. All the regular characters have had their back story told by now. Even if we haven't gotten all the answers to their pasts yet, we've got some idea of where these people have been. With all the important people having flashback episodes already, it's just about time to move on to other characters. But the show doesn't seem to be ready for flashbacks of Rousseau, Henry or the Others. So this episode flashes back to the only recurring characters from 815 not to receive back stories, Rose and Bernard.

Episode plot: As Rose and Bernard start stocking the new supplies of DHARMA food, Bernard is wondering out loud where it all came from. He's also getting upset about why people are settling down on the island when they should be asking more questions and find a way back home. But Rose is a bit more reluctant to share this line of thinking.

Bernard starts gathering some of the survivors and asks for their help in a plan. He wants to build an S.O.S sign on the beach that will be spotted by planes and satellites. However, he does not get much support for this plan, even by Rose, who argues that Bernard is giving people false hope.

Undeterred, Bernard sets about putting the sign together, but few people are helping and most of the ones that do quit. Rose again criticizes him for his leadership skills and always trying to do something, to which Bernard snaps back that she wouldn't be alive if he didn't.

By the end, everyone on Bernard's team has quit, leaving him alone to work on the barely finished signal. Finally Rose comes by and the two discuss the other time Bernard refused to give up on something this badly, which is when Rose got cancer. Rose says that Bernard's efforts didn't end up healing her, but staying on this island has. Realizing that being here has helped Rose get better, Bernard finally gives up his mission to leave the island.

Other stuff: Locke is now obsessed with remembering the hidden map on the blast door, while wondering if Henry was telling the truth about the button being useless. As for Henry, he is treated by Jack while he tells him that he's going to trade him back to the Others, in order to get Walt back. But all Henry says is "They'll never give you Walt." Jack then takes Kate with him to track the Others down.

In the hatch, Locke is becoming more and more unglued with his doubt. Ana Lucia won't let him inside to speak to Henry, so Locke simply yells and desperately asks if Henry pressed the button. All Henry does is smile as Locke starts to lose it.

Jack and Kate's trek in the jungle is interrupted when Kate picks up a doll, which sets up one of Rousseau's net traps. Kate tries to get Jack's gun from his pocket to shoot them loose. This creates some obviously awkward touching and closeness between Jack and Kate, but it works.

After Rose's argument with Bernard, she finds Locke sitting on the beach, vowing that he's done with the hatch. Rose says he'll be up and about in no time, though Locke says that Jack told him he'd heal in 4 weeks. Rose then cryptically says that "you and I both know it's not gonna take that long." This actually seems to cheer Locke up a bit. Later he returns to the hatch with a new vigor to draw the map and try to figure it out.

In the jungle, Jack and Kate finally reach the area of their last encounter with the Others. Jack begins to scream that they have Henry and that they'll have to come here if they want him back. He then yells he'll be waiting right here until they come. But by night, they still haven't arrived.

At last, just as Jack says he isn't sorry that Kate kissed him, a noise is heard. Jack and Kate go forward expecting to see the Others.

But instead, they see Michael coming forward and collapsing at their feet.

Main characters: Rose and Bernard.

Flashback details: Rose and Bernard met during a winter's night in which Bernard helped get her car out of the snow. The two hit it off and Bernard proposes to her five months later, but Rose responds by saying she has cancer and has a year to live. However, Bernard still wants to marry her and she agrees.

When the two go on their honeymoon in Australia, Bernard pulls one over on Rose by taking her to a faith healer. Despite how far Bernard went to make this arrangement, Rose is upset, saying that she has made peace with her fate. But Bernard hasn't and finally convinces her to go for his sake.

When Rose sees the faith healer, he performs a reading on her and says he cannot help her. He tells her that Rose can be healed, but this isn't the place where it can happen. Rose decides to lie and tell Bernard she really was cured, so that he will be able to enjoy his final months with her instead of looking in vain for a miracle cure.

With that, the two head onto flight 815 as Bernard is overjoyed that Rose is better. While Rose waits, she drops a medication bottle, which is picked up by a man in a chair. He hands the bottle back to Rose and she thanks him as he rolls away in his wheelchair. That man is John Locke.

Rose is the only person to know that the island made Locke walk again. This made her aware that the island cured her cancer as well.

Important details in *Lost* lore: The island is revealed to have healed Rose as well as Locke. Michael finally returns.

Amount of action: Little.

New important characters: None.

Connections between characters: Rose and Bernard's history together and struggles with her cancer are discovered. Rose realizes that both she and Locke were healed by the island, as proven by their brief meeting before the plane crashed. Henry pushes Locke's crisis of faith to the breaking point. Jack and Kate have yet another occasion to flirt as they go after the Others and get caught in a net.

***Lost* mysteries referenced:** The button, the invisible map, Locke being healed by the island, Henry Gale, whether Henry pressed the button, the fate of Michael.

***Lost* mysteries introduced:** The island's role in healing Rose, how Michael got back.

Questions raised: Why did the island heal Rose as well as Locke? Is Locke's crisis of faith really over? Where has Michael been and how did he get back? Why did Henry take such satisfaction in hearing Locke break down?

Talking points: Devoting an episode at this late stage in this season to two minor characters is a bit of a risk for *Lost.* The show is already accused of stalling enough on explaining things. But this episode did tie Rose and Bernard into the bigger mystery of the island's healing powers. The island curing Locke's paralysis is one thing, but also getting rid of cancer indicates an even bigger trend.

Other key issues: It was pretty convenient for the island to let it rain just as Jack was giving a big screaming speech to the Others, wasn't it?

Must see episode?: The trend continues of an episode's main plot being good for character development, but not really big in the larger story. The subplots, particularly those with Henry, are really the things moving *Lost* along now. But things finally start to develop faster from here on in.

TWO FOR THE ROAD

As the final month of Season Two approached, it was just about time for *Lost* to finally get down to business and resolve at least a few issues. With Locke actually asking questions about the hatch and the button, they would have to actually answer if it did anything. With one of the Others finally getting some face time in Henry Gale, some light had to be shown on them. And with Michael's recent comeback from sabbatical, plus the arrival of May sweeps, a war had to come at the end of this season.

People expected a lot, even those that had been burned so far by this season. But no one could have seen how this final run of Season Two episodes would kick off. And no one could have ever expected what one character would resort to doing.

Episode plot: While Locke is sleeping, Ana Lucia goes into the armory to talk to Henry, who isn't eating anything or talking anymore. Ana taunts him by talking about how she's been around a lot of killers. This makes Henry whisper something, but when Ana gets closer, Henry attacks her suddenly. While strangling her, Henry hisses about how she killed two of his people, calling her the real killer. Before Henry can hurt her further, Locke comes up and knocks Henry out with one of his crutches.

Later, Henry is tied up again in the armory, with Locke wanting to know why he tried to kill Ana but not him. Henry says that Locke is "one of the good ones" but doesn't go any further. He is convinced that he'll either die by Jack's hand or by the Others soon enough, since their leader is not a forgiving man. Henry says that he failed in his mission, stating that he was heading for the camp because he was coming to get Locke. Before Locke can inquire further, Jack and Kate return with Michael.

Outside, Ana is determined to get revenge on Henry and asks Sawyer for a gun, but he refuses. When Ana tries again, she gets a little more aggressive and the two wind up having sex. Meanwhile back on the beach, Hurley wants to put together a picnic for him and Libby.

In the hatch, Michael is finally well enough to start talking to Jack and Kate. He tells them that he saw the Others camp, which is run down and populated by dirty, ragged people that are barely armed. He swears that they can go take them down and once he's well, he will lead them to their camp and get Walt back.

With both Jack and Locke now ready to wage an attack, they go off to get the guns back from Sawyer, with Ana volunteering to stay behind in the hatch. But when Jack and Locke go confront Sawyer, he realizes that Ana has taken his own gun. Locke realizes why she did it right away.

Ana opens the armory and points Sawyer's gun at Henry, telling him to cut himself loose. As he does so, Henry comments about how Goodwin insisted that she was a good person and she could change, but it cost him his life when he was wrong. With no more to say, Henry stands up as Ana gets ready to shoot.

Moments later, Michael gets up and sees Ana sitting on the couch with the gun. She tells him about Henry and how she wanted to kill him, but she couldn't do it, saying "I can't do this anymore..." So Michael suggests doing it for her. Ana reluctantly agrees and tells him the combination to the armory.

Michael takes the gun and says "I'm sorry."

Ana asks "For what?"

And then with one shot, Michael shoots Ana Lucia dead in the chest.

All of a sudden, Libby then appears, having gone to the hatch to get blankets for Hurley's picnic.

Before Michael can even think, he has shot her twice as well.

Nearly in tears, Michael finally brings himself to open the armory. Henry then rises up and sees Michael, staring at him without a change in expression.

Michael then points the gun at his own arm and shoots just as the shot cuts to black.

Main character: Ana Lucia Cortez.

Flashback details: A week after Ana Lucia executed the man who shot her while she was pregnant, his body is found. Her mother and captain suspects she did it, which leads Ana to quit the force. She gets a new job as a security officer in an airport, where one day she has a talk with a man at the airport bar. He tells her he's a former doctor whose son ratted him out and made him lose his license.

Though he doesn't tell Ana his real name, we know this is Christian Shephard. He asks her to come with him to Sydney, Australia to be his bodyguard, chalking it up to fate. She agrees, with the two doing pretty much nothing until four days into the trip, as Christian calls on her to drive him to a house. There, he drunkenly yells to a woman that he wants "to see my daughter" but he is kicked out. Ana gets him back to the car and drives him away.

The next morning, the two are still in the car, parked next to a bar. Fed up with Christian, Ana asks what he's doing. He replies that since he couldn't apologize to his son, he ran away just like she did. Christian suggests they go into the bar and drink, but Ana has had enough. Christian goes into the same bar where he talked to Sawyer in "Outlaws", saying he can't ever go back.

On the day of the plane crash, Ana is standing behind Jack as he makes his plea to get Christian's body on the plane. She then calls her mother to apologize and say she is coming home.

Important details in *Lost* lore: Michael kills Ana Lucia and shoots Libby, then appears to let Henry go. Ana manages to have sex with Sawyer before she dies, however. She is also revealed to have traveled together with Christian Shephard in Australia right before he died. It also turns out Christian might have a daughter.

Amount of action: Heavy.

New important characters: None.

Connections between characters: Ana Lucia becomes determined to kill Henry, even going so far as to have sex with Sawyer to get it done, but she can't do it. Henry plants one last question in Locke's mind by saying he was coming to get him all along. Ana Lucia is found to have a pre-flight connection with both Jack and his father, albeit in different ways. In the flashback, Christian almost hits Sawyer with his car door moments before they have their talk in the Australian bar.

***Lost* mysteries referenced:** What happened to Michael, Henry Gale, and the state of the Others.

***Lost* mysteries introduced:** Why Michael could have possibly killed Ana Lucia and Libby just to let Henry go, whether Henry really was coming to get Locke, who Christian Shephard's daughter is.

Questions raised: What happened at the end? Why has Michael become a killer? What became of him while he was away to make him do this? What will become of Henry now that he may be gone? What will happen when Jack, Locke and especially Hurley find out that Ana Lucia and Libby are shot?

Talking points: All the discussions about Henry and Ana Lucia's battles, Henry's cryptic confession to Locke, Michael's assessment of the Others and even Ana and Sawyer having sex take a back seat to the final minute of the episode.

For once, the ABC publicists didn't promote ahead of time that someone would die at the end of this episode. This actually made it surprising, unlike when Boone and Shannon eventually died. And once again, the victims of surprise deaths are characters that never really got approval in the *Lost* fandom, so they didn't exactly risk fan backlash by killing them off. But even the most ardent haters of Ana Lucia probably didn't see her going out this way.

This also brings an end to Ana's involvement in the triangle with Jack and Kate. For someone who was teased as being Jack's new love interest, she never really got anywhere with him at all and had more action with Sawyer, as it turned out. And she had more interaction with Jack's father in the past, as it further turned out. Somewhere along the line, the creators kind of forgot that love angle. They also forgot the one where Jack and Ana were going to form an army.

Other key issues: Jack's father continues to get around in the past, with past connections to Sawyer and Ana Lucia as well. Plus many fans suspected that since he went to Australia, his daughter might be none other than Claire.

Must see episode?: Yes. After weeks of stalling, a limited number of plot twists, and go nowhere main plots, things are finally ratcheted back into high gear as the season starts to wind down.

?

Fans were still left reeling from the shocking death of Ana Lucia and the apparent upcoming death of Libby. But with these deaths, it meant that two of the three main new characters from the tail section were gone. For all the hype and importance bestowed on these new survivors, they all seemed to be going away by the end of the season. This left Mr. Eko, the most well liked newcomer, to carry the burden of the Tailies by himself from here on in. He also winds up sharing the burden of the hatch, the major question of the entire season, with Locke in this episode.

No, the title isn't a misprint; it is an actual question mark from the mysterious blast door map. But it is probably the most fitting episode title in *Lost* history, considering the nature of this show. Even the answers we get in this episode are still left to interpretation about how true they are. One just has to take it on faith, as Locke and Eko usually do. But whose faith is really the strongest?

Episode plot: Eko is still working on building a church when Ana Lucia appears to him. When she starts bleeding from the mouth and stomach, it's clear this is a dream and a vision. She says "You need to help John" then Eko is seen at the hatch. What's more, he sees his dead brother Yemi, who tells him that Locke has lost his way and he needs to find "the question mark." Eko then wakes up from his sleep.

After finding out about what happened in the hatch, Eko volunteers to find Henry and asks Locke to come with him. But Locke soon figures out that Eko has no intention of finding Henry. Eko tells Locke to take him to the question mark, which Locke refuses to talk about. But he changes his mind after Eko head butts him. Locke explains about the map, with Eko preferring to wait for "further instructions" from his dreams to find the symbol, as they rest near Yemi's burned plane.

The next morning, Eko awakes to find Yemi standing over him, telling him to climb the nearby cliff. When he does, he finds Yemi at the top saying "Wake up, John." As it turns out, this was Locke's dream. But it gives Locke and Eko the idea to climb the cliff for real. Eko goes up and doesn't see anything at first, then looks down to see a giant question mark in the soil below him.

Once Locke and Eko go back down, they discover the door to another hatch that's under the plane. They open it and head inside, where there is a room with several television screens on a wall. One of those screens shows what's going on in the Swan hatch, as it appears this is a monitoring station of all DHARMA hatches. The two look around further and find a printer where paper is sticking out, displaying a log of notes from whoever lived in this hatch. Soon after, they find another DHARMA orientation video.

Once again, the video is hosted by Dr. Marvin Candle, only now he calls himself Dr. Mark Wickman. He says that this is an orientation for Station 5, called "The Pearl" It is a monitoring station where the two men inside will "observe a psychological experiment." And that experiment is inside the Swan. The workers in the Pearl must take notes of everything the people in the Swan are up to, as they believe to be doing something that actually isn't real, which would be pressing the button. This would appear to be proof that the button is not real.

When it's all over, Eko is actually convinced that pressing the button is even more important than ever, while Locke is convinced it was all a lie as Jack told him over and over. He declares his entire life is as useless as the button, demanding to know how Eko can tell him otherwise.

Eko explains about his brother, how they were separated and how he found his body again on the island. Now Eko is convinced that just as he was meant to be on this island, he was meant to press the button, even if Locke refuses to keep pushing it. He takes the papers from the printer and heads off.

Other stuff: Jack, Kate, Locke and Sawyer head back to the hatch minutes after Michael's murderous actions. Henry is gone, with Michael saying that Henry shot him in the arm and killed Ana Lucia and Libby. Ana Lucia is indeed dead, but Libby is still alive, albeit barely. This makes Michael a bit nervous.

Jack works to treat Libby, but she is in shock. He asks Sawyer to find the Virgin Mary statues Locke took from Charlie, so that Jack can inject Libby with the heroin. He then tells Kate to go with her so she can finally find out where Sawyer kept the guns. With no choice, Sawyer shows her that he hid the guns under his tent all along. Before they can get away with the heroin, Hurley comes up to them and asks if they've seen Libby.

Though Jack gives Libby the heroin, it is of little use. Hurley is barely able to say goodbye to her as she slips away. Libby calls out "Michael..." in an attempt to warn the others about him. Unfortunately, they interpret her statement as expressing concern for him, telling her he's okay.

At last Libby passes away as the group mourns her and Michael watches from Henry's old cell.

Main character: Mr. Eko.

Flashback details: After the events of Yemi's death in Nigeria, Eko has made himself into a real life priest working in Australia, though he plans to head to America. Before that, he is called upon to investigate a miracle, in which a child was resurrected a day after she drowned in a river.

Eko visits the girl's examiner, who tells him she came back to life during the autopsy, playing him an audio tape of the event. When he sees the family for himself, the mother tells him not to come by.

Eko is then met by the girl's father, who is Claire's former psychic, Richard Malkin. He explains that his wife faked the report of his daughter coming back to life after discovering he was a fraud as a psychic. Eko reports that this was not a miracle and prepares to fly for America on flight 815.

Before he boards, the girl visits him at the airport, telling him she knows about Yemi. She claims to have talked to him while she was "between worlds." She says that although Eko isn't a real priest, Yemi still has faith in him. This leaves Eko momentarily stunned before he boards the plane.

Important details in *Lost* lore: Libby officially joins Ana Lucia as a murder victim of Michael's. A new DHARMA station is discovered which may prove that the button is not real. However, Eko makes it his mission to continue pressing it as Locke renounces the hatch. The guns that Sawyer was hiding are also finally discovered.

Amount of action: Fair.

New important characters: None.

Connections between characters: Claire's psychic, the one who may have set Claire up to get on 815 and crash on the island, reappears in Eko's flashback and reveals himself as a fraud. Locke and Eko pair up once again to find "the question mark" but end on far separate terms. Hurley must say goodbye to his new love Libby.

***Lost* mysteries referenced:** The button, the map in the hatch, Michael's murder spree, where Sawyer hid the guns.

***Lost* mysteries introduced:** Whether the information on the Pearl orientation video really is accurate or not.

Questions raised: Is Locke's faith destroyed for good? Has Eko taken on a fool's errand in taking over the button, or he is correct to do so? What will Locke do as a result? What is Michael about to do now that Ana Lucia and Libby are both dead? What will Jack, Kate, Sawyer and Hurley be prepared to do now that they think Henry is responsible? Why did the host of DHARMA's orientation film go under another name?

Talking points: Locke had already finished battling a crisis of faith after Henry's various tricks, having seemed to come out for the better just two episodes ago. But that was nothing compared to the crushing blow from the Pearl orientation film. Yet Eko goes on believing it, having completed his trajectory towards becoming the old Locke.

Like the old Locke, he now believes it was fate and destiny for him to be here, only he figured that out due to seeing his brother again on the island. But knowing Eko and his faith, it does not seem subjected to the kind of self doubt and nagging questions that Locke's faith does, so it will be a little harder to shake off. Now it's a matter of finding out if this is a good thing.

Other key issues: As if the parallels with the orientation video scene from "Orientation" weren't strong enough, Eko echoes Locke's line from that scene when he asks "Would you like to watch that again?" This time, Locke has seen enough.

Must see episode?: Yes. With Locke and Eko together again, character driven ordeals go hand in hand with answering some major questions, or at least getting some brand new clues. With just two episodes left this season, things are finally getting closer to being solved.

THREE MINUTES

Through all of Season Two, only one thing has driven Michael's actions, which is the quest to get Walt back. This has been defined by his mid season departure and his endless screams of "WALT!!!" Then there was the matter of him murdering two women and freeing confirmed Other Henry Gale from his prison. How could doing all that relate to his search for Walt? What could have happened to him since he left in "The Hunting Party" episode? Could his love for Walt really drive him to turn into a killer?

Since it's the end of the season now, these are questions that will actually get answered in a hurry, as Michael begins to set things up for the second annual grand finale.

Episode plot: In the aftermath of Libby's death, Michael burns a piece of paper outside before its contents can be seen. Jack comes to call him into the hatch, where everyone is discussing what to do next. Michael argues that they must attack the Others, but only himself, Jack, Kate, Sawyer and Hurley need to go. They decide to bury Ana Lucia and Libby today and go battle the Others tomorrow morning.

Michael has some words with Eko as he cleans the blood, asking about Hell. Eko relates a story in which a child told him he killed a dog to protect his sister. He was afraid that if he did go to Hell, the dog would be waiting for him. This makes Michael go back outside and throw up out of his fear and guilt. Jack finds him again and comforts him that they will get Walt back, with Michael still insisting that only Jack, Kate, Sawyer and Hurley have to go.

Michael is later reunited with Sun and Jin, telling them that Ana and Libby were murdered. Meanwhile, Jack is gathering the guns from Sawyer's tent, which attracts Sayid's attention. When he is brought up to date, he asks to go, but Jack tells him Michael didn't want him along. However, Sawyer overrides this and invites him on the team.

Michael is upset when he finds out about Sayid coming along, later telling him himself that he can't go. He insists that Sayid will damage the mission out of his desire for revenge, though Sayid denies he would let this happen. Michael further presses that it is his decision on who goes and who stays. Sayid finally relents and wishes him luck.

Jack and Sawyer prepare for the women's funeral, as Sawyer confesses that he "screwed" Ana Lucia, since Jack is the closest thing he has left to a friend. As Michael puts the plan together, Hurley refuses to come along, which makes Michael upset again.

Sayid then takes Jack aside and says that he is sure Michael has been compromised by the Others. Knowing that a father would do anything for his son, Sayid is convinced he is leading his friends into a trap. He reminds Jack that he was also convinced Henry was one of them. Sayid warns Jack not to tip Michael off that they know anything, wanting to spend the night thinking of a plan to turn things around.

At the funeral, Jack eulogizes Ana Lucia briefly, while Hurley tearfully says a few words on behalf of Libby. This finally convinces him to join Jack, Kate, Sawyer and Michael on their attack plan.

As the funeral ends, Sun looks out into the ocean and sees a shocking sight. A sailboat is coming into view and heading towards the island.

Other stuff: Charlie tries again to reconnect with Claire, handing him a case of vaccines he found in the hatch. Claire is still upset with Charlie, but seems to be softening. Charlie later finds Eko in the hatch, wondering why he isn't building the church anymore. Eko is now devoted to pressing the button instead, so Charlie gets upset and refuses to bring Eko his things from the beach.

Charlie tries and fails to keep building the church on his own. He then sees Vincent running by, carrying one final Virgin Mary statue in his mouth. Charlie shakes his head in total disbelief, then goes to get the other five statues from Sawyer's tent. Ridding himself of temptation at long last, Charlie throws all the statues into the ocean. Locke is sitting at the beach and gives Charlie a smile at this accomplishment, but Charlie is still too mad at him to accept it.

Jack finds Eko in the hatch, as he lies and says he tried to find Henry's trail. When he is told about the funeral, Eko says he will mourn "in his own way."

Finally before the funeral begins, Locke gets up and walks away with a new sense of purpose, no longer needing his crutches.

Main character: Michael Dawson.

Flashback details: The episode first flashes back before the events of "The Hunting Party" as Michael gets Locke to give him some guns and bullets for "target practice." He instead knocks Locke out cold, then goes to the computer and types to Walt that he's leaving to find him now.

After Michael locks Jack in the armory and leaves, he heads outside to start his search. He quickly finds one of the Others, who asks if he's Walt's father. This distracts Michael long enough to be ambushed by the Others, though Mr. Friendly warns that they need him alive.

That night, Mr. Friendly has Michael gagged up just before he shows himself to Jack, Locke and Sawyer. He tells Michael to be quiet or he'll never see Walt again. Michael silently watches Mr. Friendly's confrontation with his friends from the end of "The Hunting Party" while Alex asks Michael if Claire and her baby are okay. When it's over and Jack's team leaves, Alex is forced to knock Michael out.

Two days later, the Others get Michael back to their campsite, which is run down and dirty exactly as Michael said. It is filled with huts, tents and a hatch door with a DHARMA logo on it. Michael is brought inside a tent, where a woman named Ms. Klugh begins asking him questions about Walt. When Michael can't answer, she comments that he doesn't know Walt very well after all.

Over a week later, Klugh comes to Michael again, as he wonders when he is going to be killed. She explains that Walt is outside the tent and will be given back if Michael frees Henry Gale from the hatch. When Michael doubts this claim, Klugh has Walt brought inside. Michael tearfully hugs him and asks if he's all right. Walt says that the

Others are making him take tests, as they are pretending about who they really are. Klugh threatens to put Walt in "the room" if he goes on, then has him taken away right from Michael's arms.

This finally breaks Michael as he cries over having seen Walt so briefly. Klugh gives Michael a list with four names on it…the names of Jack, Kate, Sawyer and Hurley. She orders Michael to bring only these four people with him into a trap after he has freed Henry, otherwise he won't get Walt back. Michael at last agrees to do this, then says that he wants "the boat."

Important details in *Lost* lore: Michael's time away from the camp, his capture by the Others, and his brief reunion with Walt is revealed. It is confirmed that Michael killed Ana Lucia and Libby so he could free Henry as part of a deal to get Walt back. That deal also involves leading Jack, Kate, Sawyer and Hurley into a trap. Charlie also finally eliminates the Virgin Mary statues while Eko begins his takeover of the button. Finally, a sailboat is seen heading for the island.

Amount of action: Fair.

Important new characters: Two new Others named Ms. Klugh and Pickett are introduced.

Connections between characters: Michael rounds up the chosen survivors for a rescue mission/trap, though Sayid instantly realizes Michael is lying. Charlie and Eko's friendship is strained, while Locke seems to be proud of Charlie finally getting rid of the drugs, despite their fractured relationship and his own depression.

***Lost* mysteries referenced:** Michael's time with the Others, Walt's captivity, and the button.

***Lost* mysteries introduced:** Why the Others want Michael to bring just Jack, Kate, Sawyer and Hurley into their trap, why a sailboat has now appeared in the ocean.

Questions raised: Why do the Others need Michael to bring these four specific characters? Will he get away with it now that Sayid has figured it out and told Jack about it? Will this mission still wind up in Michael getting Walt back? What have the Others done to Walt involving tests and a room? What is Locke about to do now? Has

Charlie finally started to redeem himself after his rough patch this season? What is a sailboat doing heading for the island at this stage in the story?

Talking points: Many of the pieces now seem to be set in place for the finale. We have Michael leading Jack and company into an ambush while Jack and Sayid figure out it is indeed a trap. Then there's Eko taking over the hatch and Locke certainly preparing to do something about it. In the middle of all that is a boat coming to the island, so how does that fit into the plot? Why bring up the possibility of rescue at a time when wars over the Others and the hatch are finally ready to kick off?

In the meantime, Ana Lucia and Libby are finally laid to rest in a short burial. With the boat now coming to distract the survivors, the two women seem pretty destined to be forgotten by everyone else, just as quickly as fans will forget about them. But Hurley will probably remember Libby a bit longer. So will we, since there were still a few unanswered questions about her.

Other key issues: Charlie actually had something to do in this episode other than have freaky visions, get into fights with Claire and Locke, and get close to doing drugs again. That's a good first step towards character rehabilitation.

Must see episode?: Yes, as it obviously needs to be seen to get things set for the season finale.

LIVE TOGETHER, DIE ALONE

At this point and time one year earlier, *Lost* was heading towards its first season finale with all the momentum in the world, closing what would be an Emmy winning year. Flash forward a year later as Season Two drew to a close, with the picture a little more uncertain. Though things had been picking up in the last several episodes, Season Two divided a fair share of fans. To begin the charge of getting them back, this season finale would have to deliver on and answer a lot more than "Exodus" ultimately did.

But this time, the creators had a wild card to seal the deal. This time, they pinned their hopes of a grand finale on a character that had been absent for months. Someone who made a huge debut in the early episodes of the season, then disappeared into the jungle. On this character, this mere guest star, the hope of a season and a show were now put upon.

What followed was the appearance of actual, tangible answers mixed with the grand, sad, romantic story of Desmond Hume. And like with the debut of Henry Gale, this was an episode that would ultimately be looked back on as one that changed the direction of the show forever. The seeds were planted for a new future in ways few could have imagined back then.

To start off, we go back into Desmond's very important past.

Main character: Desmond Hume.

Flashback details: Desmond is seen being released from a Scottish military prison. He takes with him the Charles Dickens book *Our Mutual Friend,* which he only plans to read right before he dies.

When he gets out, he is met by a man named Charles Widmore, the wealthy father of Desmond's ex-girlfriend Penelope Widmore. Desmond is shocked to see that his various letters to Penelope from prison were intercepted by Widmore and kept from her. Widmore offers Desmond a large amount of money if he never contacts Penelope again, figuring he'll take it because he's a coward.

Sometime later, Desmond is in a coffee shop in the U.S, where he enters into a conversation with a stranger. This stranger is none other than the late Libby. Desmond tells her he's planning on winning an around the world boat race sponsored by Charles Widmore himself. However, Desmond has no boat. Touched by his story, Libby offers to give him her boat, which was given to her by her husband before he died. It is named "The Elizabeth" after her.

On the night Desmond ran with Jack in "Man of Science, Man of Faith" Desmond first sees Penelope Widmore, as she has used her money and resources to track him down. After she asks if he read his Dickens book, she also asks why he didn't write her. Choosing not to tell her the truth, Desmond tells her his plan to win Widmore's race and come back in a year. They sadly part as Desmond vows to get his honor back.

But the actual race doesn't go so well for Desmond, as his boat goes off course in a major storm. He stores his book and his last picture of Penelope in a bag as the boat crashes. It brings Desmond to the island beach, where a man in a haz-mat suit takes him and brings him into the hatch. When Desmond comes to, the man asks "Are you him?" and "What did one snowman say to the other?" as Desmond would later ask Locke.

Desmond doesn't know what any of this means, which upsets the man. He is then revealed to be Inman, the American soldier who set Sayid onto his life of torture in "One Of Them." His full name is Kelvin Inman. A second later, the timer alarm goes off and Kelvin Inman types the numbers in robotically. When Desmond asks what he did, Kelvin monotonously replies that he's "saving the world."

Sometime later, Desmond is watching the hatch orientation video again, having already settled into his new job of pushing the button with Kelvin. For the next two years the two press the button and stage fake lockdowns. Kelvin is also shown to be the one who painted the invisible map on the blast door. Kelvin's old partner Radzinsky came up with most of it before he shot himself in the head. Desmond wants to go outside into the island, but Kelvin warns against it, saying that he'll get "infected" if he goes out there.

Later on, Desmond finds Kelvin drunk in an underground floor, lying next to a lock. He holds a key up and says that by turning the key into that lock, it causes a fail-safe that will destroy the hatch as a last resort. He later explains that "the incident" hinted at in the orientation film was an accident involving the vast electromagnetic properties of the island. By typing the numbers in every 108 minutes, it keeps the energy from leaking out and causing a disastrous electromagnetic charge. Desmond asks why they don't just use this fail safe, with Kelvin asking him if he would have the guts to "blow the dam."

A year later, Desmond sees Kelvin going outside with his haz-mat suit. He notices that there is a tear in the suit before Kelvin goes. He then goes outside into the island for the first time in three years and sees that the air is clean. Desmond tracks Kelvin to a cove, where Kelvin shows him that he has fixed the sailboat and is planning to leave.

Desmond starts to get upset as Kelvin says that he needed "a sucker" to keep pressing the button after he left. Enraged, Desmond screams that Kelvin stole the last three years of his life and attacks him. He slams him against a rock…but the collision between the rock and his head kills him instantly.

In a panic, Desmond takes Kelvin's fail safe key and rushes back to the hatch, where the countdown has reached zero. A voice says "System failure" over and over as the electromagnetic charge begins to build up and everything in the hatch is flying toward a magnetic wall. Desmond frantically tries to type the numbers in, eventually finally getting through. The timer resets and Desmond catches his breath, resigned to having to press the button alone.

Weeks later, Desmond seems about ready to end it all, holding a gun, alcohol and his book. Preparing to read *Our Mutual Friend* before he kills himself, he opens it and finds a letter inside. It's from Penelope Widmore, who stored the letter in the book before he went to prison, figuring he would read it in his despair. In the letter, Penelope reassures him of her love, saying that "All we really need to survive is one person who truly loves us. And you have her. I will wait for you. Always. Love, Penny."

Now at his absolute lowest point of heartbreak and sorrow, Desmond starts screaming "It's all gone!!" and throws around whatever he can find. But as his rage subsides, he begins to hear another voice of despair...John Locke's.

This event took place during the events of "Deus Ex Machina" as Locke beat his fists against the hatch door after Boone's fatal injury, screaming why the island did this to him. And when the hatch door lit up, it was Desmond who turned the lights on to see Locke. This event not only tempered Locke's misery, it gave Desmond a new hope as well. Days later, he would meet Locke in person for the first time.

Episode plot: Jack, Sawyer and Sayid swim out to sea to investigate the sailboat in the ocean. When they look inside, they see a drunken Desmond inside. Desmond looks up at Jack and says "You..." just as Jack did in the hatch.

Once Desmond is brought back to the beach, he explains to Jack that he tried to sail to Fiji, but he just wound up back on the island. Convinced that they are on a "bloody snow globe" Desmond proclaims that there's no outside world anymore.

Sayid is inspired to come up with a plan using Desmond's boat. While Jack, Kate, Sawyer and Hurley go with Michael, Sayid will sail to the Others camp. He will make a signal of black smoke and the survivors will go in to attack the Others together. Jack is advised not to let anyone else know of this plan, or that Michael has betrayed them.

In the hatch, Locke confronts Eko as he prepares to enter the numbers. Locke tells Eko that he will not press the button and become a slave to it like he was. Locke then takes Eko's club and tries to destroy the computer, but Eko stops him and throws him out of the hatch, telling him not to come back.

Jack and his team leave the beach the next morning, as Sayid gets permission from Desmond to use his boat. Jin and Sun wind up volunteering to go with Sayid.

Locke finds out from Charlie that Desmond has come back, and goes to see him that night. He asks the snowman question, with the answer being "Smells like carrots." Locke then gets down to business, informing him of what he found in the Pearl and his new conviction that the button is useless. He advises Desmond to sober up, as he plans for the both of them to go to the hatch tomorrow and find out what happens when the button isn't pushed.

The next day, Sayid, Sun and Jin are sailing closer to the Others camp. Along the way, they see a giant statue of a four toed foot for some reason.

In the hatch, Desmond stages a lockdown which locks Eko out of the computer room, also locking Locke and Desmond inside of it. They are now ready to wait for the timer to reach zero. Eko rushes out and asks for Charlie's help to get the doors open, convinced that everyone on the island will die if he can't stop Locke. Charlie takes him to the spare sticks of dynamite from the Black Rock.

Back in the jungle, Kate discovers two Others tracking them down. She and Sawyer shoot one of them and wound another. When they want to follow him so he doesn't give them away, Jack finally cracks and admits they already know they're coming. He then grabs Michael and screams at him to admit the truth. With that, Michael confesses to his murder of Ana Lucia and Libby, plus his plan to lead them into a trap. A distraught Hurley goes to leave, but Jack stops him and reassures everyone that he does have a plan.

Eko starts planting the dynamite on the blast door as Charlie tries to get Locke to come out before Eko blows it up. Desmond reassures Locke that the door will hold, so Locke stays put. Eko then sets the dynamite off, which soon blows up and catches Eko and Charlie in the crossfire. However, the door is still shut.

Desmond worries if they are hurt, but Locke is not so concerned, thinking they're still trying to trick him. Desmond questions Locke on his motives, as Locke explains that he thought it was his destiny to open this hatch, but that quest got Boone killed. He recalls the night the hatch door lit up and he thought it was a sign, but he quips that it was probably Desmond going to the bathroom. Desmond, remembering differently, begins to get suspicious.

In the ocean, Sayid reaches the Others camp and finds it is deserted. In fact, it's a complete fake, including the hatch doors. Sayid realizes too late that the campsite is staged.

Back in the jungle, Jack's team reaches a huge pile of pneumatic tubes, which all seem to contain log books from the Pearl station. Although the Pearl orientation video said that the Pearl station workers would be filing these tubes to DHARMA headquarters, they ended up here and unread.

At that point, Jack finds Sayid's smoke signal from very far away. Realizing Michael also lied about where they had to go, Jack confronts him before hearing the low whispers of the Others. The group is ambushed and shot with electrical stun darts, as the Others come and put bags over their heads to take them away.

In the hatch, Desmond begins to wonder if the real fake experiment was on the people working in the Pearl, not on those in the Swan. Locke doesn't want to hear it, though. Desmond starts reading the printout papers from the Pearl, reading the numbers on it until he comes to a section that says "SYSTEM FAILURE" over and over, with the date 9/22/04 next to it.

Desmond then asks when flight 815 crashed, with an impatient Locke confirming that it was on September 22, 2004. Realizing what day that was, Desmond utters in shock "I think I crashed your plane."

Jack and his team are lead to a dock by the Others. Kate comments that she knows their tattered clothes are fake, as Mr. Friendly confirms it by taking off his fake beard. Just then, a boat arrives and parks next to the pier. The man driving it steps forward and shows himself to be the leader of this group.

That man is Henry Gale.

In the hatch, Charlie is waking up from the blast and trying to find Eko, while Desmond and Locke argue inside the computer room. Desmond tries to tell him that the day of the crash was the day he failed to press the button in time. That caused the electromagnetic leak that resulted in the crash of flight 815. The button is indeed real.

But Locke still believes what he saw on the Pearl orientation video, yelling that none of is real. Desmond then vows to press the button himself, but he is stopped when Locke takes the computer and smashes it on the floor. Locke is convinced he "saved us all" while Desmond is sure he's killed them.

In a flash, Desmond gets the blast doors open and rushes to get *Our Mutual Friend* from the bookshelves. Inside is Kelvin's fail safe key. He goes back inside and tells Locke about how he heard him outside the hatch days before they met. To Desmond, Locke saved his life so that Desmond could save his in return. He's now ready to "blow the dam" telling Locke that it's all real, and now he's going to "make it all go away." Desmond says he'll see him in another life and goes to the underground floor, towards the fail safe lock.

Just then, the timer hits zero and the phrase "System failure" is heard. Like it did on September 22, 2004, the hatch begins to shake as all the metal objects inside fly towards the magnetic wall. Charlie finds Eko and tries to get him out, but Eko pushes Charlie out inside and tries to find Locke.

Everything is falling apart and crashing as Desmond gets closer to the lock below. The timer is crushed as Eko finally finds Locke. With a tear running down his face, Locke simply admits "I was wrong" to Eko as they stand together and wait for the end.

Desmond finally reaches the lock and takes out the key. He remembers Penelope's final words from her letter as he puts the key inside. He says out loud "I love you, Penny" and with no further hesitation, he turns the key.

Outside, the people on the beach, those on the dock and those on Sayid's boat watch and cover their ears as the sky literally turns purple. A low humming noise drowns out everything else as everyone on the island can barely stay on their feet. Only Henry Gale stands perfectly still and looks directly up at the sky. After several seconds, the sky finally turns back to normal. Soon after, the "Quarantine" labeled door to the hatch lands right on the beach. The hatch is no more.

When everything settles down, the Others return to business. Henry gives Michael his boat and the directions to head home. He reminds him that he probably won't tell people what happened because of what he did to get Walt back. Michael asks in disbelief "Who are you people?" as Henry just smiles and says that they're the good guys.

Finally Michael sees Walt coming out of the boat. He hugs him and tells him that they're going home. As they prepare to go, Ms Klugh unties Hurley and tells him to go back to his camp, where he will instruct the other survivors that they can never come here.

As for Jack, Kate and Sawyer, Henry says they are coming "home with us."

Michael sails off with Walt and shares one more look with his betrayed friends before leaving. Hurley heads away as the Others start putting bags back over their captives' heads. Jack and Kate share one last glare before they are hooded.

On the beach, Charlie has come back, but Locke, Desmond and Eko are nowhere to be found. But few seem to care as they repair the camp. Claire and Charlie even share a romantic moment as they seem to be back on track.

Finally, the scene switches to, of all places, the Arctic. Two men speaking Portuguese are playing chess until an alarm goes off on their computer. It reads that an electromagnetic anomaly has been detected, which is likely the result of Desmond destroying the hatch. One of the men tries to read it while the other comments that they "missed it again" As the first man gets the coordinates from the anomaly, he yells at the other man to make a call.

The man dials the phone and asks for "Ms Widmore." He then says "I think we found it."

On the other end of this call, lying in bed with a picture of Desmond on her bureau, is Penelope Widmore. Shock overcomes her face as she realizes what the man has told her. They've not only found "it" which likely means the island, they may have found where Desmond is as well.

With that, the season is over.

Important details in *Lost* lore: Desmond's three year stint in the hatch is revealed, as well as his partnership with Kelvin Inman, who was seen in Sayid's flashback in the middle of the season. Desmond is also seen to have met Libby, who gave him the sailboat he used to try and sail around the world. Desmond's relationship with Penelope Widmore is also introduced.

Jack, Kate, Sawyer and Hurley are led into a successful trap by Michael. Henry Gale returns and is quite possibly the leader of the

Others. Michael and Walt sail off the island as Jack, Kate and Sawyer are taken to the Others home. A four toed giant foot is also discovered for some reason.

The button is indeed real, as the real fake experiment took place in the Pearl. The electromagnetic leak caused by Desmond not pressing the button resulted in the crash of flight 815. But Locke destroys the computer anyway and another massive leak occurs, stopped only when Desmond destroys the hatch for good.

For the first time, the outside world is seen in the present time, destroying the Purgatory theory for good. It is also shown that Penelope Widmore is searching for Desmond and the island, with the hatch explosion revealing the island's coordinates.

Amount of action: Heavy.

New important characters: Penelope Widmore and her father, Charles Widmore.

Connections between characters: Desmond's past connections to Inman, Libby, and even Locke are uncovered. Michael makes his ultimate betrayal of his friends to get back home with Walt. Charlie and Claire finally get back together.

***Lost* mysteries referenced:** Desmond's time in the hatch, the button, the Others, the crash of 815, Henry Gale, the fate of Walt.

***Lost* mysteries introduced:** The fates of Locke, Eko and Desmond, the other fates of Jack, Kate and Sawyer, Penelope Widmore's search for Desmond and the island.

Questions raised: Where are Jack, Kate and Sawyer going? Are Locke, Eko and Desmond still alive? Is rescue on the horizon thanks to Penelope Widmore? If Penelope is searching for Desmond, how does he know he's on the island? Where is the Others real home? What is Henry Gale's position of power among the Others? Will Michael and Walt ever be seen again? What will Sayid, Sun and Jin do now in the ocean? Are there any lasting effects to destroying the hatch? Why was a four toed foot introduced?

Talking points: In comparison to last year's two hour episode that barely gave any answers, this episode provided a near overload of them.

It brought a climax to the season long hatch plot, instead of cutting to the end before we found out more, like last season. It brought the promise that when Season Three rolls around, we will get much more information about the Others, including Henry Gale. It even teased that there might be a chance of the outside world finding the island. In this case, it ultimately will take a while for that plot to fully be revealed in Season Three, but it will prove to be excessively important.

Another case of symmetry is at work, as the show perhaps says goodbye to Michael and Walt while bringing Desmond and Henry into the mix as regulars for next year. Despite all the fuss over the new survivors from the tail section, it was these two guest star characters that ultimately were the most important newcomers. While yet again, new information was discovered about Libby that still has not been fully explained.

Other key issues: The people on the island are probably used to fantastical events by now, but the quick way they all shrugged off the sky turning purple is something else.

Must see episode?: Undoubtedly. These two hours ended the season on a much needed high note and made up for at least most of the less than stellar parts. The implications of this episode and what it introduced are still being felt to this day, in ways no one could have seen coming yet. But such knowledge would come eventually in Season Three.

SEASON THREE

CHARACTERS YOU NEED TO KNOW FOR SEASON THREE

Benjamin Linus-- played by Michael Emerson: The real identity of Henry Gale. The powerful, manipulative and brilliant leader of the Others.

Juliet Burke-- played by Elizabeth Mitchell: A ground breaking fertility doctor brought to the island to help their dying pregnant woman.

Richard Alpert-- played by Nestor Carbonell: Ben's right hand man and recruiter, who may be hundreds of years old for all we know.

Mikhail Bakunin-- played by Andrew Divoff: A one eyed Other who mans DHARMA's communication station, and is pretty hard to kill.

Jacob: A mysterious...someone or other who serves as the island's all powerful leader and the only person Ben answers to.

Alex-- played by Tania Raymonde: The lost daughter of Danielle Rousseau, but who is now Ben's fake daughter.

Karl-- played by Blake Bashoff: Unlucky young Other who faces Ben's wrath because of his love for Alex.

Tom Friendly-- played by M.C Gainey: The Other who commanded the kidnapping of Walt way back in Season One.

Naomi Dorrit-- played by Marsha Thomason: A woman who mysteriously parachutes onto the island.

Anthony Cooper-- played by Kevin Tighe: Locke's rotten con artist father who stole his kidney, and has even greater crimes revealed in Season Three.

Nikki and Paulo-- played by Kiele Sanchez and Rodrigo Santoro: Don't ask.

A TALE OF TWO CITIES

Another season of *Lost* begins with no real sense of where they could possibly go. Jack, Kate and Sawyer were left in the care of the Others, but that could mean anything. Locke, Eko and Desmond were probably still alive after the hatch blew up, but without it, what could they do now? This season's format was also brand new, having the first six episodes air in the fall while airing the final 17 in a row from January to May. The creators and the network were really counting on this new strategy to get some buzz back.

One thing *Lost* is good at is starting seasons with a bang in the very beginning. The pilot introduced Jack amidst the horrifying aftermath of the 815 crash. Season Two's opening scene gave a unique way to finally answer what's in the hatch. And Season Three's opening is no different. It answers another long time mystery in a rather surprising method, while introducing us to a character that would become one of the season's most important figures.

Season Three begins now.

First flashback details: As a record plays Pasty Kline's "Downtown", a blond woman is staring in the mirror, trying not to cry. She pulls herself together and smiles, but sees she has burned some muffins. She then welcomes another woman inside as a man is doing the plumbing outside.

Inside the house, a book club meeting is taking place. The people inside are debating *Carrie,* with a man commenting about how much "Ben" would hate it. This sets off the woman, now identified as Juliet, as she defends the book. But she is interrupted when the ground briefly shakes. When it stops, Juliet and her book club head outside.

They are seen in a community filled with nice, small houses in a barracks. But there are some sights that poke holes into this normal setting. The first is when the man working on the plumbing shows himself to be Ethan Rom. The second is when another man rushes outside, showing himself as Henry Gale. The third is when they all look up to see Oceanic Flight 815 breaking apart.

Henry then calls Ethan and Goodwin and gives them their orders to spy on both the crash sites, wanting lists of the survivors made in three days. Once they leave, Henry notices Juliet and comments "So I guess I'm out of the book club." An overhead shot officially confirms that this community is located on the middle of the island.

Which means that the people living there are the Others.

Episode plot: Jack wakes up inside a large cell, with chains on the ceiling, a table at the center, a security camera and a thick glass wall nearby. He yells for Kate but no one is seen or heard. Eventually, Juliet comes in and introduces herself, standing behind the other side of the glass.

Jack demands to know what's going on and where his friends are, but Juliet coolly deflects his comments. He stands on the table and grabs the chains, which doesn't impress Juliet as she leaves.

Juliet returns later on and offers to give Jack a sandwich, but only if he moves away from the door, which he refuses. She asks about his life and what he did back home, to which Jack lies about. Juliet, seeming to know better, plays along. She tells him that he can trust her, but he's still defiant.

However, Jack is getting dehydrated and needs some food. Finally, Juliet gets him to accept the food and he moves back as Juliet comes in. But with swift motion, Jack jumps her and forces her outside the cell into a hallway. Jack finds a door and orders Juliet to open it, but she says she can't.

At that point, Henry Gale appears and says that if Juliet opens the door, they will all die anyway. Jack is not convinced and makes her open it. He is rewarded by having a giant gush of water come out. Before he and Juliet can escape, Henry leaves and locks them in. The two swim to the door and manage to close it, then Juliet knocks Jack out.

When Jack wakes, he is back in the cell with Juliet behind the glass again. Juliet explains that the hatch they are in is an underwater DHARMA station called the Hydra. Jack theorizes that she and the Others are what's left of DHARMA, to which Juliet remarks that it doesn't matter who they used to be. To prove it, she displays a huge file which contains every detail of Jack's life and of everyone he knows, including his former wife.

This finally gets through to Jack, as he contemplates asking who his ex left him for. Instead, he asks if she's happy, and Juliet says that she is. Overcome with emotion, Jack is subdued as Juliet agrees to keep bringing him food, knowing he won't try to escape again.

As Juliet leaves, Henry sees her and complements her work. Juliet only replies "Thank you, Ben."

Other stuff: Kate wakes up in a bathroom, with Mr. Friendly watching nearby. He hands her new clothes, telling her to take a shower and get dressed.

As for Sawyer, he wakes inside a zoo like cage. Other cages are nearby, one of which contains a younger prisoner. Inside Sawyer's cage is a larger button with images of a knife and fork on it. Sawyer figures it will provide food, but it instead shocks him when he pushes it.

Once Kate is freshened up, Friendly takes her to a beach, where Henry has set up a table with food and coffee for her. After Kate handcuffs herself to her chair, she asks about Sawyer and Jack. Henry comments that she asked about Sawyer first, to Kate's annoyance. He further explains that he set this up so Kate would feel like a lady, have a nice view and have some nice memories to hold to. Because according to him, the next two weeks are going to be "very unpleasant."

Sawyer tries to figure out the button while the other prisoner picks his lock and escapes. But he doesn't get far as Juliet quickly appears in front of him. Calling him Karl, she tasers him with an electric dart and takes him away.

Eventually Sawyer figures out how to press the button and get water and food out of it. The food is only a big fish biscuit with the word DHARMA on it, but he eats it anyway. Friendly says that it took the polar bears two hours to figure this out, as he puts Kate in Karl's old cell. Sawyer tosses her what's left of his biscuit as the two settle into their new surroundings.

Main character: Jack Shephard.

Flashback details: Jack's marriage has ended and he has become obsessed with finding out who Sarah left him for. She won't tell him however, which only makes Jack more determined. He goes so far as to call Sarah's various contacts, as Christian advises him to just let it go. But at that moment, Jack discovers Christian is one of Sarah's contacts, turning his suspicion towards him.

Jack begins to follow Christian around, figuring he'll find him with Sarah. He tracks him to a hotel, then finds Christian at an AA support group, trying to cure his alcoholism. This doesn't make Jack any less convinced that his father isn't Sarah's lover. He trashes Christian right to his face and turns away, as Christian once again yells "Let it go!" With that, Jack runs to Christian and tackles him to the ground.

Sarah later bails Jack out of jail, having called him a cab. Jack sees a man at Sarah's car, but she still refuses to reveal his identity. She reveals she found out about Jack's arrest through Christian, as he was already drunk and has fallen off the wagon for good. Sarah comments that Jack has something else to fix and leaves him forever.

Important details in *Lost* lore: The Others are seen in lovely suburban barracks in the middle of the island on the day flight 815 crashed. Jack is revealed to be in a cell located at an underwater hatch, while Kate and Sawyer are in cages above ground. Juliet is introduced, as Henry is now referred to as "Ben." Jack accuses his father of sleeping with his ex-wife in the past, which leads to Christian becoming a full blown alcoholic for the remainder of his life.

Amount of action: Fair.

New important characters: Juliet and Karl.

Connections between characters: Juliet interrogates and manages to break down Jack, with additional hints that she has some kind of relationship with Henry/Ben. In the past, Jack becomes wrongly convinced that his father and ex-wife had an affair.

***Lost* mysteries referenced:** The Others, where Jack, Kate and Sawyer have gone.

***Lost* mysteries introduced:** The character of Juliet and her connection to Henry Gale, the Others not looking like scary island people after all, the new station called the Hydra.

Questions raised: How could the Others possibly look this...normal after all we've seen of them so far? Who is Juliet? What is her connection to Henry? Why is she questioning and taking care of Jack? Why will the next two weeks be unpleasant for Kate? What are the cages Kate and Sawyer are in? Who is Karl? How does Juliet know everything about Jack? Why are Jack, Kate and Sawyer here in the first place?

Talking points: The ghosts of the Season Two opening are quite explicit. That scene introduced a new character in Desmond and showed us the inside of the hatch, which we didn't realize until the last minute.

This opening introduces Juliet and shows us the homes of the Others, which we don't realize until the end and can still hardly believe, considering how regular it all looks. We knew the Others weren't hillbillies and only dressed up in tattered rags, but we didn't think they lived in nice homes and had book club meetings. How does that match up to what we've seen and heard of them so far? It barely does.

The episode is also big for introducing Juliet, who already shares more of a connection with Jack than him and Ana Lucia ever struck. Somehow, she knows exactly how to deal with Jack and match wits with him. The added knowledge of knowing everything about him probably helps. But the *Lost* creators are never ones to waste a literary name, so they must have named her Juliet for a bigger reason.

Other key issues: Jack and Christian's relationship ended when he drunkenly killed a patient in surgery. But if this flashback is to be believed, he only became a full blown alcoholic because Jack ruined his recovery. This sheds another new light on their relationship, as Jack now doesn't seem so squeaky clean in Christian's downfall, with Christian not seeming as completely rotten.

Must see episode?: Yes, since it is the season premiere. The stunning opening and the debut of Juliet are classic highlights, but the rest of the episode doesn't always succeed that highly, once again repeating Jack's trademark flashback issues.

THE GLASS BALLERINA

The second season ended with fans wondering what happened to Jack and his friends with the Others, as well as Locke and his people at the hatch. But behind those plot threads, there was a third team of survivors whose fates were in the air. Though Sayid, Sun and Jin weren't captured or blown up, they were still left in the ocean not knowing what to do next. So now they move to take matters into their own hands. But for Sun and Jin in particular, that has risks of its own.

In the meantime, we get a second look at Jack and his friends in captivity, leading to an ending that had a special appeal to Boston viewers.

Episode plot: After Juliet brings Jack some soup in the Hydra, she and Henry are told by an Other named Colleen about Sayid, Sun and Jin. Henry is taken aback that they have a boat, ordering Colleen to get the boat before they find the Others location.

On the sailboat, Sayid, Sun and Jin argue over their next move. Jin tries to take charge since he knows how to sail, but Sun also knows how, helping Sayid head to the mountains to start a new fire.

Once they get to land, Sun questions Sayid about his plan, suspecting he is lying. He confirms it, believing correctly that Jack and the others have been captured. He wants to set the fire so the Others will come out to investigate, leaving Sayid ready to attack them and find out what they know. He asks Sun to keep this from Jin for a while longer.

However, Jin later says in Korean that he understands English better than they thought; having figured out that Sun has lied to him. He asks for a gun to help Sayid in his trap, as Sun goes to the boat.

That night, the Others do come, but they come for the boat and bypass Sayid and Jin's trap altogether. Alone, Sun sees Colleen enter the lower deck and points her gun at her. Colleen refuses to let her off the boat, using Sun's full name and saying she knows who she is. She warns that the Others are not the enemy, but that's what they will become if Sun shoots her.

Just then the engine is turned on, causing Sun to shoot Colleen by accident. She then jumps into the water to escape gunfire by the Others, as Sayid and Jin finally notice them. They drive off with the boat, avoiding the shots. Jin jumps into the water and swims after Sun in a panic, embracing her tightly once he finds her.

Once they get back to the beach, Jin declares he doesn't know what he'd do without Sun and her baby. Sayid advises them they have a long walk back to their camp.

Other stuff: Kate and Sawyer have been put to work by the Others, as they break rocks for an unknown purpose. They are supervised by an Other named Pickett, who is Colleen's husband and who shocks Sawyer whenever he is out of line.

Kate has a brief encounter with Alex, who is hiding out in the bushes and asking about Karl. Later, Sawyer suddenly goes over to Kate and kisses her very deeply. Pickett goes to separate them, but Sawyer punches him in the face, having planned for this to happen. He takes Pickett's gun and tries to get out, but Kate is then taken at gunpoint by Juliet. This makes Sawyer put the gun down, as he is shocked into submission again.

At night, the two are taken back to their cages. After joking about their kiss, Sawyer explains that he was testing how strong their guards are. The more Sawyer sizes them up, the more prepared he'll be to plan their escape. But as he talks, Henry is sitting inside the Hydra, watching them on a room filled with monitors.

Henry then goes to talk to Jack in his cell, commenting about how their roles were reversed just a week ago. He makes a more formal introduction this time, saying that his real name is Benjamin Linus and that he's lived here all his life. When Jack refuses to shake his hand, Ben Linus has a TV brought to the other side of the glass. He tells Jack his friends are close and that if he cooperates, he will send Jack home.

Jack doesn't believe that he has the power to leave the island, but Ben corrects him by saying they do have contact with the outside, listing all the major events that have happened since the crash. Jack laughs when Ben says the Red Sox won the World Series. But he quiets down when the TV shows a video tape of the final out of the 2004 Series. Ben repeats that if Jack does what he says, when the time comes he will take him home.

Main characters: Sun and Jin.

Flashback details: As a young girl, Sun began a life of lying by blaming her maid for the destruction of a glass ballerina. As a woman, Sun continues her deception by having an affair with Jae Lee, though she wants to end it. Jae Lee professes he wants to live with her in America, until Sun's father, Mr. Paik, enters the room and finds them together.

Mr. Paik later summons Jin and tells him that Jae Lee has "stolen" from the company, ordering Jin to kill him. Jin refuses, but Mr. Paik calls him his son and tells Jin that he shares his shame.

That night, Jin finds Jae Lee and begins to attack him. Jae Lee is convinced Jin has found out about his affair with Sun, though Jin still has no idea. Before he kills him, Jin changes his mind and orders Jae Lee to leave Korea. Instead, Jae Lee jumps out of the building.

Sun watches Jae Lee's funeral from a distance with her father. He asks Mr. Paik if he will tell Jin about the affair, but he says it isn't his place to tell.

Important details in *Lost* lore: Sayid, Sun and Jin have their first action since the finale. Sun is confirmed to have had an affair with Jae Lee, who killed himself when he thought Jin knew. Henry Gale's real name is Benjamin Linus, who tempts Jack with the promise of going home if he does something for him. Sawyer and Kate have another big kiss.

Amount of action: Fair.

New important characters: Others Colleen and Pickett.

Connections between characters: Sayid, Sun and Jin continue to work together, despite some friction between Sun and Jin at first. Sawyer and Kate get even closer as they share captivity. Ben tries to make a deal with Jack.

***Lost* mysteries referenced:** Whether Sun had her baby with Jin or Jae Lee.

***Lost* mysteries introduced:** Ben's potential deal with Jack, Sawyer and Kate breaking rocks for the Others.

Questions raised: What will Sayid, Sun and Jin do now? Will Sun's lies catch up to her, now that it's even more likely she might have had her baby with another man? Why are Sawyer and Kate being put to work? What is Ben Linus going to make Jack do for a trip home?

Talking points: The initial roles continue to be reversed for Sun and Jin. Whereas Jin was the bad husband and Sun was the innocent wife, now Sun is shown to be more and more of an expert liar while Jin is more and more of a pawn. Perhaps Sun can now add manslaughter to her list of sins after her shooting of Colleen.

Sawyer returns to his old bad boy, anti hero roots by pretty much impersonating Paul Newman in *Cool Hand Luke.* But Newman didn't get as much kissing action in that movie.

Other key issues: Fans may remember Christian Shephard's ironic comment before his death, when he said the Red Sox would never win the World Series. They have extra reason to remember since his son Jack actually got to see the Sox win the Series himself.

Must see episode?: Yes, but much like with many episodes last season, the character driven material takes up the main plot while most of the really important new details are shown in the subplots.

FURTHER INSTRUCTIONS

The first two episodes this season caught up with the fates of Jack and Sayid's teams. But the hatch trio of Locke, Eko and Desmond still hadn't made a peep, which would change with this episode. Even though they are all alive, they all have to move in new directions with the hatch gone, especially John Locke.

Season One Locke was *Lost's* most beloved character, or at least one of them. But Season Two, stuck in the hatch Locke was a bit less liked. It was well past time for the former man of destiny to get back to some real business. Now that it really wasn't his destiny to work the hatch, it was time to get back to finding his real purpose. Is it too late for Locke to get it back? At the least, it isn't past time to have some freaky visions and battle another bear.

Episode plot: In the aftermath of the hatch's destruction, Locke is lying in the jungle, unable to speak. He finds Charlie and is unable to communicate with him at first. After a while, he uses a combination of charades, a pen and paper to say he needs to "speak to the island."

Locke goes into Eko's barely finished church and turns it into a sweat lodge. He creates the same kind of pudding he used to trigger Boone's visions in "Hearts and Minds" using it on himself this time. As a result, he is reunited with Boone.

After Locke tries to apologize for Boone's death, Boone leads Locke into a new vision, but Locke needs his wheelchair. A paralyzed Locke is seen in the Sydney airport.

Boone rolls him through, saying someone needs his help. Locke has a vision of all the characters, but Boone rules them out as the ones he's talking about. When he sees Jack being scanned by Ben, Locke tries to get his attention, but Boone says he has to clean up his own mess before helping them. At last Locke climbs up an escalator and finds Eko's club, as Boone tells him "they've got him." Locke then returns to the present, exits the lodge and speaks out loud that he has to save Eko's life.

Charlie accompanies Locke on their search, as they determine Eko has been taken by one of the island polar bears. They also find the large crater which is all that now remains of the hatch. As they go further, they find Hurley returning from the Others dock. After he explains what happened to Jack, Kate and Sawyer, Locke tells him to go back to camp and inform everyone else.

Locke and Charlie find the polar bear's cave, as Locke goes in alone. Armed with only hairspray and a torch, Locke finds a badly hurt Eko inside. The bear then shows itself and tries to take Eko back. However, Locke sprays the hairspray on his torch and blinds the bear with the increased fire, which allows him to get Eko out in time.

As Locke tends to an unconscious Eko, he apologizes again for everything that happened in the hatch, realizing that he could have helped Jack, Kate and Sawyer instead. Eko awakes and reassures Locke that he will find them, since he is a hunter. Charlie returns as Locke then sees Eko is actually still unconscious. Locke takes Eko back to camp and vows to the other survivors that he will find Jack, Kate and Sawyer.

Other stuff: After Hurley leaves Locke and Charlie, he discovers Desmond. All of Desmond as it turns out, since he's naked. Once Desmond gets some clothes on, Hurley learns about the hatch explosion and repeats what happened to Jack, Kate and Sawyer. Desmond responds that Locke will find them, like he said in his speech. Hurley is taken aback, remembering that Locke only said he'd go after Eko and the bear.

But later, when Locke does indeed make a speech to the camp that he will find them, Hurley comments that he got deja vu. He then looks at Desmond, wondering how he could have known about Locke giving a speech.

Main character: John Locke.

Flashback details: After his breakup with Helen, Locke retreats from civilization and joins a commune of farmers. He picks up a hitchhiker named Eddie and gets him into the community. After six weeks, Eddie asks to be let into a greenhouse that only the commune leaders are allowed in.

Locke promises to talk to them, but then finds out that the leaders are growing marijuana. They also know Eddie is an undercover cop trying to gather information about them. Worried that Eddie will break up his new family, Locke volunteers to protect them.

Locke takes Eddie hunting, where Eddie figures out Locke wants to kill him. He confesses that his bosses wanted him to get close to Locke since he was new in the commune and easy to manipulate. Locke tears up and aims the gun, but Eddie knows he won't shoot since he's not a killer, he's a farmer. Locke argues that he's a hunter, but he can't bring himself to shoot Eddie as he leaves.

Important details in *Lost* lore: Locke returns from the hatch and has a vision of Boone, who tells him to save Eko's life. Another polar bear is spotted as Locke saves Eko from it. Hurley starts to suspect Desmond can see into the future. During the final scene in the camp, two background survivors named Nikki and Paulo are briefly introduced.

Amount of action: Little.

New important characters: Nikki and Paulo, technically.

Connections between characters: Locke gets to see Boone one last time in his vision, then manages to save Eko's life. Locke also reconnects with Charlie, who helps him despite still having hard feelings towards him. Hurley encounters Desmond and figures out his new abilities.

***Lost* mysteries referenced:** The fate of Locke, Eko and Desmond after the hatch blows up.

***Lost* mysteries introduced:** Desmond's new powers.

Questions raised: Will Locke be able to save Jack, Kate and Sawyer? Will Eko be all right? Does Desmond really have the power to see the future?

Talking points: Locke's flashback really doesn't gel with his other ones, which were all about his father and Helen. The fact he was in a marijuana growing commune and got manipulated yet again really doesn't shed light on anything, or state anything we didn't already know.

Locke's vision of Boone and the airport may go down as *Lost's* weirdest scene ever. This time they seem to be making a vision that looks like a drug trip on purpose.

Other key issues: Since female fans have already memorized how Sawyer looks shirtless, they can move on to trace Desmond's naked chest for a while.

Must see episode?: Not really. The vision trip has some nostalgic value and we are introduced to Desmond's new power. But other than that, this is by far Locke's worst flashback episode.

EVERY MAN FOR HIMSELF

As Jack, Kate and Sawyer are forced to become the Others captives, the Others have to also work towards keeping them in line, whatever that line is. Juliet has already broken Jack's will to escape, while Ben is dangling the promise of home to him. In contrast, Sawyer is already making plans to escape with Kate, figuring that a few of his usual cons and tricks will free them.

They've always worked for Sawyer before, but he never really had a worthy opponent before. Perhaps even worse for Sawyer, he never had something to care about as badly as Kate. But Henry Gale proved that he can take advantage of anyone, which is hardly any different now that we know he's Ben.

Episode plot: Pickett and the Others become preoccupied once Colleen is brought back and near death. This gives Sawyer the opening to carry out his escape plan, as he connects the electricity from the cage button to a puddle of water. He will use it to electrocute the next Other who steps in the puddle, then get the keys to the cage. However, he doesn't plan to look for Jack, telling Kate it's every man for himself.

Ben then approaches the cage, asking Sawyer about his age and weight. Once Ben steps into the nearby puddle, Sawyer grabs him and kicks the button, but nothing happens. Since Ben could see and hear everything Sawyer did, he knew of his plan and turned off the electricity. He takes out a baton and beats Sawyer with it until he is out cold.

When Sawyer comes to, he is inside the Hydra and tied to a table. The Others tell him to bite down on a stick as they inject his heart with a needle, knocking him out again. This time when he wakes, Ben has a cage that contains a bunny with the number 8 on its fur. Ben shakes the cage over and over until the bunny dies.

The bunny had a pacemaker implanted in him and died when his heart rate went up. This illustrates the point that they injected a pacemaker into Sawyer as well. Ben gives Sawyer a watch, saying that if his heart rate goes over 140, he will die. Kate will get a pacemaker as well if Sawyer says anything.

When Sawyer is brought back into his cage, he refuses to tell Kate what happened, as Ben ordered. Sawyer also refuses to take part in any more escape plans, which makes Kate worried.

Later, Pickett returns outside after Colleen dies, attacking Sawyer out of blind rage. He repeatedly asks if Kate loves Sawyer as he keeps punching him, only stopping when Kate finally screams she does love him. As he recovers, Kate climbs her cage and squeezes through the top bars, calling for Sawyer to do the same. But he still refuses, which scares Kate more than ever. Even when she tries to pick his lock, he tells her to go alone, repeating that it's every man for himself. But Kate returns to her cage, choosing to quote Jack's "Live together, die alone" motto instead.

The next day, Ben wakes Sawyer up and takes him for a walk. As they climb up a ridge, Sawyer's heart rate climbs back to dangerous numbers, but it doesn't matter. Ben confesses they never gave Sawyer a pacemaker, and he never killed the bunny either. After Sawyer punches Ben as payback, Ben shows Sawyer another surprise…they aren't even on the regular island.

The Others have taken Jack, Kate and Sawyer to a smaller neighboring island. Ben has shown Sawyer this to prove that there is nowhere for him to go, having conned the resident con man. He notes that Sawyer only started to give up when Kate was threatened, using a quote from *Of Mice and Men* to back it up. Now fully defeated, Sawyer is led back to his cage by Ben.

Other stuff: Juliet visits Jack's cell with food, as Jack questions her over Ben's authority. When Juliet says Ben doesn't make all the decisions, Ben barges in and tells Juliet to come quickly. Juliet leaves to treat Colleen as she is brought inside, but later she goes back to Jack and asks for his help.

Jack is led past the cages with a hood on his face, with an alarm drowning out Kate and Sawyer's calls. Ben is upset to see Jack brought in, but Juliet points out he's the only one that can save Colleen. So Jack preps for surgery with Juliet, noting some x-rays on a wall before going in.

Despite Jack's efforts, he is too late as Colleen dies. He is later handcuffed inside the Others ER as Juliet returns. After telling her there was nothing she could do, he changes the subject to the x-rays he saw, which weren't of Colleen. They were of a 40'ish man with a spinal tumor, which leads Jack to question just who he is really here to save.

Back on the beach, Desmond asks to fix the roof on Claire's tent. Although Claire says it is fine, he isn't that convinced as he goes off. He borrows a golf club from Paulo and constructs a tower near Claire's tent. Hurley is confused, but Desmond tells him to wait a minute. Just then a rainstorm falls and breaks Claire's roof, then a lightning bolt strikes Desmond's tower, preventing the lightning from striking the tent instead. Desmond smiles as Charlie is now very confused.

Main character: Sawyer.

Flashback details: Sawyer is in prison, where he meets an inmate named Munson who stole 10 million government dollars. He tells Munson that the warden will try to find the location of the money by using his wife, which seems to come true. After this, Munson confides to Sawyer where the money is and asks him to move it.

But before this, Sawyer gets a visit from his former girlfriend and con artist partner Cassidy, who he conned out of $600,000. Cassidy tells him that she is the mother of a baby girl named Clementine, who she says is Sawyer's child. Sawyer abruptly denies this and leaves.

In the end, Sawyer gives up the location of Munson's money to the warden in return for a commuted sentence. He says that he wants the money put in an Albuquerque bank under Clementine's name, with no way of knowing who the money is from. With that, Sawyer is a free man.

Important details in *Lost* lore: Jack, Kate and Sawyer are revealed to be on another island. Jack realizes he has been brought there to save a man who has a spinal tumor. Juliet's past job was as a fertility doctor. Colleen dies from being shot by Sun. Sawyer possibly has a daughter. Desmond's tower provides more proof that he may be seeing the future.

Amount of action: Fair.

New important characters: Sawyer's daughter.

Connections between characters: Kate and Sawyer's relationship gets most of the focus. Jack and Juliet share more time and perform surgery together. Ben and Sawyer match wits, with Ben getting the best of him. Pickett goes mad over the loss of his wife.

***Lost* mysteries referenced:** Desmond's new powers.

***Lost* mysteries introduced:** The identity of the man who Jack may have to operate on, whether Sawyer really has a daughter.

Questions raised: Where did this new island come from? Has Sawyer been defeated? Is escape possible? Who has the spinal tumor, and has Jack really been captured just to fix it? Will Pickett try to kill Sawyer for revenge? Why did Desmond build the tower?

Talking points: Sawyer becomes the latest of the captured trio to be defeated by the Others. Jack was broken down by Juliet and may have found out his real task, while Sawyer now knows there is no escape. Kate is now the only one who still has hope, but that could go away real fast.

Even though Sawyer is the one making progress with Kate, Jack is still very much on her mind as she worries about where he is and even quotes his famous mantra. It seems that even without Jack around, Sawyer can't quite take a commanding lead over him in the triangle.

Other key issues: Those who freaked out about the needle injecting scene in *Pulp Fiction* probably got some flashbacks from this episode.

But fortunately, Sawyer's ordeal couldn't be as graphic as the movie, since it was on a network and all.

Must see episode?: It moves some things forward and reveals a few new things, but things are starting to slow down and get a little anti climactic as this opening string of episodes winds down.

THE COST OF LIVING

It was becoming clear that Season Three's main objective was to introduce the real world of the Others. By necessity, this would have to do better than one of Season Two's main objectives, to introduce brand new survivors of 815. By and large, fans rejected the idea and the writers eventually seemed to agree with them. With Ana Lucia and Libby killed, Bernard being just a semi-recurring character and all the other tail section survivors killed or captured, it seemed introducing these people was a waste of time. You could have taken them out of *Lost* altogether and it would have barely changed anything in the grand design.

The only one of these characters this wouldn't apply to is Mr. Eko, who gained a lot of support and made a big difference by the end of the season. However, with the hatch destroyed and Eko barely recovering, it turned out he was no less expendable.

Episode plot: Eko is still sick after his attack by polar bears, lying in his tent. He soon sees a vision of his dead brother Yemi, telling him to find him if he wants "to confess." The tent is set on fire as Charlie manages to pull Eko out in time. As Locke takes notice, Eko disappears.

The next morning, Locke makes his plan to find Jack, Kate and Sawyer. To make contact with the Others, he plans to go back to the Pearl and look for them on the station's monitors. After Charlie tells him that Eko muttered something about his brother last night, Locke realizes Eko will be heading to the Pearl as well, since that's where Yemi's plane is. Unlike Jack, Locke invites anyone who wants to come with him to go along, an offer which Sayid, Desmond, Nikki and Paulo take.

As Eko stumbles through the jungle, the black smoke monster is heard nearby. Eko then has visions of some of his former victims, who tells him to confess as well. Before the monster comes back, Eko finds Locke and his team. Once they meet up, Locke asks some questions about Yemi which Eko does not want to answer. When Locke finds out he saw the monster, he comments about how when he saw it, he saw a beautiful bright light. But that is not what Eko saw.

Locke and his team go down to the Pearl as Eko explores the plane, seeing that Yemi's body is now gone. Down in the Pearl, the survivors examine the computer equipment. Sayid works on it until he gets a picture to appear on one of the monitors. It promptly shows a man with an eye patch looking right at the camera and turning it off. Locke anticipates that this man will be expecting them.

As for Eko, he sees Yemi standing at the question mark clearing and chases after him, asking why he wants to hear a confession now. He finally catches up to Yemi, who is ready for Eko to confess his sins. Eko kneels down and speaks, but he does not confess to any sins. Saying that he has done what he needed to survive, Eko brings up how he killed a man to save Yemi's life as a boy, which he is not ashamed of, but proud. Though he did not choose this life, he did his best with it. But this is not what Yemi wants to hear.

He merely responds "You speak to me as if I were your brother."

Now realizing that this vision isn't real, Eko demands to know what this version of Yemi really is. It runs away with Eko chasing him, but what Eko finds instead is the smoke monster, rising up menacingly towards him. Eko begins to recite the 23'rd Psalm before the monster grabs him with its tentacles of smoke. Whereas Eko survived his previous confrontation with the monster, this time it crushes him against several trees and throws him to the ground.

Locke and his team come back and find Eko's body. Locke kneels down to him as Eko whispers out some final words, as images of the young Eko and Yemi are seen leaving together. Once Eko passes away, Sayid asks what he said to Locke, who replies "He said we're next."

Other stuff: Jack is taken outside to watch the Others perform a funeral service for Colleen. Before that, he talks to Ben and asks about his spinal tumor, now knowing that Ben suffers from it after seeing his x-rays. Ben denies it, but the secret is pretty much out now.

The next day, Ben interrupts one of Jack and Juliet's conversations and asks to speak to him alone. Once Juliet leaves, Ben comments on how his plans to break Jack into wanting to perform surgery on him have been "shot to sunshine." Jack is amazed that all this has been done because Ben wants him to save his life, though Ben adds he wants him to *want* to save his life. But since he can't use any more tricks to make Jack want to do it on his own, Ben asks that Jack think about it.

Juliet later returns and offers to play *To Kill A Mockingbird* on the TV behind the glass. Jack doesn't want to see it, but Juliet insists he watch. The video actually shows Juliet holding up a series of cue cards to talk with Jack. While Juliet talks out loud to convince Jack to save Ben's life, the video has Juliet showing cue cards that say differently.

Her cue cards say that some of the Others want change and hint that Jack could kill Ben during the surgery, making it look like an accident. Juliet's cards also say that she would protect Jack if anything went wrong. The final card tells Jack to say out loud to stop the movie. Jack follows this instruction and Juliet turns off the tape, saying out loud that Jack should think about what she said.

Main character: Mr. Eko.

Flashback details: Immediately after Eko's plane flew a dying Yemi away, Eko is mistaken for a priest and begins to take Yemi's place at his church. But things do not go so smoothly when a militia arrives. This army had made Yemi give 80% of his vaccine shipments to them for "protection." which Eko is expected to continue. Instead, Eko prepares to sell them on the black market.

The militia finds this out and prepares to chop off Eko's hands. But this makes him revert back to his old self, as he takes their machetes and kills all of them. Although this ends the threat, the village has to close the church since it has been desecrated by Eko's violence. He is told to repent and that he owes Yemi a church.

Important details in *Lost* lore: It is confirmed that Ben has a tumor on his spine that he needs Jack to operate on. Juliet hints on a video that she would like Jack to kill him in this surgery. Mr. Eko is killed by the monster, which appears to have taken the form of Yemi beforehand. Locke discovers the existence of an eye patched man in one of the DHARMA stations.

Amount of action: Fair.

New important characters: The eye patch man.

Connections between characters: Juliet gets closer to Jack and offers to protect him if he kills Ben. Locke and Eko have their final confrontations together. Eko is manipulated by the monster, who poses as Yemi to make him confess his sins, then kills him when he doesn't. Nikki and Paulo make their awkward and unpopular attempts to get involved in the adventures.

***Lost* mysteries referenced:** The monster, the purpose of Jack's abduction.

***Lost* mysteries introduced:** Ben's spinal tumor, Juliet's offer for Jack to kill Ben, the eye patched man, Eko's final warning.

Questions raised: Are Eko's last words to be believed? Why did the monster want Eko's confession and kill him when he didn't give it? Will Jack perform surgery on Ben or kill him? Why does Juliet want Ben dead? Will Locke be able to find the eye patched man?

Talking points: With no more major tail section characters left, this episode officially brings that failed experiment to an end. Ending it by killing the only popular character in the group didn't gain much approval either. But the creators insisted that both Michelle Rodriguez [Ana Lucia] and Adewale Akinnuoye-Agbaje [Eko] were only signed on for one season anyway and that's why they were killed off.

The most lasting new info from Eko's death is that the monster took on the role of his judge, jury and executioner in confronting him. We now know it can take human form and seems to have the same ultra strict moral code as the Others do. Is there a connection between the two?

Must see episode?: As a farewell to Mr. Eko and as a new look at the monster, yes. But this sudden death is a worse handling of Eko's departure than he deserved. Plus the ultimate revelation that Jack has been captured just to perform surgery is quite underwhelming.

I DO

This episode would end the first half of the season, although the first half was just six episodes long. After it aired, *Lost* would go into hiatus until February, then air 17 straight episodes without reruns. That plan would have to work better than this six week long first half, as fans were turning against the show. *Lost* was actually beginning to lose it's time slot and fans were already tired of seeing Jack, Kate and Sawyer separated from the other survivors. To keep fans pacified for a 13 week long break, a major cliffhanger would have to take place. But that big finale bang wasn't to come here.

Episode plot: Jack is going over Ben's x-rays in his cell, saying that Ben doesn't have long to live with his tumor. Ben is ready to go, but Jack only says he wanted to tell Ben how he's gonna die. Even after Juliet's request, Jack doesn't trust any of them to take him home after doing the surgery.

Sawyer and Kate are taken back to the rock quarry by Pickett, but their shift is interrupted when Alex charges in, taking out guards with a slingshot. She demands to know where Karl is and what happened to him, further demanding to speak to Ben. She is instead taken away as Alex warns Kate that they're going to kill Sawyer too.

Later, Juliet confronts Kate and asks to come with her, saying it's the only way to keep Pickett from killing Sawyer. She is brought to Jack, seeing him for the first time since their abduction. Kate begins to try and get Jack to do the surgery, which makes Jack suspicious and worried. She soon breaks down and cries that they're going to kill Sawyer if Jack doesn't agree. However, Jack still doesn't believe that the Others would spare them if he agreed, and calls out that they're done. A seething Ben watches from his monitoring station and orders Juliet to take Kate away.

Kate is shoved back into her cell by Pickett, who tells her that if she has anything to say to Sawyer, she needs to do it tonight. Soon after, she gets out of her cage again and pleads with Sawyer to come with her, breaking his lock. With that, Sawyer finally admits that they are on another island and that there's nowhere to run to. He kept this from Kate so she would still think they had a chance.

After two seasons of flirting, this is what gets Kate and Sawyer to finally have sex.

Back inside the Hydra, Jack finds that the door to his cell is now open and leaves. He then notices Ben's monitoring station and looks inside. After he finds a gun, he sees that one of the monitors now show Kate and Sawyer lying naked together in the cell. Jack is crestfallen as Ben appears, expecting Jack to shoot him now. But instead, Jack volunteers to do the surgery tomorrow, insisting that he needs to "get the hell off the island" and Ben agrees.

The next day, Ben is prepped for surgery on the operating table, briefly asking about Alex before he is put under. Once the surgery begins, Pickett leaves to go kill Sawyer. In the pouring rain, he takes Sawyer out of the cell and prepares to shoot.

Inside, Jack suddenly makes a cut into Ben and knocks out one of his guards. He yells that he cut Ben's kidney sac and he will die in one hour if Jack doesn't fix it. But Jack will not repair it unless he talks to Kate and Sawyer. Jack then demands that Friendly give him his walkie talkie.

Outside, Kate tearfully begs Pickett not to kill Sawyer, who merely tells Kate to close her eyes as he awaits death. But right before Pickett shoots, Friendly calls him on his walkie and tells him to give it to Kate, saying that Ben will die otherwise.

Once Kate gets the walkie, Jack talks to her, saying she and Sawyer have an hour long head start to get to the beach. If Kate does not call Jack in an hour and tell him the story Jack told her on their first day on the island, Jack will know something went wrong and he'll let Ben die.

Kate pleads that she won't leave without Jack, but he yells "Kate, damn it, RUN!!!"

Other stuff: Locke prepares to bury Eko right where he died, instead of at the beach. He claims that Eko must have been killed by a bear, but he and Sayid both know it was the monster. Locke suspects Eko died for a reason, but he doesn't know what yet.

Once Eko is buried, Locke makes a brief eulogy, then looks at Eko's club and sees the words "Lift up your eyes and look north" with "John 3:05" carved below. Locke interprets this as a sign for what he must do next.

Main character: Kate Austin.

Flashback details: Kate is in a hotel room and is visited by a policeman named Kevin. Instead of being arrested, Kate makes out with Kevin as it becomes clear they are engaged. Kate is calling herself Monica, however, since she's still on the run.

After the two are married, Kate makes a call to her old nemesis Edward Mars, asking him to call off his manhunt. Realizing that Kate's in love, Mars counters that he'll stop when Kate "stops running." But Mars knows that Kate will never be able to do that, which makes Kate hang up, worried that he's right.

Indeed he is right, as Kate begins to realize this after a false pregnancy scare. She confesses to Kevin about her past and says she can't live this life of secrecy with him. He then passes out, having been drugged beforehand by Kate, who goes back on the run yet again.

Important details in *Lost* lore: Kate and Sawyer finally have sex, which Jack discovers later on. Jack performs the surgery on Ben, but threatens to let him die if Kate and Sawyer aren't freed. Kate's former marriage is detailed. The missing Karl is revealed to be Alex's boyfriend.

Amount of action: Fair to heavy- not counting the sex action.

New important characters: Kate's ex-husband. Pickett also brings up that Jack wasn't on the list of someone called "Jacob."

Connections between characters: Kate and Sawyer finally make the ultimate connection, though Kate still can't leave Jack behind at the very end.

***Lost* mysteries referenced:** Ben's spinal tumor, the condition of Karl, Kate's former marriage.

***Lost* mysteries introduced:** Whether Jack will let Ben die, whether Kate and Sawyer can escape.

Questions raised: What will happen to Jack, Kate, Sawyer and Ben? How will Kate and Sawyer's sex affect the triangle from here on out? How did Jack bring himself to try and save Kate and Sawyer after what happened between them? How will Kate and Sawyer get off this smaller island even if they get free from the Others? What is Locke going to do now? Why did Ben ask about Alex? Why did Pickett bring up that someone named Jacob had a list?

Talking points: As a cliffhanger meant to keep people salivating for almost three months, this one didn't have a huge amount of suspense. Even though *Lost* had tended to kill off people after they had sex, like Shannon and Ana Lucia, there was no way they could kill off Sawyer despite all that teasing and rain. Plus with fans tired of seeing Jack, Kate and Sawyer being captured, Kate and Sawyer will have to be able to escape after all. In addition, it's too soon for Ben to die now.

Like with Jack, Kate's flashbacks now tend to repeat the same point over and over in different ways. Just as we learn time and again that Jack can't "let it go" we learn over and over that Kate can never stop running away.

Other key issues: Jack seems to have finally gotten wise to Ben's tricks for once, doubting his word and Juliet's even after they used Kate against him. But seeing Kate and Sawyer naked can override all critical thinking, nonetheless.

Must see episode?: Yes, if only to see things move along and fulfill the Kate/Sawyer shippers dreams. But as an episode that is meant to be a serious cliffhanger, it fails. By the end of this pod of episodes, *Lost* was now at its biggest crisis point in terms of losing fans and interest. At this point, the final 17 episodes this season would either make or break it for good.

NOT IN PORTLAND

The first half of Season Three offered an odd contradiction in criticisms. People complained that *Lost* was spending too much time with Jack, Kate and Sawyer in the Others lair while ignoring every other survivor. Although they didn't like that plot, they didn't have as much criticism for one of the major new players in it. Juliet, the newest Other, had already made her mark despite the show's history of poor new characters.

Even among the ever mysterious Others, she was an especially mysterious and hard to pin down figure. What were her real feelings toward Jack and Ben? What explained her various attitudes? Could she even begin to be trusted? *Lost* would make a first step towards getting some goodwill back by giving new clues to these questions.

Episode plot: The second after Jack yells for Kate to run, she and Sawyer overpower Pickett and rush out into the jungle. Inside the operating room, Juliet defies Jack's ultimatum. She orders the Others to go get Kate and Sawyer and kill them if necessary, figuring that Jack won't really let Ben die. Jack counters by telling Friendly that Juliet wanted Ben dead all along.

Kate and Sawyer avoid being shot by the Others and get to the beach, realizing they need to sail across the ocean back to their island. Kate radios Jack and asks for a boat, but the Others return and shoot the walkie talkie. As they're cornered, they are saved by Alex, who brings the two to a hiding place. Alex will help them escape, but only if they recover her boyfriend Karl first.

As Jack and Friendly discuss Juliet, Ben somehow manages to wake up. He slowly asks "Tom" that Juliet be brought to him. Juliet is brought back and Ben asks to speak to her alone. As Jack watches, Friendly reintroduces himself as Tom and points out that Ben and Juliet "have history." When Juliet emerges, she tells Jack to finish the surgery while she goes to make sure Kate and Sawyer escape.

Alex brings Kate and Sawyer back to the Hydra. She shows herself to a guard who comments that "her dad" doesn't want her here, then Kate and Sawyer subdue him. They go inside and find Karl in "Room 23" where he is being brainwashed *Clockwork Orange* style with a weird video. They free Karl and leave just before Juliet and Pickett show up outside. Juliet tells Pickett that Ben wants them to leave, but Pickett wants them dead anyway, not even caring if Ben dies anymore.

Alex brings out a canoe for Kate and Sawyer, while confirming Sawyer's suspicion that she is Ben's daughter. Before they can go, Pickett comes up and is ready to shoot. Shots are indeed fired, but by Juliet, who comes up and kills Pickett. Juliet tells Kate and Sawyer to go with Karl, but Alex must stay. She hands Kate her walkie talkie.

As Jack finishes the surgery, Kate retells Jack's story from the first day they met, just as Jack ordered. Now knowing she's safe, Jack makes Kate promise that she will never come back for him. After sadly agreeing, Kate sails off with Sawyer and Karl.

Juliet returns to the Hydra and sees the surgery was a success. Jack comes up to her, learning that he'll go back to his cell until further instructions are given out. He then asks Juliet what Ben told her that made her help Kate and Sawyer. Juliet recounts that she has spent over 3 years on the island. Overcome with emotion, she admits that Ben promised he would let her finally go home.

Main character: Juliet Burke.

Flashback details: Juliet is seen living in Miami, treating her sister Rachel with some medicine. She works in a medical laboratory under her ex-husband Edmund Burke, performing secret research behind his back. But he does find out about it and that her "guinea pig" is her own sister. He tells her to collaborate her research with him so that it will become cutting edge, otherwise it will raise ethical and criminal concerns.

The next day, Juliet has a meeting with a man named Richard Alpert, who works for an organization called Mittlos Bioscience. He wants to hire her as a department head in their headquarters at Portland. Alpert mentions Juliet's research on being able to impregnate a male mouse, offering her the chance to do even more ground breaking work on fertility if she takes the job. But Juliet turns it down, saying Edmund wouldn't let her leave short of getting hit by a bus.

Juliet returns home and finds out that Rachel is pregnant, all thanks to her medicine. Now with the leverage to leave Edmund, she confronts him and refuses his offer. As Edmund argues with her, he goes into the street...and is promptly hit by a bus.

Juliet is later seen at the morgue, identifying Edmund's body. As she cries, she is met by Richard Alpert and his associate, Ethan Rom. She then remembers her comments to Richard about Edmund getting hit by a bus, but Richard claims not to remember. He makes his offer again, inviting her to come to his facility just for six months. Juliet asks if she can bring her sister, which makes Richard admit that it would be difficult since their facility really isn't in Portland.

Important details in *Lost* lore: Kate and Sawyer finally escape, with Jack staying behind and finishing Ben's surgery. Juliet kills Pickett to ensure their escape, revealing that Ben promised to let her leave the island in return. We find out Juliet's past as a fertility researcher whose medicine got her sister pregnant, which got the attention of the Others. Also, Alex is Ben's fake daughter.

Amount of action: Heavy.

New important characters: Richard Alpert and Juliet's sister Rachel.

Connections between characters: Jack parts from Kate and Sawyer, seemingly wanting Kate to never see him again. Alex is shown to be Ben's daughter, though they're not on good terms since Ben locked up her boyfriend.

***Lost* mysteries referenced:** The surgery, Juliet's past.

***Lost* mysteries introduced:** Why the Others recruited Juliet, Room 23.

Questions raised: What will the Others do to Jack now? Will Ben recover from surgery? What is Ben and Juliet's history? Will Juliet now be sent home? Will Kate really never come back for Jack?

Talking points: Many *Lost* characters often act the same on the island as they do in their flashback scenes. But Juliet's flashback, if viewed without the present day action, wouldn't give you the idea of the kind of woman she is on the island. Whereas she is enigmatic and hard to read in the present, going so far as to kill someone in this episode, Juliet is more of the meek, unconfident type in the past. It seems being on the island and being on it longer than she wanted has really changed her, but how has it? And to what extent?

In addition, *Lost's* latest account of borrowing a philosopher's name comes from Edmund Burke, of the famous "The only thing necessary for the triumph of evil is for good men to do nothing" quote.

Other key issues: *Lost* returned from it's absence by making another scenes that fans have to TiVo and study over for weeks, in this case Karl's brainwashing video from Room 23.

Must see episode?: Yes, as *Lost* begins it's road to recovery by bringing the captivity plot closer to an end, while shedding new light on the still mysterious Juliet.

FLASHES BEFORE YOUR EYES

Lost is a show that includes all kinds of fantastic sci-fi elements. Pretty much the only major element they hadn't included yet was time travel and seeing the future. So they quickly brought an end to that by giving those abilities to Desmond. Since he no longer had to live in the hatch or press the button, he probably needed something to fill the void.

To explain his new ordeals, this episode introduced a brand new storytelling format. Episodes usually balance present action with flashbacks, as this is technically a Desmond flashback. But it is one that is unlike any that has come before, so you will need to pay pretty close attention to this one.

Episode plot: Charlie, Hurley and Desmond go over to meet Locke, who tells them Eko is dead and that they should help maintain calm on the beach. But Desmond suddenly runs away and heads for the beach, where Claire is drowning. Charlie tries to go in, but Desmond beats him to it, saving her life. Charlie can't understand how he knew Claire was drowning from so far away, so Hurley informs him that he can see the future. To find out for sure, they vow to get him drunk.

That night, the three are drinking by the fire, yet Charlie gets nowhere with his questions. Desmond walks away, leading Charlie to call him a coward. This makes Desmond attack Charlie, yelling "You don't wanna know what happened to me!!" After spending the majority of the episode finding out what did happen, we go back to the present at the very end.

Once Desmond calms down, he apologizes to Charlie and tells him what he wants to know. When he built the tower near Claire's tent and rushed to save her from drowning, he didn't foresee Claire dying. Both times, he saw Charlie dying trying to save Claire. Desmond has tried twice to save Charlie, but he knows that no matter what he does, eventually Charlie is going to die.

Main character: Desmond Hume.

Flashback details: Desmond is seen turning the hatch key once again, then he sees a flash of light before his eyes. The next thing he knows, he is lying on a floor with blood around him. However, it is just paint, as he appears to be back in his flat on the mainland. What's more, Penelope Widmore is there as well.

Desmond has gone back in time to when he lived with Penny, coming to believe he just had a bad dream about being on the island.

As he returns to his life with Penny, Desmond still sees the numbers in various places. But he goes on as he visits Charles Widmore to apply for a job at Widmore Industries. Instead he tells Widmore about his relationship with Penny, saying he wants to marry her.

In response, Widmore draws his attention to his bottles of whiskey and how much they are worth, which is even more than Desmond. He goes on to say that offering him a drink of it would be an insult because he will never be a great man. As such, if he isn't even worthy of drinking the whiskey, he can never be worthy of Penelope.

Desmond goes outside and sees Charlie playing guitar for a small crowd. This triggers memories of seeing Charlie on the island, as Desmond begins to remember his time there.

He then rushes to his friend Donovan, a physicist whom he asks about the concept of time travel. Though Desmond realizes he might have gone back in time, Donovan doubts it. He looks up at a soccer game telecast and tries to predict what will happen, but he is incorrect. This tempers Desmond's worries for the moment. Then after Penny comforts him for not getting a job from her father, he vows to marry her as planned.

However, when Desmond goes to pick a wedding ring, the elderly female shop keeper says he won't take it. The woman tells him he's not supposed to take it. What he's supposed to do is get cold feet, break up with Penny and wind up on the island.

Desmond is brought outside by the woman, who dodges his theory that she is his subconscious. She explains that fate cannot be changed, since the universe has a way of "course correcting itself." Even if Desmond tries to avoid his destiny of landing on the island, it won't make a bit of difference in the end. Desmond denies this and still takes the wedding ring, more determined than ever to propose.

Desmond meets up with Penny where they get their picture taken, which is the same picture Desmond still carries around with him on the island. With that, Desmond remembers how this scene went the first time and winds up repeating the same thing all over again. He tells Penny they're not supposed to be together, which makes Penny call him a coward and leave.

Back at the pub, Desmond ponders over having left Penny for the second time. He looks up at another soccer game playing on TV, realizing that this time he can make the right prediction of what happens. He looks ready to try and change his fate after all, but this ends when a man comes into the bar and Desmond is hit by his bat.

With that blow, Desmond is sent back to the hatch right after it blew up, naked and alone. He finds his picture of Penny and pleads to be sent back, but nothing happens. From then on in, Desmond is able to have flashes of the future instead.

Important details in *Lost* lore: Desmond is literally sent to the past after destroying the hatch, relieving how he broke up with Penelope and learning from a mysterious woman that his fate cannot be changed. He then reveals that Charlie will die in the future.

Amount of action: Heavy with all the time travel details.

New important characters: The woman in Desmond's flashes, named as "Ms. Hawking."

Connections between characters: Charlie tries to get information out of Desmond, finding out a bit too much due to Desmond's predictions of his death. The end of Desmond's relationship with Penny is shown all over again for Desmond.

***Lost* mysteries referenced:** Desmond's future flashes, what happened to him after the hatch blew up and how his relationship with Penny ended.

***Lost* mysteries introduced:** Whether Charlie really is about to die, who "Ms. Hawking" is.

Questions raised: Why did Desmond get to time travel after destroying the hatch? Is fate really unchangeable? As such, is Charlie doomed as a result?

Talking points: In one of *Lost's* most unusual episode formats, a character literally flashes back to the past instead of us seeing his or hers past in flashbacks. If we can attribute Desmond's flashes as created by the island, or a higher power, it's a bit puzzling as to why it would give Desmond this trip now. Why does Desmond need to be convinced that his fate is set in stone? And how does that connect with him being able to see the future?

Other key issues: *Lost* takes a break from borrowing the names of philosophers, taking one from a scientist by giving Desmond's "subconscious" Stephen Hawking's last name.

Must see episode?: Yes, as it creates a bold new experimental format to introduce brand new elements in the *Lost* story, while teasing the possible death of Charlie to wrap things up.

STRANGER IN A STRANGE LAND

The mid season return of *Lost* was paying off early with two straight strong episodes. Kate and Sawyer were heading home, Jack would have to be sent back soon and things were starting to move forward. But just when the show was getting on a mini-roll, this episode happened.

Of all the mysteries and questions one can devote an episode to; fans wouldn't name Jack's tattoos on his arm as one of them. One wouldn't include Jack taking a trip to Thailand in the equation either, but they did anyway. The result is one of *Lost's* most mocked and low rated episodes.

Episode plot: Jack is back in his cell as Tom Friendly comes to get him. He expects that the Others will kill him soon enough, rattling off their previous crimes, but Tom just asks if he wants stones for his "glass house." Tom leads Jack past Juliet, who is being held prisoner herself. Jack is put inside Sawyer's old cage.

Juliet is soon sent to Jack, asking him to treat an infection on Ben, but he refuses. That night, Jack is visited by a woman named Isabel, designated by Tom as their "sheriff." She makes some comments about the meaning of the tattoos on Jack's arm, then brings him into the Hydra and asks him questions about the surgery. However, Jack now denies that Juliet asked him to kill Ben, saying he lied to get an advantage on the Others. Isabel knows he's lying and sends him back.

Jack remains in his cage as one of the former tail section survivors, Cindy, watches him along with the kidnapped kids from the tail section. Soon after, Alex visits him, telling him that they will probably kill Juliet for killing Pickett. After finding out that she did so to save Kate and Sawyer's lives, Jack asks to be let out so he can see Ben.

Ben is in the operating room lying in recovery. Jack informs him that his infections might prevent Ben from walking again unless he treats him. Ben realizes that Jack is going to extort him again, as Jack asks that Juliet's life be spared. Ben warns him that Juliet will always be "one of us" but agrees to the deal. Instead of being killed, Juliet is "marked" by being branded on her back.

Juliet later brings Jack food as he helps tend to her mark. He vows that he will make Ben keep his promise to let them leave together. But for now, Jack and the Others are going back to the regular island, where Jack will be kept in the Others barracks.

That night before they leave, Isabel informs Jack that his tattoos says "He walks among us but he is not one of us" in Chinese. Jack replies that it's what they say, but not what they mean.

Other stuff: Despite Kate's objections, she and Sawyer sail back to the island with Karl. Sawyer makes camp at the shoreline despite Kate's desire to go right back to the main camp and find Locke and Sayid. That night, Sawyer and Kate talk to Karl about the Others, but he is thinking about Alex.

Later on, Karl has left the camp and Sawyer finds him crying over what has happened. He advises that if he feels that strong about Alex, he should go back to get her. Karl finally heads off over Kate's objections. Sawyer argues that Kate has been mad at him out of guilt for having slept with him, which he thinks she only did because he was about to die. Kate has nothing to say to that as the two start their trek back home.

Main character: Jack Shephard.

Flashback details: Jack is seen in Thailand, where he meets a Thai woman named Achara. The two hit it off although she keeps coming and going, with vague hints that she has "a gift." Finally Jack tracks her down and follows her to a tattoo parlor. He makes Achara confess that she has "a vision" to see who people are, which she marks with her tattoo. Jack angrily asks if she can envision him, although she is not supposed to do this for outsiders.

But he eventually makes Achara do it as she says he is a leader and a great man, but lonely and angry as well. Jack then makes her give him the tattoos to mark this. As a result, the next day Jack is beaten up by a group of Thai men and ordered to leave the country.

Important details in *Lost* lore: Jack's tattoos are translated, if that indeed is important. Sawyer and Kate head home with Karl leaving them to find Alex, while Jack is finally taken off the Hydra island with the Others.

Amount of action: Little.

New important characters: Isabel and Achara.

Connections between characters: Jack and Juliet bond further as they vow to make sure Ben sends them off the island together. Sawyer and Kate have a fight as Sawyer accuses her of having sex with him out of pity. Karl heads off out of love for Alex.

***Lost* mysteries referenced:** Jack's tattoos, Ben's condition, Kate and Sawyer's trek home, Cindy and the captured children of the Others.

***Lost* mysteries introduced:** Whether Jack and Juliet will be sent home after all.

Questions raised: What will happen to Jack and Juliet now that they're heading back to the island? Will the new rift between Sawyer and Kate be repaired? Will Ben continue to stay immobile?

Talking points: As noted above, few people liked this episode at all. It certainly raises the question of how the *Lost* writers can do a whole episode about Jack's tattoos while still ignoring 500 more important details to devote an episode to. The show has stalled for time in answering things and moving things along before, but this is a far too glaring example of that trend.

All this to reveal that Jack's tattoo reads "He walks among us, but he is not one of us" a motto and theory fans could have figured out themselves.

Other key issues: One would think *Lost* would be above such eye rolling endings as having separated lovers Alex and Karl stare at the stars at exactly the same time, even though they're at very different places. But they did anyway.

Must see episode?: Nope.

TRICIA TANAKA IS DEAD

While some characters have been plenty busy this season, a few have been left in the dust. A common complaint was that there wasn't much time spent with survivors other than Jack, Kate and Sawyer in the early going. That would certainly apply to Hurley, who has done little since returning from the Others dock.

Even with this time to himself, the death of Libby and other dreary ordeals has brought the former jolly character down hard. Hurley can usually be counted on to lighten up some moods and help people out, but not lately. This pretty much symbolizes the current state of the show as a whole. But at just the right time, Hurley finally decides to turn things around.

Episode plot: While standing over Libby's grave, Hurley talks about his recent troubles, which now includes Charlie's potential death. Just as he starts to believe that is also part of his curse, he sees Vincent the dog run by with a skeleton arm. Hurley follows it until he finds an overturned van. This makes him determined to fix it, but only Jin winds up helping him.

Hurley and Jin see that the skeleton inside the van belonged to a DHARMA worker named Roger, who is labeled as "Workman." There is also a huge supply of very old beer inside. Sawyer then shows up, which further convinces Hurley their luck is changing. Bribing him with the beer, he gets Sawyer's help to work on the van.

After they push the van back up, Hurley tries to turn it on but the engine fails. However, he keeps trying, determined to get a victory. Once the van rolls down a hill, he gets an idea. Hurley rushes to get Charlie, wanting him to find some hope as well so both their fates will change. Hurley's plan is for Jin and Sawyer to push the van down a bigger hill, which will allow him to pop the clutch. With Charlie at shotgun and Hurley at the wheel, Jin and Sawyer push the van.

Muttering over and over that he can make his own luck after all, Hurley pushes the clutch right before the van crashes into the rocks, which succeeds perfectly. Rejoicing, Hurley begins to drive the van around as Jin and Sawyer cheer from above. Jin, Charlie and Sawyer return to camp with some new optimism as Hurley continues to ride in his new van.

Other stuff: When Kate and Sawyer initially return to camp, Sawyer isn't in much of a mood to speak to her. The survivors are happy to see them nonetheless. Once Kate tells Sayid what happened, she vows to go back for Jack despite his wishes. But first, she's going to get help.

That night, Kate finds that Locke and Sayid have followed her. They offer their help just as Kate finds who she's looking for. Danielle Rousseau comes out of the jungle, wondering what they're doing here. Kate asks for her help in finding the Others, telling her that while she was captured, she met a girl who helped her escape. A girl who is 16 years old and who Kate correctly believes is Rousseau's daughter, Alex.

Main character: Hurley.

Flashback details: When Hurley was young, he was actually skinny until his father turned him onto candy bars. He instructed him that one has to make his own luck, then left for the Grand Canyon and never came back.

Many years later, Hurley has his lottery money and is in the middle of his curse. A reporter named Tricia Tanaka is interviewing him after he purchased the chicken shack he once worked for. As Hurley lists all the bad things that have happened since he won the lottery, he is interrupted when a meteorite strikes the shack, killing Tricia Tanaka.

This furthers Hurley's desire to go to Australia and investigate the cursed numbers, but he is then stunned to see his father has finally come back. He moves back in as his mother thinks he can help Hurley with his claims of a curse…plus help with her own desires as well. Hurley and his dad eventually go to a psychic who says she can remove the curse, but Hurley soon figures out his father put the psychic up to this.

Finally Hurley makes his plans to go to Australia. Before he leaves, his father admits he came back for the money, but advises Hurley to make his own luck. If he has to, he can give up the money and leave enough to fix their family Camaro. After a pause, Hurley goes off anyway, with his father insisting he'll be here when he returns.

Important details in *Lost* lore: Hurley's estranged relationship with his father is revealed. He also discovers a DHARMA van and gets it to work, creating a rare victory. Kate, Sayid and Locke team up with Rousseau to begin searching for Jack. Rousseau is finally told that her daughter is actually alive.

Amount of action: Little.

New important characters: Hurley's father, the skeleton of a DHARMA worker named Roger.

Connections between characters: Hurley teams up with Jin and Sawyer to work the van, then gets to share his success with a depressed Charlie. Kate, Sayid, Locke and Rousseau form a new team.

***Lost* mysteries referenced:** Desmond's visions of Charlie's death, the numbers.

***Lost* mysteries introduced:** The mysterious DHARMA van and the dead man inside.

Questions raised: Have things finally turned around for Hurley and Charlie? Will Kate's search team succeed in finding Jack? Will Rousseau finally be reunited with her daughter after all?

Talking points: By all accounts, this episode should fail the way "Stranger in a Strange Land" did, with a seemingly useless plot out of nowhere involving a DHARMA van and action that doesn't really move anything forward. But the results are different when they involve

Hurley, Jin and Sawyer, things are actually funny and there's a hopeful ending for once.

Hurley becomes the latest character to suffer from having a bad father nonetheless. But his dad is really just the garden variety "walks out on his kid and comes back for money type" not the kidney stealing type or the rotten, not really dead doctor type. And he's played by Cheech Marin, so we couldn't take it seriously if he was one of those really evil dad figures anyway.

Other key issues: Sawyer taught Jin the English words "I'm sorry" "You were right" and "Those pants don't make you look fat" to deal with women. The man should teach a class.

Must see episode?: Technically it's a comedic episode which doesn't move things around too much. But it's a refreshing chance of pace from all the drama. Plus one shouldn't be so quick to forget about the van, as this isn't the last we've heard of it.

ENTER 77

What would *Lost* be like without a few episodes in which teams of survivors journey through the jungle? Jack and Kate usually have all the fun wandering around and running into adventures, with occasional support from Hurley, Locke, Charlie and Sayid. This time with Jack gone, Kate, Locke, Sayid and Rousseau form a new team of their own. Their latest marching order is to find Jack and the Others.

To start off, their first little obstacle is to encounter a man Locke saw on a monitor a while back, and discover a new DHARMA station along the way. Jack could probably do it in half an episode while these guys take the whole show, but one has to start somewhere.

Episode plot: Locke leads Kate, Sayid and Rousseau through the island with the bearing of 305, which he got from Eko's stick. Sayid questions the wisdom of this move, but is proven wrong when he hears a cow. He hears someone whistle for it and discovers a station with a giant satellite dish on top. Outside of it is the man with an eye patch that Locke saw on the Pearl monitor days before.

Sayid makes a plan to come towards the man unarmed, with Kate and Locke as hidden backup. Once he comes out, Sayid is shot by the man, who speaks with a Russian accent and yells that "we have a truce!" Sayid realizes that he thinks he's an Other, so he distracts him before

Kate and Locke show to disarm him. The man says his name is Mikhail Bakunin, the last living member of the DHARMA Initiative.

Mikhail brings them inside the station and treats Sayid's wounds. He explains that he was a former Soviet Army member who joined DHARMA over 10 years ago. He lives in a station called the Flame, which was used to communicate with the outside world. Soon after he arrived, DHARMA was wiped out by the Others in what Mikhail calls "The Purge." Since then, Mikhail made a truce with them to stay in the Flame, which the Others aren't interested in because the satellite doesn't work.

But all this does not convince Sayid, who deduces that Mikhail really is an Other. He continues to play along however, getting out of Mikhail that the Others probably have a submarine. Once Sayid brings up how one of the Others was killed on his former sailboat, Mikhail breaks his ruse and attacks, but Kate brings him down.

During all this, Locke is preoccupied with a chess game on Mikhail's computer. Even as he is told to watch Mikhail's unconscious body, he goes back to play it. As he plays, a video clip is shown of Dr. Marvin Candle. He offers instructions on what buttons to push for various things, which Locke plays along with until Candle says "Has there been an incursion on this station by the Hostiles? If so, enter 7-7." Before Locke can, Mikhail arises and grabs him.

Meanwhile, Sayid and Kate find a hatch door on the ground, going downstairs to find C4 explosives all over the place. They also find DHARMA manuals and protocols. Finally, they discover another Other, Ms. Klugh, who Kate recognizes from the dock. They bring her back up, where Mikhail has Locke at knife point. Klugh starts arguing with Mikhail in Russian as Kate, Sayid and Locke talk over them. Finally Klugh yells "Do it!" and Mikhail eventually shoots and kills her. This gives Sayid the opening to capture him.

By the time it's night, Sayid, Kate and Locke have the map to the barracks where the Others live and where Jack likely is. Rousseau argues that they should kill Mikhail. But Mikhail is Sayid's prisoner and he decides not to kill him, taking him along as his captive.

Locke and Kate return, with the Flame station blowing up into flames seconds later. Locke found time to enter 77 after all, which destroyed the station. Sayid argues that Locke may have destroyed their hopes of contacting the outside world.

Other stuff: On the beach, Sawyer is wondering where Kate has gone. He also becomes upset that his stash has become public property now. So he offers to play anyone in a game of ping pong to get his supplies back. Sun makes it interesting by saying that Sawyer can't say any nicknames for a week if he loses. Finally Hurley steps up as Sawyer's opponent.

In no time, Sawyer is defeated and he has to actually abide by the no nickname rule. But Hurley does give Sawyer his pornography collection back and reassures him that Kate will be fine with Sayid and Locke.

Main character: Sayid Jarrah.

Flashback details: Sayid works at a kitchen in Paris, until he is kidnapped by a man named Sami and his wife Amira. He is kept in their basement, as Sami explains that his wife was one of Sayid's torture victims while he was in Iraq. Sayid says he never tortured any women, but Sami beats him and orders him to confess under penalty of death.

Amira talks to Sayid alone the next day, telling him about her pet cat and how she rescued it from torture. Though it bites, she shares the cats fear that she will never be safe, all because of Sayid. This finally touches Sayid as he breaks down and confesses, saying her face has haunted him. With that, Amira plans to tell her husband they have the wrong man and they should let Sayid go. In this way, she will not become like Sayid and the people that hurt her cat.

Important details in *Lost* lore: Sayid, Kate and Locke discover a DHARMA communications station called the Flame, which is destroyed by Locke. They also meet and battle with an Other named Mikhail, who tells them that DHARMA was wiped out years ago in a "Purge" by the Others.

Amount of action: Heavy.

New important characters: Though he was seen before, Mikhail has his first official appearance.

Connections between characters: Kate, Sayid and Locke begin their trip together, though Locke manages to leave a destroyed station in their path. Hurley defeats Sawyer in ping pong and gets him to lay off his trademark nicknames.

***Lost* mysteries referenced:** The DHARMA Initiative, the Others.

***Lost* mysteries introduced:** The Purge, the Flame station, Mikhail, the Others submarine.

Questions raised: Will Kate, Sayid and Locke find Jack in time now that they know where to look? What will they do with Mikhail? What was the Purge? Was Locke really being clueless when he entered 77, or was it on purpose? Why did Klugh order Mikhail to kill her? Can Sawyer really come up with no nicknames for a week?

Talking points: Sayid's last flashback revealed the origin of his torture career and showed him coming out of retirement to beat up Ben. In contrast, this one shows him facing the consequences of his career in the past. In deeper contrast, Sayid doesn't revert back to torture or death in dealing with Mikhail, choosing not to kill him. Sayid has tried to give up his violent tendencies before on the island, which hasn't worked too well. Can this new change be any different?

The episode also shot down the theory that the Others are leftovers from DHARMA. Mikhail introduces the notion that the Others killed off DHARMA when they intruded on them. But people like Mikhail and Juliet were recruited later on, so not all of the Others could have lived on the island during DHARMA's time.

Other key issues: Locke is making a history out of blowing stuff up. He blew up the hatch door in Season One and made it necessary to destroy the hatch itself in Season Two, plus he's now destroyed the Flame to boot. Has this begun to become a trend?

Must see episode?: Yes, as it introduces Mikhail and gives a few more key nuggets into DHARMA and the Others. But the episode is really a set up one, as the real action is still a few episodes off.

PAR AVION

Claire is a character who tends to fade in the background when she's not raising Aaron or dealing with Charlie. In Season One her main mystery was when she would give birth to Aaron, which she finally did. In Season Two, her main mystery was in trying to recover her memory, which she also managed to do. Since then, she's gone back to reconnecting with Charlie and caring for Aaron. But with her one designated episode this season, she reopens another left in the dust possibility of actually trying to find rescue. She becomes even more important in the past, as the show confirms a long suspected connection between her and the still missing Jack.

Episode plot: Charlie is all set to spend the day with Claire, until he receives Desmond's latest death prediction that he will die around her. Just then, Claire comes up with an idea that might get them rescued. She sees a pack of gulls migrating south that are being tagged by scientists. If she catches one and attaches a message about the survivors to its leg, she thinks scientists will be able to find it and get them rescued.

Sun and Jin aid her, but Charlie doesn't, convinced that doing so will kill him. Desmond even tries to stop her by firing a rifle in the air. When Claire doesn't get any answers about why they're trying to stop her, she follows Desmond for herself. She finds him getting one of the gulls from the ocean, as Claire wonders how he could have known it was there. Desmond finally confesses that he saw Charlie trying to save this bird and get it for Claire, where he would have died by slipping in the ocean.

Now knowing about Desmond's powers and Charlie's possible fate, Claire is able to get Charlie's help this time and they both attach a note to the gull. As it flies off, Claire reassures Charlie that she won't give up on him and will help him try to avoid death.

Other stuff: Locke, Kate, Sayid and Rousseau continue their route to the barracks with Mikhail as their prisoner. As they do, Mikhail tells them how he was recruited and how he got to the island on a submarine. The sub can still leave the island, but can't come back since communications were destroyed after the hatch exploded.

Kate can't understand why the Others would stay on the island, but Mikhail explains that they couldn't understand, since they're not on any of their lists. Only those who aren't "flawed" are put on it by the man who brought Mikhail and all the Others recruits to the island. However, this great leader is not Ben. Mikhail goes on to demonstrate just how much he knows about Kate, Sayid and Locke, including their flaws and full names. But before he can reveal that Locke was paralyzed, they discover a series of sonar posts. They make up a security fence that surrounds the barracks, as it will electrocute anyone who walks through it.

To prove this, Locke shoves Mikhail between the posts. After Mikhail thanks him, he is electrocuted and falls down, apparently dead.

Sayid is now fully suspicious of Locke's actions, especially when he sees that Locke found time to recover C4 explosives from the Flame before he blew it up. But the four are able to use a tree to climb over the sonar posts and arrive at the barracks. The barracks are the same location seen in the opening scene of "A Tale Of Two Cities" as the Others are seen outside.

That includes Jack, who is actually playing football with Tom Friendly.

Main character: Claire Littleton.

Flashback details: As a younger girl, Claire was in a car accident which put her mother in a coma. Though it may be permanent, the costs have been paid for by an unknown benefactor.

One day, Claire goes into the hospital to find a doctor watching over her. Her aunt Lindsey then sees him and becomes angry at him. As they fight, Claire is confused as to what this is about. The man then explains that he is Claire's father.

That man is also Dr. Christian Shephard himself.

Christian and Claire talk in a coffee shop, where Christian explains that he had a fling with Claire's mother years ago. He visited Claire a few times as a baby, but the fact he had "another family" made Claire's mother kick him out. He says that her coma is so severe that it may be better to let her die, which sets Claire off. She leaves without wanting to know Christian's name.

Years later, Claire is seen visiting her still comatose mom just before she leaves for flight 815. She apologizes for arguing with her right before the car accident and wishing she was dead.

Important details in *Lost* lore: Claire makes a plan to get rescued, also finding out about Charlie's potential death in the process. Christian Shephard is revealed to be Claire's father, making her Jack's half-sister. Mikhail reveals how much the Others know about the survivors, that the Others have a sub and that their true leader is not Ben. Then he is electrocuted by Locke. Jack is seen at the Others barracks happily playing football.

Amount of action: Little.

New important characters: Claire's comatose mother.

Connections between characters: Claire's ultimate connection to the Shephard family is discovered. Charlie and Claire now seem to be fully back together. Locke's strange actions arouse suspicion from his current teammates.

***Lost* mysteries referenced:** Christian's daughter, the Others and their lists, Jack's current state.

***Lost* mysteries introduced:** Jack having fun with the Others, Mikhail's claims that Ben is not "the magnificent man" who leads the Others.

Questions raised: Will Claire's rescue plan have any luck? Will she be able to help Charlie stay alive? Why is Jack enjoying himself at the barracks? What will Kate, Locke, Sayid and Rousseau do to get him out? Why has Locke been blowing things up and killing people lately? Will Jack and Claire discover their true connection? How do the Others know so much about Kate, Locke and Sayid? Who does Mikhail refer to as "the magnificent man" that isn't Ben?

Talking points: It wasn't a huge surprise to many about Claire's family ties to Christian Shephard, since fans suspected he went to Australia to find her in the "Two for the Road" flashbacks. By now, *Lost* could pretty much become a "Six Degrees of Christian Shephard" game.

Unlike most of the Others, Mikhail actually seemed to be clearing up things, answering questions and giving things away. So for that, he had to be shocked to death by Locke, of course. And why has Locke been more trigger happy than usual these last two weeks, anyway?

Other key issues: Break out the history books, as Claire turns out to have slightly more mother issues than daddy issues, which is pretty much a show first.

Must see episode?: It connects Claire and Christian and lets Mikhail give out some juicy details before biting it. But other than that, it's just one long setup for the next episode.

THE MAN FROM TALLAHASSEE

This season faced criticism that *Lost* was wasting time, just like Season Two often did. Though the show was still capable of providing great individual parts, there wasn't really a full complete package of an episode yet. Each show either had useless subplots, questionable calls or at least one or two head shaking moments. We didn't have a real instant classic episode yet like in the good old days. By this point, with *Lost* facing its harshest critics yet, it needed one now.

Thanks to John Locke, a long awaited reunion between him and Ben, the solving of one of *Lost's* longest lasting mysteries and a final surprise cameo, that instant classic comes just in time.

Episode plot: Stunned that Jack could be having fun with the Others and shaking hands with a wheelchair bound Ben, Kate wants to go get him now. But Locke argues Jack must have a good reason, offering to wait till night to get him out if he wants to.

That night, Kate finds Jack in a house, playing piano. Once Jack sees her, he tells her to leave as he is being watched by cameras. But the Others guards barge in and capture her, bringing Sayid in as well. Kate tells them no one else is with them.

But Locke is out and about, arriving inside Ben's bedroom. Ben wakes up and is shocked to see Locke for the first time since he left the hatch. Locke tells him he's not here for Jack. He wants to find the submarine Mikhail told them about.

Just then Alex enters and is grabbed by Locke. He takes her into a closet as Tom and Richard Alpert come in and update Ben. Before Richard leaves, Ben orders him to bring "The Man from Tallahassee." Afterwards, Locke tells Alex to find the package of C4 that is in Sayid's backpack.

When they're alone, Ben tells Locke that he knows the explosives are from the Flame, figuring out that Locke wants to destroy the submarine. Ben claims "I know you, John Locke" proving this by talking about Locke's life and that he has spent the last four years in a wheelchair. Ben also knows how Locke ended up in it, asking "Did it hurt?"

Ben later shares how much he wanted to ask Locke about his recovery in the hatch, but he couldn't without giving himself away. Locke notices that Ben is worried that he hasn't recovered so quickly, wondering how he even got sick in the first place.

Jack visits Kate at a rec room where she is being held prisoner. He tells her that he made a deal with the Others, where he and Juliet will leave on the sub tomorrow morning. Jack vows that he can bring back help. Despite the fact Kate broke her promise not to come back, he will come back for her.

Back in Ben's house, Locke wheels Ben to the living room and eats some chicken from the fridge. Ben starts to explain that he would have a problem with his people if the sub blew up. Most of the Others were recruited to the island, as they need to know they can leave if they want to. The sub being destroyed would end that "illusion" since most of them haven't made a full commitment to the island, unlike Locke.

Ben offers to show Locke things that he wants to know about the island, using the metaphor of a "magic box." But Locke is not deterred, arguing that Ben has lost touch with the island and compares him to a Pharisee. After all, although Ben's lived here his entire life, he is in the wheelchair and Locke isn't.

Alex returns with the dynamite, after a captive Sayid tells her that she looks like her mother, who Alex thought was dead. Locke takes her with him to the sub, ignoring Ben's claim that even if he lets the sub go, no one will ever find the island. As Locke and Alex go, Alex tells him that Ben really wants him to destroy the sub and is making it look like Locke's idea. In the background, Rousseau watches and gets a look at her daughter for the first time in 16 years.

Jack and Juliet prepare to go, first getting Ben to promise that he will let Kate and Sayid go once the sub departs. Once they get to the docks, they see Locke coming out of the submarine. Locke tells Jack he's sorry, then the sub explodes behind him, destroying Jack and Juliet's chance to leave.

Locke is now held in a room as Ben returns in his wheelchair, with Locke realizing Ben really did want him to destroy the sub. Ben explains that his people would have turned against him if he let Jack and Juliet go and was defeated, but they would have also turned on him if they saw him break his word. With Locke having solved this for him, it made his "dreams come true."

Locke is led out of the room as Ben clarifies his question of whether Locke's paralysis hurt. He wanted to know what it was like knowing his own dad tried to kill him. He states that Locke destroyed the sub because this is the one place Anthony Cooper can't get to him.

But Ben wants to help him, due to his communion with the island, as well as the fact that Ben's in a wheelchair and Locke isn't. Ben then shows him one final thing.

A door is unlocked revealing a man who is bound and gagged. Shock and disbelief registers on Locke as he sees the man, then asks "Dad?"

Anthony Cooper is "The Man From Tallahassee" Ben had asked for.

Main character: John Locke.

Flashback details: Locke is suffering from depression as a young man named Peter visits him. Peter's wealthy mother is marrying a man named Adam Seward, who got a kidney from Locke. Adam Seward is really Anthony Cooper, which Locke doesn't tell him about. Instead he confronts his father yet again and orders him to call off his latest con, or else he'll rat him out. Cooper eventually agrees, but Locke is soon shocked when police ask him about the death of Peter.

Locke finds Cooper at his apartment and demands to know if Cooper killed Peter. Cooper responds that the wedding was called off only after the boy's death, saying that he isn't a murderer. If Locke doubts this story, she can call the mother himself. Locke then goes to the phone and asks for her number.

Cooper instead tackles Locke and pushes him out of the window, which is eight stories above the ground.

Locke is left paralyzed as Cooper disappears into Mexico.

Important details in *Lost* lore: Locke was paralyzed because his father threw him out of an eight story window four years ago. In the present, Locke destroys the Others sub before Jack and Juliet can leave the island. Kate and Sayid are left as prisoners. As a reward for Locke destroying the sub, Ben shows Locke that Anthony Cooper is a captive of the Others. Rousseau finally gets a look at Alex, who briefly hears about her mother from Sayid.

Amount of action: Heavy.

New important characters: None.

Connections between characters: Jack and Kate reunite, as Jack vows to come back for her before being denied his trip home. Locke and Ben are also reunited as they combat each other about the sub and the island itself. Locke and Cooper's final devastating confrontation is revealed, before they are brought together again on the island.

***Lost* mysteries referenced:** The origin of Locke's paralysis, Ben's sickness, the Others sub, Jack's care by the Others.

***Lost* mysteries introduced:** The appearance of Anthony Cooper, Ben's "magic box."

Questions raised: What is Anthony Cooper doing as the Others prisoner? Why did Ben bring him there? What is Locke going to do about it? What will become of Jack and Juliet now that they can't go home? How will Kate and Sayid be dealt with? Will Alex become suspicious that her mother might not be dead, as Ben told her? How is Ben going to help Locke? Will Ben ever walk again? Why has the island healed Locke and not Ben?

Talking points: At last, after several Locke flashbacks, this one finally explains how he got in that pesky wheelchair. The answer is pretty the same reason for all his pre-island misery: Dad did it. As Ben suggests, this is really why he doesn't want off the island or want anyone to find it, because his dad can't get to him here. That would seem a might ridiculous until seeing that Anthony Cooper did find him on the island, albeit after being taken there by the Others.

In addition to solving the mystery of Locke's paralysis, this is also really the first time he could talk about it to someone else. He briefly mentioned it to Boone and shared a knowing conversation with Rose, but Ben is really the first person who understands what happened to him and can talk about it with him. Or at least wants to know so he can get cured himself.

When Locke brings up that Ben is a hypocrite for relying on technology and not showing devotion to the island, he is one to talk. After all, Locke relied on the technology of the hatch and lost his connection to the island all throughout Season Two. But then again, that might be why Locke gets so mad at Ben for not knowing the island as well as he should, because he's been there and suffered the consequences for it himself.

Other key issues: Rousseau lost her usefulness to the rescue team pretty quickly, as she dropped out to finally get a look at Alex. Yet she didn't show herself to her and only let herself look, despite all her misery since losing Alex. But that might be balanced by Sayid planting the idea in Alex's head that she's being lied to about her family.

Must see episode?: The most must see of the season thus far. After a whole season and a half of waiting, the true John Locke is finally back. Being paired up with Ben again and reestablishing his connection to the island has given him his mojo back. Emmy voters agreed, as this episode finally won Terry O'Quinn his overdue Emmy award. The tide began to turn back into *Lost's* favor starting with this episode.

EXPOSE

Since *Lost* began, about 10-15 different survivors have been the main characters. However, there are more than 40 total survivors of flight 815. While Jack and company have their adventures, there are many extras in the background who no one hears about. What do they do while the regulars go have their fun, and who are they? By creating the former background survivors of Nikki and Paulo in Season Three, *Lost* attempted to answer this question. Problem is, no one liked it.

Of all the things fans have turned against from this show, Nikki and Paulo were the things they turned on the quickest. No one liked how they were put in all of a sudden, no one was entertained by their newfound interaction with the regulars, while even the survivors were asking out loud who they were. So this episode was created to answer who they were and put their existence into the context of the rest of the show. But in the end, it mainly satisfied the fans bloodlust.

Episode plot: Nikki is seen digging a hole and then running through the jungle. She stops and sees Sawyer and Hurley, saying something the two can't understand. She then drops, as Hurley realizes Nikki's dead, though Sawyer still doesn't even know who she is.

Sawyer and Hurley are joined by Sun, Jin and Charlie to investigate. Hurley comes to believe Nikki said "Paulo lies" and they go to find him. But when they do, Paulo is dead as well. With the mystery fully on, the investigators have various theories of who killed them. Soon Sawyer comes to believe they were moles for the Others.

Hurley learns from Desmond that Sawyer was arguing with Nikki hours earlier, turning his suspicions on him. Sun still believes it was the Others, since they attacked her earlier. But this makes Charlie finally confess that he did it on behalf of Sawyer. When they confront Sawyer, he admits to arguing with Nikki, but he didn't kill her. He noticed that Nikki's nails were dirty and she must have been hiding something. And he's right as he found a pouch of diamonds on Paulo's body.

The two bodies are buried, as Sun hands the diamonds back to Sawyer since they're useless here. She comments that she won't tell Jin about what Sawyer did to her since they'd have to dig another grave afterwards, then slaps him. Hurley soon delivers a eulogy for Nikki and Paulo, which doesn't consist of much since they still didn't know them too well. Sawyer puts the diamonds in the grave and they start to bury Nikki and Paulo.

Main characters: Nikki and Paulo.

Flashback details: In her past, Nikki was a guest star on a hit syndicated TV show called *Expose,* which co-stars Billy Dee Williams. Nikki was having an affair with the series creator, but was working a con on him with Paulo in which they stole a bunch of diamonds. The two get on flight 815 to escape, having gotten away with their crime.

During the first moments on the island, Nikki looks for Paulo after having run into Dr. Arzt. She finds Paulo and asks where the bag of diamonds is.

During the events of "White Rabbit" Nikki and Paulo search the luggage for the diamonds and meet up with Ethan, then watch Jack's "Live together, die alone" speech.

Days later, Nikki gets to know Dr. Arzt and his collection of spiders, as he draws a map for her to find debris from the plane. Paulo is jealous, but he and Nikki follow Arzt's map to the Pearl station, having found it long before Locke and Eko have. They don't go in, however.

During the events of "Whatever The Case May Be" Nikki and Paulo find out from Shannon about the case of guns found under a waterfall. Figuring that might be where the diamonds are, they go down there. Paulo dives under and finds the bag, but keeps it to himself.

Several days later, Paulo has dug the bag under the beach, but Locke comes to see him. Though he doesn't ask what he's doing, he advises Paulo that the beach will erode soon and that he should find a new hiding place for his pouch. So Paulo goes back to the Pearl and hides the diamonds inside that hatch's toilet.

In the process, he oversees Ben and Juliet entering the station. They look at Jack on a monitor while discussing their plans to capture him and make him do Ben's spinal surgery, as Paulo watches.

On the day Locke invited Nikki and Paulo to go to the Pearl in "The Cost Of Living" Paulo takes the diamonds back and hides them in his pants, covering it up by flushing the toilet.

Hours ago, the two lie together on the beach. Paulo leaves to get breakfast, while Nikki goes to ask Sawyer for a gun. He refuses and she storms off. Hours later, she finds Paulo in the jungle, having figured out he had hidden the diamonds on the beach. She reveals a jar containing one of Dr. Arzt's former spiders, which can paralyze someone for eight hours and make it appear that they're dead, though they're really not.

She flings a spider at Paulo and it bites him, leaving him paralyzed and allowing Nikki to search his body. After she finds the pouch, Paulo admits he didn't want to lose her if she did find the diamonds, then falls unconscious. Just then, many more spiders arrive and one of them bites Nikki, making her run away until she falls unconscious as well.

Eight hours later, Nikki's eyes open just as the survivors finish burying her and Paulo. What she really tried to say to Sawyer and Hurley was "paralyzed." But now it's too late. The two have been buried alive and this is how they finally die, with no one noticing or caring.

Important details in *Lost* lore: The story of Nikki and Paulo, plus their background appearances in several key *Lost* moments, is discovered. The two are finally buried alive when everyone thinks they died, but were really just paralyzed by spider bites.

Amount of action: Little.

New important characters: None.

Connections between characters: Nikki and Paulo have various meetings with many now dead characters, like Shannon, Boone, Ethan and Dr. Arzt.

***Lost* mysteries referenced:** Who Nikki and Paulo are.

***Lost* mysteries introduced:** None.

Questions raised: What was the point of this episode?

Talking points: Basically, Nikki and Paulo are the Forrest Gump, or the Rosencrantz and Guildenstern of *Lost.* Gump was digitally enhanced into historic events, while Nikki and Paulo also suddenly appear in past *Lost* moments. Rosencrantz and Guildenstern were minor *Hamlet* players whose full lives were revealed in a famed Tom Stoppard play, just as Nikki and Paulo's lives are revealed here. But that play didn't have diamonds and spiders and characters no one liked.

This episode is really just one big parody of itself. It's basically a clip show except with new characters put into the clips. It outwardly spoofs just how useless Nikki and Paulo really were. In fact, the whole reason this episode existed is because the fans loathed them. The creators had bigger plans for them, but when they realized they were so unpopular, they created this episode to get rid of them. So this was technically the first and only collaboration between the creators and their fans.

Other key issues: When Hurley read Nikki's script for *Expose,* he was stunned that the character of Mr. LaShade played by Billy Dee Williams was "The Cobra" and the mastermind behind everything. Many fans took that as a possible clue to *Lost*'s own mysteries.

Must see episode?: This episode is the very definition of a one shot that has nothing to do with the main story. *Lost* turns itself into a self parody for this one show, which is especially glaring after this directly followed the brilliant "Man From Tallahassee." For those who want to see a real *Lost* episode, this isn't it. But for those who want to see this kind of silly spoof and get pleasure from Nikki and Paulo finally going away, watch this when you have nothing else to do.

LEFT BEHIND

When Juliet was introduced, she became the new mystery Other and someone who could shed new light on them. But in a more shallow sense, she was really the new potential love interest for Jack. Ana Lucia was introduced to possibly drive a wedge between Jack and Kate, but it didn't work out. Juliet has had better luck, as she and Jack have already bonded. But inevitably, this was going to bring her into conflict with Kate as well. And in this episode, that's exactly what happens as *Lost* introduces the concept of a cat fight

Episode plot: Kate's still held captive in the rec room. She tries to attack Juliet when she comes in to bring her food, but Juliet flips her instead. Later Locke comes in and tells her the Others are leaving, as he is going with them. Kate is being left behind due to her past crimes. Sometime afterwards, the Others do leave and throw gas canisters in the room, which knock Kate out.

When she comes to, she is in the middle of the jungle and handcuffed to, of all people, Juliet. Kate finds a knife on her and takes it, but Juliet then wakes and grabs her. The knife can't pick their lock, so they're stuck together.

That night it is pouring rain and Kate, dragging Juliet with them, tries to follow the Others trail. Juliet is amazed she's going back to find

Jack, blaming her for stopping their chance to leave. With that, their cat fight is on.

It is ultimately won by Kate when she breaks Juliet's shoulder by accident. They are stopped when they begin to hear the black smoke monster. Kate brings Juliet behind the trees, but the monster comes up in front of them and light comes out, as it seems to be scanning the women.

The monster finally leaves, but the two have to spend the night in the trees. While they wait, Juliet tells Kate how Jack saw her and Sawyer together, which made Jack tell Kate not to go back because she broke his heart. Eventually, Kate is able to pop Juliet's shoulder back into place.

The two leave the next morning, as Juliet counters Kate's claim that she doesn't know anything about Jack by retelling his past history. This latest argument is interrupted by the monster again, as the two rush to the sonar fence of the barracks. Juliet claims the fence is turned off, but Kate doesn't believe her. So Juliet gets out a key and unlocks their cuffs, leaving her free to get behind the fence and turn it back on. When the monster comes, this fence blocks it from coming closer as Juliet stares it down.

Once it leaves, Juliet admits she knew about the monster's existence, but Kate is more concerned that she had a key. Juliet confesses that she thought Kate would leave her behind if she knew the cuffs could be unlocked. With that, they trudge back to the barracks and Kate finally finds Jack in his temporary house. She apologizes for everything, but Jack just asks where Juliet is. Once Kate says she was left behind, Jack makes the decision to finally head back to the beach.

Jack and Kate then find Sayid, who confirms that all the Others are gone. Jack announces that Juliet is coming with them back to camp, since she was left behind too.

Other stuff: Hurley informs Sawyer that he might be banished from the camp, due to his growing unpopularity. He advises Sawyer to act nice, but Sawyer turns that down until he sees how difficult it would be living on his own.

So Sawyer helps Claire with Aaron, aids Desmond in a boar hunt and roasts a boar that they find. But then Hurley admits to him that he was never going to be "voted off" having actually conned him into being nice. Hurley argues that with Jack still gone, Sawyer will be looked upon as a temporary leader.

Main character: Kate Austin.

Flashback details: Kate's latest adventure involves Cassidy, the former love interest of Kate's future love interest Sawyer. The two connect after Kate spots her performing a con, as Kate needs some help to find and talk to her mother. Cassidy agrees to help, still smarting from when Sawyer conned her out of her money.

Cassidy is used as a decoy as she knocks on Kate's mother's door and sees Edward Mars and the U.S Marshals there, while Kate watches. When Cassidy returns, Kate tells her what she did to her father Wayne, as she's here to ask her mother why she turned Kate in.

Eventually, the two find Kate's mother at her diner. Cassidy spills soup on Kate's mother, who has to clean her clothes. This is where she finds Kate, who asks her the questions. Her mother still loved Wayne despite his abuse, as she explains that Kate killed him for her own good and not for her mother's. Though she won't give Kate up, she vows to scream for help if she ever sees her again, which she did in "Born to Run."

With her quest over, Kate thanks Cassidy for her help, advising her to turn in the man who conned her, which is what she ultimately did to Sawyer.

Important details in *Lost* lore: The Others leave the barracks along with Locke, leaving Kate and Juliet in the middle of the jungle. They have it out and face off with the monster before finding Jack and Sayid, leaving them and Juliet ready to head back to camp. Kate's past connection to Sawyer's former girlfriend Cassidy is discovered.

Amount of action: Fair.

New important characters: None.

Connections between characters: Kate has another connection to Sawyer through her past partnership with Cassidy. Kate is even the one who convinced Cassidy to ultimately put Sawyer in jail. Kate and Juliet literally brawl over Jack.

***Lost* mysteries referenced:** The monster.

***Lost* mysteries introduced:** Locke's partnership with the Others, how much the Others know about the monster, why Juliet was left behind.

Questions raised: Are Kate and Juliet ever going to get along? Has Jack's devotion transferred to Juliet now? What will happen when Juliet joins the camp? Where have Locke and the Others gone? Does Juliet know more about the monster than she lets on? Why did the monster scan her and Kate at night?

Talking points: After the camp that was the entire "Expose" episode, *Lost* takes another step towards cheesiness by having Kate and Juliet brawl in the rain. It seems that this season, Kate has really had nothing to do other than go back and forth between Jack and Sawyer. Even when she has a fight scene with Juliet, it's all about Jack.

The monster seemed to be scanning Juliet just like it did with Mr. Eko way back when. That didn't end well for Eko ultimately, so Juliet may have had extra reason to watch out.

Other key issues: It took long enough, but *Lost* finally openly referenced *Survivor* with Hurley's lie that Sawyer could be voted off the camp.

Must see episode?: Really just a set up episode for next week's action.

ONE OF US

Juliet Burke and Benjamin Linus have a lot of things in common. They're both Others, they're both hard to figure out, they both have their share of dirty tricks, plus there's supposed to be this history between them. The parallels are even stronger with the title of this episode. When Ben first arrived as Henry Gale, his first episode was titled "One Of Them." His introduction to the survivors was a good beating by Sayid. Now Juliet is labeled as "one of them" when she arrives at the survivors camp. Since they can't beat her up, they are just left to suspect her as Jack maintains that she is "One Of Us."

But who is she "one of" really? This episode reveals more about her than ever before and yet still doesn't bring us any closer to figuring it out.

Episode plot: Jack, Kate and Sayid start heading back to camp with Juliet. Once Sayid gets her alone, he says he wants to know everything about the Others and about her. Juliet claims he'll kill her if she tells him everything, but Sayid just replies "What do you think I'll do if you don't?" But Jack stops him, ordering that no one will question her until she's ready.

The next day, Charlie cares for Aaron after seeing that Claire isn't well. When she wakes up, she looks even worse. But just then, Sun looks out and sees Jack coming. The whole camp rushes to reunite with their long departed leader. They also happily welcome back Kate and Sayid as well. Sawyer is pleasantly surprised to see Jack, then hugs Kate. But his good mood disappears when he sees Juliet nearby, as the whole camp now notices her for the first time.

Juliet stays on the beach as Jack discusses her with the other survivors, trying to convince them she can be trusted. No one believes it, as they are further put on edge after finding out what Locke did to the submarine. Their debate is interrupted when Claire coughs up blood and looks even more gravelly ill. Once she notices this, Juliet rushes to Kate and asks to see Jack, telling her she knows what's wrong with Claire. She's sick because she did this to her.

Juliet reveals why the Others really took Claire. For the last several years, every single woman who's gotten pregnant on the island has died during their pregnancy. Ethan was sent to the survivors' camp to take blood samples from Claire, as Juliet was going to give her medication that would save her life. But when Ethan was discovered as a mole, he went overboard and took Claire too early. Yet when Claire was in their care, Juliet's medicine helped her survive to give birth to Aaron.

However, Claire is now suffering from withdrawal and needs to be injected with the medicine again. Ethan had a hiding place for this medicine in the jungle, as Jack agrees to let her go get it.

The next morning, Juliet arrives at a tree to get a case of Ethan's medicine underneath. But Sayid and Sawyer have tracked her down, demanding answers from her and not moved by Juliet's claims that Claire needs the medicine right away. So Juliet expresses amazement that these two have become the "moral police" of the island, recapping all of their past crimes. She argues to be let go to help Claire, since they don't need even more blood on their hands. Juliet takes the medicine and heads back, injecting the medicine for Claire under Jack's supervision.

The medicine works and heals Claire, which results in Juliet being allowed to stay in camp for now. Still, they'll want answers soon enough. But Jack never needs them, as he explains that he knows she wants to leave the island more than anything, just like they do. That makes Juliet "one of us."

Main character: Juliet Burke.

Flashback details: Juliet and her sister Rachel head for the headquarters of Mittlos Bioscience, the Others front company. Juliet parts with Rachel, believing she'll be back in six months to see Rachel give birth. Richard Alpert and Ethan bring her inside, as Juliet starts to get second thoughts once they tell her to drink a tranquilizer for the trip. But Richard recaps how Juliet's research made her sister pregnant and how she can accomplish great things with them. This makes her drink up.

When she wakes up, she is inside the Others submarine, which has arrived on the island. She gets herself out and is greeted by Benjamin Linus, who gets her onto the dock and leads her into the island. This took place in September 2001.

Sometime later, Juliet fails to save a pregnant woman from dying and heads out in distress. Ben comes to comfort her, as Juliet states how pregnant women die on the island soon after conception. She offers to take them off the island for further testing, but Ben rules it out. Juliet tells him that since there's nothing else she can do, it's time for her to go home since her initial six month commitment is up.

Ben then informs her that Rachel's cancer has returned and she will soon die. Unless Juliet stays, in which case Ben will have her cancer cured, since no one on the island can get cancer. He explains that "Jacob" said he would take care of it.

On September 21, 2004, Juliet is lying in her bed with Goodwin. Afterwards, she is given some x-rays and becomes stunned. She rushes to Ben's house and tells him that his x-rays have returned, which confirm Ben has a fatal cancerous tumor on his spine.

Ben is in shock, which Juliet takes note of, since Ben told her no one could get cancer on the island. This makes Juliet convinced he also lied about curing Rachel's cancer. She angrily demands to speak to her, as Ben says Rachel is fine. Juliet breaks down in fury as she screams that Ben lied to her, but Ben, despite his fragile state, insists that he gave her his word. Juliet sobs and pleads for Ben to let her go, but he can only say no.

The next day, Juliet is seen once again in the opening scene from "A Tale Of Two Cities" as it is now clear that she was near tears because of Rachel. Once that full scene is replayed, Ben talks to Juliet after he sends Ethan and Goodwin away. He takes her to the Flame station, where

Mikhail has already found out the crashed plane is Oceanic 815. He has already started to make detailed files for every single passenger on board. But Ben is here to talk to Richard, who is off island in Miami.

A TV monitor shows a newspaper from September 22 in a Miami park. It then displays Rachel, who is alive and playing with a boy. Juliet starts to cry in joy as she looks on, while Ben explains that Rachel's cancer did disappear and she named her healthy baby boy "Julian." Juliet is even happier while Ben instructs Richard to come back, since the island has "new visitors." Mikhail turns off the monitor over Juliet's pleas.

Ben insists again that he is not a liar, but Juliet just asks once more to go home. However, she can't go until her work is finished, as they'll go through as many expectant mothers as possible until it is. Ben even remarks that there might be one on the plane.

One final flashback takes place in Ben's house. Juliet is asked to go over "the plan." She says she will take Kate into the jungle and handcuff them together, so she will be allowed to go back to the beach camp. Ben says that an implant in Claire has been activated to make her sick, just so Juliet can cure her and gain the trust of the survivors. Though Juliet looks a little uneasy, she insists she's fine. Ben gives her a gas mask and wheels off, saying "See you in a week."

Juliet is still working for Ben after all.

Important details in *Lost* lore: Juliet's time on the island is revealed. Pregnant women on the island have been dying, which Juliet was hired to fix. It is also the reason why Claire was abducted by Ethan in the first place. But all Juliet wants is to go home to her sister, which Ben has kept her from doing. The Others have found out everything about the survivors due to Mikhail's research. Juliet appears to have had a love affair with late Other Goodwin.

In the present, Juliet is integrated into the survivors' camp after saving Claire's life. However, the sickness was caused by Ben as part of a plan to plant Juliet in the camp. The purpose of this plan will be revealed in a week.

Amount of action: Heavy with information.

New important characters: None.

Connections between characters: Juliet meets the rest of the survivors for the first time, as Jack protects her from questioning. Juliet's past with the Others, Ben and Goodwin is revealed further.

***Lost* mysteries referenced:** Juliet's experience on the island, Claire's abduction, Jacob, why Juliet was left behind by the Others.

***Lost* mysteries introduced:** Why pregnant women die on the island, what Juliet and Ben's plans are for the camp.

Questions raised: Why is Juliet still working for Ben? Why does Ben want her in the camp? What will he be doing in a week? Could Jack really be this blind in trusting her? Will the other survivors ever be able to get answers out of her? Why do pregnant women die on the island? Does this mean Sun is in danger as well? Who is Jacob? Will Juliet ever see her sister again? Why did Ben get cancer on the island?

Talking points: More important answers are included in this episode than in any since "Live Together, Die Alone." In finally answering the purpose of Claire's kidnapping and the Others obsession with children, it still introduces even more questions. With this new mystery of pregnant women dying on the island, it also brings Sun into big trouble with her little growing miracle.

Juliet's flashbacks certainly put a lot of her actions into perspective. But even though her actions are done out of love for her sister, it is still very clear that she is capable of betraying anyone to get it done. She's even still working for Ben despite all her knowledge of his past lies. Will anyone be safe in Juliet's way, or is there a line she will not cross for her own desires?

Ben's claim of not being a liar has to be questioned. However, we saw in "The Man From Tallahassee" that he was afraid of the consequences of not keeping his word. Perhaps in his own mind, all his actions really aren't lies. At the least, he certainly wants Juliet to know he can keep his word. He even tried to do so in the midst of finding out he got cancer. But now we have another reason to ask why the island made Ben sick while it made Locke better.

Other key issues: Ethan has officially made more appearances after his death than he ever did while he was alive in Season One.

Must see episode?: An absolutely essential episode as major answers and major new plot lines are introduced. In addition, Juliet's ever growing legacy is assured, as we both fear and feel sorry for her in equal amounts throughout the entire show, powered by Elizabeth Mitchell's tour de force performance. After mixed episodes in the two weeks after "Man From Tallahassee" the show returns on its newest roll.

CATCH-22

For Desmond, his bad breaks and weird situations just keep on coming. More than almost any other *Lost* character, he is a pawn of fate and other forces beyond his comprehension. According to his last time traveling experience, he was always supposed to lose his beloved Penny, land on the island, push a button for three years, crash flight 815 and finally destroy the hatch. On top of all else, he has to deal with seeing Charlie die in various ways and narrowly stopping it. The man just cannot get a break from being used by some cosmic force.

But in this episode, Desmond finally comes to see some kind of hope and the possibility of a long awaited reunion. Of course he doesn't get exactly what he wants, but it does begin the show's most important plot line in a long time.

Episode plot: Desmond's newest future flash involves him, Charlie and Jin walking through the jungle. There, Charlie is killed when one of Rousseau's traps goes off and shoots an arrow in his neck. But Desmond then sees images of someone in flight gear and a helmet hanging in a tree. This convinces him that someone is coming to the island.

One other image he sees is Hurley pushing the underwater cable Sayid tripped over early in Season One. He gets Hurley, Charlie and Jin to come with him towards the cable. Charlie worries that he saw another vision of his death, but Desmond lies and says he didn't. They march to the cable and Hurley and Jin push it, so they set camp to see what happens next.

Charlie and Jin tell scary stories as Desmond looks at his photo of Penny, becoming convinced that she's the one he saw in the tree and she's here to save him. Just then, the group hears a helicopter and sees it crash into the water. However, they see a red light sailing through the sky and realize someone has parachuted onto the island. After some debate, they agree to go looking at daybreak.

The next morning, the group goes into the jungle and finds some debris. One of the items is the book *Catch-22*, which contains a copy of Desmond and Penny's photo inside. Desmond is now certain Penny is on the island, but also knows that according to his vision, Charlie dies during their trip.

Afraid that if he saves him, it won't be Penny after all, Desmond still keeps that part of the vision to himself. But when the time comes and Charlie steps on Rousseau's trap, he finally leaps into action at the last possible second and pushes Charlie clear of the arrow.

After they all recover, the groups split up with Charlie coming with Desmond. Charlie realizes Desmond knew all along what would happen, as Desmond explains that he had to follow the flashes perfectly or else the overall vision would change. As he questions the value of even saving Charlie time and again, Jin shouts out and the group reunites to see the parachutist stuck in the tree.

Desmond climbs up and cuts the figure loose, as the gang uses her parachute to catch her. Hurley soon hears the parachutist moan. Realizing she's alive, Desmond rushes over to take off her helmet, fully expecting it to be Penelope after all. Instead, it is a completely different woman.

However, the woman recognizes Desmond and says his name before passing out.

Other stuff: Kate settles back into camp and tries to talk with Jack at night. But he doesn't say too much, not even responding to Kate's intentional flirting. Once Kate sees Jack going to eat with Juliet instead, she rushes to Sawyer's tent and heatedly makes out with him, which Sawyer ultimately doesn't mind.

The next morning, Sawyer and Jack play a friendly game of ping pong, where Sawyer learns Jack was eating with Juliet just before Kate went to his tent. He realizes just why Kate "jumped him," later telling her that all she has to do is ask next time.

Main character: Desmond Hume.

Flashback details: Before Desmond even knew Penelope, he was training to be a monk in Scotland. He is ordained by Brother Campbell, who Desmond got his "brotha" catchphrase from. But Desmond's new existence is interrupted when a man comes by and punches him in the face. This man is the brother of Ruth, a girl who Desmond left a week before their wedding.

Desmond goes to visit Ruth, telling her that he got drunk out of fear, then Brother Campbell saw him on the street and asked if he could help. This made Desmond think he had a higher purpose and had to sacrifice everything for it. Ruth counters that he left because he was a coward.

Later one night, Desmond finds Brother Campbell drinking from a supply of wine they are packing. There, Campbell tells Desmond he isn't cut out to be a monk. Although Desmond does have a higher purpose, this isn't where he was meant to end up. Desmond is left at a loss at what to do next, planning to leave the next morning. He says goodbye to Brother Campbell, who offers that another monk can give him a ride home if he helps with a customer.

Outside, the wine crates are being loaded in the customer's car. The customer is Penelope Widmore, who Desmond meets for the first time. The two hit it off right away, as Penny invites Desmond to help her bring the crates to the town of Carlisle.

Important details in *Lost* lore: Desmond has a vision of a woman crashing on the island. Believing its Penny, he nearly lets Charlie die to make sure the vision comes true. The woman isn't Penny, but it's someone who knows Desmond and has a picture of him and Penny together. In the past, Desmond and Penny first meet right after he was fired as a monk.

Amount of action: Fair,

New important characters: Brother Campbell and the new woman who crash landed on the island.

Connections between characters: Desmond, Charlie, Hurley and Jin form a new search party, as Desmond narrowly saves Charlie from death again despite his reluctance. Kate literally jumps Sawyer's bones after Jack shows her no interest. In Brother Campbell's last scene, there is a picture of him and Ms. Hawking, the mysterious woman from Desmond's time traveling trip in "Flashes Before Your Eyes."

***Lost* mysteries referenced:** Desmond's visions, Charlie's potential death, the cable in the water.

***Lost* mysteries introduced:** The passed out woman and how she knows Desmond.

Questions raised: Why did a woman parachute onto the island? What was a helicopter doing near the island to begin with? How does this woman know Desmond? Will she recover in time to answer these questions? Did Desmond really change his vision of the future by saving Charlie?

Talking points: Although Locke has been labeled *Lost's* man of destiny from day one, it seems he might have some competition in Desmond. If his last two episodes are on the level, it seems he was only meant to be a monk long enough to meet Penny and fall in love. This in turn, made it necessary for him to leave her and stumble onto the island and the hatch.

The blink and you'll miss it connection between Brother Campbell and Ms. Hawking suggests even more hands of destiny and fate into Desmond's journey. Was he meant to be the major man of destiny all along, or is his destiny a wild card in this game we call *Lost*?

Desmond's fear that he literally changed Penny into this new mystery woman by saving Charlie does open some new cans of worms. But the show couldn't be that weird. Plus, it was made explicitly clear to Desmond in "Flashes" that fates could not be changed, since the universe course corrects itself every time. But if Desmond was only meant to be a monk long enough to find Penny, maybe he's meant to find this woman long enough to find Penny again.

Maybe it will at last bring back Season Two's final cliffhanger of Penelope possibly finding out where the island is, after such a long time of waiting for that to be explained.

Other key issues: Kate sets a brand new record of being indecisive between Jack and Sawyer, by literally doing it with Sawyer when she couldn't have Jack. It is not one of her prouder moments. But she's been having less and less of those this season.

Must see episode?: One of those episodes that sets the stage for some large events to come, but other than that, it doesn't have the mind blowing zeal of Desmond's last few flashbacks.

D.O.C

The episode "One Of Us" had very big revelations about the danger of pregnancy on the island. It made people realize that this offered very real danger for Sun, the island's latest pregnant woman. Back in Season Two, her pregnancy was seemingly introduced just to give her something else to do with Jin, but now it directly ties her to one of the island's biggest mysteries. Sun already has enough to fear, considering she doesn't know if Jin is the real father of her child. Now, not only could the answer end her marriage, it could determine whether she may face the end of her very life.

Episode plot: Sun is suspicious when Jack asks her a series of questions about her pregnancy. She now questions Jack's loyalty, considering the time he spent with the Others and his new connection with Juliet. Once Kate gives away that Juliet's a fertility doctor who did "research" on Claire's baby, Sun rushes to Juliet and demands to know what happens to the island's pregnant woman. Juliet simply replies that they all die.

That night, Juliet goes into Sun's tent and covers her mouth, telling her to come with her. She offers that there might be hope for her to live, but they have to go to the Others medical station. There, Juliet will determine when the baby was conceived. If it happened before she came to the island, she will live like Claire did. But if it was conceived on the island, she is likely to die. It also means the baby won't be Jin's if it was conceived off the island.

The two go inside a nursery room where all the pregnant mothers eventually died. Juliet desperately hopes to tell Sun that the baby will be fine, after having lost so many mothers and giving so much horrible news over the years. An ultrasound is set up, as Sun explains Jin was infertile and couldn't be the father. But Juliet counters that being on the island dramatically increases a man's sperm count, which could work in Jin's favor.

And it does, as it confirms the date of conception was 53 days ago, while she was on the island. Sun cries in happiness that the baby is Jin's, even though this also means she is likely to die.

The next morning, the women leave the station as Juliet explains that Sun has two months before her symptoms begin. Sun reassures Juliet that she gave her good news after all, since Jin really is the father. She thanks Juliet, who then goes back into the station. There, she makes a recording for Ben that Sun is pregnant, and she will work towards finding out if any other women are pregnant, including Kate. But after she turns off the recorder, Juliet sadly mutters, "I hate you" and leaves the recording in a locker.

Other stuff: Desmond, Hurley, Charlie and Jin try to figure out how to save the parachutist's life. There is a branch that has pierced her lung and is killing her. Desmond wants to run to get Jack, but it is too dangerous to run alone. Hurley winds up accidentally firing a flare gun as Desmond and Charlie keep arguing, then someone comes out of the bushes. It is Mikhail Bakunin, the Other who was supposed to have died in "Par Avion."

Jin chases after him and the two have a huge brawl, which Jin wins. They then overhear the woman talking in different languages, which Mikhail understands. He offers to help treat her, but in return, they have to let him go. Over Charlie's objections, Desmond agrees.

Mikhail is eventually able to take out the branch and treat the lung, mentioning that the injury should heal quickly thanks to the island. The woman tells Mikhail something in Portuguese, which Mikhail translates as a thank you, but fans figured out the correct translation was "I am not alone."

As Mikhail leaves, Jin finds that he has taken a satellite phone from the woman and catches him in time. Charlie yells that they can't let him go, but Desmond keeps his word and lets Mikhail head off. Charlie, Desmond and Jin then work on creating a stretcher to take the woman to camp.

Meanwhile, Hurley plays around with the satellite phone just as the woman wakes up. He introduces himself and says he's a survivor of flight 815. But the woman says that's impossible.

According to her, they found the plane at the bottom of the ocean. There were no survivors.

Hurley quietly asks "What?"

Main character: Sun.

Flashback details: In the early months of Sun and Jin's marriage, Sun encountered a woman who claimed to be Jin's mother. She believes Jin's parents are dead, but the woman demands $100,000 dollars or else she'll reveal that she's both Jin's mother and a prostitute.

Sun figures out where Jin's father really is and meets him. Mr. Kwon admits that Jin's mother was a prostitute who left Jin with him as a baby. Knowing that Jin hid that his father was alive out of shame because he's just a fisherman, Mr. Kwon tells Sun not to let Jin know about his mother either.

So Sun goes to her father, Mr. Paik, and asks for $100,000 with no questions asked. Otherwise, she will stop pretending about the kind of work her father really does. Mr. Paik agrees, but as a result, Jin has to repay the debt by working directly for him, which is how Jin became his enforcer.

When Jin finds the money one day, Sun claims that her father gave it to her for a honeymoon. But Jin asks for her to return it, saying he can provide for her and he doesn't want to owe Mr. Paik anything. Sun uneasily agrees, but later gives the money to Jin's mother. Sun warns her that although Jin merely thinks she is dead, she should not make that a reality.

Important details in *Lost* lore: Sun finally finds out that Jin is the father of her baby, but it also means she could be the latest pregnant woman to die on the island. It is shown that Jin became Mr. Paik's enforcer because Sun borrowed money from her father to pay off Jin's mother. Juliet's mission for Ben is to find out how many women in the camp are pregnant, though her loyalty to him has shaken. Mikhail returns and helps the parachutist recover. The woman then tells Hurley that flight 815's wreckage was found and all the survivors were found dead.

Amount of action: Fair.

New important characters: Jin's mother.

Connections between characters: Sun and Juliet are the main pair, as Juliet confirms Sun's date of conception and begins to regret her mission for Ben as a result. Desmond and Charlie fight again, this time over Mikhail.

***Lost* mysteries referenced:** The parachuting woman, who Sun's baby's father is, Sun's possible death via pregnancy, Juliet's undercover work for Ben.

***Lost* mysteries introduced:** The new woman's claim that flight 815 was already found and everyone is dead.

Questions raised: Will Sun be able to make it through her pregnancy? Now that she knows Jin is the father, will he ever find out that Sun was afraid he wasn't? How committed is Juliet to her mission now? How did Mikhail come back to life? Will sparing his life cause trouble later? What did the woman mean when she said everyone on flight 815 is dead?

Talking points: After spending almost three seasons convincing fans that the island was not purgatory, the creators just gave the theory new life with the parachutist's statement that the survivors are dead. At least they did for a few weeks.

The rabbit hole of Sun's lies and secrecy goes down to new heights, as it was her mission to pay off Jin's mother that began Jin's future brutal life. More and more, it looks like Sun was reaping what she sowed in her past, although she dodged a bullet about her baby's father thanks to Juliet. Other than the fact her life's in danger now.

Mikhail makes a comeback and raises new questions about the island's healing powers. Yet Ben's tumor remains a glaring exception. Does the island get to pick and choose who is made better?

Other key issues: Jin almost rivals Sayid in kicking someone's butt, as proven by his fight scene with Mikhail.

Must see episode?: Yes, though most of the strength comes through the character work between Sun and Juliet. But it is a little less necessary in furthering other key mysteries. However, the really big stuff is on its way as the season hits May sweeps.

THE BRIG

The island tends to make people confront the horrible things in their past. However, rarely has it done so as specifically as it has for Locke. Days ago, Ben showed them that the Others had Anthony Cooper, the father who hurt Locke in so many physical and emotional ways. Now Locke is about to see if he can take his revenge for it, and whether he can take his first steps towards finding out what the island really is as a result.

But even if he doesn't, he comes to find out that there is someone else he knows that could. Someone that has even more of a reason to do it than Locke does, though he doesn't know it yet. But he will.

We will start off with some on island Locke flashbacks.

Main character: John Locke.

Flashback details: Seconds after Locke finds Anthony Cooper tied up and gagged, Ben claims that Locke brought him here. Locke ungags Cooper and he bites him, saying "Don't you know where we are?" Locke is led out and Ben gets him to agree to come with them to a new campsite.

Days later, the Others are all outside in tents with Locke, who has attracted a lot of attention. Locke goes to see Ben, who tells him about his plan to take the pregnant women from the beach. He then gets out of his wheelchair, now able to walk with a cane ever since Locke arrived. Ben says he wants to show him the island's secrets, but first Locke has to make a gesture of free will by killing Cooper.

That night, Ben wakes up Locke and brings him to Cooper, tied outside to a large pillar. Ben hands Locke a knife and tells him to kill Cooper, who taunts that Locke is too spineless to do it. Locke raises his knife, but despite Ben's goading, he finally can't do it. Ben knocks Cooper out with his cane and tells the audience of Others that Locke isn't who they thought he was.

The next day, Locke sits on a hill overlooking the camp as Richard Alpert comes to greet him. Richard explains that Ben knew he wouldn't kill Cooper. All he wanted was for Locke to fail so that the Others wouldn't believe Locke was special. The news about Locke's newfound ability to walk had made the Others remember their larger purposes on the island. Richard further argues that Ben is wasting their time with his fertility obsession and other "novelties."

Richard would like to help Locke realize his greater purpose, but to do that Cooper has to die. Since Locke can't do it, Richard gives him the file of a man who might. Locke is surprised to see that this is a file of Sawyer, not understanding why Richard would give him this until he keeps reading.

A day later, Ben and the Others are leaving the camp. However, Locke and Cooper are not going with them. Locke says he can't do this, but Ben uses Locke's famous "Don't tell me what I can't do" line right back at him. They will leave a trail for Locke to track, but he shouldn't bother unless he has Cooper's body with him.

Episode plot: Sawyer heads outside to pee at night, where Locke is waiting for him. He says that he's been working undercover all along, as he has just captured Ben. He wants Sawyer to kill him, which takes him aback. Locke brings up that Sawyer's killed a man before, which makes Sawyer follow him.

The next morning, Locke explains that he read the Others file on Sawyer, asking him about what happened to his family and why Sawyer chose his name. This makes Sawyer attack Locke, yelling that he won't be conned by him. He demands to know why Locke can't kill Ben himself, to which Locke can only cry out that he can't.

Sawyer argues that they're going to take Ben back to camp and he won't kill him. Locke insists that when he hears what Ben has to say, he'll change his mind.

Locke takes Sawyer to the Black Rock ship, as it seems he has Ben locked in the brig. Sawyer goes inside and sees a man in chains with a bag over his head. Just then Locke locks Sawyer inside.

As Sawyer yells to be let out, he takes off the captive man's bag and sees it's not Ben, but Anthony Cooper. Locke stands guard outside, while Rousseau shows out of nowhere and takes some of the ship's remaining dynamite.

In the brig, Cooper starts talking and tells Sawyer that Locke is his son. He explains that while he was driving in Tallahassee, a car crashed into him and the next thing he knew, he was on the island. But he believes this is Hell, since Locke is walking again and the rest of the world believes him and everyone on Oceanic 815 died months ago. If this isn't Hell, "then where are we?" Cooper asks.

Once Cooper mentions he conned Locke out of his kidney, Sawyer takes an interest and asks for his name. Cooper mentions the various con names he's used, one of which is Tom Sawyer.

Now it finally dawns on Sawyer who this man really is.

Sawyer asks if Cooper's been to Jasper, Alabama, which he confirms. With that, Sawyer gets out the letter he wrote as a kid to the "Sawyer" who destroyed his family. He asks Cooper to read it, but he only gets halfway through. Once Sawyer mentions his mothers' name, Cooper remembers her.

This is the final proof that Anthony Cooper is the same con man who Sawyer has looked for all his life.

Sawyer now screams for Cooper to finish reading his letter, but he tears it to pieces. In blind fury, Sawyer takes Cooper's chains and wraps them around his neck until he finally collapses, dead for real. When it's over, Locke comes in and thanks Sawyer.

Sawyer heads outside to vomit. Locke goes on to tell him that Juliet works for Ben, who plans to capture the pregnant women. He hands him Juliet's recording for Ben, which Sawyer can use as evidence against her. But Locke is going back to the Others, on his own path to find out the truth about the island.

Sawyer asks if Locke was really a cripple, to which Locke says "Not any more." Locke then takes a bag with his dead father's body in it and leaves to find Ben.

Other stuff: Desmond, Charlie, Hurley and Jin are hiding the parachutist in a tent, away from Jack since they don't trust him anymore. But they bring the more trustworthy Sayid into the loop so he can ask her why she's here.

The woman's name is Naomi, as she claims she was hired by Penelope Widmore's company. She was on a freighter that was ordered to go to specific coordinates, even though there appeared to be no land there. She found the island on her helicopter and then bailed out before it crashed.

Her freighter is 80 miles off shore, but her satellite phone doesn't work well enough for her to contact it. She also confirms that the remains of what looked to be Oceanic 815 were found in an underwater trench weeks ago. Obviously it was a fake.

As Sayid tries to work the satellite phone, Kate oversees him and finds out the truth. Sayid tells her not to tell Jack, but she does the exact opposite. She finds Jack and Juliet sitting together and tells them about Naomi, informing Jack that no one else trusted him because of Juliet. All Juliet says is "We should tell her" but whatever they have to say, Jack says "Not yet."

Important details in *Lost* lore: Locke's recent time with the Others is revealed, as he fails to kill his father. But he learns from Richard Alpert that Anthony Cooper is the same con man that conned Sawyer's parents' decades ago, so he gets Sawyer to kill him. Ben has plans to capture the pregnant women on the island. Naomi reveals the existence of a freighter that can rescue the survivors. Jack and Juliet are working on some kind of secret plan.

Amount of action: Heavy.

New important characters: None.

Connections between characters: Locke and Sawyer are both connected due to the pain Anthony Cooper has caused both their lives. Richard Alpert seems to go behind Ben's back to help Locke. Jack loses the trust of many more survivors due to his relationship with Juliet.

***Lost* mysteries referenced:** Locke's recent activities, Sawyer's search for "Sawyer", Naomi the parachutist.

***Lost* mysteries introduced:** Jack and Juliet's plans, Ben's scheme to capture the pregnant women, Naomi's freighter, Locke's mission to make Ben reveal the secrets of the island.

Questions raised: What will Locke find out now that he's killed his father? Why didn't Ben want people to believe Locke was special, as Richard claims? Now that Sawyer's life long quest is over, what will become of him? What are Jack and Juliet up to? Can Jack restore his good name with the survivors? Why did Rousseau stop by the Black Rock to get dynamite? Is rescue possible?

Talking points: Another long suspected answer has come true, as Anthony Cooper is indeed Sawyer's "Sawyer" as some suspected since Season One. But it doesn't make Sawyer's long awaited confrontation with him any less brutal. Of course, since Cooper thought he was already dead, that probably gave him more room to be more psychotic than usual.

For the first time, we get a sense that Ben's position as leader is less stable than it looks, if Richard can be believed. The comparisons between Ben and Locke may now go beyond Locke being healed by the island and Ben getting a tumor. Perhaps Ben's throne has become a little up for grabs now.

If it's May sweeps, it's time to tease the possibility of the survivors getting rescued again. This really should be impossible, since the show would end if that happens and it can't end now.

Other key issues: Ben may not be physically imposing, but he can certainly smack people around with batons and canes.

Must see episode?: Yes, as it gets the ball rolling for one of the most important series of episodes in the show's history.

THE MAN BEHIND THE CURTAIN

It cannot be overstated how crucial the addition of Benjamin Linus was to *Lost.* Not only did it give the show its major villain, it got us into the world of the Others and even further into the history of the island. But although we have a greater idea of the Others past and history, we still don't have one of the DHARMA Initiative, whom the Others supposedly wiped out. To fix that, we have Ben to thank yet again as his long awaited first flashback episode goes back to his island childhood and the days of DHARMA.

After a season of waiting, it was time to find out what made Ben into the scheming genius he is today…at least some of what made him that. And while meeting young Ben and young DHARMA, we got to know someone named Jacob as well.

Episode plot: Ben sits in his tent staring wistfully at a wooden doll, as it is his birthday today. But he's interrupted when Locke returns with Cooper's body, wanting Ben to tell him everything about the island.

As they meet in his tent, Ben is more reluctant. He explains that he really isn't the leader of the Others, as instead it is a man named Jacob. However, Jacob only talks to Ben and no one else has ever seen him, which convinces Locke that Ben is a liar equivalent to the Wizard of Oz.

Mikhail rushes into camp, informing Ben of Naomi and her arrival to the island. Ben offers to deal with it during their mission to capture the pregnant women, but Locke interrupts to say he and Ben are going to see Jacob. To illustrate this point, he beats up Mikhail when he objects, leaving Ben no choice but to take him. Alex later gives Locke a gun and sarcastically wishes Ben a happy birthday.

That night, Ben and Locke approach a circle of volcanic ash. Inside this circle is an eerie, small, dilapidated cabin. Ben lights a lamp and warns Locke that there's no turning back, but Locke just steps forward. So Ben opens the door and the two go into the light free cabin. Ben goes next to an empty chair and says "Jacob, this is John."

But Locke can't see anyone in the chair.

Ben continues to speak to, and argue with, the chair as if someone was sitting there. Locke is convinced Ben is crazy and really knows nothing about the island. Ben maintains there's someone there, but Locke turns to leave. Just as he opens the door, he hears a gravelly voice slowly say "Help me..."

Locke asks Ben what he said, but Ben claims he didn't say anything. As Locke lifts up the lamp, the room shakes and many items are thrown around and destroyed. Ben rushes to the chair and is pushed back by something unseen…but Locke very briefly sees a man sitting there after all. He rushes out and Ben joins him a minute later.

The next morning, when Ben asks what Jacob said, Locke maintains that Ben was putting on a show for him and he's a fraud. Ben then admits that some of what he's said isn't true, including that he wasn't born on the island. So he takes Locke to show where he did come from.

They arrive at a pit filled with skeletons of dead DHARMA Initiative workers. Ben says that these are his people, who had to go when they couldn't co-exist with the island's original inhabitants. Ben was one of those smart enough not to end up in that ditch, which makes him smarter than Locke.

Realizing what that means, Locke turns to attack, but Ben shoots him. He falls in the pit, then Ben again asks what Jacob said to him. Locke tells him that he said "Help me" which shocks Ben. He hisses to Locke that he hopes Jacob helps him, leaving him to cling to life in the pit.

Other stuff: Sawyer returns to camp and hands Sayid the tape Locke gave him, which proves Ben and Juliet are working together to take the camp's pregnant women. By then, the whole camp now knows about Naomi and her freighter.

That night, they all discuss this before Jack and Juliet come by. Jack then reveals that Juliet told her of Ben's plan a few days ago, which he didn't reveal because he hadn't figured out what to do about it yet. So Jack admits that they have some catching up to do.

Main character: Ben Linus.

Flashback details: In the early 1960's, a woman named Emily is giving birth prematurely in a jungle. Her husband Roger helps her give birth, but she still looks sick. He takes her to a road, as they are actually 32 miles from Portland. A car stops near them and another couple, Horace and Olivia Goodspeed, try to help them. But Emily slips away, right after she tells Roger to name the newborn boy Benjamin.

Years later, the young Benjamin Linus arrives with his father to the island, which is occupied by the DHARMA Initiative. Horace Goodspeed is a DHARMA member who has gotten Roger Linus a job on the island. However, Roger is only hired as a "workman" as young Ben meets a girl named Annie.

Ben is then seen at a DHARMA school taught by Olivia Goodspeed. Their lesson is interrupted by a siren and gunshots. Ben and the children duck and cover as Olivia exits the room with a gun. Roger is in this crossfire of an attack by the island's "natives." That night, Ben hears his father lash out at Horace, then goes to his room and sees his dead mother standing outside for a brief moment.

On Ben's birthday, Annie gives him the present of a wooden doll representing her, while Annie keeps a wooden doll representing Ben, so they "never have to be apart." But Ben's father forgets his birthday, as he is drunk. Roger tells Ben that he killed his mother by being born so early, which left Roger stuck on the island with him.

Ben runs out in tears and heads to the sonar fence around the barracks. He once again sees his mother, now behind the fence, but she tells him "It's not time yet" as Ben cries for her.

The next day, Ben turns off the fence and heads into the jungle. He is met by Richard Alpert, who aside from having longer hair, does not look any different than he does in the present day. Ben says he is looking for his mother even though she's supposed to be dead.

Richard actually seems to believe him and takes great interest in his story. Ben then pleads for Richard to let him join his people. Richard says that it may be possible, but Ben has to be very patient.

Years later, Ben is an adult and a DHARMA workman himself. On the day of his birthday, he puts Annie's doll in his pocket and goes to join his father at work. Roger offers to take Ben out for a drive in his van before they go deliver beer to the Pearl station.

Once they park, Ben asks his dad if he really blames him for his mother's death, but he has no real answer. Ben keeps looking at his watch as Roger promises to remember his birthday next year.

However, Ben says that won't happen, recounting how he's had to put up with his father all these years. To him, doing so required a lot of patience. Ben then puts on a gas mask and sets off a canister of poisonous gas. It kills Roger as Ben sits still, unable to directly look at his father die.

Ben returns to the barracks and sees that every DHARMA worker has died from more poison gas attacks. He stops to see Horace Goodspeed's body, then closes Horace's eyes. The rest of the Others and Richard appear with gas masks and guns. Ben instructs them to leave his father's body in the van. With that, the DHARMA Initiative has been purged from the island.

Important details in *Lost* lore: Ben's mother died giving birth to him. Years later, he arrived on the island when his father worked for DHARMA, but his dad was a drunk who blamed Ben for his mother's death. Ben's only friend as a child was a girl named Annie. Ben first found the Others after he saw visions of his dead mother. Richard Alpert is seen looking almost the same age in the past as he does in the present.

Years later, Ben helps the Others destroy DHARMA and kills his father as part of "The Purge." The VW van Hurley found in "Tricia Tanaka Is Dead" is the same one where Ben killed his dad years ago, as Roger Linus's skeleton was the one in the van.

In the present, Ben introduces Locke to the Others true leader, Jacob, whom only Ben can see. But Locke eventually hears Jacob call for help. In response, Ben shoots Locke and leaves him for dead. Juliet has told Jack of Ben's plans for the island's pregnant women, which has made Jack come up with a secret plan.

Amount of action: Heavy.

New important characters: Roger and Emily Linus, Horace and Olivia Goodspeed, Annie, Jacob.

Connections between characters: Ben's past family life is shown, while in the present, he faces off with Locke and later tries to kill him. The survivors continue to distrust Jack, who has been keeping secrets of his own.

***Lost* mysteries referenced:** The DHARMA Initiative, Ben's past, the Purge, Jacob, Jack and Juliet's plans, the old DHARMA van.

***Lost* mysteries introduced:** Young Ben's visions of his mother, Richard Alpert's true age, Ben's friendship with Annie and relationship with Horace Goodspeed, Ben's past with the Others, the nature of Jacob, Locke's shooting.

Questions raised: Who or what is Jacob? Why is Ben the only one that can see him? Why did Jacob say "Help me" to Locke? Will Locke survive? Is Ben losing his favor with the Others? What was the history between the DHARMA Initiative and the Others? Why did young Ben see his dead mother? What happened between the day Ben first met Richard and the day of the Purge? Was the Purge Ben's idea? What was Ben's relationship with Horace Goodspeed? Is Richard unable to age? What became of Ben's friendship with Annie? What is Jack and Juliet's plan to stop the Others?

Talking points: This was our first hints at Ben's past and his back story. And yet, there are so many more questions left about it than there are answers, much like Ben himself. Yet in the end, it seems so much could have been avoided if Ben didn't have a bad father, like 70% of the *Lost* characters.

Did Ben really see his mother on the island, or did the island create these visions for him? Is he some kind of chosen one? The idea of someone seeing a dead person certainly didn't seem to faze Richard in his first meeting with Ben. This only raises even more unanswered questions about who the Others were back then, and about their war with DHARMA that Ben helped them win.

The most glaring unanswered plot point was Annie, who gave Ben a birthday gift which he still carries around to this day. How important is she to the gap of years between young and adult Ben?

As for Jacob, he gives *Lost* another excuse to reference *The Wizard of Oz,* whom Locke compares Ben to. The wizard was the man behind the curtain, as Locke believes Ben to be. But if Jacob is indeed real, then he would be the real man behind the curtain after all.

Other key issues: Michael Emerson's real life wife, Carrie Preston, played Ben's mother in the flashback scenes. This is an Oedipal occurrence which resulted from some jokes Emerson made that Preston, who was a big *Lost* fan from day one, should play his mom in a flashback.

Must see episode?: Unbelievably important to the past of Ben, DHARMA, the Others and the island, as well as the present with Jacob and his scary cabin. Do not miss this one.

GREATEST HITS

Nearly everyone who's ever lived has wondered how they would like to die, what they've achieved and what they would like to accomplish before death. For Charlie, these questions have become necessities since Desmond warned of his coming demise. But instead of making a bucket list, Charlie looks back on his life instead as he finally realizes how and why it must end. Whereas he has narrowly avoided death before, now his departure could mean the salvation of Claire and his friends, which is a better way to die than he hoped. However, Ben and the Others still have a say in the whole thing.

Episode plot: Jack has taken the survivors to the middle of the island. He admits he knew about the Others plan to capture the pregnant women, but instead of running away again, this time they will fight back.

With help from Rousseau, they have gotten dynamite from the Black Rock to use on the Others. Juliet will mark the tents on the beach, and when the Others go to the tents to take the women, they will find dynamite instead that will "blow them all to hell."

Meanwhile, Sayid is working on how to contact Naomi's freighter. Rousseau's 16-year-old distress call is blocking the signal and must be turned off at a radio tower. However, Juliet explains that Ben has blocked all transmissions from the island, at an underwater station called The Looking Glass.

Charlie discovers Desmond's latest flash. This time, he has seen Claire and Aaron getting into a helicopter and getting rescued. But for that to happen, Charlie must go to a hatch, flick a switch next to a yellow light and drown. Desmond says that this time, Charlie has to die to ensure rescue.

Sayid uses Mikhail's maps to find the Looking Glass's underwater location. Someone will have to swim down, enter through a pool and turn off the transmission. Ben had told Juliet that the station was flooded, so this would be a suicide mission. Charlie overhears this and realizes this is what Desmond talked about, so he volunteers. But Jack overrules him, focused on the Others.

Soon after, Karl is seen running onto the beach, trying to warn them about the Others attack. The survivors had thought they were going to attack tomorrow, but Karl warns that they're coming right now. Hours earlier, Ben returned to his camp after shooting Locke and ordered his people to attack the camp tonight. Alex overheard this and told Karl, who she had hidden in the jungle, to warn the survivors. With that, the survivors plan must be altered.

Sayid, Jin and Bernard will have to stay behind and shoot the dynamite when the Others approach it. Jack plans to take everyone else to the radio tower, giving Charlie the task of swimming down to the Looking Glass after all. He goes to see Claire and takes one last look at Aaron, then tells Claire not to worry about him. They share a brief kiss before Charlie heads away.

Charlie and Desmond then make their plans to canoe into the ocean, as Hurley volunteers to go. Fearful that Hurley will see his death, Charlie says he's too fat and can't come. But Charlie then gives him a final hug goodbye. After Hurley leaves, Charlie and Desmond swim out. When they get to the right position, Charlie hands Desmond his "Greatest Hits" list, which lists the five greatest moments of his "sorry excuse for a life."

Desmond now volunteers to go down in Charlie's place, thinking he's supposed to do so all along. As he prepares to go, Charlie knocks him out with the oar, knowing it really has to be him. Charlie dives underwater and finds the large Looking Glass station, swimming to the pool. The hatch isn't flooded after all, as Charlie pulls himself to the surface and screams that he's alive.

Just them, two women enter the area and point their guns at Charlie.

Main character: Charlie Pace.

Flashback details: The five greatest moments of Charlie's life are shown. Number 5 is the first time he and Liam heard "You All Everybody" on the radio.

Number 4 features Charlie as a young boy, as his father teaches him to swim in a public pool.

Number 3 is a Christmas morning where Liam gives him the Pace family heirloom ring as a gift.

Number 2 is the time Charlie saved a woman's life from a mugger. That woman is Sayid's lost love Nadia, who calls Charlie a hero.

Number 1 is the first time Charlie met Claire after the plane crash, as Charlie writes it was "The night I met you."

Important details in *Lost* lore: Charlie is now likely to die from turning off a jamming signal from the Looking Glass underwater station. This will allow Jack and the survivors to call Naomi's freighter and get rescued, after they turn off Rousseau's distress call at the radio tower. But Ben orders the Others to attack the camp now, as Sayid, Jin and Bernard are left to blow them up with dynamite. Charlie now appears to be taken prisoner by women inside the Looking Glass.

Amount of action: Fair.

New important characters: The women at the Looking Glass.

Connection between characters: Charlie says his last goodbyes to Claire, Aaron and Hurley. Jack and Sayid clash over their various plans. Alex, now officially working against her father, has Karl warn the survivors about the Others. Charlie is revealed to have saved Nadia years ago.

***Lost* mysteries referenced:** Charlie's possible death, Naomi's freighter, the Others upcoming attack and Jack's plans to fight them.

***Lost* mysteries introduced:** The Looking Glass, Jack and the survivors road to the radio tower, the fate of the dynamite plan, Charlie's capture.

Questions raised: Will Charlie die, and if so, will his death lead to the survivors rescue? Will these women in the Looking Glass stop him? Will the dynamite plan work? Will Jack and company make contact with the freighter? Will Ben discover Alex and Juliet's betrayals?

Talking points: In essence, this was Charlie's farewell episode. Usually characters get big, final flashbacks on the episode that they die, although Charlie was still alive at the end here. But killing Charlie right before the season finale wouldn't be big enough.

Like Desmond, Charlie is now motivated by love, in the hopes that Claire and Aaron will be rescued due to his sacrifice. All of Desmond's visions have come true and helped Desmond stop Charlie's previous deaths. So could this one, the one that really counts, be any less accurate?

Sayid once again proves to be more of a stable and smart leader than Jack, as he sets him straight on his priorities. Yet Jack is still the one unofficially in charge.

Other key issues: Sayid's hint to Alex in "The Man From Tallahassee" that her mother isn't dead seems to have really made her think, as she now wonders if Ben's her real father. It seems she got suspicious at just the right time.

Must see episode?: It serves as the bridge to the big finale, though not as huge and mind blowing as the previous two episodes. Still, the stage is set to change *Lost* history.

THROUGH THE LOOKING GLASS

So now it comes to this, yet another *Lost* season finale. However, one would have to wonder beforehand how thrilling it could be. The Others and Ben would probably be defeated, yet the survivors couldn't be rescued by Naomi's freighter at this early stage. After all the events of last week's show, it was almost a foregone conclusion that Charlie would die. Plus the episode was labeled a Jack flashback, which seemed very puzzling. His flashbacks were getting extremely old and repetitive, so what would a two hour Jack flashback have to tell us about him that we didn't know?

Oh, what we did not know.

The second half of the season had gotten fans back and erased the year's poor start, but people still didn't know what they were in for with this episode. New shocking answers and clues were finally coming at a steady pace, but no one knew the bombshells yet to come. Unless they had read Internet spoilers, no one in the *Lost* fandom could have expected what was to come here.

What was to come? Nothing less than the twist that ensured *Lost* would return on top for good.

Episode plot: Jack and the survivors head off to go to the radio tower, while Sayid, Jin and Bernard stay to carry out the attack on the

Others. In the Looking Glass, Charlie is being beaten and interrogated by Greta and Bonnie, two women working in the station.

After Charlie talks about Juliet's betrayal of the Others, the women contact Ben and tell him everything. Stunned, Ben orders Mikhail to go to the Looking Glass. However, Ben can't contact the attacking Others to warn them, due to radio silence.

The team of attacking Others have already arrived at the beach. When they get to the marked tents, Sayid and Bernard shoot their guns and blow the tents up, killing seven Others. Jin's shot misses, as he is captured by the Others and they get Sayid and Bernard. In the distance, the survivors are worried that they only heard two explosions, but Jack says to keep going.

When Ben finds out what happened at the beach, he tells Tom to kill Jin so that Sayid and Bernard will talk. Bernard finally cracks, confessing that Karl warned the survivors about the attack. He also gives away the plan to go to the radio station and make contact with Naomi's freighter. As Ben realizes Alex betrayed him as well, he informs Tom not to kill the captives yet.

The next morning, Ben orders Richard to take the remaining Others to "The Temple" while he goes to find Jack. He invites Alex to go with him, also proclaiming that he's going to talk Jack out of calling the freighter.

In the ocean, Desmond awakes just as Mikhail starts shooting at him from the beach. Desmond dives underwater and swims to the Looking Glass. Charlie then distracts Greta and Bonnie long enough for Desmond to hide. Mikhail then swims up and is surprised to see the women. There, he finds out for the first time that the Looking Glass wasn't flooded, as well as its use to jam all transmissions.

Mikhail calls Ben, who frantically explains that the island is under its greatest threat in years, which is why he had to lie to everyone. Ben orders Mikhail to kill Charlie and the women so that the jamming signal will remain on.

In the jungle, Kate tells Sawyer they should go back for Sayid, Jin and Bernard, but he doesn't have much of a reaction. She realizes Sawyer has been withdrawn since he returned from his trip with Locke. However, Sawyer later volunteers himself to go back to the beach without Kate.

Juliet wants to go too, saying she knows where to find guns. Before she goes, she kisses Jack on the lips. Juliet and Sawyer leave, though there is no supply of guns. Hurley rushes after them, wanting to help, but Sawyer argues that he'll just get in the way and leaves him behind.

Ben is now close by, as he tells Alex that he's giving her away to the survivors. She asks why he can't just let them leave the island, but he only answers "Because I can't."

Locke is then seen in the DHARMA pit for the first time since he was shot. He can't move his legs, which makes him convinced he is paralyzed again. Locke takes a gun and is ready to shoot himself, but he sees a shocking sight standing over him. Walt is now standing next to the pit. He tells Locke he can walk and instructs him to get up, saying he has work to do. A relieved Locke smiles widely.

As Jack's team continues on their trek, he tells Kate for the first time that he loves her. Soon after, he finds Ben standing in front of the group, inviting Jack to talk. He goes off with Ben by himself.

Ben starts by saying that Naomi is not who she says she is. Instead, she represents "the bad guys" who have been trying to find the island. If Jack calls her freighter, everyone on the island will be killed. So Ben tells Jack to get Naomi's satellite phone and give it to him. When Jack refuses, Ben takes his walkie and radios the beach to confirm that Sayid, Jin and Bernard are held at gunpoint. Unless Ben calls them back in one minute, the Others will kill them. But Ben won't call the Others unless Jack gives him the phone.

Jack still announces he's getting everyone off the island, as Ben taunts that Jack has nothing to go back to. But Jack lets Ben's countdown go to zero, after which three shots are heard. Believing that his friends are dead, Jack tackles Ben and beats him mercilessly. He radios Tom to tell him he's going to get everyone rescued, then come back and kill him.

In the Looking Glass, Mikhail kills Greta and wounds Bonnie, then Desmond emerges from a locker and shoots Mikhail with a spear gun. He gets Charlie free and they go to a dying Bonnie, as Charlie asks her to give him the code to turn off the signal. Bonnie finally confesses that the code is set to the tune of "Good Vibrations" having been programmed by a musician.

Jack drags Ben back to the survivors, ordering him to be tied up. Alex then finally meets her real mother, Rousseau, for the first time. She tearfully holds Alex and asks for help in tying Ben up.

On the beach, it turns out Ben only ordered the Others to fire bullets into the sand, as Sayid, Jin and Bernard are still alive. Sawyer and Juliet are nearby as they try to figure out a plan, but then they hear an engine. Hurley drives the VW van into the beach, running over an Other. Sawyer and Juliet rush in and free their friends, killing the remaining Others except for Tom, who surrenders. But Sawyer shoots him in the chest, exacting his revenge for Tom's attack on the raft in "Exodus." Hurley then contacts Jack, who now realizes his friends are alive after all, as the survivors rejoice.

Charlie goes into the Looking Glass communications room and plays "Good Vibrations" on the control pad, turning off the signal. Just then, an incoming transmission begins to come through. Charlie looks on the monitor and sees a woman trying to make contact. That woman is Penelope Widmore.

Charlie says he's a survivor of 815 and tells her that Desmond is alive. He asks about Naomi and the freighter, but Penelope doesn't know what he means. This means she doesn't know Naomi after all.

Outside, Desmond sees Mikhail's body is gone, then Charlie sees Mikhail outside the window and in the water. Smiling sadistically, Mikhail holds up a hand grenade and activates it. He blows himself up, which destroys the window and results in the room starting to flood. But Desmond is rushing in, having seen Penny on the monitor. To save Desmond's life, Charlie locks himself in.

As more water rushes into the locked room, Charlie takes out his pen, frantically trying to write a message on his hand. Once he sinks underwater, Charlie holds up his hand to the door window, showing Desmond the message "Not Penny's boat." Desmond sadly gets the message as Charlie finally drowns.

Back on the island, Naomi sees a green light on her phone, which means the jamming signal is off. All they have to do is turn off Rousseau's call and she can contact the freighter. The survivors finally reach the radio tower and do just that. Naomi goes back outside to get a signal as Ben, now tied to a tree, makes one last desperate plea for Jack to stop. To him, making the call is "the beginning of the end!"

But Jack is no longer listening to Ben, as Naomi finally gets a signal...then a knife is thrown into her back. John Locke shows himself as the man responsible.

Locke pulls out a gun and orders Jack not to pick up Naomi's phone. Jack does it anyway, telling Locke he's done keeping him on the island. Locke threatens to shoot, but he can't do it. He can only quietly plead that Jack isn't supposed to do this. But Jack makes the call anyway, getting through to a man named Minkowski. Jack says he is a survivor of Oceanic 815 as Locke slips away.

Minkowski says they'll be right over, as the survivors celebrate that they will be rescued and Jack smiles in tearful joy.

Main character: Jack Shephard.

Flashback details: Jack has a heavy beard as he flies on an Oceanic plane. He reads an obituary that later causes him to cry in his car. He calls someone to talk about it, but gets no answer. So Jack goes to a nearby bridge, steps on a ledge and is about to jump, whispering "Forgive me." But before he jumps, a car crash occurs behind him, so Jack rushes to the scene to save the day.

Jack is later treated at the hospital, where he has an uneasy reunion with his now pregnant ex-wife. Later, he's at the bedside of the woman he saved from the crash, while taking some pills. Jack is instructed to go home, though he wanted to do the surgery.

Soon afterwards, Jack drives to a funeral home, after again failing to contact the person he's trying to get a hold of. He enters the home and sees he's the only one there. When he's asked if the dead man was friend or family, Jack says "Neither." But he almost breaks down again standing over the coffin. Still, Jack doesn't open it as he realizes he's out of pills.

Jack tries to get a refill using his father's prescription. When the man behind him recognizes Jack and calls him a hero, Jack storms off. He later breaks into the hospital to get more pills, but is discovered by the head doctor. Jack is then questioned about just how he got to the car crash so quickly. He then goes on an out of control rant, asking the doctor to call his father and see if Jack is drunker than he is. Jack leaves while rambling that no one can help him.

Finally, Jack is seen in his wreck of a home, with maps and atlases everywhere. He finally gets a hold of the person he wants to see, as they agree to meet at the airport. Jack goes to the airport gate and sees a car coming. The person driving it then gets out.

It is Kate Austin.

Jack asks her if she went to the funeral, but Kate asks why she would want to go. Jack goes on to talk about how he's been using a Golden Pass from Oceanic to fly every Friday night across the Pacific Ocean. There, he actually prays that he'll crash so that he can "go back."

And now it has become clear what this scene is.

This is not a flashback.

It's a flash forward.

In the future, Jack and Kate have gotten off the island. But Jack is "sick of lying" and says that they were not supposed to leave.

Kate's eyes well up, as she says she needs to go home or "he's" going to wonder where she is. She says goodbye to Jack and drives away in tears, as Jack makes one final plea.

"We have to go back, Kate.....we have to go BACK!!!"

Important details in *Lost* lore: The Others plan to attack the beach fails as they all get killed, including Tom. Ben tries to convince Jack not to call Naomi's freighter, since she's one of "the bad guys" who Ben says will kill everyone on the island. Walt returns to see Locke, telling him he has work to do. Alex and Rousseau are finally reunited.

Charlie turns off the Looking Glass jamming signal, then receives a call from Penelope Widmore, who confirms Naomi was not hired by her. Mikhail finally kills Charlie by blowing himself up in the ocean and flooding the room, as Charlie writes a final message to Desmond that it's "Not Penny's Boat." Jack manages to contact them anyway, as Locke kills Naomi but fails to stop Jack.

But the episode's flashback is a flash forward, as a bearded, drunken Jack mourns a dead man he knew, and wants to find the island again to fix his "mistake."

Amount of action: Heavy.

New important characters: None.

Connections between characters: Charlie and Desmond work together one last time, though it doesn't stop Mikhail from killing Charlie. Jack pummels Ben when he believes his friends on the beach were killed. Jack shares a kiss with Juliet, although he later tells Kate he loves her. In the future, Jack and Kate are estranged, as Kate is living with someone else and doesn't want to go back to the island.

***Lost* mysteries referenced:** Naomi's freighter, Walt, Locke's fate, the Looking Glass, Charlie's potential death, the radio tower.

***Lost* mysteries introduced:** "The Temple" that Ben sent Richard and the remaining Others to. Who Naomi's freighter really works for. Who Ben believes the "bad guys" are. How Walt returned to help Locke. Why future Jack believes leaving the island was a mistake, and what happened to everyone other than Jack and Kate. Who future Kate has to go home to. Who the man in the coffin is that wasn't Jack's friend or family.

Questions raised: How do Jack and Kate leave the island? Why was it a mistake? Were Ben and Locke right all along? Has Naomi's freighter really come to kill everyone? Has Charlie's death mission not brought rescue, but doom for the survivors? Why have future Jack and Kate grown apart? Who is future Kate living with? Who else got off the island? What is the state of the island in the future? Why is future Jack sick of lying and what was he lying about? How did Walt get back to help Locke? Where are the remaining Others heading to? If the episode was a flash forward, why did future Jack talk about his father as if he were still alive? Who is the dead man that future Jack nearly killed himself over?

Talking points: For all the action, suspense, death and drama of the first 98% of the episode, all that was later discussed was the final twist. To this day, the introduction of the flash forward is regarded as the twist that brought *Lost* back to life.

Beforehand, it looked like Jack's drunken, pill addicted condition was brought on after his wife left him. Sarah Shephard came back to add to the misdirection, and Jack even brought up his father to make us believe this was taking place before Christian's death. But some astute viewers figured out that Jack's cell phone had to have been made after 2004, the year of the plane crash.

For the record, the obituary that Jack read from seemed to say that the dead man's name was "John Lantham" who was dead of a suicide in New York, survived by a teenager. Michael lived in New York and Walt was a teen by now, so he became the prime suspect. Ben and

Locke were suspects since they were far from friends or family to Jack. But the future events may have convinced him they were right to try and stop him.

Ben sank to the most extreme depths of evil behavior he has ever gone to, ordering many people to be killed and making Jack believe he let his friends die. However, the flash forward and Charlie's final discovery points to Ben telling the truth for the first time ever. If the freighter doesn't belong to Penny and the future is so horrible that it makes Jack admit his mistake, Ben could have been the good guy after all.

With the episode title "Through the Looking Glass", the Looking Glass station, and how Jack has gone through the looking glass of the island to suffer on the other side back home, the *Alice in Wonderland* series now rivals *The Wizard of Oz* as the most referenced novel on *Lost.* "White Rabbit" previously made heavy references to it way back in Season One.

Other key issues: Nothing marks a long awaited reunion between long lost mother and daughter Alex and Rousseau like tying up Alex's bloody and beaten father together.

Some quick witted fans realized the big twist when they saw the name of the funeral parlor. It is called "Hoffs/Drawler" which is an anagram for flash forward.

Must see episode?: Not only must see, but historic. From this moment on, all the preconceptions about how *Lost* could end and where it could go for future seasons were shattered forever. The show's place as a one of a kind, rule defying program was assured. Fans would have an eight month wait ahead for Season Four, which felt even longer after this one. The sluggish pace and wasted strings of episodes on this show are over.

SEASON FOUR

CHARACTERS YOU NEED TO KNOW FOR SEASON FOUR

Daniel Faraday-- played by Jeremy Davies: A brilliant and very odd physicist who has a special knowledge of the island's special powers.

Miles Straume-- played by Ken Leung: An abrasive man towards the living while he's not communing with the dead.

Charlotte Staples Lewis-- played by Rebecca Mader: An anthropologist with at least some basic knowledge of DHARMA and the island.

Frank Lapidus-- played by Jeff Fahey: A helicopter pilot who was originally scheduled to fly flight 815.

Charles Widmore-- played by Alan Dale: Penelope Widmore's father who plans to take over the island from his old nemesis Benjamin Linus.

Martin Keamy-- played by Kevin Durand: The bloodthirsty head mercenary of Charles Widmore.

Matthew Abaddon-- played by Lance Reddick: Mystery man who helped arrange the freighter mission and had an important past encounter with John Locke.

THE BEGINNING OF THE END

The introduction of flash forwards to *Lost* wasn't the only thing that had recently changed. Damon Lindelof and Carlton Cuse had declared that *Lost* would end after six seasons, setting an official end date of 2010. There would be only 48 more hours of episodes over these three seasons, averaging out to 16 episodes a year.

As a consequence, each of the last three seasons would begin in January, meaning an eight month wait for each season. Yet it meant 16 straight weeks of episodes each January to May. But the writers strike derailed that plan in Season Four, cutting this season's supply of episodes down to 14 hours. So when Season Four premiered on January 31, 2008, it would be the first of eight straight episodes until a five week break.

Season Four's sky was the limit. With flash forwards, we would see who else left the island with Jack and Kate and lived to regret it. With the freighter arriving to the island, we would meet brand new characters and see if they were the bad guys Ben said they were. The biggest sign that things were changing was that Jack wasn't the star of this season premiere, Hurley was. Through him, the term "Oceanic 6" would be a permanent part of *Lost* vocabulary.

Season Four begins now.

Episode plot: In the jungle, the survivors are getting ready for rescue. A still tied up Ben pleads for Rousseau to get Alex out before everyone dies, but Rousseau hits him again.

On the beach, Hurley rejoices that once he returns home, his cursed money will be gone and he'll be free. He does a cannonball dive, but then sees Desmond return from the Looking Glass, warning that the people on the boat are lying. But Hurley is the only one to ask where Charlie is. Desmond's sad silence gives him his answer.

Jack gets another call from Minkowski, saying that he needs to readjust the phone's signal. He asks for Naomi, but Jack says she went to get firewood, then sees that Naomi's body is gone. There is a trail of blood which Jack and Rousseau plan to follow, keeping Ben close by. Kate hugs Jack goodbye and Ben sees her take the satellite phone from Jack, planning to find Naomi herself.

The team on the beach goes into the jungle to warn Jack, with Hurley leading the way. But he soon becomes separated from the group. While trying to find them, Hurley instead discovers Jacob's cabin. Hurley carefully comes closer to it, looking through the window to see a man sitting in Jacob's rocking chair. For a second, that man is identifiable as Christian Shephard.

Just then Hurley sees an eye looking right at him and he falls back. Believing he is imagining the cabin, Hurley tries to will it to go away. The cabin door opens by itself almost invitingly, but soon enough, it disappears from view. When Hurley opens his eyes again, he sees Locke standing over him. The two then make plans to talk Jack out of calling the freighter.

Jack and Rousseau get nowhere in finding Naomi, but Kate does as Naomi jumps from a tree to tackle her. She demands that Kate give her the satellite phone. Once she does, she calls Minkowski and says she got hurt from a fall, not from being hurt by Locke. Naomi fixes the phone so that the freighter can recapture the signal, saying "Tell my sister I love her" before finally dying.

The rest of the survivors finally reunite with those from the beach in the middle of the jungle. When Locke returns, Jack punches him and takes his gun. He pulls the trigger to kill Locke, but there are no more bullets. Locke repeats his warning that the freighter has come to kill everyone, urging the survivors to come with him to the Others barracks.

No one agrees until Hurley speaks up, telling everyone about Charlie's death and how he tried to warn them about the freighter before he died. Hurley announces that he isn't listening to Locke or Jack, he's going to listen to his friend. Once he goes to Locke's side, Claire, Sawyer, Rousseau, Alex, Karl, Ben and several other survivors go with him. With the group now separated in two, Locke's new team leaves for the barracks.

Afterwards, Jack and Kate reflect on Charlie's death near the remains of Oceanic 815's cockpit. Just then a helicopter flies over them as a light falls out. The two rush over and see a man landing on the ground. He takes off his helmet, asking "Are you Jack?"

Main character: Hurley.

Flash forward details: In the opening scene of the season, a Camaro car is being pursued by police. When it stops, Hurley comes out of the car. As he's arrested, he yells "I'm one of the Oceanic 6!"

Hurley is later questioned by Ana Lucia's former partner, who recounts that Hurley left a convenience store in a crazed rush. Once the cop leaves, Hurley has a vision of Charlie swimming up to the interrogating room window, with the words "They need you" on his hand. Hurley freaks out again and is sent back to his old mental institution, which actually makes him relieved.

As Hurley settles back in, he gets a visit from a man claiming to be an attorney from Oceanic Airlines. His name is Matthew Abaddon. He offers to put Hurley in a better institute, but he turns him down. Getting suspicious, Hurley asks Abaddon for a business card, which he doesn't have. Hurley goes to leave, but Abaddon asks him "Are they still alive?" This makes Hurley panic and scream that the man is after him, making a scene as Abaddon slips away.

Later, Hurley is sitting outside where he gets another visit from Charlie. Hurley denies that he's really there, like he was at the store. Charlie replies that he is dead, "but I'm also here." The two talk about Charlie's death, then Charlie brings up that he's here to tell him something. Hurley covers his ears as Charlie says "They need you" and that he knows they need him. But finally, Charlie disappears.

Hurley is then seen playing basketball as Jack, who isn't a bearded miserable wreck just yet, comes to visit him. They have an uneasy reunion as Hurley says Jack wanted to know if he was "gonna tell." Jack starts to leave as Hurley apologizes for going with Locke on the island, but he also says that they didn't do the right thing. He says "it" wants them to go back, but Jack yells that they will never go back. Hurley says to never say never as Jack goes off.

Important details in *Lost* lore: Hurley also got off the island with Jack and Kate, as those who did get off the island are labeled "The Oceanic 6." Hurley is sent back to the mental institution, where a man named Abaddon asks him if "they" are still alive. Hurley sees Charlie in the future, who convinces him that "they" need him.

In the present, Naomi finally dies and the survivors are split up. Locke and Hurley convince several other survivors that rescue is not imminent, taking them to the barracks. Hurley sees Jacob's cabin, briefly finding both Jacob and Christian Shephard inside. Jack and Kate have their first meeting with someone from the freighter at the end.

Amount of action: Fair.

New important characters: Matthew Abaddon and the man Jack and Kate meet in the end.

Connections between characters: Hurley mourns Charlie's death but gets to see him again in the future. Hurley also meets Ana Lucia's ex-partner after he's arrested, but Hurley doesn't admit that he knew her. Hurley unknowingly sees Jack's father inside Jacob's cabin. The survivors are split up for good thanks to Locke and Hurley's warnings about the freighter.

***Lost* mysteries referenced:** The freighter, Jacob's cabin, the fact some survivors leave the island, Hurley's hallucinations.

***Lost* mysteries introduced:** Matthew Abaddon, the "Oceanic 6" and their secrets.

Questions raised: Who makes up the rest of the "Oceanic 6" along with Jack, Kate and Hurley? Why have only six people left the island? What happened to everyone else? Why does undead Charlie say they need Hurley? Why does Matthew Abaddon ask if "they" are still alive?

Who does Abaddon really represent? What secret do future Hurley and Jack share? How can Hurley see Jacob's cabin? Why was Christian Shephard inside? What will Locke's new group of survivors do to avoid the freighter? Who is the man Jack and Kate have just met? Why did Naomi say "Tell my sister I love her" before dying?

Talking points: It is now official that the flash forward is here to stay, at least for this season. It appears this technique will be used for the other three Oceanic 6 members and potentially for Jack and Kate again.

Jack's future is miserable, but in this episode, he's still healthy and beard free. Plus he's pretty much in denial about whatever happened to get him home. Hurley's future is no less worse, as he has reverted back to his old crazy self. However, that could actually be useful if he takes Charlie's warnings seriously.

When Hurley was revealed to see imaginary friends in "Dave" it seemed like a minor twist that really had no bearing on anything. But now, Hurley's hallucinations seem extremely important, as not only could he see Charlie in the future, he could see Jacob in the present. Only those with a very special connection to the island can see Jacob, as Ben and Locke can. Now that Hurley is one of those "special" people, he may provide a whole new key to the Jacob mystery.

Though it may have happened too quickly for people to glance at first, pausing the episode confirms that it really was Christian in Jacob's rocking chair. Remember, his body was never found by Jack and he was seen walking around on the island way back in Season One. Now he too is tied to Jacob's ever growing circle.

Other key issues: Even when tied up and beaten to a pulp, Ben still senses things the others don't, like when he figured out Kate's trick on Jack. But now he's Locke's problem, and we'll see just how well he can put up with Ben after he tried to kill him.

Must see episode?: Yes, as it introduces the mystery of the Oceanic 6 and sets the rest of the bleak future into motion. It also sets the stage for the "beginning of the end" and also lets Hurley reestablish himself as the emotional center of the show.

CONFIRMED DEAD

The show's troubled history of bringing in new characters is well known. The tail section survivors largely failed while Nikki and Paulo failed even worse. The only time new characters have worked is by accident. Ben and Desmond were both guest characters that eventually turned into regulars and became invaluable to the show's core. As a result of Ben's rise, Juliet was introduced and made it big as well. The show has a shakier history of creating new characters that are supposed to be new regulars from the start. But that would have to change this season.

For Season Four, four new characters were introduced from the now infamous freighter. These people are the one who would either rescue everyone, be the cause of the horrific future for those who left the island and those who didn't, or do both. Now we would finally find out if Ben's claim of their danger was true for ourselves. Along the way, we would see just how fitting it is that these four newcomers are on the island. But whoever brought them there may really be the ones to fear.

We will start by introducing them in their flashbacks.

Flashback details: These flashbacks take place on the day the phony wreckage of Oceanic 815 was found at the bottom of the ocean. Our first new character is the same man Jack and Kate met at the end of the last episode. His name is Daniel Faraday, a physicist who is crying over the TV report of Oceanic 815's recovery for reasons even he doesn't know.

The second new character is an Asian man named Miles Straume. On the day the fake wreckage was discovered, he goes into the house of an elderly woman. He enters the room of her dead grandson, activates a strange device, and actually seems to be communicating with this dead person. Miles tells the dead grandson to leave, though not before finding a bundle of hidden cash.

The third new character is a female anthropologist named Charlotte Lewis. On the day the wreckage was discovered, she was in Tunisia, reading about the wreckage in different languages and not believing that it's true. She gets her way into an excavation site where bones are being dug up. They are the bones of a polar bear, which has a collar with the logo of the DHARMA Initiative around it. Charlotte smiles, not seeming the least bit surprised about the collar.

The fourth new character is a helicopter pilot named Frank Lapidus. On the day the wreckage was discovered, he is watching the TV report in Hawaii. When he sees a close up of the body of pilot Seth Norris, Frank calls Oceanic Airlines. He says that the body can't be Seth's, since it doesn't have his wedding ring on his hand. He is asked why he knows this, as Frank says it was because he was supposed to be the pilot of Oceanic 815 that day.

A final flashback shows Naomi examining the photos of Daniel, Charlotte, Miles and Frank. Matthew Abaddon is there as well. He has chosen these four to go to the island with Naomi, saying each of them was hired for specific purposes. Naomi asks what to do if she finds survivors of Oceanic 815 on the island, but Abaddon cryptically insists that there are no survivors. She is instructed to do her job and complete their mission without anyone getting killed.

Episode plot: Daniel Faraday is pushed out of the helicopter and lands on the island. There, he introduces himself to Jack and Kate, who give him Naomi's phone to contact Minkowski. Daniel tells him he doesn't know where his partners are, but the phone's GPS unit will allow him to track them. As he talks, Kate notices a gun in Daniel's back pocket.

The next morning, Locke instructs his new team about how he saw Walt and is going to look for him, also looking to find Jacob's cabin. Ben finds time to taunt Sawyer about how he went with Locke because he has no use back on the mainland, getting another beating for his trouble.

Jack, Kate and Daniel try to track Miles's signal, discovering equipment that was thrown out of the helicopter. When Jack finds a bag with gas masks in it, he begins to question Daniel, who now admits that rescuing the survivors is not their "primary objective." He then picks up Miles's signal before he is asked any more questions.

They find Miles lying on some rocks near the ocean. He quickly gets up and points his gun at Jack, demanding to know where Naomi is. Naomi's final words "Tell my sister I love her" were a code to indicate danger. Kate confesses Naomi is dead, saying that Locke killed her and not them. But Miles still wants to see the body to find out if this is true. Once he does, he uses his powers to confirm they're telling the truth.

Soon after, Jack instructs Miles and Daniel to put away their guns, or his people will fire. Miles doubts this until Sayid and Juliet come in with guns pointed at them. After they're disarmed, they now look for Charlotte's signal. But Charlotte has landed in a river, where she is picked up by Locke's people. She offers to take them back to their helicopter, but Locke is taking her with them, saying they don't want to be found. Soon after, Jack and his team gets Charlotte's signal, but her GPS tracking unit has been put on Vincent, as Jack realizes Locke has her.

Frank Lapidus is on the ground, managing to shoot his flare gun. Charlotte sees it, but Locke insists they're not going near it. Charlotte starts to leave, but Ben, having taken a gun from Karl, shoots her in the chest. Sawyer beats him again as Locke runs to Charlotte, seeing she has a vest on.

Jack and his team find Frank, who shows them that he landed the helicopter safely on the ground. As they prepare to fly out, Frank questions Juliet. After finding out her full name, he realizes she wasn't on 815, having studied the flight manifest thoroughly. Miles then yells to her "Where is he?!" and finally admits why his team has come to the island. He announces that they're here for Benjamin Linus.

Ben is at gunpoint as Locke is finally ready to kill him. Ben pleads that he has answers for him, but when he won't confirm it by answering what the monster is, Locke cocks the gun. Ben then yells out Charlotte's full name and every detail about her, including the names of her teammates. He says if Locke kills him, he'll never know how great a threat these people are. Ben also knows that they're here to come get him. Locke then asks how Ben knows all this.

He knows because he has a spy on the freighter.

Important details in *Lost* lore: Daniel Faraday, Charlotte Lewis, Miles Straume and Frank Lapidus are introduced and given brief backgrounds. They seem to have been hired by Matthew Abaddon and are on a mission to capture Ben, who admits that he knows this already because he has a man on their boat. We also see the day Oceanic 815's fake wreckage was found.

Amount of action: Heavy with information.

New important characters: Daniel, Miles, Charlotte and Frank.

Connections between characters: The four new characters were recruited by Naomi and Abaddon. Frank has direct ties to the pilot of Oceanic 815. Sawyer becomes the latest character to give Ben a beating, while Locke finally has enough of Ben until he reveals his info.

***Lost* mysteries referenced:** The freighter and the people on it, Abaddon, Oceanic 815's phony wreckage, Walt's appearance to Locke.

***Lost* mysteries introduced:** Miles's ability to speak to the dead, Frank's role as the original pilot of 815, Charlotte's discovery of DHARMA polar bear skeletons, Ben's spy on the boat, the freighter's mission to snatch Ben, the helicopter's supply of gas masks.

Questions raised: What else makes up the back stories of these four new characters? Why was Daniel crying over the TV report? What is with Miles's abilities? How much does Charlotte know about DHARMA? Why didn't Frank fly Oceanic 815? Why and how did Abaddon recruit these people? What do they want with Ben? Who is Ben's spy on the boat? How did he even get one?

Talking points: This is just like the old days of Season One, which showed flashbacks for characters we didn't know about yet. But here, with four characters to flashback to, there is only a taste of what their pasts are.

What is clear is that they were not employees of whoever hired them until just a few weeks ago, since they were all seen in different places and jobs the day Oceanic 815's "crash site" was discovered. So in the power structure of this mission, they seem to be just hired hands. The real men behind the curtain who set up this trip are still hidden, save for Abaddon.

These people individually do not seem like threats. Daniel is twitchy and eccentric, Miles may be dangerous but he's more abrasive than rotten, Charlotte came prepared but she seemed happy to be here at first, while Frank is smarter than he first appears. Thanks to Ben's warnings, it was expected that this group was more sinister, but that doesn't appear to be so. Yet that also means they could have been tricked and manipulated into doing evil by the people behind this mission.

However, the startling thing about each of them is how they fit right into the island. Daniel has already started studying the island's properties, noting how the light scatters differently. Miles's powers to hear the dead are useful on an island filled with spirits. Charlotte already has some past knowledge of DHARMA, while Frank already knows the cover story of Oceanic 815 is bogus. Abaddon hinted these people were chosen for specific purposes, which seems to be a dead on statement. Whoever else hired them also must know the island pretty well.

Other key issues: The full name of Charlotte is Charlotte Staples Lewis, as Ben yelled out. She has the same middle and last name as famed fantasy writer C.S Lewis, as her joyful arrival to the island is another *Chronicles of Narnia* reference as well.

Must see episode?: Yes, as it introduces the new characters and ensures they will fit right in, unlike some of the other newbies of the past. But it's Ben who has the real mind blowing final words to top it all off.

THE ECONOMIST

Many huge mysteries surround *Lost* this season, most of all surrounding "The Oceanic 6" who are the only group of survivors confirmed to have left the island in the future. Jack, Kate and Hurley are three of them, leaving three spots to go. Quite simply, whoever has flash forward episodes this season gets to be an Oceanic 6. But even that isn't as simple as it appears to be.

However, this episode definitely gives the fourth spot to Sayid, which makes sense. His survival skills, brute strength and capable leadership makes him someone that is very easy to see getting off the island. But like everyone else, his future isn't that bright as he resumes old habits in a brand new way...along with brand new allies.

Episode plot: Jack debates with Miles over what to do next, as Miles wants to go get Charlotte back from Locke. Sayid offers to get Charlotte freed, but without any violence. He makes a deal with Frank that if he can do this, Sayid will be taken to the freighter. Jack has Kate go with him as Miles comes along as well.

Locke and his team are still walking through the jungle. Sawyer fails to make Ben tell him who his spy is, since he would be killed right afterwards. Locke arrives at where he thinks Jacob's cabin is, but it's not there. After Ben quips that Locke was looking for someone to tell him what to do, Locke vows to head for the barracks as planned, keeping Charlotte as a hostage.

Sayid, Kate and Miles arrive at the barracks as well, which now looks deserted. They hear a thumping sound and go into a house, seeing Hurley tied up in a closet. Hurley says Locke left him behind and headed for Ben's house.

The three head inside Ben's house, as Sayid discovers Ben's hidden closet filled with fake passports, fake ID's and money from all over the world. Kate goes into the bedroom and finds Sawyer entering. Sayid soon finds Locke pointing a gun at him, as it appears Hurley helped lead them into a trap.

Sayid is taken to the rec room where Ben is already captive. Kate stays in the bedroom with Sawyer, who tries to convince her that they could live here and there's nothing to go back home to. Miles is nowhere to be found, but Locke insists he's fine.

Sayid confronts Locke and asks him to give up Charlotte. He agrees that the freighter isn't here to rescue them, but if he can get onto the freighter, he can find out their real intentions. But Sayid knows Locke won't give up Charlotte for nothing, so he allows Locke to keep Miles.

Juliet brings Desmond to the helicopter, as he wants to know why Naomi had a picture of him and Penelope. Desmond asks Frank to confirm that he's never heard of Penelope Widmore, but he looks uneasy. So Desmond vows to go onto the helicopter once it takes off. Sayid then returns with Charlotte safe and sound.

Frank starts up the helicopter as both Sayid and Desmond go on board, while Charlotte and Daniel stay behind with Jack. Daniel urges Frank to follow an exact bearing of 305 back to the freighter before they go. With that, Sayid and Desmond are taken off the island.

Other stuff: While Jack and company wait for Sayid to get back, Daniel performs a little experiment. He sets up a beacon with a clock on it, contacting a woman named Regina on the freighter and asking her to send a payload. She does, but when it is supposed to arrive, it doesn't. However, the payload, which is a small rocket, arrives much later on. The rocket has a clock in it which says it is 3:16. But Daniel's clock on the island reads 2:45. Having proven a significant difference in time between the island and the outside world, Daniel starts to worry.

Main character: Sayid Jarrah.

Flash forward details: Sayid plays on a golf course, as he makes a bet with another player. Sayid starts to explain he can afford this due to his settlement from Oceanic Airlines, introducing himself as one of the Oceanic 6. The man becomes nervous and starts to leave, then Sayid calls him "Mr. Avellino" and shoots him dead right on the course.

Later, Sayid is in Berlin making a date with a woman named Elsa, who works for "an economist." Once they make the date, Sayid calls someone and says he has "made contact." Sayid and Elsa get closer, until one day when Sayid urges her to leave Berlin. People will start to ask her what happened to her boss, as Sayid has really gotten closer to Elsa to find and kill her employer.

Elsa starts to get mad, as Sayid starts to explain that her boss isn't an economist. But Elsa returns from the bathroom and shoots him. She then calls her boss and says that Sayid hasn't given the name of his employer, but she will bring him to a safe house. Sayid quickly gets out his gun and kills her just before she can shoot back.

Later on, Sayid goes to a veterinarian's office to be treated by an unseen person. Still upset over what he had to do, Sayid explains that Elsa is dead. He says she wanted to know who he worked for. A deep voice says "Of course she did" and Sayid's boss reveals himself.

It is Benjamin Linus.

Ben mocks Sayid for caring about Elsa, saying her people don't deserve sympathy. He brings up what they did the last time Sayid "thought with his heart instead of his gun" which is how he made Sayid agree to kill for him. Ben reminds him that all this is to protect his friends, then says he has a new name for him to target. Resigned, Sayid mentions that "they" now know he's after them.

Ben only replies "Good."

Important details in *Lost* lore: Daniel confirms that time on the island runs different than time on the outside. Sayid retrieves Charlotte from Locke, but leaves Miles and Kate behind. Sayid and Desmond leave the island with Frank to go to the freighter. In the future, Sayid is an assassin working for an unknown employer, who later turns out to be Ben. Somehow, he's off the island too.

Amount of action: Heavy.

New important characters: Elsa and her unseen boss known as "the economist."

Connections between characters: Hurley begins to question Locke's leadership, though he helps Locke capture Sayid, Kate and Miles. Sayid comments that the day he trusts Ben is the day he were to "sell his soul" yet he winds up killing people for him in the future.

***Lost* mysteries referenced:** Jacob's cabin, Ben's spy, the Oceanic 6.

***Lost* mysteries introduced:** Daniel's time experiment, why Sayid is Ben's assassin in the future.

Questions raised: Why could Sayid possibly have agreed to kill for Ben? How did Ben get off the island? What did "these people" do to Sayid? How is their killing protecting Sayid's friends? Who exactly are they targeting? What will happen to Sayid and Desmond in their trip to the freighter? What will Locke do with Miles? Will Sawyer get Kate to "play house" with him? Where has the cabin gone?

Talking points: Yet again, someone who leaves the island has a miserable future. As Jack became a pill addict and Hurley went back to the mental institution, Sayid went back to a life of killing. What's more, he's doing it for Ben, who seems to be no stranger to going around the world.

But rather than Sayid turning evil, it could be that his work for Ben further legitimizes Ben's claims that he is the good guy, or at least fighting people worse than he is. How it protects Sayid's friends as Ben claims, we don't know. Nor do we have any idea who they're targeting yet.

Fans can be forgiven for thinking that much of this plays like a spy movie/spoof, as Sayid literally seems to be impersonating James Bond with Elsa. It skirts very close to parody until the final revelations.

Once more, Hurley speaks for the rest of the fans when he compares Miles to being "another Sawyer" just as fans were calling him.

Other key issues: Yet again the Red Sox are mentioned, as Jack asks Frank to confirm that the Sox really did win the 2004 Series. Whether it speaks well about Frank that he "bleeds Yankee blue" we don't know.

One of Ben's fake passport names is "Dean Moriarty" an almost intentional callback to the evil genius that battled Sherlock Holmes.

Must see episode?: It slows down a bit from the pace of the first two, and the flash forwards initially walk a fine line between gripping and spoofy. But the final scene is among the biggest and most jaw dropping revelations yet.

EGGTOWN

Kate's shocking arrival at the end of "Through the Looking Glass" confirmed that Jack's flashback was a flash forward in the future. Two other smaller mysteries then rose up. The first was who Kate was rushing to go home to, assuming it wasn't Sawyer. The second is how the heck she was even free to see Jack in the first place. After all, she was on the run and must have been brought up on charges for her crimes when she got back. So what was she doing free?

All this is answered here, though as usual, not in the ways one expects.

Episode plot: Ben is held in his basement as Locke now lives in Ben's house. Locke brings Ben breakfast and tries to ask again who his spy on the boat is, but Ben brings up how Locke has hit a dead end yet again, just like old times. Locke takes the breakfast and leaves, then smashes the plate against the wall as Ben listens from his cell.

Kate is outside with Claire, turning down Sawyer's offer to live with him. The possibility that Kate might have gotten pregnant from Sawyer is brought up awkwardly. Kate then goes to see Locke, asking to talk to Miles. Locke immediately refuses, but Kate finds out where Miles is through Hurley.

She finds Miles in a boathouse, asking him if he knows who she is and what she did. Miles will tell her, but first he wants one minute alone to talk to Ben. So she goes to Sawyer and gets his help with a plan. Sawyer distracts Locke by playing backgammon with him, just long enough for Kate to bring Miles into Ben's basement.

When Miles sees Ben, he asks if he knows who he is and who he works for, which Ben does. Miles comments that he could tell his boss where Ben is, or he could lie and say Ben is dead. In return, he wants Ben to give him 3.2 million dollars.

Ben asks where he's going to get that much money, but Miles assures him that he knows Ben can make it happen. He makes Ben agree to get this done in a week as Kate forces him out. With that, Miles admits that his people know about Kate's crimes and everyone else on 815. Locke then returns and orders Kate back to her house.

After Kate tells Locke about Miles and Ben's meeting, Locke orders her out of the barracks by morning. She stays with Sawyer, who offers to keep her safe and they make out. The next morning, Kate confirms that she is not pregnant after all, then gets upset when Sawyer is so relieved. She goes to leave, but Sawyer figures she'll go back to him after she finds a reason to be mad at Jack, causing Kate to slap him and go.

Locke visits Miles at the boathouse, introducing himself as the man responsible for the island's well being. He gets a grenade, pulls the pin and shoves it in Miles' mouth, insisting that he will eventually tell him why his people are here. Locke then leaves Miles in his new position.

Other stuff: Daniel and Charlotte are brought to the beach camp, as Jack explains they are making arrangements to get the survivors rescued. Jack and Juliet then try to use the satellite phone to find out about Sayid and Desmond. Charlotte gets them through to the emergency line, which Regina answers. When asked about the helicopter, Regina says that she thought the helicopter was still on the island. It's been almost a day since the helicopter took off, but Sayid and Desmond still aren't on the freighter.

Main character: Kate Austin.

Flash forward details: Kate is finally on trial for her various crimes, pleading not guilty. Her lawyer suggests they bring "him" into the courtroom to give Kate sympathy, but she argues that they will not use "my son" in that way. However, Jack is called in to give testimony. He lies that after 815 crashed, Kate saved the rest of the Oceanic 6 and two others who died later on. Jack says she took care of them, but Kate can't hear any more.

Later, Kate's wheelchair bound mother, who is the prime witness for the prosecution, visits her. With little time to live, she offers not to testify against Kate, but only if she can see Kate's son. Kate rejects this and leaves. However, her mother does not testify after all due to her ailing health. With the jury already sympathetic to Kate, the prosecution offers to give Kate 10 years of probation, in which she cannot leave the state. Kate quickly agrees.

When it's over, Jack and Kate meet in the parking lot. Kate reflects on how often Jack's told the fake story of them on the island, then invites Jack to her house. He is reluctant, as Kate says she knows why he doesn't want to see her son. But until he gets over it, they can't be together. She then takes a cab and heads into her large house, going upstairs to a bedroom. A boy who is only a few years old wakes up in his bed, saying "Hi mommy" to Kate as she hugs him.

Kate says "Hi, Aaron."

Important details in *Lost* lore: Kate finds out that the freighter people know of her past, yet she leaves Sawyer to go back to Jack's pro-rescue team. Miles tries to blackmail Ben into giving him 3.2 million dollars not to turn him over to his boss. Sayid and Desmond's helicopter is nowhere to be found. In the future, Kate escapes jail time for her crimes. The "he" Kate referred to living with in the future is not Sawyer or Jack. It is Aaron, who is now Kate's son.

Amount of action: Little.

New important characters: None.

Connections between characters: Kate and Sawyer separate again. Locke is once again driven to anger by Ben, as he banishes Kate and shoves a grenade in Miles mouth. Ben knows who Miles works for. In the future, Jack and Kate's relationship is strained due to Jack's hesitation around her son, who is actually Aaron.

***Lost* mysteries referenced:** Whether Kate is pregnant, who Kate is living with in the future, how she escaped jail time, who Miles and the freighter people work for.

***Lost* mysteries introduced:** Kate claiming Aaron as her son in the future, why Jack doesn't want to be around them, Miles's demand for 3.2 million out of Ben, the state of the helicopter.

Questions raised: Why and how is Aaron living with Kate in the future? What happened to Claire? Why is Jack uneasy around Aaron? Why does Jack have to tell a cover story about what happened to them on the island? Is Aaron one of the Oceanic 6? Has Locke finally lost it? Can Ben get Miles his money? Who does Miles work for? Will Kate just go back to Sawyer yet again later on? What happened to the helicopter?

Talking points: Unlike everyone else so far, Kate actually seems to have a happy future, with a new big house and freedom. However, the fact she is raising Aaron as her own son indicates this too came at a horrific price.

Ben's mythic powers continue to grow as Miles suggests he knows Ben can raise 3.2 million dollars easily. He also makes history repeat itself as he once more makes Locke destroy a plate in anger, as Locke's leadership becomes more and more unstable.

Other key issues: Sawyer accurately sums up the love triangle better than anyone else so far, getting slapped for it as a result.

Must see episode?: The final revelation is a big twist, though not as big as the last episode. Otherwise, this is one mainly for the shippers and the first less than stellar episode this year.

THE CONSTANT

Ever since losing Penelope Widmore, Desmond's road back to her has been filled with near misses. When he destroyed the hatch, it appeared that Penelope's people had found the island's location and she had sent the freighter to rescue him. However, the freighter wasn't hers. Worse yet, Desmond was prevented from speaking to Penny as Charlie locked himself in the Looking Glass to die.

Now Desmond has had enough near misses, wanting answers on the freighter. He gets answers all right, but not about Penny. He instead finds out about his own time traveling powers and the consequences of leaving the island all too well, literally putting his brain in danger of collapsing. To follow along with this episode, your brains may collapse as well.

Episode plot: The helicopter carrying Sayid and Desmond is flying into a storm, as Frank has to follow Daniel's exact bearing of 305. But the storm knocks them slightly off course as Desmond watches.

Just then, Desmond is seen waking up in a military barrack. He has flashed back to the time he was in the Scottish military. Convinced he had a dream, he gets ready to perform his duties.

At that point, Desmond literally flashes back to the present as he's still in the helicopter. But now, he doesn't know where he is and who

Sayid is. He becomes very disoriented as the helicopter finally lands on the freighter. However, due to going off on a different bearing, they have landed almost a full day into the future, which is why Jack couldn't contact them the previous night.

As they get off the helicopter, Desmond continues to lash out. A man named Keamy offers to take him to sick bay, as Desmond insists he's not supposed to be here. But when he finishes his sentence, he is seen back with the military regiment in the past.

Desmond remembers he had a picture of Penny on the boat and rushes to call her. Before he can, he is flashed back into the present and on the boat. He is brought down to sick bay, where he sees a man tied down to a bed who says "It's happening to you too, isn't it?"

Sayid gets Frank to give him his satellite phone so he can call Jack. He is confused about Desmond's strange behavior, but Daniel Faraday seems to understand exactly what's going on. People can experience side effects when going back and forth from the island if they don't follow the right bearing of 305. Because Desmond was exposed to large doses of electromagnetism when the hatch exploded, his side effects are more severe, as his mind is traveling back to the past.

Desmond is then visited by the freighter doctor, as the tied up man explains that these side effects will happen to everyone when they get to the island. As the doctor turns to examine Desmond, he goes back to the past. There, he gets a hold of Penny, who doesn't want to hear from him since they were broken up at this point. As Desmond pleads to see her in person, he flashes back to the present. Apparently his body stood completely still as his consciousness traveled to the past.

Just then Sayid barges into the room with the satellite phone, blocking the door so no one can get in. He gives the phone to Desmond as Daniel starts talking to him. Daniel soon finds out that Desmond thinks the year is 1996. He then tells Desmond that when he goes back to the past, he must go to Oxford, where he will find Daniel in 1996. He instructs Desmond to tell the past Daniel to set a device to 2,342 and oscillate to 11 hertz, and that he knows about "Eloise."

Desmond then flashes back to 1996 and goes to Oxford, finding the past Daniel Faraday. He says he's from the future, which Daniel believes to be a prank until he tells him about the device and Eloise. So

1996 Daniel takes Desmond to his private lab, where he is working on an experiment. Eloise is a rat Daniel is testing on.

Using a bright red light, he sends Eloise's consciousness mind ahead an hour into the future, when Daniel was to teach her how to run through a maze. When Eloise awakes in the present, she knows how to do it. Confused as to how this helps him, Desmond's consciousness mind then returns to the present.

The man in the bed overhears Desmond's name, revealing himself to be Minkowski, the man Jack first talked to on the phone. As the communications officer, Minkowski often got incoming calls he was ordered never to answer. Those calls came from Penelope Widmore.

Desmond then returns to 1996, as his body went catatonic in 1996 for five minutes. Eloise has died, as Desmond now worries this will happen to him. Daniel explains that Desmond needs a "constant" which is something that Desmond really cares about that is in both 1996 and 2004. If he gets one, it will stabilize his mind. Desmond goes off to talk to his "bloody constant" Penny, then collapses and goes back to 2004.

Present Desmond realizes he needs to call Penny on the freighter. Minkowski then points out that the door to the sickbay has been opened. Desmond and Sayid take Minkowski out, as he explains he got these flashes when he went to see the island on a raft. They get to the radio room, where all the equipment has been destroyed, likely by Ben's spy. As they start repairing it, Desmond goes back to 1996.

Desmond goes to an auction house, where the journal of the Black Rock is being auctioned off. Charles Widmore is there as he successfully purchases the journal. Desmond finds him and asks where Penelope is living now. Widmore snidely comments that Desmond probably wants another chance, after his cowardice prevented him from proposing to her. But Widmore, wanting Desmond to see how much Penny hates him now, gives him her address anyway.

Desmond then returns to 2004 as Minkowski, suffering from having no constant, finally dies when he can't return to the present. Sayid fixes a phone, but Desmond doesn't know what number to call. He is then sent back to 1996, where he goes to Penny's new address.

Desmond begs Penny to give him her number, saying he's going to call her on Christmas Eve 2004. Wanting him to leave, Penny tells him the number as Desmond asks her not to change it. She sends him away as Desmond pleads for her to trust him, then he goes back to 2004.

Now knowing Penny's number, Desmond recites it as Sayid dials the numbers. The phone only has enough power to last for a minute. Desmond waits by the phone, hoping for any answer. Finally, he hears Penny say hello. Desmond answers as his flashes now appear to be stopping.

Back in London, Penny is seen at her house beginning to cry happily as she hears Desmond's voice. Desmond rejoices that Penny still cares for him, as she says she's been looking for him for three years. She knows he's on the island and has been trying to research it, but she only knew for sure that Desmond was still alive when she talked to Charlie. The two declare their love for each other as Desmond vows to come back and Penny vows to find him. As they say "I love you" together, the phone's power dies down.

Desmond now remembers who Sayid is, shaking his hand in thanks. When Sayid asks if Desmond's all right, he responds that now he's perfect.

Back on the beach, Daniel looks through his journal and reads the words "If anything goes wrong, Desmond Hume will be MY constant" smiling in relief.

Important details in *Lost* lore: Desmond's consciousness jumps back and forth from 1996 to 2004 after the helicopter leaves the island. Daniel reveals that people experience these flashes if they don't follow the right bearing across the island, especially if they were exposed to electromagnetism as Desmond was.

Desmond meets Daniel in 1996, as he performs time experiments on a rat. 1996 Daniel informs Desmond that he needs a constant in both times to end these flashes, which in Desmond's case is Penny. Desmond finally makes a call to her as they talk for the first time in three years. Penny confirms she knows about the island and has been looking for it and Desmond. In the past, her father Charles Widmore wins the journal of the Black Rock in an auction.

Amount of action: Heavy with information.

New important characters: Two new people on the freighter named Keamy and Omar, as well as a freighter doctor. Minkowski is seen in person for the first time as he dies from his flashes.

Connections between characters: Desmond and Daniel meet and help each other in both 2004 and 1996. Desmond doesn't recognize Sayid or anything else until he recovers after finding his constant, Penny. Daniel plans to make Desmond his constant if "anything goes wrong."

***Lost* mysteries referenced:** The status of the helicopter, the difference in time between the island and the outside world, Desmond's flashes, Penny's search for Desmond and the island.

***Lost* mysteries introduced:** Daniel's experiments and whether he has flashed back and forth through time himself, who destroyed the freighter's radio room, Charles Widmore's purchase of the Black Rock journal.

Questions raised: Are Desmond's flashes over? Will Penny be able to come for him now? How did she find out Desmond was on the island? Why might Daniel need Desmond to be his constant? How does Daniel know so much about the island and the properties around it? Why has Charles Widmore bought the journal of the Black Rock, the slave ship that crashed on the island?

Talking points: Desmond's previous episodes stretched the limits of science fiction, time travel and other odd elements. But this episode takes the cake, creating an even wilder new format of telling a story than "Flashes Before Your Eyes." The concept of time travel becomes even bigger now, though Desmond didn't literally disappear into different times. His conscious mind only went to one time while his body in the other time was catatonic.

Daniel Faraday becomes even more helpful in both time periods, as his connection to the big questions of the island seems to be stronger than any other new character.

Let's recap the time travel rules one last time for those confused readers. The helicopter was sent forward almost a day in time because it traveled through the wrong bearing. It made Desmond experience flashes to 1996 because of his massive past exposure to electromagnetism, as well as his pre-existing condition of seeing into the future. So not only is there a time difference between the island and the rest of the world, traveling to and from it can cause grave consequences if you don't use the precise bearing of 305. Hope that repairs your mind a little bit.

Other key issues: The brief scene of Charles Widmore buying the journal of the Black Rock is not one to be dismissed, as it is put in a greater context in the very next episode.

Must see episode?: If one can follow the format of the episode and how the various time travel elements work, yes. If one watches for the emotional aspect, they will be greatly rewarded when they see Desmond and Penny's tearful phone call. Technically this is a one shot episode that only moves forward the concept of time travel and time differences on the island. But even if it's not that essential otherwise, it is regarded as one of *Lost's* most mind bending and moving episodes.

THE OTHER WOMAN

The episode title could very well be Juliet's motto. She is the "other woman" because she is an Other and because she is the other woman in the Jack/Kate/Sawyer love triangle. She is also revealed as the other woman in her affair with doomed Other Goodwin. But she is also Ben's other woman. Although we suspected he had feelings for her before, the truth is far more unsettling, even by Ben's standards. But while Ben sinks to new lows in the past, he has some of the most valuable information of the season to reveal in the present, as Locke must turn to him yet again.

Episode plot: Daniel and Charlotte are nowhere to be found, as Jack forms a search party after them. Juliet goes along, but soon meets a former associate of hers, Harper. She says that Daniel and Charlotte are going to "The Tempest" DHARMA station to unleash poison gas that will kill everyone on the island. Harper states that Ben would like Juliet to stop them, then disappears. When Jack finds Juliet, she gets him to help although she doesn't reveal everything.

Daniel and Charlotte are indeed on their way to the Tempest station, but Kate finds them on her way back to Jack's camp. Charlotte knocks her out with her gun, as Kate is found by Jack and Juliet sometime later. Juliet offers to get Kate water, but instead goes to the Tempest.

Inside the station, Daniel is working on computers as Juliet points her gun and orders him to stop. When he doesn't, Charlotte attacks Juliet and the two fight. Charlotte then argues that they're really trying to contain the gas, as Ben had set it to go off before he was captured. Coming to believe her, Juliet lets Daniel render the gas inert just before it is released.

Jack and Kate arrive as Charlotte offers to explain everything. Jack and Juliet stay behind, with Juliet commenting that Ben manipulated her. Juliet tells Jack that these people are here to wage war on Ben, a war which Ben will win. When he does, Jack can't be near Juliet since Ben knows how she feels about him. But Jack kisses her and says that Ben knows where to find him.

Other stuff: Locke becomes frustrated again as he is getting nowhere. So he goes to Ben, who points out that Locke's people will become more upset with him when they see he has no plan. Ben offers to tell Locke who sent the freighter, in return for getting his freedom back.

Locke takes Ben to his living room, where Ben takes a tape out of a safe. The tape shows the man who Ben says has sent the freighter. It is a recording of Charles Widmore.

On the tape, Widmore is beating up an Other who was caught on the mainland. Ben claims that Widmore wants to exploit the island for its powers. He gives Locke a file of everything he has on Widmore, but Locke also wants the identity of Ben's spy on the freighter. Ben agrees, saying Locke might want to sit down.

Sometime later, Hurley and Sawyer are shocked to see Ben walking around outside, as he calls out "See you guys at dinner!"

Main character: Juliet Burke.

Flashback details: On her first week on the island, Juliet meets with Harper, who was the Others psychologist. She is taken to her new home, which has been set up by Ben.

As Juliet begins her work, she meets Goodwin, who is Harper's husband. The two get close, even though there are hints that Ben is annoyed by it. When Juliet meets Harper for a session, she talks about Ben's interest in her, as Harper comments that Juliet "looks just like her." She reveals that she knows about Juliet's affair with Goodwin, warning her that she doesn't want Goodwin to be hurt by Ben as a result. But he would be hurt when Ben sent him to spy on the tail section.

One night Ben invites Juliet to a private dinner at his house. Juliet wonders why Goodwin hasn't been called back yet, as Ben argues that he's staying to try and help Ana Lucia. But that is not the truth, as Juliet realizes when Ben takes her to see Goodwin's dead body days later. She now knows that Ben left Goodwin there, hoping that the tail section people would kill him.

Ben is shocked that Juliet would ask why he did this. After everything he's done to get her to the island and keep her here, he asks how she could possibly not understand, in his own words, "that you're MINE!!" Ben soon calms down from his outburst, telling Juliet to take as much time as she needs.

Important details in *Lost* lore: Juliet's affair with Goodwin is detailed, as well as Ben's possessiveness of Juliet. Ben even let Goodwin die at the tail section camp because of his relationship with her. In the present, Juliet thinks Charlotte and Daniel are about to poison everyone, but instead they stop the gas from being released. Jack and Juliet share a kiss when it's all over. It is revealed that Charles Widmore sent the freighter, as he wants to capture Ben and control the island.

Amount of action: Fair.

New important characters: Harper, who was Goodwin's wife and Juliet's shrink.

Connections between characters: Ben's obsession with Juliet is shown in the past. Juliet had an affair with Goodwin, the husband of her island shrink. Jack and Juliet kiss fully for the first time. Charles Widmore is the man who sent the freighter to the island.

***Lost* mysteries referenced:** Juliet's affair, Ben's spy, the freighter's mastermind.

***Lost* mysteries introduced:** Why Charles Widmore has sent the freighter, where Harper came from, how Charlotte and Daniel knew that they had to turn the gas off.

Questions raised: Why was Juliet manipulated to ensure the gas would be released into the island? Are Jack and Juliet going to get closer? Why does Ben believe Juliet is his? Who is the woman from Ben's past that Juliet looks just like? Why is Charles Widmore really out to find the island? How will Locke's people react to Ben being set free? Who did Ben say his spy was?

Talking points: As the final blanks are filled in on Juliet's island life, it appears all her mystery has gone with her. This episode had no hints of the cool, mysterious and unpredictable Juliet we saw in much of Season Three, though we saw Goodwin's death may have turned her into that type of character. But the more she turns into a good guy, the less interesting she has become.

In contrast, Ben manages to stay mysterious, interesting and complex the more we find out about him. In this instance, his creepy obsessive stalker side is introduced. Even when trying to make Juliet a romantic dinner, he's still unsettling.

More importantly, this is the episode that introduces Charles Widmore as the man behind the curtain of the freighter. It now appears that when Penelope Widmore's people briefly found the island's location, her father found out too and was quick to send the freighter. How he did this behind Penny's back is still a mystery.

Other key issues: Still another Red Sox reference is made, as Ben taped over the Sox 2004 World Series win to videotape Widmore.

Must see episode?: The main plot is the most disappointing of the season, using fake suspense and eroding most of the mystery and complexity Juliet had in Season Three. Skip that part, but Ben's subplot and what he has to tell is much more important.

JI YEON

With only two slots left open for the Oceanic 6, there is no shortage of candidates. One very likely one is Sun, as she needs to get off the island to survive her pregnancy. As different as *Lost* is, one doubts they could depict a main character dying from childbirth. And so they didn't, as although Sun begins to have doubts about everything on the island, she is seen alive in the future and ready to give birth. That fills the fifth spot, but what about the final Oceanic 6? The answer to who that is appears to be certain. Or does it?

Episode plot: After Sun finds out what happened at the Tempest, she begins to question the truth about the freighter's mission. She asks Daniel point blank if they're here for rescue, but he says it's not his call. That's all the proof Sun needs, as she tells Jin that they're going to join Locke's camp.

When Juliet finds out, she tries to talk Sun out of it due to her pregnancy. But Sun now even doubts Juliet's stories of dead pregnant women are true, since Claire turned out okay. As Sun and Jin leave, Juliet keeps trying and failing to talk them out of it.

So out of desperation, Juliet drops her ultimate trump card. She tells Jin that Sun told her she had an affair and she was afraid the baby wasn't Jin's. After Sun slaps Juliet for revealing her secret, Jin storms back to camp. He is no mood to talk to her, but accepts Bernard's invitation to go fishing.

There, Bernard talks about married life to Jin, bringing up how Rose was healed by the island. But she didn't go with Locke because he's a murderer, bringing up karma and how good things happen after making good choices. Back on the beach, Juliet confronts Sun and now successfully convinces her of what will happen if she doesn't get off the island.

That night, Jin finds Sun, telling her that he realizes Sun had her affair because of how he was before they came to the island. Bad things happened when he made bad choices. So Jin forgives her and promises that he will get her and the baby off the island alive.

Other stuff: On the freighter, Sayid and Desmond find a note slipped under their door, saying "Don't trust the captain." They soon find out Frank has left, taking the helicopter back to the island. As they try to find out why, Regina jumps off the freighter wrapped around in chains. Before anyone can jump after her, the freighter's captain, whose name is Gault, appears and orders them to stop.

Sayid and Desmond confront Captain Gault, who explains that many people on the freighter have gotten odd sicknesses due to being so close to the island. They cannot move back because the engines have been destroyed by a spy. He mentions that the boat was hired by Charles Widmore, then brings Sayid and Desmond to his quarters.

There, he shows them the black box from the supposed wreckage of Oceanic 815. He knows it was staged, questioning how much money and time went into setting it up, as well as how they got 324 dead bodies to put in the plane. He says that is one of the many reasons why they want to seize Benjamin Linus.

Later, the freighter doctor leads them back to their room, ordering a deck hand named Kevin Johnson to clean up a suicide. As the deck hand comes into view, Sayid recognizes who it really is...none other than Michael. This means Michael is Ben's spy.

Main character: Sun.

Flash forward details: Sun is alive off the island, finally about to give birth to her baby. Meanwhile, Jin is seen frantically trying to purchase a large toy panda. In the hospital, Sun is about to give birth while yelling for Jin, as Jin tries to get the panda. Finally, Sun gives birth to a baby girl. But when Jin gets to the hospital, he gives the toy panda to the daughter of an ambassador, on behalf of Mr. Paik. As he leaves, he comments to a nurse that he's only been married for two months.

Jin's portion of the flash forward was actually a flashback to when he worked for Sun's father, while Sun's part was the only one set in the future.

After Sun returns home, she is visited by Hurley, who has not yet gone insane. The two then go to a grave site…Jin's grave site. The grave reads that Jin died on the day of the crash, which can't be true. Sun talks about giving birth to the baby, saying she named her Ji Yeon as Jin wanted. She cries about how much she misses him, but whether he's really dead or left behind on the island is not made clear.

Important details in *Lost* lore: Sun is the fifth member of the Oceanic 6 as she succeeds in giving birth to her baby. But Jin is not an Oceanic 6, as his flash forward was actually a flashback. In reality, Jin has a gravesite and the world believes he died on the plane crash, though it's not answered if he's really dead. In the present, Jin finds out about Sun's affair and eventually forgives her, while Sayid and Desmond meet the freighter captain and wind up seeing Michael.

Amount of action: Little.

New important characters: Captain Gault, Ji Yeon and "Kevin Johnson" who is Michael's alias.

Connections between characters: Sun and Jin hit a big snag but manage to get past it, while Sun and Juliet confront each other over Sun's possible death from pregnancy. Sayid and Desmond find out that Michael is on the boat.

***Lost* mysteries referenced:** Sun's pregnancy, the Oceanic 6, Ben's spy, the fake Oceanic 815 wreckage.

***Lost* mysteries introduced:** Michael's appearance on the freighter, Captain Gault's claim that Ben planted the 815 wreckage, whether Jin is alive or dead in the future.

Questions raised: Why isn't Jin with Sun in the future? Did he die, or is he still on the island while the Oceanic 6 have made the world believe he died in the crash? Who really planted the fake 815 crash? Why is Michael on the boat? Will Sayid give him away? Can the captain be trusted?

Talking points: Many people were a bit confused as to the eventual structure of the flash forwards, as it turned out to mix with a flashback. It was a narrative trick that likely won't be used again and probably shouldn't. But with this, the official list of the Oceanic 6 is Jack, Kate, Hurley, Sayid, Sun and Aaron.

Those with TiVo's were able to see that Jin's gravestone had the date 9/22/04 on it as his date of death. Even if Jin died, he didn't die on the plane, so that must be part of the Oceanic 6's cover story of lies. Why have they made up so many lies, especially if Jin and others are alive on the island?

The return of Michael on the boat is not a shock. Fans knew for months that Harold Perrineau, who plays Michael, was coming back to the main cast. And after they found out Ben had a spy on the boat, they thought it would be Michael for weeks. So this "shocking twist" is really the least shocking thing *Lost* has ever done.

Other key issues: Bernard's discussion of karma makes one believe the writers of *My Name is Earl* came to visit the set for a day.

Must see episode?: At least for the key twists and new information, plus the official conformation of Ben's spy. But other than that, this is one of the least action packed shows of the season, with a somewhat too tricky structure at the end.

MEET KEVIN JOHNSON

This episode was the last of the first eight episodes this season. By this time, the strike was over and it was announced *Lost* would go on a five week break, then wrap up the season with five straight episodes. So as the mid-season finale, this episode would have to provide big cliffhangers and bigger answers.

As such, it seemed fitting that Michael was back to reveal what he's been doing lately, and why he is now working for Ben to sabotage Charles Widmore's freighter. People had been wondering about these things since Michael's return was announced, so now they would get answers. But sometimes there are things on *Lost* that are more straightforward and uncomplicated than others.

Episode plot: Sayid and Desmond go to the deck at night to see Captain Gault beating up two people before they can leave the freighter. He yells that he's trying to save their lives, considering everything that's happened to people who have gotten close to the island. As soon as they fix the engines, they'll be okay. Sayid then finds "Kevin Johnson" a.k.a. Michael. He asks what he's doing here, as Michael just replies that he's here "to die."

The next morning, Sayid and Desmond get to Michael alone, as Sayid now forcefully asks him to tell them exactly how he got on the boat. He spends the rest of the episode telling that story.

When it's over, Sayid is more focused on the revelation that Michael works for Ben. So he drags him to Captain Gault's quarters and gives him away as the spy, calling him a traitor.

Other stuff: At the barracks, Locke has a meeting in which he gets Miles to admit the freighter is out to capture Ben. But they can't turn Ben over, because the orders are to kill everyone else on the island once Ben is taken. The others doubt the wisdom of protecting Ben, so he tells the truth by admitting his spy on the boat is Michael.

When the meeting is over, Ben calls Alex over and gives her the map to "The Temple" where the remaining Others are hiding. He worries that if his enemies found out that Alex was Ben's daughter, they would capture her. So Alex, Karl and Rousseau go off to find the Temple.

The next day, the three are resting in the woods, as Karl says he has a bad feeling about this. His suspicions are confirmed when shots come out of nowhere and kill him. Rousseau takes a crying Alex away and instructs her to run away. She tells Alex she loves her, then goes off on the count of three…and is shot herself.

As Alex hears the people who shot them come closer, she gives herself up and yells "I'm Ben's daughter!"

Main character: Michael Dawson.

Flashback details: After returning to the island, Michael is all alone without Walt. He goes to his car and pins a suicide note to his chest, then drives the car into a pier. But Michael survives this crash, though he has a brief vision of Libby in the hospital.

Once he recovers, he goes to his mother's house, where Walt is staying. She argues that Walt wants nothing to do with him and she doesn't even know why, or what happened to them after the crash. When he can't answer, he goes off. Walt briefly sees him from his window, but turns away.

Michael then trades Jin's former watch for a gun at the pawn shop, determined to shoot himself. Before he does it, a man in the shadows asks for the time. He then steps forward and calls Michael by his name. Michael then sees that it is Tom Friendly, the man who led the abduction of Walt.

Michael attacks Tom but he gets the best of him, although Michael pleads for him to shoot. Tom explains that the Others need his help. Michael is incredulous, as Tom realizes that Michael told Walt about what he did to Ana Lucia, Libby and his friends.

This is why Walt is separated from Michael, who wants to die as a result. But Tom calls out that he can't kill himself because "the island won't let you!" Tom invites Michael to meet him at a hotel once he realizes this.

Michael returns home and tries to shoot himself again, but the gun jams although it's fully loaded. Before he tries again, he sees a TV report that Oceanic 815's wreckage has been found. With that, he goes to find Tom and wants to know what the plane is doing there. Tom tells him that the wreckage is fake, having been planted by Charles Widmore. He did this so no one would find it on the island before he does.

In a few days, Widmore will be sending the freighter to the island. The Others have already gotten Michael a job on the boat as a deck hand named Kevin Johnson. Tom says that if Widmore's people get to the island, they'll kill all of Michael's friends. Michael can finally redeem himself by saving them, then when his work is finished, the island will allow him to die. But Michael's not going to go back to the island, as he is ordered to kill everyone on the freighter before they get there.

Michael heads to Fiji and boards the freighter, as there is a package there for him already. Tom calls him and tells him not to open it before they get into the ocean. Days later, after Michael sees Keamy and his team fire guns for target practice, he opens the crate. Inside is a bomb, which Michael gets set to activate. Awaiting death, Michael instead sees a flag pops up that says "Not yet."

Soon afterward, Minkowski tells Michael he has a phone call from someone named Walt. Michael rushes to the radio room expecting to hear from Walt, but instead it's Ben. He explains that he planted the fake bomb to show him that, unlike Widmore, Ben would not kill innocent people in war.

Instead, Michael is to gather the names of everyone on the freighter, so Ben can research them and determine which ones are innocent.

Then Michael will destroy the radio room and the engines so that the freighter can't get to the island. Once Michael finally agrees, Ben tells him to consider himself "one of the good guys" and hangs up.

Important details in *Lost* lore: Michael is officially confirmed as Ben's spy, as Sayid turns him in to Captain Gault. Walt has disowned Michael after finding out about his murders, but although Michael wants to kill himself, the island won't let him. Instead, he is chosen by Tom Friendly to go undercover on the freighter. It is also hinted that Charles Widmore really planted the fake Oceanic 815 wreckage. On the island, Karl is killed and Rousseau is wounded by unseen people, who Alex gives herself up to.

Amount of action: Fair.

New important characters: Michael's mother.

Connections between characters: Michael is reunited with the man who took Walt, Tom Friendly, as now he sets Michael up for his mission on the freighter. Michael sees two visions of Libby, one of his murder victims. Alex loses both Karl and her mother as she is captured by some unknown shooters.

***Lost* mysteries referenced:** What happened to Michael after leaving the island, his new job as Ben's spy, the fake Oceanic 815 wreckage, Charles Widmore's mission to take the island.

***Lost* mysteries introduced:** Why the island won't let Michael kill himself, who killed Karl and shot Rousseau, whether Charles Widmore really planted the fake 815 crash.

Questions raised: What will happen to Michael now that he's exposed? Did Sayid make a mistake turning him in? Who shot Karl and Rousseau and captured Alex? Has the war for the island now begun? How is the island able to prevent Michael's death? How could Walt have visited Locke in last season's finale if he was home in New York? Is Ben telling the truth that Widmore's people will kill everyone once they have him?

Talking points: The episode created a time line that was rather confusing to many. We are led to believe that Michael returned to the island, got separated from Walt, tried to kill himself, recovered from a car crash, met Tom Friendly again and was put onto the freighter all in the span of about two weeks.

Fans expected something like time travel and other powers would get Michael back that quickly, but it didn't happen. People also rushed to figure out when Tom could have gone to the mainland to find Michael, as well as when Ben could have contacted him on the radio. Figuring all this out creates more of a headache than usual.

The notion that the island has special powers even on the mainland isn't a huge stretch. It was later confirmed that Jack is also protected by the island, as a car crash occurred to keep him from killing himself in "Through the Looking Glass." Hurley's visions of Charlie in the future and his claims that he is needed could have been made by the island as well. So even when people leave the island, it seems the island isn't done with them until it gets what it wants.

People were also left wondering if Alex's family was shot down by killers on the freighter, or if Ben sent them into a trap so Karl and Rousseau would die. After Ben left Goodwin to die in "The Other Woman" fans were more inclined to believe Ben would do this to Alex's other loved ones. However, that was far from the case, which would become a horrifying truth in the next episode.

If Michael's job was to stop the freighter from coming to the island, it failed anyway since the helicopter brought killers there. So why didn't Ben plan ahead to sabotage the helicopter too? Or did Michael just not get to tell him about it?

Other key points: The suspicion that Tom Friendly was gay is confirmed as he sent his boyfriend away before he talked to Michael in the hotel. This was suspected since he told Kate she "wasn't his type" in the Season Three premiere.

Must see episode?: If only to see what Michael has been up to, as well as the revelation of a few new island powers and the setup for the island war to come. However, this episode is a disappointingly straight forward and almost surprise free account of Michael's experiences after leaving the island. In addition, the supposed death of Rousseau is a very disappointing end for her, as the shootings of her and Karl are a rather weak cliffhanger to hold fans over for five weeks. For the second straight season, a "mid-season" finale has a hard time delivering the goods.

THE SHAPE OF THINGS TO COME

Ben Linus, for the most part, has always been in control of everything. He's used and tricked the survivors countless times, especially John Locke. He maintains power over his subordinates even when they should know better by now. Even when his apparent enemy Charles Widmore found the location of the island, he got Michael to spy for him despite everything he did to Walt. No matter what the occasion, Ben has found a way to win or at least stay in the game. The man is a savant at plotting, with no emotions in his way.

But what if that isn't always true? What if Ben was capable of making a big mistake in strategy? What if the man untouched by emotions or guilt did have a heart and was emotionally vulnerable? And what if that heart could be shattered for all time with the worst kind of tragedy? When these questions are brutally answered, the rules of this game and the entire series change forever.

Episode plot: Alex's captors bring her to the sonar fence, where she turns it off. This sets off a phone call to Ben's house, as Locke picks it up and hears "Code 14-J." He goes to find Ben, who is playing a piano, and asks him what this means. Ben instantly realizes it means one of his people was captured, as his enemies have finally arrived.

Ben, Locke and Hurley fortify Ben's house as Sawyer goes to find Claire. But the attackers then open fire on him, blowing up Claire's house with a rocket. Yet when Sawyer rushes to the wreckage, she is alive. He carries Claire to Ben's house, but Ben won't open it. So Hurley breaks open the window for them to get in.

Ben tells Locke that they both need to stay alive, since they need to find Jacob so he can tell them what to do next. They also need to bring Hurley since he last saw the cabin. Soon the doorbell rings and Locke opens it to bring Miles in. He was given a walkie talkie by the mercenaries, who want to talk to Ben. He refuses until Miles says they have Alex.

Ben calls them and is put into contact with their leader Keamy, who introduces himself as an employee of Charles Widmore. Ben looks outside the window to see him, as Keamy tells him that he'll leave if Ben comes out. But Ben knows Keamy would kill everyone on the island if he did, citing specific information about Keamy's mercenary past. With that, Keamy ends the formalities and brings Alex out, threatening to kill her.

Ben is stunned, but he still counter-proposes that Keamy and his men leave right now. Alex is given Keamy's walkie to say goodbye, as she pleads for Ben to save her. Keamy then says Ben has 10 seconds.

In desperation, Ben says that Alex is not really his daughter, calling her a pawn. Even though he is shaking slightly, Ben yells that Alex means nothing to him and he's not coming out.

Just as he finishes, Keamy shoots Alex in the head.

Ben stands perfectly still, emotionally comatose from seeing his daughter killed. Sawyer argues that they should give Ben up as Ben continues to stand in saddened shock. He finally mutters that "He changed the rules..." then proceeds to lock himself into his secret closet. There, he goes to another secret room and enters a strange passageway. When Ben emerges, he is covered in soot. He then informs everyone to leave the house in one minute.

Just then, monstrous sounds are heard. Ben looks out to see that the black smoke monster has come out into the camp and is about to attack the mercenaries. Ben sends everyone out, as they go outside to see the monster's attack, seemingly under Ben's command. The group heads to the creek as Ben stays behind to say goodbye to Alex. As the monster finishes its assault, Ben stands over Alex's body and collapses to his knees. Crying openly, he kisses Alex's forehead and closes her eyes.

When Ben returns, he tells everyone that they are headed to Jacob's cabin. But Sawyer is done with them, as he plans to go back to the beach with Claire, Aaron and Miles. Yet Locke insists that Hurley is coming with him and Ben. Hurley finally agrees, as Sawyer threatens Locke's life if anything happens to him. Once Sawyer's team leaves, Locke, Ben and Hurley head off to find Jacob.

Other stuff: The people on the beach find a dead body washing up on shore. Daniel and Charlotte recognize him as the freighter's doctor, Ray. They then work to repair their satellite phone to find out what happened, as they are able to use Morse code.

That night, Daniel types out the code to ask what happened. When they get a response back, Daniel says that it means the helicopter will return for them in the morning. But Bernard knows Morse code, saying that the message really said the doctor was fine.

Jack gets upset that Daniel was lying, finally asking if the freighter ever planned to rescue anyone from the island. When Daniel at last admits that they weren't, Jack leaves in increasing pain.

Main character: Ben Linus.

Flash forward details: Ben suddenly seems to awake in the middle of the Sahara, wearing a heavy DHARMA parka. Two Arab men on horses come towards him, but Ben uses his baton to subdue them, heading off on their horses. He arrives in Tunisia and checks into a hotel under the name Dean Moriarty, after confirming the date is October 24, 2005. Just then, he sees a TV report of Sayid heading to the funeral of his wife.

As it turns out, Sayid found his lost love Nadia after leaving the island and married her, but she has just died. Ben goes to Iraq and finds Sayid, who is stunned to see him. Ben tells him that he's here to find the man who killed Nadia. His name is Bakir and he works for Charles Widmore, as Ben shows Sayid that Bakir was at the site where Nadia was killed.

Later, Ben tracks down Bakir, who then holds him at gunpoint. Ben tells him he has a message for Widmore, which gives Sayid time to shoot Bakir in cold blood. When it's over, Sayid stops Ben from leaving, as he wants to go on and help Ben hunt down Widmore and his people. Ben seems reluctant, but finally agrees...then he leaves with a growing smile on his face.

Sometime later, Ben is seen entering a London hotel. He takes the elevator up to a penthouse suite, where a man is sleeping. Ben says "Wake up, Charles" as Charles Widmore turns the light on from the bed. He had been expecting Ben to show up eventually, as it becomes clear that they've known each other for some time.

Widmore asks if Ben has come to kill him, but Ben says they both know he can't do that, instead blaming Widmore for Alex's death. But Widmore counters that they both know it was Ben who ultimately killed her, ridiculing Ben's notion that he's the victim. Widmore says he knows who and what Ben really is, claiming that everything Ben has, he took from him. He asks again why Ben's really here.

Ben replies he's here to tell him that he's going to kill Penelope Widmore. Once she's dead, Widmore will understand how Ben feels and he'll wish he hadn't "changed the rules." But Widmore is convinced he'll never find her. He goes on to say the island is his and always has been, and will be again. Ben quips he'll never find it either, as Widmore declares that the hunt is on for both of them. Ben tells him to sleep tight and leaves the suite.

Important details in *Lost* lore: The barracks come under attack from Widmore's mercenaries, as their leader Keamy kills Alex in front of Ben. Ben then appears to summon the smoke monster to attack them. Ben, Locke and Hurley go on their own to find Jacob as Sawyer, Claire, Aaron and Miles head for the beach. On the beach, the body of the freighter doctor washes up, but when contacting the freighter, they say he is fine. Jack then finally realizes the freighter was never going to save them.

In the future, Ben is somehow in the Sahara wearing a parka. He finds Sayid, who has married Nadia but is burying her in Iraq. Sayid becomes Ben's assassin after he learns Widmore's men killed Nadia. Later, Ben confronts Widmore in London and says he's going to kill Penelope.

Amount of action: Heavy.

New important characters: Bakir.

Connections between characters: Ben and Alex's connection is severed forever as Keamy kills her. Ben's connection to the smoke monster is uncovered as he sends it after the mercenaries. Ben, Locke and Hurley then join up to find Jacob. In the future, it is revealed how Sayid and Ben joined forces to kill Widmore's men. When Ben and Widmore confront each other, we get various hints to their past relationship and current war, as Ben vows to target Penelope as revenge for Alex's death.

***Lost* mysteries referenced:** The smoke monster, Jacob, who captured Alex, how Sayid came to kill for Ben.

***Lost* mysteries introduced:** How Ben got to the Sahara wearing a parka, how Claire survived her house getting blown up, how Ben can control the smoke monster, why the doctor is dead on the island but apparently alive on the freighter, the nature of Ben and Widmore's past, whether Ben will kill Penelope.

Questions raised: How could Ben have gotten things so wrong for once? What are "the rules" between Ben and Widmore which Widmore broke? What does Widmore mean when he says the island has always been his, and that Ben stole it from him? Will Ben get to Penelope? Why did Widmore's people have Nadia killed, if it really was them? How can Ben control the smoke monster, and has it killed Keamy and his team? Will Ben, Locke and Hurley find Jacob? Will Sawyer and his new team get back to the beach safe? What happened to the doctor? Why does Jack appear to be in a lot of pain? Now that the camp knows the freighter won't rescue them, what will they do?

Talking points: For only the second time and first since last season's finale, Ben's plans fail miserably. But losing Alex is obviously a lot harsher. What's more, Keamy actually shoots Alex right after Ben stops talking, instead of pausing a few seconds to increase the tension like most other TV and movie deaths. This helps makes Alex's death *Lost's* most brutal ever.

So how could the doctor be dead on the beach while the freighter claimed he was fine? The now traditional answer to time related questions on this show is that island time just doesn't match with real world time.

It's been a while since an Other countered someone's claim that they don't know anything about them by reading a laundry list of their past. Ben took care of that by bringing up Keamy's, but in context, it wasn't a wise move.

When Ben is in his parka, it shows the name "Halliwax" which is one of the names of DHARMA's orientation video host, Dr. Marvin Candle. Ben claimed he got off the island using Desmond's sailboat, but that hardly appears to be the case.

There are almost too many little clues in the meeting between Ben and Widmore to go over. All of them hint to a relationship and war between them that strikes to the core of this entire island. To film this historic scene, the *Lost* crew and Michael Emerson actually filmed it in London, since Alan Dale, who plays Widmore, was doing *Spamalot* in the London theater and couldn't go to Hawaii.

Other key issues: There were those who wondered how Claire could have survived her house blowing up. This isn't an unimportant question, as future episodes would explain.

Must see episode?: One of the most pivotal episodes of all time. Alex's death, the smoke monster's attack and Ben's meeting with Widmore are among the biggest scenes in show history. Nearly everything you thought about Ben is shattered in this episode, powered by the great Michael Emerson. "The Shape Of Things To Come" indeed.

SOMETHING NICE BACK HOME

For the entire season, we've been waiting to figure out how the heroic Jack Shephard of the island could turn into the wretched, desperate to go back Jack of the future. In flash forwards this season, Jack appears to still be stable, as he managed to stay in denial about whatever happened. In the present, he's been waiting patiently for a rescue, but now he finally figured out the freighter will not give it to him.

So, aside from realizing Locke was right all along, which he would never do, what can Jack do now? And what miseries have we yet to see during his time home? As usual, the answers involve two very common things for Jack in both times, which are pain and Kate.

Episode plot: As the beach camp is trying to get answers from Daniel and Charlotte, Jack is coming down in even more pain. Juliet takes charge and figures out his appendix is about to rupture. She plans to perform surgery, sending Daniel, Charlotte, Sun and Jin to the medical hatch. Jack insists on staying awake through the surgery and wants Kate to help.

During their trip to the medical hatch, Jin realizes that Daniel likes Charlotte and that Charlotte can understand Korean. He tells Charlotte in Korean that he will hurt Daniel if they keep lying, insisting that when the helicopter returns, Sun will be put on it first.

Juliet sets up a tent for the surgery. Kate holds up a mirror while Jack looks into it to instruct Juliet what to do. As the pain gets worse, Juliet sends Kate away and tells Bernard to knock Jack out. But eventually, the surgery succeeds. Kate thanks Juliet for saving Jack, as Juliet tells her that Jack kissed her, but that he still loves Kate all along.

Other stuff: Sawyer, Claire, Aaron and Miles are on their way back to the beach, as Sawyer becomes protective of Claire when Miles keeps looking at her. Soon they are found by Frank Lapidus, who warns them to hide before Keamy and the mercenaries come back. Indeed, although they are banged up, they survived the smoke monster attack. Keamy suspects there are people hiding, but Frank convinces him to go so he can fly them back onto the freighter before dark.

That night, Claire awakens and sees someone holding Aaron by the fire. It is Christian Shephard, who is both Claire's father and still dead, if one remembers.

The next morning, Sawyer wakes up to see Claire gone. Miles says he saw her go with someone she called "Dad." Sawyer calls for her, then sees that Aaron has been left alone in front of a tree.

Main character: Jack Shephard.

Flash forward details: Sometime after Kate's trial, Jack finally connected with her and they now live together, as Jack helps her care for Aaron. But one day, he gets a call from the mental institution where Hurley lives.

Jack goes to see Hurley, who has gotten worse and is now convinced him and the Oceanic 6 are dead. He's still talking to Charlie, who told him Jack was coming and gave him a message, which is "You're not supposed to raise him, Jack." Hurley asks if that refers to Aaron, as Jack grows worried and goes to leave. However, Hurley also says that someone will be visiting Jack soon.

After some uneasiness, Jack recovers and goes back home to propose to Kate, who says yes. But one night when Jack is working, he hears someone call his name from the lobby. Jack then sees his father sitting on a couch. Before Jack can confront him, another doctor soon comes in to end this reunion. Jack then asks for a prescription for sleeping pills.

Not long after that, Jack is already drunk as he waits for Kate to get home. Suspicious of where Kate has been, he asks for her to tell him. Kate keeps on avoiding the question until she admits she was fulfilling a promise she made to Sawyer. Jack gets upset, proclaiming that he's the one who came back for her and saved her.

Breaking down, Kate tells Jack he can't be like this around her son, which makes Jack explode and yell that she's not even related to Aaron. Just then, Aaron walks into the room, as Jack leaves while Kate goes to her "son."

Important details in *Lost* lore: Surgery is performed on Jack. In the jungle, Claire disappears with her late father Christian Shephard. Christian also briefly appears to Jack in the future, which forces him to begin his addictions and end his relationship with Kate.

Amount of action: Little.

New important characters: None.

Connections between characters: Juliet saves Jack's life, then takes herself out of the running in the love triangle with him and Kate. Sawyer watches over Claire in the jungle, but loses her when she goes off in the middle of the night with Christian. Jack and Kate are living together in the future and are briefly engaged, but break up when Jack begins to fall apart.

***Lost* mysteries referenced:** Jack's new pain, Christian Shephard's life after death, Kate being Aaron's mother in the future, Jack's future addictions, Hurley's future talks with Charlie, the premonition that no one other than Claire must raise Aaron.

***Lost* mysteries introduced:** The fate of Claire.

Questions raised: Why did Jack get sick now? Will he recover fast enough to secure rescue? Is Juliet no longer interested in Jack romantically? Where has Claire gone with Christian? Why did they leave Aaron behind? Why was Miles paying so much attention to Claire? What are Keamy and the mercenaries going to do when they return to the freighter?

Talking points: Having Jack get sick is a cheap ploy to generate suspense when it's clear he'll be off the island in three episodes. The only interesting point made was by Rose, who comments that people get better, not sick on the island. The island chose to heal Locke and Rose, while it kept Jack and Michael from killing themselves back home. However, it almost killed Ben and allowed Jack's appendix to nearly burst.

It has become clear that people who live on the island only stay alive as long as the island lets them and needs them. Why was Jack suddenly not useful? Or did the island just want him sidelined for a while?

The suspicions are growing that Claire actually died when her house blew up in the last episode. After all, she left with the dead Christian Shephard, and she was examined by Miles, who would know if she was dead due to his powers. Is this why Aaron has to be left in Kate's care?

Way back in Season One, Claire's psychic predicted disaster if anyone other Claire raised her baby. Now, with Hurley giving the message that Jack isn't supposed to raise him, this ominous proclamation may have become crucial to *Lost* once again.

Other key issues: The smoke monster is losing its touch, as it certainly didn't kill too many of Keamy's people even though Ben must have really wanted it to.

Must see episode?: The flash forward and the two returns of Christian Shephard are, but the rest can be skipped over.

CABIN FEVER

If there's one thing we know about Locke, it's that he's convinced he's special. After all, the island gave him his legs back, he is regularly called upon to protect it, plus he's one of the few that has heard from Jacob. It seems Locke has led a blessed life for the most part on the island, while having a rotten one off of it. But the notion of Locke being special wasn't a recent phenomenon.

There have been many terrible things in Locke's past life, but there have been many more opportunities to fulfill his destiny a lot earlier. John Locke is a man of destiny, but we're about to find out how far back that destiny goes.

Episode plot: Locke, Ben and Hurley are getting nowhere trying to find Jacob's cabin. But that morning, Locke has a vision as he sees someone cutting down trees. It is Horace Goodspeed, the DHARMA worker who brought Ben and his dad to the island, but who died 12 years ago in the Purge. As Horace chops down trees on a loop, he tells Locke that when he finds him, he'll find Jacob. Locke then wakes up and knows where to go.

He takes Ben and Hurley to the pit of dead DHARMA workers. As Locke looks for Horace's body, Hurley and Ben discuss the Purge. Ben says he didn't kill off DHARMA, as it was a decision made by the Others former leaders, not him. Locke finds Horace's skeleton and finds the blueprints to Jacob's cabin, which Horace built. Now knowing where the cabin is, he leads Ben and Hurley off.

That night, Ben questions whether Locke is going the right way, as Locke assures he was told where to go. Ben bitterly reflects on how he was told he was special and chosen, as all he got for it was a tumor and Alex's death. He tells Locke he too will face consequences for being chosen, because destiny is "a fickle bitch." Their discussion is interrupted when Hurley finds the cabin. Ben chooses to stay behind, saying that his time in charge is over.

Locke enters the cabin and sees a man in the shadows. The man says he's not Jacob, but he can speak on his behalf. He then shows himself as Christian Shephard. After Locke confirms he was chosen to be here, he notices that Claire is sitting nearby and is smiling.

When Locke asks where Aaron is, Christian says he's not supposed to be here and tells Locke not to say anything. He then points out that since the people from the freighter are coming back, none of Locke's other questions matter one bit. Locke's only question that does matter is "How do I save the island?"

Locke soon leaves the cabin and tells Ben and Hurley what Jacob wants them to do.

He wants them to "move the island."

Other stuff: The helicopter returns to the freighter, as Keamy is becoming more unhinged. He now plans to work on a secondary protocol that Charles Widmore set up for him. It tells him where Ben is going to go next, since Ben knows that they're going to "torch the island." All this is news to Captain Gault.

He later tells Sayid and Desmond to hide, but Sayid knows that the only way to survive is to get everyone off the island before Keamy's people kill them. Gault allows him to use the freighter's Zodiac raft to get back to the island and start bringing people on the boat. Desmond stays behind as Sayid drives off.

Frank visits Michael in his cell, as Michael pleads for him not to bring Keamy back to the island. That night, Frank does refuse to fly Keamy back. Since Keamy can't kill him, he instead slits the freighter doctor's throat and throws him overboard, where he will float back onto the island two days earlier.

Captain Gault then shows and points his gun at Keamy. But Keamy has some kind of device attached to his arm, which distracts Gault long enough for Keamy to kill him. Finally Frank relents and flies him and the mercenaries off the boat.

On the beach, Jack is in recovery from his surgery, although he's not lying around. The helicopter then flies over them as a package is dropped off. Jack picks it up to see a satellite phone that's tracking the helicopter's location, thinking they want the survivors to find them.

Main character: John Locke.

Flashback details: In the mid 50's, a young girl rushes off to meet her boyfriend who is twice her age. But then a car crashes into her, which induces her pregnancy. Though she is only six months pregnant, she gives birth to the baby. As it's taken away, she asks to name it John. This is how John Locke was born.

As baby Locke lies in an incubator, his mother gets cold feet and rushes off. Her own mother makes plans to put Locke in adoption, only stopping when she sees someone standing outside. She denies he knows him, but she seems to recognize him. The man is Richard Alpert, who once again looks the exact same as he does 50 years later.

When Locke is five years old, Richard comes to visit him again in his foster home. He says he runs a special school that he is considering Locke for, which is obviously on the island. Richard lays some items on the table in front of Locke, telling him to pick the items that "belong to him already."

Young Locke picks a container of dirt, a compass, and looks to be picking out a book of laws. He picks a knife instead, which angers Richard as he now says Locke isn't ready, then leaves.

When Locke is 16 years old, he is a bullied high school student being stuffed into lockers. A teacher informs him that Locke was offered a chance to go to a science camp run by Mittlos Bioscience, which is the Others front company run by Richard Alpert. Teenage Locke refuses, saying he wants to do things like sports instead. The teacher tells him he will never be able to do those kind of things, but Locke says for the first time "Don't tell me what I can't do."

When Locke is grown up and crippled, he is undergoing physical therapy. Once he's done, an orderly wheels him back to his room, telling him not to give up. He calls the fact that Locke survived an eight story fall a miracle. Then the orderly is revealed as Matthew Abaddon, the mysterious man who helped organize the freighter mission for Charles Widmore.

Abaddon tells Locke he needs to go on a walkabout, which Locke doubts he can do since he's crippled. Abaddon says that when he went on a walkabout and found out who he really was, a miracle happened to him. When Locke mocks him for being an orderly, Abaddon insists he's a little more than that.

He ends by saying that Locke will listen when he's ready, and when they meet again, Locke will owe him one. This plants the idea in Locke's head to go on his walkabout. As we know, it was only after he got rejected to go in "Walkabout" that Locke arrived on the island at long last.

Important details in *Lost* lore: Locke is seen at various ages as he comes close to being brought to the island by Richard Alpert on several occasions. Finally, Matthew Abaddon gives Locke the idea to go on a walkabout, which led to him finally landing on the island. In the present, Locke encounters the late Horace Goodspeed, who built Jacob's cabin. He finds it, but encounters Christian Shephard and Claire instead. There, he gets instructions to "move the island." Meanwhile, Keamy and his team head back to the island.

Amount of action: Fair.

New important characters: A young Emily Locke and her mother, who seems to know Richard.

Connections between characters: Richard Alpert is seen to know about Locke from birth, trying a few times to get him onto the island at an early age. Matthew Abaddon also encounters Locke in the past, giving him the inspiration for his walkabout quest. Ben seems to finally pass the torch of island leadership to Locke willingly, as they and Hurley search for Jacob. Locke finds Christian Shephard instead, not knowing that he's the father of his other rival Jack.

***Lost* mysteries referenced:** Jacob, Christian's life after death, Claire's disappearance, Locke's destiny, Richard Alpert's agelessness, Matthew Abaddon.

***Lost* mysteries introduced:** Christian's connection to Jacob, Richard's interest in Locke, Abaddon's visit to Locke, what the device on Keamy's arm is, what moving the island means, who led the Others in the Purge instead of Ben, Horace's connection to the cabin.

Questions raised: What does it mean to "move the island?" Why was Christian in the cabin instead of Jacob? Why is Claire still with him? Is Ben really going to just hand control of the island to Locke now? What does it mean that Horace built Jacob's cabin? Whose idea was the Purge? Why was Locke chosen from birth to go to the island? Why did Abaddon give Locke the idea to go on his walkabout? Will Sayid be able to get his friends off the island in time? What is Keamy and Widmore's secondary protocol? Where do they think Ben is going?

Talking points: Locke's destiny now goes back even further than fans could have guessed. From his birthday, the island seems to have wanted him. It would appear that Ben was and always has been the island's second choice while it was waiting for Locke. It would explain why Ben got a spinal tumor right before the plane crash, since it, or Jacob, must have known Locke was finally coming and wanted Ben out of the way.

Abaddon's appearance to Locke seems a bit out of place. All of Locke's previous flashbacks in this episode showed how the island wanted to get a hold of him. But Abaddon was previously revealed as the one who recruited Daniel, Charlotte, Miles and Frank for Charles Widmore's mission to take control of the island. So what does it mean that Abaddon is the one who set Locke off on his walkabout quest? It probably means Abaddon knew Locke would finally go to the island once they rejected him for the walkabout. But who did he do this for?

If Abaddon is working for Widmore, then perhaps Widmore also knows that Locke was chosen by the island. As such, he may have had a grand plan of his own to bring him there so Locke could supplant Widmore's nemesis Ben. If Abaddon did this on behalf of the island, then it calls into question why he's really on Widmore's team.

Richard's odd test of the five-year-old Locke is a direct reference to how Buddhists choose the reincarnation of the Dalai Llama. So now you also need a Buddhist education to follow this show.

Other key issues: Hurley sweetly finds the heart to share his candy bar with Ben while they wait outside the cabin. But it came at a price to us fans that needed information, since it interrupted Locke's conversation with Christian.

Must see episode?: It brings a whole new dimension to the destiny and purpose of John Locke as we see how important he's been to the island all his life, so yes. It also crams a few more cliffhangers in and raises the head scratching notion of "moving the island" as the season finale approaches.

THERE'S NO PLACE LIKE HOME: PART 1

Here we are again at the beginning of another *Lost* season finale. Readers will reflect that we've gotten here pretty quickly, but in real life, it was a longer wait for this episode. Like with the Season One finale, they would show an hour long part 1 and then a two-hour long part 2 and 3. Somewhere in these three hours, the answers about the present and the future that had been teased out all year would finally come.

But first, this episode sets the pieces in motion for the various forces on the island on the pivotal day of rescue. In addition, it shows the beginning of the Oceanic 6's life back home. Or truth be told, the beginning of the end for them.

Episode plot: Despite his recent surgery, Jack is still up for a trip to the jungle with Kate to find the helicopter. They turn on their new satellite phone and overhear Keamy say that they will deploy to "The Orchid." Daniel looks through his journal and realizes exactly what that means, telling Charlotte they have to leave the island right now.

Jack and Kate soon find Miles, Sawyer and Aaron. Sawyer says they lost Claire and tells Jack about the mercenaries attack on the barracks. But Jack brushes this aside, still wanting to get the helicopter and leave the island. He gives Aaron to Kate and goes off, with Sawyer following him.

On the beach, Sayid has returned with the Zodiac raft. When he tells everyone what's going on, Juliet informs him that Jack has gone off towards the helicopter.

Ben, Hurley and Locke are going off to "move the island." To do this, Ben is taking them to "The Orchid" a DHARMA greenhouse station. He explains he didn't do this before the mercenaries arrived because moving the island is a last resort. Ben then finds a box with a mirror inside, using it to communicate with someone on the hills.

On the beach, Daniel volunteers to start bringing people back to the freighter. Once Kate comes back and tells Sayid what happened, the two make plans to go back in the jungle. Kate gives Aaron to Sun as she and Jin board the raft, then Daniel drives them away.

Ben, Locke and Hurley soon arrive at the Orchid, but Ben anticipates that Keamy and his men are already there under Charles Widmore's orders, which they are.

On the freighter, Daniel brings Sun, Jin and several other survivors on board from the raft, then goes back to bring the next batch on. Right afterwards, Sun and Jin see Michael for the first time since he left the island. Michael has finished fixing the engines and the freighter should be ready to head for the beach. However, Desmond finds that a signal from somewhere onboard is blocking their fathometer.

In the jungle, Sawyer and Jack find Frank handcuffed to the helicopter. Frank says that he threw the satellite phone so they could find him and he could fly them off before the mercenaries returned. As Jack and Sawyer try to unlock him, they find out that the mercenaries are waiting for Ben. After Sawyer reveals that Hurley is with Ben, Jack realizes they have to go get him.

On the freighter, Michael tries to explain himself to Sun and Jin, until Desmond yells that he needs him. They go inside a room where there is 500 pounds of C4. Jin sends Sun and Aaron away as he, Michael and Desmond stay to try and disarm the explosives.

In the jungle, Kate and Sayid find fresh tracks right behind them. They yell for whoever's there to come out. Soon Richard Alpert appears, along with an army of Others who trap Kate and Sayid.

At the Orchid, Ben instructs Locke on how to find an elevator that will take him to the real Orchid station underground. Locke asks what he's supposed to do about the armed men, but Ben answers he'll take care of it, reminding Locke that he always has a plan. Ben then heads off to the Orchid.

In a final montage, Jack and Sawyer head towards the Orchid, Kate and Sayid are led away by Richard and the Others, Sun takes Aaron to the dock of the freighter, Locke and Hurley remain in the bushes, while Ben shows himself to the mercenaries. He reintroduces himself to Keamy, who promptly hits Ben in the forehead with his gun.

Main characters: The Oceanic 6.

Flash forward details: A plane is transporting the Oceanic 6 back to the mainland. Oceanic employee Karen Decker instructs them that their families are waiting for them, giving them the option of not having to talk to the press. Jack agrees to the press conference, while none of the other survivors speak up. When Decker leaves, Jack reminds them that they all know their cover story and they don't have to answer if the press asks too many tough questions. Soon, the plane touches down.

The cargo door opens and the Oceanic 6 take their first steps back home. Hurley finds his parents waiting, Jack is greeted by his mother, while Sun is hugged by her parents. Hurley introduces Sayid to his parents, but Kate is all alone with Aaron, having no one waiting for her.

At the Oceanic 6 press conference, Decker tells the press that the survivors washed up on an island near Indonesia, close to the fake Oceanic 815 wreckage. The story is that they found a raft and sailed to the island of Sumba, where they were discovered and brought back by the Coast Guard.

The survivors then take questions, as Sun uneasily explains that Jin died in the plane crash and Sayid flatly denies there are any more survivors. When it's over, Decker tells Sayid that a woman named Nadia claims she knows him. He goes out back and sees Nadia for the first time in years, as the two hug and kiss tearfully.

Sometime later, Sun is seen at her father's company, still pregnant. She goes to see her father and informs him that she used her settlement from Oceanic to buy a controlling interest in the company. Sun yells that Mr. Paik ruined Jin's life and he is one of the two people responsible for his death. Once Sun has her baby, she will take an active role in running her father's company.

Hurley is then seen at his mansion, as he receives a surprise island themed birthday party. There, Hurley's father shows him that he fixed the family Camaro while Hurley was away. But when Hurley gets inside, he sees the numbers 4, 8, 15, 16, 23 and 42 on the speedometer. Freaking out over seeing the numbers again, Hurley runs away.

Sometime after that, Jack gives the eulogy at Christian Shephard's wake. Afterwards, he is confronted by an Australian woman who says she knew Christian. This is Claire's mother, who has awoken from her coma and tells Jack that Christian had a daughter. What's more, she was on Oceanic 815 with Jack. She tells him that Claire was his sister, which shakes Jack to his core. Claire's mother then goes to Kate and tells her that her baby is beautiful, not knowing that Aaron is her real grandson. But Jack now knows that Aaron is his nephew.

Important details in *Lost* lore: The Oceanic 6's first days back home are revealed, as Sun buys out her father's company, Sayid finds Nadia again and Jack finds out Claire was his sister. On the island, a new DHARMA station called the Orchid is discovered, which has the power to "move the island." Jack and Sawyer head there to find Hurley so they can fly off the island, Kate and Sayid are captured by Richard Alpert and the Others, and Locke is instructed to go inside the Orchid while Ben gives himself up to buy time. Daniel brings Sun and Jin to the freighter where they reunite with Michael, then discover that there are C4 explosives onboard.

Amount of action: Fair.

New important characters: Oceanic representative Karen Decker.

Connections between characters: The Oceanic 6 are seen returning home. Soon after, Jack discovers his family connection to Claire and Aaron. In the present, Jack and Sawyer delay their ride home to find Hurley, as Sun and Jin see Michael again. Kate and Sayid are caught by Richard and the remaining Others.

***Lost* mysteries referenced:** The Oceanic 6's return home and their cover story about where they were, the concept of "moving the island."

***Lost* mysteries introduced:** The Orchid station, Daniel's knowledge of what the Orchid does, the C4 explosives on the freighter.

Questions raised: What is the Orchid, and how does it move the island? Will Locke be able to move it? Will Ben survive being captured by Keamy? Will Jack and Sawyer retrieve Hurley in time to leave the island? Why are Richard and the Others in the jungle? Where did the C4 explosives on the freighter come from? Will Desmond, Jin and Michael be able to defuse them? What does Daniel know about the Orchid? Who else is responsible for Jin's supposed death?

Talking points: After being forgotten about for a few episodes, Daniel's knowledge of weird island stuff like the Orchid comes back into play. As well as his inability to actually explain more about what he knows, which is weird since he can't lie well and has the worst poker face on the show.

Sun's buyout of her father's company could be very crucial, since it has been suspected that Mr. Paik is one of Charles Widmore's business allies. With that kind of access and wealth, Sun would have a fair shot to find the island again if she wants to.

After being pretty much out of it in the last episode, Ben reverted back to his old "I always have a plan" mode literally overnight. Although Locke was told to move the island, Ben's the one that knows how, which makes him holding all the cards once more.

The Orchid is a location that has been teased for almost a year to *Lost* fans. In their presentation at Comic-Con the previous summer, *Lost* showed the orientation video for the Orchid, hosted again by Dr. Marvin Candle. But this version was disrupted during filming when two bunnies with the numbers 15 and 16 on it came together, which somehow meant near disaster. Until then, Candle hinted that experiments in space and time were crucial to the Orchid. Space time elements could certainly help move an island.

Other key issues: The "wake" for Christian Shephard has got to go down as one of the more useless goodbyes to someone in history, considering he's far from being laid to rest.

Must see episode?: This part 1 merely puts the pieces in place for the two hour finale, but these pieces are very necessary to see. Coupled with a few emotionally draining, Michael Giacchino scored silent montages in the beginning and end, the stage is set for something really gigantic.

THERE'S NO PLACE LIKE HOME: PARTS 2 & 3

This is all that's left, at least for now. This is the very end of the recap and the very end of *Lost's* first four seasons. After this, there is no more to tell or see until late January 2009, when Season Five begins. If you are reading this in late January and have everything finished, you are one short step away from being fully caught up to *Lost.* Then again, there's nothing short about this two hour episode and the many huge developments that have left fans hanging for eight months.

Some of the many questions answered here are: Who is the man in the coffin that Jack mourns in the future? How do the Oceanic 6 return home? Why are some people left behind? What is the Orchid station? How does one move an island? Why does Jack know that he has to go back? Why do the Oceanic 6 need to lie about what happened to them? Do Charles Widmore and his mercenaries succeed in conquering the island?

So many questions answered, 10 times more created as a result. Would you still be trying to catch up to *Lost* if it were any other way? Here is your final episode to read up on.

Episode plot: Jack and Sawyer arrive at the Orchid to see Hurley and Locke. Jack prepares to leave with Hurley until he learns that Keamy and his men are bringing Ben back to the helicopter.

There, the mercenaries are met by Kate, who claims that she's being chased by Ben's people. This sets up the mercenaries to be ambushed and brought down by the Others. Kate runs off with Ben as Keamy gives chase, but he is tackled by Sayid. The two get into a major brawl, yet Keamy finally gets the advantage. Before he chokes Sayid, he is shot in the back by Richard Alpert. With the battle over, Richard tells Ben that he allowed Kate and Sayid to leave the island in exchange for their help. Ben agrees to let Kate and Sayid take the helicopter.

On the freighter, Desmond, Jin and Michael are trying to figure out how to disarm the C4 explosives, which can be triggered remotely once a red light flashes on.

Back at the Orchid, Locke requests to have a talk with Jack. He tries to convince him not to leave the island, saying that Jack knows he's here for a reason and that knowledge will eat him alive until he decides to go back. But Jack isn't listening, so Locke now tries to convince him to lie about the island when he goes home. Jack still doesn't believe him, dismissing Locke's claims that miracles happen here.

Ben then returns, going on to show Locke where the Orchid elevator is. He tells Jack that Kate and Sayid are at the helicopter and his people from the beach are heading for the freighter, advising him to leave within the hour. Locke makes one more request that Jack lie about the island before going underground with Ben.

On the freighter, Michael's plan is to freeze the bombs with liquid nitrogen, claiming that it will ensure the explosives don't go off the second the red light goes on. Back on the beach, Daniel has returned and prepares to get the next batch of people on the raft. Miles says he's staying on the island, cryptically asking Charlotte why she would leave after all the time she spent trying to get back.

Jack, Hurley and Sawyer reunite with Kate and Sayid at the helicopter. After finally getting Frank's handcuffs off, he gets them onboard and flies them off the island.

Back at the Orchid, the still alive Keamy emerges. His bulletproof vest stopped Richard's shot, as Keamy calls for Ben to come out. He then shows the device on his arm, which is connected to the C4 explosives.

If his heart stops, it triggers the explosives to go off and destroy the freighter. Keamy practically dares Ben to take a shot, but stops when he sees Locke coming to try and reason with him.

Just as Keamy goes to attack Locke, Ben comes out of a locker and hits Keamy with his baton. He then grabs Keamy's knife and madly stabs him in the neck out of rage over Alex's death. Locke proclaims that Ben just killed everyone on the freighter, to which Ben replies "So?"

On the beach, Charlotte tells Daniel that she's staying, as she claims she's "still looking for where I was born." After she says goodbye, Daniel goes to the raft, as Juliet finishes getting people on board. She says she promised not to leave until she got everyone else off. Daniel parts with Juliet, seeming to realize that she won't be able to leave herself, then drives the raft away.

The helicopter is flying over the ocean, but is losing fuel because a bullet went through the fuel tank. They try to dump extra weight off, but it's not enough. Frank offers to fly to the island to refuel, but Jack orders him not to. However, there may be no choice.

Sawyer thinks things over in the back, seeming to come to a decision. He asks Kate to do something for him, then whispers his request in her ear and gives her one last kiss. With that, Sawyer jumps off the helicopter and lands in the ocean, emerging to swim back to the island as Kate watches him go in tears. But soon enough, the helicopter finds the freighter and now has enough fuel to make it.

At the Orchid, Locke frantically tries to keep Keamy alive, but it's no use. Keamy's final words are to tell Ben that no matter where he goes, Widmore will find him. Once he finally dies, his device beeps.

Back on the freighter, the red light is now on, but Michael has frozen the radio enough to delay the explosion. Desmond leaves to tell everyone to evacuate the freighter, then sees that the helicopter is about to land. Desmond screams that there's a bomb, but Frank still needs to refuel. He and the survivors rush to get it done as Sun starts to panic that Jin's not back, giving Aaron to Kate.

Inside, Michael runs out of nitrogen, telling Jin to go and get back to Sun. Jin thanks him and leaves as Michael stays behind. Jin gets on deck just as the helicopter takes off. Sun sees him and screams for them to land, but Frank says they can't do it.

Back inside, Michael starts to hear whispers and then sees someone in front of him. Christian Shephard is there, telling Michael that he "can go now."

A second later, the freighter explodes and sinks into the ocean. Sun yells in terror for Jin, pleading for the helicopter to try and find him. But Jack doesn't see Jin's body and is convinced he's gone. With no choice now, he tells Frank to fly back to the island as Sun cries at the top of her lungs.

In the Orchid, Locke yells at Ben for dooming the freighter, as a now calm Ben explains that he let his emotions get in the way. He then activates the vault with the metal inside it, which results in a hole being blown up in the back.

On the beach, a shirtless Sawyer has managed to swim all the way back to the island. He notices Juliet sadly drinking rum, as she can see the smoky remains of the freighter from far away. Sawyer notices it too, fearing that Kate and the others may have died in the explosion.

Back in the Orchid, Ben has put on the same parka he wore in the Sahara in "The Shape Of Things To Come." He explains that although Jacob told Locke to move the island, he didn't tell him how because he wants Ben to do it and suffer the consequences. Because once you move the island, you can never come back.

So Ben tells Locke to leave and find the Others, who are already waiting for him to take command. He offers his hand to Locke, apologizing for everything he did to him, as Locke finally shakes the hand of his former rival. Locke returns to the jungle and discovers the Others, as Richard tells him "Welcome home" causing Locke to grin.

Ben goes through the open hole in the vault, crawling inside a passageway. He finds a small icy surface, which he breaks to reveal a frozen room below him. He climbs a ladder down to the room, but slips and hurts his arm. Getting up, Ben goes to what he's looking for...a wall with a large, frozen wheel in the center. Ben takes the frozen wheel, looks up and says "I hope you're happy now, Jacob."

Ben tries to turn the wheel, though it is almost too heavy for him. But finally it begins to move as Ben keeps pushing it forward. A light begins to glow from the wheel, as a humming noise is heard from the jungle, the beach and from the ocean where Daniel and his raft of survivors are. Ben makes the final push as he actually begins to cry. The light finally covers him and he closes his eyes in both relief and grief.

Another larger light begins to cover the entire island and Daniel's raft. Those in the helicopter are also able to see it. When the light finally fades away, the island is gone.

Frank keeps asking where the island is, as Hurley is the only one who understands what just happened. But now there's nowhere to land and the helicopter is out of fuel for good. The survivors put life jackets on, as Sayid throws down a life raft he got from the freighter. The helicopter crashes and breaks apart in the ocean.

Minutes later, Jack awakens and sees the other survivors swimming into the raft. He finds an unconscious Desmond and brings him on board, performing CPR until he is resuscitated. With that, the future Oceanic 6, Desmond and Frank are all on the raft, stuck in the middle of the ocean.

That night, Hurley expresses amazement that Locke actually moved the island. Jack disagrees, but Hurley points out that the island did indeed disappear. At that moment, Frank sees a light approaching, realizing there's a boat. The rest of the survivors call for help as Jack stays quiet, now seeming to finally realize what Locke did, as well as what he was asking him to do. He now understands that they need to lie.

So Jack tells everyone that they have to cover up everything that happened to them and everything about the island. He quickly recaps that someone put fake wreckage of Oceanic 815 in the ocean and tried to have them all killed. The only way to protect those they left behind from any future attacks is to convince the world they weren't on that island. Jack says he'll do the talking as the boat now approaches them. A man onboard notices them and calls for "Ms. Widmore."

Desmond now looks up in shock, as a second later, Penelope Widmore appears on the boat and orders her crew to bring the survivors up. Desmond rushes up into the ship and finds Penelope. The two happily embrace and kiss for the first time in many years. Penelope tearfully says that she used her tracking station in the Antarctic to trace her phone call with Desmond and begin searching. Desmond vows that he loves her and will never leave her again. Soon, the rest of the survivors are on the boat, but Jack soon tells Penelope that they need to talk.

A week later, the Oceanic 6 are preparing to sail on a raft to the island of Sumba, where they will be found by the Coast Guard. They have spent the last week developing their cover story with Penelope about what happened to them. Desmond is staying behind with Penny, ready to go into hiding so Widmore doesn't find him. Jack says his goodbyes to Desmond and Frank, then he, Kate, Sayid, Hurley, Sun and Aaron board the raft. Eight hours later, they arrive on the island and are noticed by villagers, as they make their way to finally return home.

Main characters: The Oceanic 6.

Flash forward details: Picking off right when the flash forward scene in "Through the Looking Glass" ended, the future bearded Jack yells to Kate that they have to go back to the island. This makes Kate drive back to Jack, mad at his suggestion. She then brings out the obit for the man in the coffin, who Kate calls Jeremy Bentham. This man also visited Kate and told her she had to return. Kate thought he was crazy, yet Jack listened to him. She tells Jack definitively that she is not going back.

Later, Hurley is seen in the mental institution, as Michael's mother has brought a teenaged Walt to visit him. Walt tells him that Jeremy Bentham also visited him, as he wonders why the Oceanic 6 are lying about what happened. Hurley says it's the only way to protect everyone.

Late at night, Sayid also goes to the mental institution, killing someone who is watching from the parking lot. Sayid finds Hurley's room and tells him Bentham is dead, discounting the report that it was a suicide. Hurley almost calls Bentham by his real name before Sayid stops him, saying they are being watched. Sayid wants to take Hurley to "somewhere safe." Hurley agrees, though not before finishing his chess game with the ghost of Mr. Eko.

In London, Sun is on the phone with her toddler daughter Ji Yeon, as she says to her nanny that she is finishing some business. She looks over to a restaurant and sees Charles Widmore coming out. Sun introduces herself to him, as Widmore asks about her father. She then asks if he's really going to deny who she actually is, pointing out that he knows the Oceanic 6 have been lying to the world.

Sun says she and Widmore have common interests and invites him to call her, also noting that the 6 aren't the only ones who left the island. As Sun leaves, Widmore asks why she would want to help him, but she doesn't answer as emotions begin to overtake her.

At Kate's house, she is woken up from her sleep by noises. The phone then rings and plays a backwards message, which actually means "The island needs you. You have to go back before it's too late." Kate gets up as she hears footsteps coming towards Aaron's room and opens it, seeing someone over the bed. That someone is Claire.

Kate steps back in shock as Claire tells her "Don't you dare bring him back!"- then Kate wakes up from her dream/vision. She then goes to Aaron's bed for real, as she starts to cry and mutter that she's sorry.

Finally, Jack is seen driving back to the funeral parlor. He breaks in and goes to the coffin where Jeremy Bentham is held. He opens it and looks at the body in sadness, then jumps back when he hears a voice say "Hello, Jack."

Ben Linus is now in the room.

Ben asks Jack when "Bentham" came to see him. Jack tells him he saw Bentham a month ago. When he did, he was told that "very bad things" happened after he left the island. Bentham said that it was Jack's fault for leaving and that he had to go back. Ben knows that Jack has been flying on airplanes since then, hoping that they would crash.

But Ben is here to say that the island won't let Jack go alone. All of the Oceanic 6 have to return. Jack points out that he doesn't know where Sayid is, Hurley is insane, Sun blames him for what happened to Jin, and Kate won't see him anymore. Ben offers his help, saying that this is the only way as the Oceanic 6 have to do this together. He already has a few ideas on how they can return. At last, Jack makes his choice as he agrees to unite with his old enemy.

But before Jack leaves, Ben points to Bentham's body and says that they have to bring him too.

And then at long last, the body of John Locke is seen in Jeremy Bentham's coffin.

Important details in *Lost* lore: After Keamy's team is taken out, Jack, Kate, Sayid, Hurley and Sawyer leave the island on the helicopter.

However, Sawyer jumps out and swims back to the island when they're low on fuel. Ben and Locke go down to the Orchid, which is where DHARMA conducted space time experiments. The still alive Keamy goes down there as well, where Ben kills him, but it triggers a device which will blow up the C4 explosives on the freighter. Sun and Desmond board the helicopter before the freighter blows up, killing Michael and seemingly killing Jin.

Ben sends Locke away and goes below the Orchid station to a frozen wheel, where he turns it and is able to make the island disappear, which also sends Ben to the Sahara desert 10 months into the future. But the helicopter then crashes into the ocean, leaving the survivors stranded until a boat run by Penelope Widmore saves them. A week later, the Oceanic 6 have their cover story set to protect those left behind, as they sail off while Desmond stays with Penny.

In the future, the man in the coffin is revealed to have the fake name of Jeremy Bentham. Sayid breaks Hurley out of the mental institution while Kate receives a vision of Claire telling her not to bring Aaron back. Sun begins to enter into business with Charles Widmore in London. Jack goes back to the funeral home and finds Ben, who offers to bring the Oceanic 6 back to the island. They also have to bring Bentham, who is finally revealed to be a dead John Locke.

It is also hinted that Charlotte may have been born on the island, as she elects to stay behind.

Amount of action: Heavy.

New important characters: None.

Connections between characters: Sawyer parts with Kate as he jumps off the helicopter to save the survivors. Ben and Locke part ways as they seem to finally make peace. Sun is snatched away from Jin as he seems to die in the freighter explosion, to which she blames both Jack and her father. Christian Shephard appears to Michael before he dies. In the future, Kate sees a vision of Claire that tells her not to bring Aaron back, Sayid and Hurley are going into hiding while Sun makes an alliance with Charles Widmore. Finally, Jack joins forces with Ben to go back to the island with the Oceanic 6 and Locke's dead body.

***Lost* mysteries referenced:** The departure of the Oceanic 6, the fate of Jin, the Oceanic 6's cover story, the Orchid, the notion of moving the island, Penelope's search for Desmond, Keamy's device on his arm, the man in the coffin from Jack's first flash forward.

***Lost* mysteries introduced:** The revelation of John Locke as the dead man in the coffin, his name change to Jeremy Bentham, where the island has gone, what happened to those left behind on the island over the last three years, Charlotte's past on the island, whether the freighter explosion killed Jin, what Ben's ideas are to bring the Oceanic 6 back, why Locke's dead body has to go with them.

Questions raised: Why and how is John Locke dead under the name Jeremy Bentham? What very bad things happened on the island after the Oceanic 6 left? Who is responsible for these very bad things? What has happened to everyone else still on the island? How did Locke get back to visit Jack, Kate and Walt? How will Ben reunite the Oceanic 6 and bring them back? Why must the dead Locke be brought back too?

Where did the island go after Ben moved it? Did Jin really die on the freighter? Why is Sun forming an alliance with Charles Widmore in the future? Why has Claire told Kate not to bring Aaron back to the island? Where are Sayid and Hurley going to go? Will Walt figure into the Oceanic 6 and Ben's plans? What will become of Desmond and Penny now that they're together again? Will Charles Widmore find out about them, or does he know already?

Talking points: Every year the creators make up a weird name to designate the big scene in their season finales. This year's nicknamed scene was "the frozen donkey wheel" but for the first time, their nicknames were accurate as Ben literally turned a frozen wheel to move the island. Many fans were taken aback by the creators actually giving that away under their noses.

It would also appear that turning the wheel sent Ben halfway around the world to the Sahara and 10 months into the future, where he was seen in "The Shape of Things To Come."

The question of whether Jin is alive or dead is still open. We never saw him blow up, and one would think he'd get a bigger death. Besides, Michael went to a lot of trouble to get him out in time, then was told by Christian Shephard that he can finally die. Would the island finally let Michael die if he didn't succeed in getting Jin out fast enough for him to live? The island probably has stricter standards than that. Jin could be in a position to get picked up by Daniel and his raft.

In addition, if Jin was alive Locke would certainly know about it. Locke was revealed to have visited many Oceanic 6 members as Jeremy Bentham. Is it a stretch to imagine he saw Sun too and told her Jin was alive? It might be a more flattering explanation as to why Sun is trying to join up with Charles Widmore, perhaps to use him in order to find the island and Jin again. If not, it will be a lot trickier getting her to join the Oceanic 6's trip back.

Even though it took place after the island left, Locke finally got through to Jack when he realized they had to lie. Jack made it look like lying was his idea, which is how Ben usually convinces people to do anything, if you want to compare Locke and Ben in that way.

But in terms of blame for why the Oceanic 6 left and others were left behind, it would appear that is a blameless act. The Oceanic 6 were in circumstances beyond their control, as it wasn't really their fault that the freighter blew and the island moved before more people could get off. As usual, Ben takes the rap for those bad events.

However, the ultimate question is how he failed in the overall mission. The island moved to stop Charles Widmore from finding it again, which it seems he still hasn't. In that case, why has the island gone to Hell anyway? If Widmore didn't cause terrible things to happen on the island while the Oceanic 6 was away, who did? Were Richard Alpert and the Others responsible? Might Jacob and/or Christian Shephard have something to do with it? Are there forces on the island that are on Widmore's side? Is it possible that Ben was the only thing holding the island together?

Months and months worth of questions.....

Other key issues: The number of fat jokes at Hurley's expense really increased in the last few episodes, as he ate candy bars and 15-year-old crackers, dreamed about mallomars, then looked uneasy when Frank suggested they dump a few hundred more pounds off the helicopter.

Must see episode?: All season finales are by necessity, a must see. But this episode is more action packed, filled with twists, stuffed with iconic scenes and revelations, and is more thrilling than almost any *Lost* episode ever.

By the time you read this, the long long wait for the next chapter of the *Lost* story will hopefully be over and we can pick up where we left off from this thriller.

Printed in the United States
129714LV00004B/11/P

9 781440 10288